SEEING RED

By
C E Allardyce

Seeing Red

Copyright © 2025

All rights reserved. No part of this book may be used or reproduced in any form whatsoever without written permission except in the case of brief quotations in critical articles or reviews.

This book is a work of fiction. Names, characters, businesses, organisations, places, events and incidents either are the product of the author's imagination or are used fictitiously. Any resemblance to actual persons, living or dead, events or locations is entirely coincidental.

For more information contact:

claire@ceallardyce.com
http://www.ceallardyce.com

Cover design by Ed Simkins

ISBN – Paperback: 9798298278454

First Edition: September 2025

Dedication

To those special people who are no longer with us – I was a little lost without you until I started putting pen to paper (actually fingers to keyboard in a creative way, but you know what I mean!). Who knew writing would be so therapeutic? I hope you know how much I miss you and would want to share this with you.

To those wonderful souls who supported me through this process – I will be eternally grateful to you for listening to me ramble on and of course reading my work (despite the numerous versions).

To all those women out there – the strong, independent women who face adversity every day. This one is for you ☺

To George, most of all. You're the best son a parent could wish for. You're a rock star and I am so very proud of you.

Contents

Dedication iii
Contents iv
Chapter One 5
Where It All Began 21
Echo 42
Enigma 59
Information Gathering 75
Meeting at the Café 95
Revelations 104
Journey Home 124
A New Threat 137
Arrivals 182
Church Goes Solo 197
Irritation 209
Charity Fundraiser 233
Joint Op 262
Site B 279
Showtime 298
Sierra Building 310
Archers, Scorpio and Echo 328
Takedown 338
The Demonstration 349
Operation Cerberus 359
The End? 370
A New Hell 388
Tall Pines 396
About the Author 413

Chapter One

Geoff Abraham

Geoff Abraham sat, nervous and sweating, on the edge of his leather executive chair, his long legs jerking restlessly. The chair was the only luxury item in his boxy office, which overlooked the adjacent building not far from Canary Wharf. His fingers drummed on the desk as he pondered his decision and its implications. It was certainly a risk, it might cost him his career, perhaps even his life. But it was a risk he couldn't afford not to take.

He was a plain man. His Savile Row suit had cost more than he paid his cleaner in a year. Now the fraying jacket stretched over his widening waistline, so he rarely fastened the buttons. His Ralph Lauren shirt had faded to a greyish off-white and was missing a button. He kept his thinning grey hair swept back from his face, limp tendrils brushing the collar at the back of his neck.

He drank too much and smoked too many cigars, but it was too late to quit now. And why bother? Life was meant to be enjoyed, but he wasn't enjoying it any more. Debts were piling up faster than he could pay them off.

Geoff had worked at EMP, a successful pharmaceutical company based in London, for thirty years as Chief Financial Officer. Yet his salary didn't come close to covering both his gambling habit and his ex-wife. The other executives at EMP all enjoyed far more lavish work environments. Most had views of the Thames, but his repeated faux pas had earned him his current location as punishment.

Decision made, Geoff reached for his mobile. With a shaking thumb, he entered the number from memory, hoping it was still current. The line rang, then after a few quiet clicks, the call connected to silence. He waited a beat, but no greeting came.

"Doctor?" His voice trembled.

There was no reply.

He took a deep breath and pressed on. "I have some information you may be interested in. Can we meet?" He swallowed hard. He longed for a drink, his tongue felt like sandpaper. "The programme. The recruits. This information could change things dramatically for you. Potentially a very profitable enterprise."

"What is it?" a woman asked impatiently.

"Not over the phone, please."

"I'll send someone to you."

The line went dead.

Geoff sat on a bench in the park near his office building, where he usually ate lunch on dry days. Today was windy and cold. He watched as the leaves skipped and swirled across the grass. He turned up the collar of his beige wool overcoat.

A homeless man stumbled along the path towards him, stopping passers-by to beg for change. As the scruffy man approached the bench, Geoff averted his eyes, if he pretended the man didn't exist, maybe he'd go away.

"The Doctor sends her regards," the man mumbled from under his hood.

Geoff looked up in surprise. This was who she'd sent? A homeless man? Surely not. This was important. Though, on closer inspection, the stocky man appeared well-nourished, with huge arms and thick fingers.

"I don't have long," Geoff said.

"Get on with it then, man," he said through gritted teeth, his Geordie accent cutting through.

"She's not here?" Geoff asked, glancing around the park.

"What do you think?" the man said sarcastically.

Reluctantly, Geoff shoved a hand into the pocket of his overcoat and pulled out a USB stick. He wrapped it in a banknote and held it out. "This is a summary. I can get the rest, but it will take time. I need certain assurances first."

"You get nothing until she commands it," the man sneered, snatching the note from Geoff. He suddenly leaned down and grabbed Geoff's wrist in a large, strong hand. "You're not to contact her again. We'll be in touch."

Geoff looked alarmed and shrank back. He nodded in agreement and the man released him.

It was getting dark. The wind had died down, leaving behind a bank of heavy grey clouds. Geoff was back at his desk, the company's ledgers open on the screen in front of him. But he wasn't looking at them. He was watching the people leaving the neighbouring building, all young and energetic, hurrying away with sprightly steps.

His mobile vibrated once in the breast pocket of his shirt. He snapped out of his reverie and checked the screen.

Unknown number:
Download Signal app

He followed the instructions and waited. The thought of speaking to the Doctor again filled him with a mix of excitement and dread. This was his chance to redeem himself in her eyes. Would she forgive him? His past transgressions had ended their business relationship, mistakes he deeply regretted. Nothing had been the same since she cut him off.

His phone remained silent on the desk. He willed something to happen. Another text. A call. Anything. All he wanted was to hear her voice again. But the screen stayed dark, as if mocking him.

After a long wait, he decided to head home. There was no point staying in the office. He was planning to play poker later that night with some old colleagues and friends, a monthly event held on the last Friday of the month, close to payday, with the venue rotating. Tonight's players weren't very skilled, so it was a chance for Geoff to recoup some of his recent high-stakes losses. The night usually involved copious amounts of beer and whisky. He'd already bought a bottle of Talisker, a fine single malt, in preparation. At least that would bring some temporary solace.

He shrugged on his overcoat, grabbed his battered briefcase and headed for the lift. He walked to Canning Town station, where the tube journey home would take about an hour and a half. He didn't notice a stocky man following him. The man was no longer dressed like a homeless man, now in clean, designer jeans, trainers and a baggy khaki green hoodie.

The man followed Geoff all the way to the street where he lived, in a leafy suburban area of Stanmore. He stopped at the corner and watched as Geoff unlocked his front door and stepped inside. The man pulled a mobile from his back pocket and made a call.

"Nothing to report. He went straight home. Spoke to no one. Made no calls," he said.

"Is he alone?" the Doctor asked.

"Yes," he confirmed.

"I'll put him out of his misery," the Doctor said, then hung up.

Geoff had just pulled off his tie, standing inside his lounge, when his mobile buzzed. He fumbled to retrieve it from his pocket. It was an incoming call on the Signal app.

"Hello?" he answered nervously.

"You're home late," the Doctor said smoothly.

"I had a meeting," Geoff said, twitching the curtains to look out of the window. He couldn't see anyone, though his view was partially obscured by the trees lining the street.

"The information looks quite interesting," she said.

"I hoped as much."

"Where's the rest of it?" the Doctor asked.

"My debts," he said. "I have some creditors to settle with. In addition to the normal fee..."

Was that too bold? Was he pushing his luck? He knew how valuable the information was. The line was silent for a few agonising moments.

"Consider them cleared," she said quietly.

Geoff let out a sigh of relief. "Thank you." He closed his eyes and murmured a prayer. "One point five?"

The Doctor didn't answer straight away. She certainly knew how to make a man sweat.

Eventually she asked, "When can you obtain the rest of it?"

"Next week, there's a big conference. All the senior operational staff will be there. I'm staying behind. Romano..." He realised he was babbling and closed his mouth. He waited a moment, then realised she had already hung up.

Edward Cavendish

Edward Cavendish said his goodbyes to his drunken friends and hurried from Geoff Abraham's house, making a call on his mobile.

"Pick up, pick up, pick up," he chanted quietly. He knew it was late, but needs must. He jumped into his wife's car and the driver pulled smoothly out into the empty street. The call went to voicemail.

"Kenny," he said after the tone. "It's Edward. Sorry about the hour, but this is time critical. That proposition we discussed... it's now or never. Call me as soon as you get this." He hung up and prayed Kenny would call back.

Edward didn't feel guilty, EMP owed him. Big time. Geoff was considering stealing Edward's life's work and Edward wasn't going to let that happen. If anyone was going to get their hands on it, it was going to be him. Screw EMP and screw that damn Italian bitch, Romano, who'd forced him out of his own company.

Geoff

Geoff arrived at the office on Monday morning at half past eight. He was still slightly drunk from his weekend of celebration, but nothing a hot shower, several espressos and some mouthwash couldn't disguise. The smell of cigar smoke lingered around him in an invisible haze. He stopped at the café in the entrance lobby to top up his travel cup. He really should have added a finger or two of whisky to smooth the edges, but he needed a clear head.

He stepped out of the lift and into the open-plan finance department. Something was seriously wrong. The usual calm, quiet atmosphere was noticeably absent. People were speaking urgently on phones in hushed tones. One of the admin girls trotted past and stopped when she saw him.

"Oh, Mr Abraham," she said breathlessly. "You're here." She sounded surprised. "Miss Romano has called an emergency meeting. Didn't you get the notification?"

"What's going on?" he asked. "The conference... why isn't everyone there?"

"Can't say." She looked at him expectantly. When he didn't move, she pointed upwards with a finger. "Boardroom. Meeting started five minutes ago."

Geoff checked his watch and swore under his breath. He returned to the lift and pressed the button. After a few moments, he gave up waiting and took the stairs. The boardroom was only two floors up.

Antonia Romano

Antonia Romano, CEO of EMP, scrutinised the ageing, suited men seated around the large, polished table. Her board of directors.

Incompetent, pathetic misogynists, she thought. *Which one? Who has the balls to try to steal from me?*

The door opened and Geoff entered, slightly dishevelled, flushed and out of breath.

"Apologies," he mumbled, taking his seat.

"Thank you for attending this crisis meeting," Antonia began, looking each bewildered face in turn.

"What's the crisis this time, Toni?" asked Andrew Eakins, the Operations Director, his tone implying scepticism. He thought Italian women were prone to being overly dramatic. "We should all be at the conference, not sat here..."

"There's been a breach, Andrew," Antonia replied coolly, cutting him off. "Files have been stolen. Confidential files."

She paused for effect, watching the board members exchange glances. Some muttered in disbelief. "Stolen, removed without authorisation and deleted. The backups have also been compromised. We have a leak. I am asking you to sanction the resources to fix this. Quickly and quietly."

"Which files?" Andrew asked.

"A Research and Development project," she replied evasively. "I don't need to tell you, if news of this reaches our competitors..." She left the rest unsaid. "I need to know exactly what happened and who is responsible. We must retrieve every byte of data."

"Which project?" Andrew pressed.

"The name is irrelevant," Antonia snapped. "You are not aware of it because it is at a critical phase and hasn't yet been approved." She addressed the room. "This could be the biggest project this company has ever seen. If the preliminary results are as promising as they look, we're looking at a substantial return on investment."

Geoff swallowed hard and reached for a glass of water from the centre of the table. He hoped, prayed, that Antonia wasn't referring to the project known as *Warrior IV*. The information he planned to deliver to the Doctor later that day.

Had someone beaten him to it? Who?

"I need your agreement. Now," Antonia continued. "We can't trust anyone until the leak is found. I expect your reports by the end of the day. Leave no stone unturned, especially those members of staff who didn't turn up for work today." Her eyes fell on Geoff.

"How..." The words stuck in his throat. He coughed loudly into his fist. "How much are we talking about?" He was acutely aware of the entire board looking at him.

Antonia held his gaze. "Whatever it takes, Geoff."

He tugged at his tie. "I can certainly move things around, adjust the budget, transfer funds from other projects."

"Perfect." She smiled at him, though it didn't quite reach her eyes.

Geoff

Geoff returned to his office and sank heavily into his chair. He spun around to face the window and loosened his tie. What was he going to do? Decisively, he turned back to his laptop and jabbed a finger at the space bar to wake the screen. He entered his PIN and navigated through the various project folders. He ran the cursor down the list. The one he was looking for was missing, *Project 20050604WIV*. He ran a search. Nothing. He tried again, using several different combinations of keywords. Same result. Every search returned zero results.

How could nearly twenty years of information be gone? Formulas, spreadsheets filled with test results, reams of reports and analyses, risk files, lists of variations... all just gone. *Warrior IV* was gone and with it, his hopes of selling it to the Doctor had just been obliterated.

Geoff picked up the phone and viciously jabbed in the numbers for an internal extension. He needed answers and there was no better place to start than with the Research and Development department.

"Hello?" a stressed male voice answered.

"Can I speak to Kenny? It's urgent."

"He's not here," the voice replied, impatiently.

"Off sick?" Geoff asked.

"No. Family holiday."

"Who is this?" Geoff pressed.

"Interim Head of Research. I've been transferred here from Paris. Can I help you? I don't mean to be rude, but we're really up against it down here. I've got both IT and the Security Department tearing the lab apart." His voice trailed away. "Now they want access to all the offices too... sorry, I've got to go." He hung up, leaving Geoff staring at the receiver in disbelief.

As the realisation sank in, Geoff cradled his head in his hands. He was too late. Someone had reached the information before him, removed it and deleted it. How was he going to explain that to the Doctor?

He briefly considered throwing himself from the window. His office was eight floors up, death would be inevitable, but then people would think he was responsible. He was innocent. Well, not entirely, he *had* considered stealing the information and selling it to the Doctor to clear his debts and retire in the sunshine.

Seeing Red

This was a disaster. Failure was not something the Doctor tolerated. He'd learnt that the hard way. He was going to pay and it wouldn't be pleasant.

Geoff's mobile buzzed, making him jump. It was the Doctor calling. He considered not answering. He should leave. Now. Then what? She would hunt him down and kill him. Begrudgingly, he accepted the call.

"What's the problem?" she snapped.

Geoff looked around his office, then nervously out of the window. Was he being watched?

"It's all gone," he said quietly. He could practically hear her disappointment in the silence that followed.

"When?" she asked eventually.

"It must have been yesterday, last night, even."

"Who knew?"

Geoff's mind reeled. "Obviously the Research and Development team, those who were working on it."

"Who else?"

"Me, some of the board members."

The Doctor remained quiet. She clearly wasn't satisfied with his answer.

"Romano, the CEO," he added. "Edward Cavendish, he wrote the original premise and developed the first iteration."

"Would that be the same Edward Cavendish you were playing cards with last night?" the Doctor asked, her tone dripping with menace.

Geoff swallowed hard. He was definitely being watched.

Edward

Edward had his own problems. He was on his knees in the server room at the deserted Torenta offices. He had emptied several drawers onto the floor and was reaching blindly into the cabinet, feeling about with trembling fingers.

His golden goose was gone. His idea had finally borne fruit, thanks to Kenny Mackay, Deputy Research Scientist at EMP, who had made a few changes to the formula and *bingo*! He owed Kenny everything, for calling him back that night and, more importantly, for meeting him with that innocuous USB stick, shaped like a carved black chess piece.

Kenny had willingly copied the project files onto the USB, then deleted all traces from the EMP servers. He had corrupted the backups and ensured the physical copies were destroyed with a single email to a junior administrator, who'd spent a few laborious hours shredding every last report. Once the job was done, Kenny walked out of the office with the USB in his pocket and met Edward for drinks.

"It's all there," Kenny had promised. "Not a trace left."

"Thanks," Edward had said, in awe of Kenny's efficiency. "What now?" he asked.

"I'm taking the girls on holiday," Kenny replied. "The files won't be missed until Monday morning, no one else is working on it. So you've got less than forty-eight hours to get away."

Seeing Red

"When all this is over, the job's yours." Edward had grinned and they clinked their pint glasses together.

The trouble was, Edward had taped the USB stick to the underside of one of the drawers in the server room for safe keeping. Now, as he tried to retrieve it, it was nowhere to be found. He searched the drawer below, then the one above. Nothing. He resorted to emptying everything onto the floor.

Edward sat back on his heels and rubbed a hand over his sandy-coloured hair. What was he going to do? Who knew it had been hidden there? He pulled his phone from his pocket and called his wife. She would know what to do.

"May, darling," he crooned when she eventually answered.

"What do you want?" May asked, impatiently.

"I've got a problem, honey. I need your help."

"What's happened?"

"I've lost something important. At work. Not lost exactly, stolen, I think."

"So?" she asked, disinterested.

"You must know someone who can help me find it."

"Why would I know someone like that?"

"You must know someone who knows someone," he pleaded. "It's crucial I get it back, it could change everything."

His wife sighed, exasperated. "I'll make a call," she conceded and hung up.

Jack Williams

Jack Williams stood on the balcony, watching his lead team, *Alpha*, put a group of trainees through their paces in one of the gyms housed within the extensive training facility. The old RAF barracks was now home to *Cactus*, Jack's international military contractor firm. A few of the new recruits showed promise, many, not so much. He was always on the lookout for fresh blood, operators with the kind of tenacity that made them worth his investment.

His mobile vibrated gently in the breast pocket of his immaculate, crisp white shirt. He pulled it out, checked the screen and smiled.

"Mrs Cavendish, what do I owe this unexpected pleasure?" he said, stepping away from the balcony.

"Jack, you whore of a man," May Cavendish replied affectionately.

Jack chuckled. "It's been a while, May. What's up?"

May sighed with contempt.

"Edward being a nuisance again?" Jack asked, rightly guessing her errant husband was the reason for her current mood.

"Again? Jack, seriously, when is he *not* a nuisance? I honestly don't know why I put up with him. Anyway, long story short, I need a favour. He's lost something at work and needs someone to help him find it."

"Animal, vegetable or mineral?" Jack asked with a smirk.

"Information, I suppose. He's pretty worked up over it."

Seeing Red

"Can he pay?"

May scoffed. "What do you think?" she replied, dryly. "I'll be expected to pay."

"Understood," Jack said. "What shade are we talking?"

"Who knows with Edward?" May said. "He's not usually one for *real* shady dealings, so I'd guess... the lightest shade of grey on your scale. Does it matter?"

"Not really," Jack admitted. "Just depends who I send."

"Don't you have good guys working for you?"

"All my people are impeccable at what they do," Jack said. "But not all are suited to that end of the shade scale. I'll send an associate of mine."

"Associate?" May questioned. "Is that a euphemism? Not an employee, then?"

"She's a former employee. She'll get the job done."

"She?" May asked suspiciously. "And here I imagined your people only left feet first?"

"Ha!" Jack laughed. "Usually, yes. Occupational hazard. But not her, she's special. One of a kind."

"High praise indeed. What's her name?"

Jack evaded the question. "I'll send her a message. Edward can expect her call within the hour."

"Okay, I won't ask. But thank you, Jack, I mean it."

Where It All Began

Claudia Church

The sound of Claudia Church's heels echoed around the eerily quiet residential street. Her long, dark red ponytail bobbed and swayed gently with her relaxed stride. She loosely held the strap of her handbag at her shoulder, while her other hand was occupied with texting on her mobile phone.

It was just after midnight and Church was heading back to the car park a few streets away. She had met her friend Annalise for dinner. They hadn't seen each other for almost a year, so there had been much to catch up on. A few bottles of wine could easily have been consumed, but Church had a meeting first thing in the morning. She had opted to drive into the city to remove the temptation.

"Get a taxi," her friend had cajoled.

"I have an early meeting. I really shouldn't," Church had said. "Next time, I promise."

Church received a text and smiled as she read it.

Annalise:
Me too! It was so nice catching up. Let's not leave it so long next time x

Church replied, then returned her phone to the side pocket of her soft leather jacket. She turned into a dark alley between the ageing university buildings. The stone was crumbling in places, blackened by time and exhaust fumes.

Someone was watching her from the shadows on the opposite side of the street. The scrawny man crouched low to the ground, keeping her in sight through the windows of the parked cars. Dressed in dark jeans and a puffer jacket, he tugged a woollen hat lower over his forehead, pulled a bandana up over his nose and silently followed her into the alley.

In a few lumbering strides, the man caught up with her. One gloved hand grabbed her wrist, the other clamped over her mouth. With a muffled scream, she was forcefully pushed into an alcove. He shoved her into the wall, his chest pressed firmly against her back.

"Scream again and I'll cut your throat," he rasped into her ear.

The hand over her mouth was removed and something cold and sharp pressed against the skin at her throat. Church froze, her nostrils flaring as she drew in air through her nose. A gloved hand roughly searched each of her pockets. It swept over the back pockets of her jeans, lingering a moment longer than necessary, feeling for more than just loose possessions.

The sound of a motorbike echoed around them. The man hesitated, waiting for the sound to pass, his hand falling away from her backside. The bike flew past the end of the alley and the engine noise faded into the distance.

Church was relieved of her phone, her handbag was torn from her shoulder. The knife whispered across her skin as he stepped back, pulling her roughly away from the wall and spinning her around to face him. The tip of the blade hovered less than an inch from her eye. Her gaze fixed on the knife, a dull, rusty blade with a dark plastic handle. He was holding it like a wand, his index finger pressed along the top edge.

Church decided, in that moment, that she'd had enough. She ducked to the side, away from the knife. A lightning-fast jab to his throat, then she slapped the knife-wielding hand away from her face. She shoved him back, pivoted on her foot and swung her left shin at his chest.

The man staggered backwards. The knife clattered to the pavement, her handbag landing with a soft thud. Blinking in surprise, the man hesitated. Church spun again, bent low and kicked him in the head. He collapsed to the ground, unconscious.

Church smoothed down her shirt, flung her ponytail over her shoulder and regarded her attacker with contempt. She stooped and frisked him quickly, finding her phone in his jacket pocket. Removing his hat and tearing off his bandana, she took several photos of his face. Standing, she retrieved her bag and swiped up his poor excuse for a knife.

As she turned back towards the street, she spotted a motorbike idling at the end of the alley. The rider was watching her. Was it the same bike she had heard moments ago? A concerned citizen or an accomplice? The rider was tall, with broad shoulders tightly clad in leather. The visor of the expensive carbon fibre helmet was heavily tinted, concealing their face.

The bike couldn't pass through the black iron bollards. What was he doing? Church kept her eyes on the rider, silently daring him to act, as she continued down the alley. Emerging into the streetlights, she purposefully lifted her phone to her ear, her thumb selecting a favourite contact. The rider revved the powerful engine and sped up the street.

"Hey, Kez," Church said without an ounce of concern, watching as the bike disappeared around the corner. "Could you make an anonymous call to the boys in blue for me? A man just tried to steal my phone and bag."

"Oh my God, Church! Are you okay?" Kez cried.

"I'm fine. Him? Not so much. He's unconscious, I don't think I broke anything," she replied, unfazed.

"Picked the wrong girl to attack," Kez said, amused.

"He caught me in a good mood. He was lucky."

"Since when has restraint been in your repertoire?" Kez joked. "Where is he now?"

"I'll send you a pin and a few mug shots, see what you can find out," Church said, reaching her car. "I'll be back in half an hour."

On Church's way home, an incoming call illuminated the console. Jack Williams's name appeared on the screen. She pressed the accept button on the steering wheel.

"Morning," she answered jovially.

"Ah, you're still awake," Jack said. He was Church's silent business partner, investor, former boss and friend.

"What's up?" she asked. Something must be wrong. Why else would he be calling?

"I have a client for you. Friend of a friend, you know. Well, actually, the husband of a friend."

Church smiled. Jack always got straight to the point. "Okay," she said amiably. "Got any details?"

"Lost something important," Jack said, as if the details were irrelevant. "His wife will pay whatever you need."

"Why aren't you taking it yourself?" Church asked, a little suspicious.

"I thought this would be perfect for you gals. Simple search and retrieve."

Jack knew she employed a balanced mix of men and women. It was her lead team, Team Archers, that happened to be all female. A coincidence, nothing more. They were her closest, most trusted friends, her family.

"Worried about our bottom line?" Church asked.

"I didn't invest in Archers purely for the profit," Jack replied.

He didn't need the return on his investment, he earned more than enough from his own company.

"I'm glad to hear it," Church said. "So, are you going to tell me anything, or are you expecting me to work it all out myself?"

"His name is Edward Cavendish," Jack said.

The name meant nothing to Church. She'd have to do her homework. "Okay, text me the number."

"Let's catch up soon," Jack said.

"Sure. If this job pans out, I'll buy you a gin or three," Church said.

"Make it at least five and you've got a deal."

"Deal. Speak soon." Church ended the call.

She messaged Kat, her second-in-command and asked her to cover the eight o'clock meeting. Church received a thumbs-up emoji in reply. She then called Edward Cavendish. Despite the hour, they spoke for a few minutes and agreed to meet at his London office at ten a.m. to discuss the details.

Preparation

The next morning, Church stood in front of the full-length mirror in her attic bedroom at Archers, studying herself critically. She was wearing a black pinstripe suit with a cream silk shirt, provocatively open at the cleavage and black Louboutin high heels. The suit was tailored to her curves and concealed her defined musculature well. With the heels, she stood a few inches shy of six feet tall.

Church told herself she could pass for a serious businesswoman. She *was* a businesswoman, though one who usually preferred combats, a cargo vest, heavy boots and her trusted Bowie knife strapped to her back or thigh.

Today's meeting required a different persona, one of many in Church's repertoire. She pulled her hair into a high ponytail and turned her body first to the right, then to the left, assessing the final touches. The movement sent a twinge of pain radiating from her lower back down to her toes. She turned away from her reflection and swiped a small pill bottle from the dressing table. Tapping two tablets into her palm, she swallowed them dry.

The pain was currently hovering around an eight on Church's personal scale, zero being *all okay* and twelve being unbearable, bone-aching agony that made her want to die. She massaged the knotted scar tissue on her lower back with her fingers. Pain had been one of her closest companions for the last three years.

It had been three years since her last overseas mission. Three years since she'd watched her teammates run fruitlessly from two Apache helos and eighteen months since she had left Cactus, following her struggle to overcome her injuries. She'd received several medical opinions stating she would never walk again, an opinion she had flatly refused to accept. Eventually, she had proved them all wrong.

After applying a dark red lipstick, matching her hair and painted fingernails, Church brushed her fingers longingly over the hilt of her knife. She wouldn't need it today, but she loathed leaving it behind. She felt naked without it. Taking a deep breath, she gave herself one last look in the mirror, then headed downstairs.

Church got into her RAV4 and drove out of the underground car park on the small country estate where her company, Archers, was based. She glided down the sweeping, tree-lined drive towards the gates, which opened automatically as the car approached.

The drive to London would take just over an hour. Twenty minutes of winding country roads would lead her to the motorway. Heading south on the M1, she would take the M25 to just past the Dartford Crossing.

As she drove, Church contemplated the significance of this meeting with Mr Edward Cavendish, CEO of Torenta Pharmaceuticals. The job details were still unclear. It had come as a personal recommendation from Jack Williams, her former Commander-in-Chief at Cactus, her mentor, Archers' primary investor and a close friend. Without his investment, Archers simply wouldn't exist.

The fact that Jack hadn't taken the job himself or passed it to someone within his vast network of employees and contacts, spoke volumes. Was it too *clean* for Cactus? She hoped that was the case. She was determined to keep Archers firmly in the light. Jack knew full well that she wanted nothing more to do with anything even remotely black.

Church was done with all that. It had nearly killed her. Now, mostly recovered from her injuries, at least the physical ones, she was focused on ensuring Archers gained a reputation for being efficient, clean and dependable. A respectable private security and investigations firm that could get the job done without a body count. Once this new potential client explained the brief, she could begin her due diligence and vet them thoroughly.

Torenta Meeting

Torenta Pharma was located in a small business park in Erith, south-east London. Church pulled into a visitor's space and looked up at the squat building. Offices occupied the front, with a large warehouse at the rear. She approached the front door and searched for an intercom. Not finding one, she tugged on the handle, it opened freely.

No wonder they lost something. Security is more than lax, she thought.

The reception area was grey and bland. A sad, neglected-looking yucca plant drooped in the corner beside a simple and conspicuously unmanned desk. The computer screen was unlocked, the email app open. Church grinned to herself, remembering the mischief that could be caused when someone left their email open for anyone to access.

She glanced at the desk, confidential-looking letters and documents were strewn across its surface. She mentally tutted. *This outfit really needs some basic pointers in security.*

"Can I help you?" a female voice called from down the corridor.

Church turned to see a young woman, with poorly bleached blonde hair and too much make-up, tottering towards her on unsteady heels.

"Morning," Church replied brightly. "I'm Claudia Church. I have an appointment with Mr Cavendish."

The woman scrutinised Church for a moment. "This way," she said.

Church followed her up a flight of stairs and was shown into a corner office overlooking the car park and a small patch of grass with a rickety picnic table on it.

The young woman disappeared from view and Church heard the floorboards creak under her retreating steps. Church glanced around the office. The furniture was basic, the floor covered in cheap, thin carpet tiles and a few certificates hung crookedly on the walls. No photos. No personal touches.

Quiet voices came from the outer office. Church leaned back slightly towards the doorway and saw the young woman standing very close to an older man with sandy-coloured hair, speaking softly into his ear. His eyes were firmly fixed on her chest as he listened. Church raised an eyebrow internally and waited. This, she assumed, was Mr Cavendish.

The man entered the office a few moments later. He left the door open and sat down behind the desk. He didn't introduce himself or offer a handshake.

"Miss Church, thank you for coming so quickly. Apologies for keeping you waiting, things are a little hectic here, as you can imagine."

Church smiled sweetly while thinking, *Hectic? Hardly, next to no staff, no phones ringing. What's going on here?*

Mr Cavendish explained the situation. Church listened attentively, making several mental notes.

"It's very important we get this back," he finished, looking at her expectantly.

"So, some company-sensitive information is on a USB device. It was last seen in the server room and only you knew it was there?" she summarised.

"Yes," he confirmed.

Church nodded. "And now it's gone. When do you believe it could have been taken?"

"Like I said, it was there last night. This morning, it's not."

"Do you normally store information this way in the server room?"

"No."

"Tell me about your security measures," Church said.

Mr Cavendish looked slightly uncomfortable. "We have closed-circuit cameras outside the building, focused on the entrances and exits and the warehouse loading bay, obviously."

"Any cameras inside?" Church asked.

"I've checked the footage, nothing of interest. I have to consider my employees' privacy."

"Of course," Church said, though more alarm bells were ringing in her head. "I understand. But you've been the victim of a crime and I'm only trying to help you recover the USB device. I have no interest in your employees, unless we discover one of them is responsible."

"No, they wouldn't do such a thing," Mr Cavendish insisted, shaking his head.

"The agreement is clear," she said, pointing to the tablet she had placed in front of him. "Once we can eliminate individuals from our enquiries, we won't pursue them further. The same goes for any company information. We will act with complete discretion, subject to clause twelve being met. You won't even know we're here. With your permission, I'd like my tech team to access your systems remotely."

"That's out of the question," he said firmly.

Seeing Red

"Mr Cavendish, the fact that you haven't called the police is telling in itself. You're willing to pay Archers to retrieve it, we will retrieve it, I can assure you."

"How?"

"By following the evidence, Mr Cavendish. It's quite simple, really." She smiled kindly. "Let us do our thing and within a few hours, we'll have some answers." She pulled a small rectangular box from her bag. "All I need is to plug this into any device connected to your network and my team will do the rest. While that's working, why don't you show me the server room?"

Mr Cavendish swallowed, then nodded his agreement.

The server room was located near the back of the office suite, close to the rear stairwell. On the way there, Church didn't see a single employee.

"Quiet up here today," she remarked. "Where is everybody?"

"Downstairs or in the warehouse," Mr Cavendish replied. He waved his keycard over the sensor beside the server room door. The sensor beeped and the small light turned green. He opened the door and gestured for Church to enter first.

The room was long and narrow, no more than six feet wide. Rows of black, open cabinets housing the servers lined each side, tangled with cables in various colours, blinking lights flickering. The room vibrated with a low, constant hum.

"This way," Mr Cavendish said, sliding past her.

He walked between the cabinets towards a cluster of four desks, partitioned by tired-looking, fabric-covered boards. The surface was strewn with assorted pieces of equipment in various states of repair. Against the back wall stood two tall metal filing cabinets.

"It was in here," Mr Cavendish said, pulling open the third drawer down.

"Who has access to this room?" Church asked.

"Me, the IT guys, the cleaner," he replied.

"May I speak to them?"

"The cleaner comes in early, before office hours… it wasn't him. The USB was already gone before he arrived."

"And where are the IT personnel now?"

"Downstairs. Working on… something else."

"Okay," Church said cheerfully. "How about we head back to your office?"

Mr Cavendish looked surprised. After a pause, he nodded and led the way with a wave of his hand.

Archers

The reason Edward Cavendish hadn't wanted Archers to view the security footage was now abundantly clear. Church's team sat along one side of the conference table, watching the main screen in front of them. Edward and the young, bleached-blonde woman were otherwise occupied in the corridor outside the server room. The time stamp read

23:22, the night Mr Cavendish had reported the USB missing.

"He gave you this?" Kat asked Church incredulously.

Katherine Jones, Church's second-in-command, was seated to her left. They had been best friends since meeting at Cactus. Kat was the tallest in the team, standing at five foot eleven. Her long, straight black hair reached her waist and her brown eyes were framed by naturally arched, quizzical eyebrows.

Church shook her head. "Kez found it in his recycle bin. I spotted the camera on the tour of the building. He failed to mention that too."

"He lied," Kat said plainly. "Did he really think we wouldn't find out?"

Kerys Davies, the Chief Technology Officer, grinned. "Sloppy," she said. "He scrubbed about an hour of footage from the server but forgot he'd emailed that section to himself. He deleted the email, but not the copy in his recycle bin. And as for keeping company-sensitive information on a USB stick, hidden in the server room..." She rolled her eyes.

Kez, the shortest member of the team at five foot five, had a voluptuous figure. Unlike the others, she wasn't a trained fighter and preferred to stick to the tech side of the business. That said, she could more than hold her own, if pushed, she was as scrappy as they came.

"Such a cliché," Jen muttered, wrinkling her nose. Jennifer Buckingham, an engineering and explosives expert, had MacGyver-like improvisation skills. With wavy blonde hair, she matched Church in height but had a thinner, willowy physique.

"So, the only two people who went near the server room that night were Mr Cavendish himself and Collette Millford?" Kat asked.

"Appears so," Church replied, indicating to Kez to fast-forward the footage by drawing a circle in the air with her finger.

Kez scrolled forward to a point where the couple parted ways. Mr Cavendish zipped up his trousers and kissed Miss Millford's cheek. He staggered towards the toilets, one hand on the wall for support. Collette lingered, then stood, swiped a pass at the sensor and slipped into the server room. She emerged less than a minute later, tucking something into her bra.

"That's Mr Cavendish's pass," Kez confirmed, having quickly pulled up Torenta's login records.

"Well, that was straightforward," Jen said. "Shall I pay her a visit and ask her straight out?"

"I have her home address," Miz announced, sending it to Jen's phone.

Marie Izzard, the team medic, had met Church shortly after Kat, when they were thrown together during the messy aftermath of a particularly nasty op at Cactus.

Jen hopped out of her seat.

"Stay safe," Church said seriously.

"Sure thing," Jen replied as she left the conference room.

Jen

Jen approached the front door of Collette's flat silently and cautiously. There were no signs of forced entry. But from the moment she'd stepped out of her car, her skin had prickled. Was someone watching? She had scanned her surroundings, a typical suburban block of flats with a car park. Nothing suspicious. Nothing out of the ordinary. So why did the unease linger?

She knocked on the door with three firm raps of her gloved knuckles. No answer. She paused to listen. The muffled sound of a television could be heard inside. She tried the handle. It was unlocked.

With a deep breath, she stepped inside.

The narrow hallway was dim. Two closed doors flanked the corridor, which led to an open-plan lounge and kitchen.

"Control?" Jen whispered.

"Receiving, Four, we're all here," Kez confirmed.

"Something's off," Jen said quietly.

"Backup is five mikes out," Kez said. "Drone is circling your location."

"You see anything odd?" Jen asked.

"Not yet. Will let you know if I do," Kez said.

Jen glanced around the corner. The living area was empty. She retreated, picked a door and entered. A small bathroom. The mirror over the sink was smashed and Collette's makeup and toiletries were strewn across the sink and floor.

The shower curtain had been ripped from its rail, which now lay askew in the bath.

She turned to the second door, took a steadying breath and pushed it open.

Collette lay unconscious on the bed, surrounded by clothes. Every drawer had been emptied. The wardrobe too.

Jen tore off her glove with her teeth and pressed her fingers to the woman's neck. "She's alive," she reported.

"We'll bring her back to Archers," Miz said, already alerting the medical centre to prepare for an incoming patient.

Jen gently manoeuvred Collette into the recovery position, then continued her sweep. The curtains billowed inward. It was too cold for the window to be open.

Approaching it, she peered out, left, right, down at the ground, then up towards the roof. Nothing. No movement. No one visible. Leaning back in, she closed the window and pulled the curtains shut.

Collette

Collette was taken to the medical centre at Archers. Eve, the Chief Medical Officer, examined her and found no injuries, she had simply been sedated. After running some tests, Eve administered an antidote to counteract the sedative.

Church was waiting at her bedside when Collette finally stirred. She blinked a few times, slowly taking in her surroundings.

Church gently took her hand. "You're safe, Collette," she said quietly, with as much kindness as she could muster.

Collette looked at her, eyes glazed. "Where am I?"

"You're in our facility. You're safe here."

"Where's here?" Collette asked, confused.

"Cambridgeshire," Church replied.

Collette tried to sit up. Her eyes widened as the memory returned. "The man… Did you send him?"

"What man?" Church asked. "We didn't send anyone to you."

"I don't know!" Collette wailed. "He came into my flat looking for the USB, but I'd already given it to the other men." She began to cry. "He scared me… he… I don't know what happened."

"Collette, it's alright," Church said soothingly. "You need to tell us everything. Let's start from the beginning. Who asked you to take the USB from Torenta?"

Eve cleared her throat to catch Church's attention. "Can't this wait?" she asked disapprovingly.

Church was about to respond when her phone rang.

Eve continued, "My patient needs rest. Come back tomorrow. I'll update you if her condition changes."

Church nodded and left the room, answering the call as she stepped into the corridor. She listened for a moment, then said, "I'm on my way." She headed back to the conference room.

A Lead

"What have you found?" Church asked as she took her seat at the conference table.

"Something and nothing. Maybe," Kat replied. "Show her." She nodded to Jen.

"I was trawling through the drone footage. Something was bugging me," Jen said, transferring an image to the screen. It showed a man in a baseball cap emerging from behind the apartment building and walking to a van parked in the car park.

"Looks innocent enough, but we did a bit of digging. The registration is fake. Facial recognition came back, this is Thomas MacDonald. Apparently, he works at a club called *Enigma* in Cambridge. You know, the one on the river? Anyway, we also identified two men on the CCTV entering the flats around the time we believe Collette was attacked. We managed to access the CCTV outside the club. Guess what? All three of them have been there most of the afternoon."

"Okay," Church said slowly, already thinking ahead. "Do we have their names yet?"

"Soon," Kez replied.

"It's Saturday night," Kat said. "I propose we have a night out, mix a little reconnaissance with a lot of pleasure!" She looked very excited at the idea.

"Hang on. Give me a minute to process this." Church held up a hand, halting Kat, who was already bouncing in her chair. "Anything else on this club?"

Seeing Red

"It's got a great reputation as a true dancery," Kez said. "Classy, modern vibe, good beats… you know. Right up our street."

"Do we have anything on the owners?" Church asked, looking around at the team.

"Can you lighten up a bit?" Kat urged. "Let's not overthink this. We get dressed up, go out and see what's what. Where's the harm in that?" She stood and flicked her hair over her shoulder.

"I'm searching now for the low-down on the club," Kez said. "Shouldn't take long. I'll get the techs to alert us when we have a hit."

"Alright, a night out it is then," Church said. "Go get ready. I'll catch up in an hour, I want to do a bit of homework first."

"Make it thirty minutes and you've got a deal," Kat said, already halfway out the door.

"Fine," Church conceded.

Kat clapped her hands excitedly and practically skipped out of the room.

"Feel free to leave me to it," Church said to the others. But Jen, Kez and Miz stayed in their seats.

"I'll drive," Jen said. "If they were casing Collette's flat, they might recognise me. I'll stay in the car."

"Nothing a wig wouldn't solve," Miz said.

"Some night out," Kez grumbled. "You can't just sit in the car all night!"

"I've got work to catch up on and you might need backup. I don't mind, honestly," Jen said with a grin. "We can always start the after-party here when we get back."

"The background on Torenta is ready," Kez said as her laptop pinged with a notification.

"Thanks. I'll look it over tomorrow," Church said.

Echo

Antonia

Antonia stood in front of the windows, overlooking the Thames and the city beyond, in her penthouse office at EMP. Having secured agreement from her senior management team earlier that morning, she dialled the number she had been given for a firm that solved problems, known simply as Echo. It was a recommendation from a friend of a friend. She tapped a toe on the marble tiles as she waited.

A deep, gravelly male voice eventually answered. "Riley."

What a way to answer a potential client!

"Mr Justin Riley?" she asked.

"Yes."

"I'm Antonia Romano, EMP Pharma. An acquaintance recommended you to me."

The line fell silent, prompting her to frown. She decided to clarify. "The Wrights of St John's Wood. Mr Wright is head of Drake Holdings, I went to university with his wife, Abby. She told me what you did regarding their daughter, Daisy. I could use someone with your expertise for a different kind of problem."

"Hmm," he growled.

"Do you recall the family?"

"Hmm."

Was that an affirmation? Antonia rolled her eyes. She should have passed this call on to someone else. But who else could she trust to get the job done? Dealing with this man was the only option. According to Abby, he could be trusted to deliver.

"Some crucial project files have been stolen from my company. I need them back."

"When?"

"When what?" she snapped, patience wearing thin. "*When* were they stolen, or *when* do I need them back?"

"Both," he said calmly.

Antonia wondered if he was capable of using words with more than one syllable. She supposed he didn't need to, given his line of work.

"We noticed the files missing first thing this morning. I don't know when they were taken but I need them back immediately." She waited for a response but none came. "What are your terms?"

"Have you checked your backups?"

She frowned again. Of course she had checked the backups! "All trace has been erased," she said through gritted teeth.

"Send me a brief and I'll get back to you."

"I was hoping to settle this now."

"We don't usually get involved in corporate theft," he said curtly.

"I can pay whatever you need to get the job done," Antonia offered. That would grab his attention. She studied her fingernails with her free hand, planning to book an appointment with Fabio, her beauty therapist, as soon as she finished here.

"Fifty upfront, a further fifty on completion," he finally growled.

"Fine," she said, unsurprised. It was a fair price considering how valuable the information could be. "I may extend the contract depending on your findings."

"That's entirely your decision, ma'am."

"So, how do we proceed?"

"I'll send you a secure email address. Email it and we'll reply with an encrypted link. We'll start as soon as the deposit is paid."

"We obviously have a leak in our system and security. I'd prefer to meet in person. I have cash." Antonia's foot tapped faster. The wind outside made the building shudder.

"I'll be at your office in two hours," he said, abruptly ending the call.

Antonia lowered the phone from her ear, surprised. Should she let this man into the building? He had left her little choice. She returned to her desk and sat down. Reaching for her desk phone, she called her security chief. He had much to answer for. She should have fired him for his incompetence. But by keeping him on, she could make his life a lot worse.

"Double security at the main entrance and outside my office for the rest of the day," she ordered.

"Certainly, Miss Romano," the security chief responded. "May I ask why? We have two officers on every level. The cyber team are monitoring all communications..."

"Just do it!" she snapped, slamming the handset down.

Justin Riley

Two hours later, Riley stood outside the EMP Pharma head office, dressed in an expertly tailored dark grey three-piece suit, white shirt with chrome cufflinks, knotted burgundy tie with matching handkerchief and immaculate brown leather shoes. His black hair shone with a touch of product and he was clean shaven for the first time in months.

He strode towards the glass doors and entered the building with purpose. Approaching the reception desk, the receptionist smiled up at him expectantly.

"Mr Riley, here to see Miss Romano," Riley announced, returning her smile.

"One moment please, take a seat," she instructed, indicating two leather sofas positioned either side of a low glass coffee table.

The receptionist took in the visitor. The well-dressed man before her was over six foot of pure toned muscle. His black hair was cut short at the back, with waves of shiny curls long enough to fall over his eyes if he chose to let them. Today, they were neatly smoothed back. His dazzling blue eyes twinkling with mystery and mischief.

His nose was straight with a slight cleft at the tip. Extremely kissable lips, the corner of his mouth twitched devilishly before his smile lit up his face. He had straight white teeth and a strong chiselled jaw. He was clean shaven and smelled divine. His broad shoulders were barely contained by his suit. Huge biceps, large strong hands. *No wedding ring!* she noticed. Her eyes travelled down his body to his slim waist…

Riley made no move to follow her direction. He held her gaze when her eyes finally returned to his, until she started to blush. She blinked rapidly and looked away shyly. She made a call and spoke quietly to whoever answered.

Turning his back to her, Riley shoved his hands into his trouser pockets and admired the atrium entrance lobby. With quick glances, he noted the number of security guards – four in total – the position of security cameras and the display board listing departments and their floors.

"Mr Riley, you can go up now," she called, offering him a visitors pass. "Just take the lift to the penthouse office, tenth floor. Someone will meet you there."

Riley glanced quickly at her name badge. "Thank you, Jessica." He grinned, taking the pass and clipping it to the breast pocket of his jacket. She had regained some composure. He winked at her mischievously and headed for the lift.

The lift doors opened and Riley was greeted by a security guard, dressed in an ill-fitting brown shirt and trousers, making him look like a UPS courier. Riley assumed the guard was meant to be intimidating, but Riley was taller and much broader across the shoulders.

"This way please, Mr Riley," the guard said politely.

Riley smiled warmly and dutifully followed. He was shown into Miss Romano's office. He stepped inside and waited for the door to close behind him.

Antonia Romano was sitting at her desk in the corner of the huge office, frowning at her computer screen. Eventually, she looked up and her eyes widened immediately in surprise.

"Mr Riley?" she asked, unable to mask the disbelief in her voice.

"At your service, Miss Romano," he responded, striding over to her desk and offering his hand. She stood and shook it with practiced confidence.

Antonia Romano was barely five foot five, even in her Jimmy Choo heels. She was curvy, dressed in a navy pencil skirt and jacket. Gold jewellery adorned her pierced ears, neck, wrists and fingers. Her dark hair, streaked with grey, was cut into a bob and tucked behind her ears. Her large brown eyes studied him.

Antonia gestured for him to sit on one of the brown suede sofas at the other end of her office.

Riley sauntered over the marble tiles, studying the room as he waited for Antonia to join him. She sat on the edge of one of the sofas and crossed her ankles gracefully. Riley unbuttoned his jacket and slowly sank down.

"You are not quite what I was expecting," Antonia admitted candidly. *Bell'uomo!* she thought. Beautiful man!

"And what were you expecting?" Riley asked, a flash of something playful in his eyes.

Antonia shook her head, dismissing the image in her mind. "Nice suit," she offered instead.

"Thank you," he said, leaning back. He casually draped his arm over the back of the sofa.

Antonia stood suddenly, strode back to her desk and retrieved a thick padded envelope from the top drawer. She handed it to him and sat down. Riley tucked the envelope into his inside jacket pocket.

To business then, he thought.

"Tell me everything you know about the missing information – what happened, when it happened, any suspicions, any recent grievances," he demanded, holding her gaze.

That was the longest sentence he had spoken. *Not so monosyllabic after all!* she reflected.

"Grievances are many and widespread," she said. "Business is tough, no?"

"Hmm," Riley agreed, noticing her Italian accent growing stronger.

"The information. Do you need to know what it is?" Antonia asked.

"Not if you'd rather not say."

"It's a research project. That much I *can* tell you. Data, formulas, reports, test results." She waved a hand. "It was last accessed early last week. Only a small number of employees were working on it." She looked at him expectantly, then shared as much as she dared. She felt she could trust him. To a point.

"Sounds simple enough," Riley observed after she finished.

"Anything you need, just ask." Her eyes flashed. "You have my number."

Internally, Riley groaned. She was all over him with her eyes. He would play along until the job was done. Clients like her, with unlimited resources, didn't come along often. This job could be financially very lucrative if he played it right.

"Tell me about your firm. I know nothing about it," she continued, leaning back in her seat and slowly crossing her legs.

"I'd like it to stay that way," Riley said firmly. "All you need to know is that we will get the job done as quickly as possible. You say this is time sensitive, so we shall start immediately. Any concerns about the amount of force we may need to use?"

"I'm not interested in your methods. I just need the information back."

"Understood, ma'am."

"Call me Toni, please," she purred.

Riley stood, buttoning his jacket. He held out his hand again. She took it but didn't let go after they shook. Instead, she stepped closer.

"It's been a pleasure, Justin," she breathed.

Enigma

Riley drove back to his nightclub, Enigma, a converted boathouse on the banks of the river just outside the centre of Cambridge. He approached the solid steel side door and heard a muffled buzzing as it was remotely unlocked. He strode down the dark corridor, passed through another reinforced, security-controlled door and finally descended wooden steps towards the control room.

The rest of the Echo team were hunched over their stations. The back wall was covered in monitors showing maps, security footage and several background checks. Audio of Miss Romano shouting orders over the phone played from one workstation.

"How'd it go?" Harris, Riley's lieutenant, asked. Charlie Harris was six foot four, with a ripped upper body, blonde hair and deep brown eyes. He had stood on Riley's left since they met during Royal Marine Commando training.

"Hmm," Riley growled noncommittally, scanning one of the backgrounds.

While he read, he pulled the thick envelope from his pocket along with a cloning device. He placed them on Ellis's desk and clapped him on the shoulder in appreciation. Ellis Clarke was their tech guy, just under six feet tall, with long brown hair tied in a bun and a wiry physique. His hazel eyes scanned the screen, absorbing the information.

Riley removed his suit jacket and waistcoat, flinging them over the back of a chair. Jonny leapt from his seat, took the abandoned items and carefully hung them on a coat hanger before disappearing from the dark room. Jonny's muscled frame almost rivalled Riley's but he was several inches shorter. He kept his brown hair cropped close to his scalp and sported a thick, bushy beard.

"Miss Power Suit hasn't given us enough to work with," Ellis complained. "We need full access to their systems to find out who did this."

"Let's start with her prime suspect, Cavendish. Anything on him?" Riley asked.

"We have eyes on him," Ellis confirmed, pointing to another screen.

"Shifty as hell," Tom said. "Sure looks guilty to me. He's working at Torenta Pharma now, thanks to his wealthy wife. Not very grateful though – he's banging one of his junior sales reps." Tom was their medic, six foot tall, brown hair and a healthy, tanned complexion.

"Hmm," Riley growled. He needed more.

"He's still in contact with a few guys from EMP. Poker nights with a finance guy, drinks with a research scientist," Tom added.

"Name?" Riley asked, unsurprised at his team's efficiency.

"Kenny Mackay," Tom confirmed, checking his screen. "Joined EMP a few years after its incorporation."

"He's one of the employees who worked on this project," Riley said. "We need to track him down."

"On it," Tom acknowledged.

"I can't access Torenta's servers," Ellis muttered. "Yet," he added. "Give me a bit more time... or we could go directly for Cavendish's laptop?"

Seeing Red

"We could pay Cavendish's bit on the side a visit," Harris suggested. "Borrow her security pass for a while?" Riley nodded his agreement. Harris headed for the door. "Tom with me."

"Take the muscle with you too," Riley said, nodding towards Jonny, who had just walked back in. "In case you get into trouble."

Harris grinned and flipped Riley the bird before leaving. Tom and Jonny followed.

Riley approached Ellis, noticing his frown. "What's up?" he asked.

"Someone else has eyes on Torenta," Ellis replied.

"Who?"

"Don't know yet, but this guy keeps popping up. Here." Ellis showed several screenshots of a man lurking outside Torenta's offices. Not very tall, burly, shoulders hunched and hood pulled low. "He's avoiding cameras, can't get a clear shot of his face."

Ellis's computer dinged and he clicked the notification. "Huh," he muttered. "He's popped up again, this time outside the girlfriend's flat."

"When?" Riley asked.

"Sunday." Ellis sighed as another notification sounded. "Could do with an extra pair of hands or three in here." He slid his chair across the floor to another workstation.

Riley removed his cufflinks, rolled up his sleeves and sat at a desk. He focused on the stocky man. Riley entered the man's characteristics into Ellis's software. About five foot eight, well-built, approximately eighty to one hundred kilos, aged twenty-five to thirty-five. He entered locations of interest to narrow the search. It didn't take long for the familiar shape to be picked up.

The man had been lurking outside EMP's offices. He walked with a swagger, feet pointing outwards. He kept his back straight and the swing of his arms gave him away. Riley set another programme running, which scrolled through the last ten years of military records.

"Who are you, you stocky little fucker?" he growled.

Echo Team

Harris – Echo Two, Tom – Echo Three and Jonny – Echo Five pulled into the car park outside Cavendish's girlfriend's block of flats in a borrowed van. The number plates had been changed and fake magnetic signs were fixed to the sides. They read *Total Maintenance Services*.

Tom slid open the side door. After a quick visual check of the area, he released a drone into the air. He remained in the van as Harris and Jonny got out and sauntered towards the entrance, dressed casually rather than in their usual combat gear.

A female resident came out of the doors and both Harris and Jonny stepped aside politely to let her pass. Harris held the door open for her.

"Thank you," she said, giving them both an admiring once-over.

Seeing Red

"You're more than welcome," Harris responded with a big smile.

"That's not her," Ellis said over comms. "Collette is blonde and much younger. You need the third floor, flat nine."

The men took the stairs. At the door to number nine, they listened for a moment before Harris knocked. A young woman answered, looking startled at the two large men filling her doorway.

"Bingo!" Ellis confirmed, watching the footage from Jonny's hidden bodycam.

Collette poked her head out into the corridor and looked down the hall towards the stairs. "You here for the USB?" she asked quietly.

"Yes," Harris answered automatically.

The woman nodded, held up a finger indicating they should wait and closed the door in their faces. Jonny glanced at Harris, who shrugged in response.

Collette returned. "Here," she said, handing Harris a black, wooden carved chess piece.

"Thank you," Harris acknowledged. He passed it to Jonny, who stashed it in the inside pocket of his jacket.

"The other guy could've been a bit more polite like you," Collette remarked, still looking at Harris.

"What can I say? My mother brought me up to remember my p's and q's," he said with a smile.

"Do you have the money?" she asked.

"No, sorry."

Collette frowned, but the expression quickly melted into fear as she looked between the two of them. "So, what happens now?" she asked, nervously stepping back. Her knuckles turned white as she clutched the door. Could she slam it before they muscled their way in? By their size, it wouldn't take much to break it down. She cursed herself for handing over the USB before receiving the promised money.

"We'll leave. They'll be in touch shortly," Harris assured her.

"When?" Collette cried, her voice trembling.

"Above my pay grade, I'm afraid," Harris shrugged.

"We've got company," Tom announced quietly over comms. "Stocky's back."

"Two, Five, get out of there and bring me that USB!" Riley commanded. "Three, keep an eye on Stocky."

"Copy that," Tom confirmed.

"I'm sorry," Harris told Collette. "We gotta go."

The men turned on their heels and strode towards the stairs.

"Stocky is heading for the flats," Tom reported.

"We'll go out the back," Harris said. With a nod to Jonny, they leapt down the stairs and sprinted to the fire escape.

From behind his newspaper, Tom watched the stocky man swagger past the front of the van. He stopped at the building entrance, entered a code into the keypad and let himself in.

Tom checked his watch and waited two full minutes. "All clear," he said.

Seeing Red

Harris and Jonny appeared from behind the building and jumped into the back of the van.

Jonny plugged the USB into a laptop. "Looks like this is it," he confirmed.

"Well, that was easy," Harris observed.

"Too easy!" Riley growled over comms.

"Not every op goes sideways," Ellis noted. "We caught a break, for once."

"What are you waiting for? Let's go," Harris urged Tom.

"We should check on the girl," Tom insisted, fingers drumming on the steering wheel.

"Get back here with that information," Riley ordered.

Tom didn't start the engine. Instead, he picked up a newspaper from the passenger seat and opened it as a car pulled into the car park. Harris and Jonny exchanged a glance, their view limited from the back of the van.

"We have more company," Tom said quietly, watching an attractive blonde woman get out of the car. She looked around then headed towards the front door.

"Stocky hasn't left the building as far as I can tell," Ellis confirmed. He sent the drone higher to widen the view.

"Control, check out the RAV4, would you?" Tom requested.

"What did your last slave die of?" Ellis grumbled.

"I'll do it," Harris offered from the back of the van. "Read me the number."

Tom read out the licence plate.

A notification dinged on Ellis's laptop. "What the…" he muttered. "Stocky's just entered the tube station. No idea how he got there – must have teleported!"

"Forget him!" Riley ordered. "He'll keep for another day."

Tom recalled the drone, Jonny slid open the side door to retrieve it and they headed back to base.

Riley retreated to his office in the back rooms of the club. The walls were bare and painted the same dark blue as the rest of the club. He sank into the leather chair behind the large, sturdy oak desk. A long dark green leather sofa sat against the wall opposite, a grey fringed throw draped over one arm.

Riley called Miss Romano on his mobile.

"Justin," she purred. "I hope you have good news for me, I could certainly use some."

"Miss Romano," Riley responded formally. "We have the files."

"Call me Toni, please. That was fast."

"When would you like us to return them? We haven't had chance to follow up yet. There's no way of telling if the information's been altered, copied or how many times it's been downloaded. We're working on that."

"Leave that to me. I have a specialist who'll handle it. Who had them?" she asked.

"An acquaintance of Mr Cavendish's."

"Which acquaintance?"

"A junior sales rep at Torenta."

Miss Romano snorted with disdain.

"I can be with you within an hour," Riley offered.

"I'll come to you," she said firmly. "Tomorrow evening."

Riley frowned. "Not today?"

"I can't tonight, I have a prior engagement."

"Tomorrow then. I'll send you the address of where we can meet. First thing suitable?"

"I'm tied up in meetings all day. Eight p.m. is the earliest."

"Fine, I'll confirm the details before lunch tomorrow."

"Your place?" she asked suggestively.

"No, ma'am."

"Pity."

Riley said nothing.

"I look forward to it," she breathed, ending the call.

C E Allardyce

Enigma

Night Out

Having successfully endured the ever-growing queue outside the club, four members of Team Archers were admitted close to eleven p.m.

The gleaming chrome bar stretched down one side of the space, the walls painted a dark blue and dotted with soft downlights. Five semicircular booths filled the far side of the spacious dancefloor, while a few sturdy chrome tables and chairs were placed at the back of the room.

The ceiling was completely mirrored and adorned with many glitterballs ranging from the size of footballs to the largest, which hung above the centre of the dancefloor. The stage was raised, with soft LED-lit material hanging behind it like a night skyscape. The table where the DJ's decks and laptop were placed was covered in black velvet. The music was expertly mixed, seamlessly melding EDM and electronic pop bangers. Right up the girls' street. The heavy bass vibrated through the air and could be felt in their chests.

"Welcome to Enigma!" a tall, blonde and particularly handsome man called over the music. He appeared as if from nowhere before they could reach the crowded bar. He wore a black long-sleeved shirt with black jeans. "Is this your first time? I'm sure I would remember your beautiful faces... here, let me escort you to one of our booths."

The man gallantly offered Kat his arm. She slid in between Kez and Miz, threw her hair over her shoulder and allowed him to lead her around the edge of the dancefloor. The rest of the girls followed, exchanging knowing looks.

"Full VIP treatment for the most beautiful ladies I have ever seen. My name's Charlie. You need anything…" He leaned closer to Kat's ear. "And I mean anything, just shout." He gave Kat a cheeky wink.

Kat turned towards Church and grinned like a Cheshire cat. Church rolled her eyes and quietly followed the group to the booth. Charlie took Kat's hand, twirled her in a slow pirouette and gestured theatrically for her to sit. He bowed before her and kissed her knuckles.

"What can I get you ravishing ladies to drink? A bottle of something special, perhaps? First round is on the house," Charlie offered, his eyes fixed on Kat.

Kat shook her head. "Iced tap water for the table, spiced Cuba Libre over ice, vodka and lemonade over ice with all the fruit, gin and tonic, bucket not tall and a vodka and diet coke over ice." She looked expectantly at him, certain he'd ask her to repeat some or all of their order.

Charlie bowed his head in acknowledgement. "Regular or diet coke with the Cuban? Ice and fruit with the gin and tonic? Fruit in the vodka and skinny coke?" he asked, without missing a beat.

"Yes, please to the ice and fruit," Miz confirmed.

"Regular, in a can, if you have it," Church requested. "No fruit pieces, thank you."

"Fruit for me, please," Kez added.

Charlie bowed again and was about to head to the bar when Kat stopped him by touching his arm. He leant down and Kat slipped her credit card into his hand.

"We'll pay for all our drinks, thank you for the offer though. And keep them coming," she instructed.

He bowed his head. "As you command." Then whispered in her ear, "May I be so bold and offer you my number?" He quickly glanced at the name on her credit card. "Katherine."

"Kat," she corrected. "We'll see." She returned her attention to her friends, effectively dismissing him.

With a quick salute, he clicked his heels once and about-faced. Within minutes, a waiter appeared with a large black circular tray with not a single error. He also knew which drink belonged to each of the group.

Church watched the waiter retreat to the bar and wondered how they did that. What code had they used? Most likely Cuban for the redhead, G and T for curly, vodka and diet coke for curvy, vodka and lemonade for the tall one...

Once the crowd engulfed the table, Church leant in towards her teammates. "Let's mingle, check out all the corners and see what we can find out," she proposed.

"I'll take Charlie Boy," Kat said immediately.

"Watch your back," Church warned.

Kat waved it off dismissively and winked. "Let's get this party started!" She downed her drink, took Miz and Kez by the hand and sashayed them onto the dancefloor.

Church

Church needed a bit more time and a few more drinks to get into the groove. She stayed in the booth, slowly scanning the club, picking out the employees from the clientele. The bartenders and waiters wore branded black polo shirts, with a large silver 'E' on the back and a smaller symbol on the front pocket. The two door attendants wore smart black shirts and ties. And then there was the all-too-charming host. Was he the owner or just the manager on shift? Church intended to find out. This was the sort of homework she would have preferred to do before coming here.

The DJ was doing a fine job, in her opinion. She couldn't see the person at the decks clearly, just a bluish glow from the laptop screen that revealed a dark head wearing large glittery headphones. Long painted nails and slender fingers appeared and pulled one side of the headphones from the DJ's ear, revealing large hoop earrings.

Girl power! Church thought and continued her surveillance.

A pair of intense blue eyes at the bar caught her attention. They looked directly at her. She sipped her Cuba Libre through the silver straw and didn't look away. He was very handsome. Chiselled jaw with a hint of dark stubble, dark hair with a slight curl. He was tall and muscular. He wore a midnight blue shirt with the top two buttons undone, revealing a hint of dark chest hair.

Careful! No time for distractions!

But just look at him!

I said no!

The man didn't seem to mind her watching him. He looked relaxed, one elbow resting on the bar. He held a crystal glass in his large hand, obscuring the contents. Whisky? Bourbon? Brandy? She decided bourbon matched his demeanour.

His expression told her nothing. He slowly raised his glass to her. She allowed herself a hint of a smile, then looked away. That was enough, for now. She wasn't here to play...

More's the pity! she thought.

Church finished her drink and sidled onto the dancefloor. The DJ was playing one of her favourite dance tunes. With a quick glance back at the bar, Mr Tall, Dark and Handsome had gone.

Church let the music consume her – her team were within shouting distance and all looked to be thoroughly enjoying themselves too. She closed her eyes and moved to the music. Slowly the crowd merged into one living, breathing being, pulsating to the beat. It felt like heaven and all the tension, including the pain, melted away. She hadn't felt this relaxed in a very long time.

Just one more tune! she promised herself. *Then back to it.*

Her edges started to blur – she revelled in the warmth and privacy the darkness gave her. She lost herself. The bass drummed in her chest like a heartbeat and she let it drive her movement. It felt pure and primal.

An unfamiliar yet very pleasant masculine scent filled her senses. She felt a presence behind her, radiating serious heat. He moved with her but didn't touch her. His breath tickled the skin on the back of her neck. It sent shivers of both excitement and irritation down her spine and arms. Could a girl not dance alone and have fun without some meathead trying it on?

She waited for the inevitable groping but he kept his hands to himself. Eventually, demurely looking over her shoulder, she caught a glimpse of strong arms in midnight blue sleeves. She smiled to herself. A little alone time with this beast of a man wouldn't hurt.

Mixing business and pleasure leads nowhere! You've got work to do!

Church ignored the snippy thought and swayed her hips in a slow figure of eight, half wishing to catch him unawares, but he seemed to anticipate her movements. He continued to sway with her, barely inches away.

She was impressed with his self-control, which made her seriously question her own. Now was not the time to get distracted, however enticing the thought of dancing with this man was. Who was he?

She glanced into the crowd and spotted Kat dancing with the host, Charlie. He looked totally mesmerised by her, not taking his eyes off her. Kat glanced towards Church and gave a discreet nod towards their booth.

Church took her time and tilted her head to the side. Her dance partner was still close. She closed her eyes and embraced the sensation. Then she spun to face him – his eyes instantly found hers. He had a look of intense concentration, dark eyebrows creased into a frown.

She placed a hand on his shoulder. He kept his hands by his sides. She could feel the warmth of his skin through his shirt. The muscles in his shoulder moved and flexed beneath her fingers. She stepped into him and rested her head against his chest.

Please don't work here! she thought.

Church glanced towards the booth. A young man was sitting with Kez. The tempo increased. Church pressed herself against her dance partner, chest to hips. She kept her eyes lowered. He softened his knees, lowering his head until he dropped into her line of sight. His hand lifted towards her chin, encouraging her to look at him without touching her. Their eyes met.

Riley

A low whistle, barely audible over the music, brought Riley out of his euphoric haze. But he didn't take his eyes off the redhead and her incredible green eyes. She was stunning and toned. She smelled like a summer meadow laced with vanilla and something spicy. He wondered if she tasted just as good. Her pale skin glowed, complementing her shimmering little silver dress. Her shapely legs were accentuated by strappy heels. Her enticing curves... curves he longed to explore.

A second whistle sounded, more urgent this time. Riley frowned at the interruption and glared towards the source. The bartender gestured at him then pointed towards the booths.

Duty calls, he thought.

Seeing Red

Riley looked down at his dance partner apologetically. Her cheeks were flushed and she was breathing heavily, her chest rising and falling in a hypnotic rhythm.

I've gotta go.

He turned towards the booths and immediately saw the problem. With one last longing look at the redhead, he shouldered his way through the crowd.

A young woman with glossy straight brunette hair was slumped over the table and a skinny kid with a baseball cap was all over her. Riley reached the booth, grabbed the kid by the back of the neck and dragged him off his feet. Backup arrived in the shape of Team Echo and they closed in around the booth, shoulder to shoulder.

The kid was sandwiched between large muscular bodies, unsuccessfully trying to slither out of Riley's grip. The kid's skin was cold, clammy and unpleasant to the touch.

Riley shoved him roughly into Jonny's hands. "Take him out back," he growled. Sudden movement by the fire escape caught his attention. A chubby kid in a fluorescent pink T-shirt was running out the door. "Ellis! Rabbit!" he growled, nodding in the kid's direction. Ellis went after him.

Riley turned his attention back to the girl in the booth. She was totally out of it, her eyes rolled back and she was limp as a rag doll. He knelt beside her and checked the pulse at her wrist. "Miss? Can you hear me?"

The girl mumbled something incoherent. Riley stood and scooped her into his arms. The remaining team members backed away and cleared a path for him towards the door marked *Private No Admittance*, next to the bar.

Riley called to Harris over his shoulder. "Tell one of her friends to come to the office."

"I'll get Kat," Harris said and headed back to the dancefloor.

Riley strode down the dark corridor and kicked the door to his office open. He laid the girl on the sofa and covered her with the grey throw.

Riley heard Harris approaching with one of the girl's friends. She was angrily demanding to know what had happened and why they had taken her friend out of the booth. As soon as Harris showed her into the office, the tall, attractive woman stopped shouting.

"Kez!" she cried and knelt in front of her friend. She glared at Riley. "What the fuck is going on?" she shouted.

"Ri," Harris said. "This is Kat."

Riley nodded in greeting as Tom stepped forward. "I can help, I have medical training," he offered.

"Touch her and I'll break every bone in that hand!" Kat spat. She turned to Harris. "Get Miz. Now!"

Harris looked confused for a moment.

"The curly-haired brunette!" Kat clarified. "Gin and tonic girl."

Harris glanced at Riley, who nodded. Tom followed Harris out.

"We found her being groped by some dopehead," Riley explained as Kat tried to rouse her friend.

"Nice joint you have here," she mumbled under her breath, loud enough for Riley to hear.

Seeing Red

"We don't tolerate that kind of behaviour or dealing here. I assure you we take this very seriously. The kid responsible and his associate are being held until the police arrive."

"You called the police?" Kat raised a dubious eyebrow.

Before Riley could lie, Harris returned with the other friend, Miz, who immediately surveyed the situation then set to work on her friend.

"She needs a drip to counteract whatever that arsehole gave her," she said, standing up. She looked critically at Riley. "Thank you, we'll take it from here."

Kat made a call on her mobile. "Jen, we need to leave. Can you meet us round the back?" She listened for a moment. "It's fine. I'll explain later."

Kat and Miz struggled to pull the girl up from the sofa. Riley stepped in. "Here. Let me," he said and lifted the girl easily into his arms. "Are you sure any of you should drive?"

Kat snorted but stepped back and let Riley lead the way. Harris and Tom flanked her and Miz followed behind.

Outside, a white Toyota SUV was idling. Harris opened the door and held it as Riley slid the girl into the seat. He started to retreat then spotted the redhead from the dancefloor in the front passenger seat. A spark ran up his spine and the corner of his mouth twitched. He was about to say something when he noticed the blonde woman in the driver's seat. She hadn't been in the club with the rest of the girls.

Alarm bells rang in his head. The blonde was at Cavendish's girlfriend's flat. The redhead held his gaze until Miz brushed past him to tend to her friend. The redhead got out, slid into the backseat and between her and Miz, they cradled the semi-conscious girl.

Miz reached for the door handle to close it but Riley grabbed the top of the door, stopping her. The girls froze and stared at him.

"Please let me know how she gets on," he said. He gave one last lingering look at the redhead and stepped back. Kat blew a kiss to Harris as she jumped into the front passenger seat. The two men watched silently as the car pulled out of the car park.

Archers

"Did you get it?" Church asked Jen as they drove back to Archers.

"I sure did," Jen said smugly. She pulled the USB out of her bra and held it over her shoulder. Church took it and closed her fingers around it. "I scrambled their CCTV and slipped in unnoticed. It's pretty impressive down there. I planted a few little toys while I was mooching around too."

"Explosive toys?" Kat asked, surprised.

Jen laughed. "No! Just a few bugs and a little something to get us into their system."

Church was relieved. Impromptu ops were risky.

"I hope it was worth it," Kez said from Church's shoulder. She opened her eyes and sat up straight.

"Great performance back there, Kezza," Kat said, turning in her seat.

"Thanks. The kid was all tongue and hands. I feel violated!" Kez complained.

"Didn't hear you complain when Mr Frowny picked you up though," Miz said, grinning.

"Well, that was different!" Kez insisted. "He was just being gentlemanly." She looked apologetically at Church.

"And good job with the chief meathead, Miss Church," Kat added. "You certainly held his attention."

Church smiled in response but gazed out of the window as the streets whizzed by. At the time, she had no idea her dance partner was the owner of the club and, more importantly, the commander of the team called Echo.

Jen had made the most of the few hours waiting in the car by doing her homework. With help from the techs back at Archers, she found all the details about Enigma, its owner Justin Riley and his team of ex-military meatheads – Team Echo, muscle for hire. Their cases ranged from protection details to hunting expeditions and more.

To make the most of the journey back to Archers, Church accessed Echo's meagre records using the link Jen had planted. The more she read, the less she understood. Echo were rivals, as she suspected. She was surprised their paths hadn't already crossed or collided. Not wholly in the business for the money, it seemed. A few noble causes, some shady dealings but mostly nothing out of the ordinary.

They didn't appear to be worthy of the label of bad guys. They had been hired to do a job and had executed it efficiently. Collette must have been collateral damage. But why drug her and ransack her place? What did that achieve? They got what they were looking for.

Well, they don't have it anymore!

Echo

The club closed its doors at two a.m. and the clean-up began. Riley retreated to his office for some solitude.

There was a knock on his door and Harris poked his head in. "I have an update for you," he began, holding two crystal glasses filled with bourbon. He slid one glass towards Riley then settled on the sofa. "The car the girls left in is also registered to Archers. Same as the car at Cavendish's girlfriend's flat."

"Hmm," Riley growled. "So, you gonna call the Amazonian supermodel?"

Harris laughed. "Well, it would be rude not to."

"Find out what you can."

Ellis appeared in the doorway. "Ri, we have a problem," he said with trepidation. Riley gestured for him to come in.

"Erm... the USB has gone."

"What?" Riley stood up. Harris spun his head to look at Ellis in surprise.

"The USB. From the girlfriend's flat. It's gone," Ellis repeated.

"I heard you! How? When?" Riley bellowed.

"Must have been earlier tonight. Jonny and Tom are going through the security footage now."

"No need," Riley growled.

"Boss?" Ellis looked confused.

"Those fucking girls!" Riley said, looking at Harris then back at Ellis. "How did they get past our security downstairs?"

Ellis shrugged. "I'll find out."

So they have skills! Riley thought furiously. *Well, so do I!*

He strode down to the control room with Harris and Ellis behind him.

Harris started to explain. "Ellis finally got into Torenta's system and tapped Cavendish's phone. Archers were hired by Torenta but Cavendish's wife is paying them. She transferred money into the company account and it went straight to Archers. May Cavendish is friendly with Jack Williams... he didn't take the job himself but minutes later Cavendish got a call from Archers." Harris waited for Riley to burst another blood vessel at the mention of Jack's name.

Riley was thinking, *Why would Williams hand over a job to a smaller outfit? Is there no escaping that man?*

He quietly fumed while watching the blank screen in front of him. It was supposed to be their security feed – instead all he saw was over ten minutes of absolute nothing.

Harris ploughed on. "The redhead used to work for Cactus, can't find out why she left or how she managed to leave without ending up in a body bag... all the girls we saw tonight also worked there. They all left Cactus at the same time."

"What's her name?" Riley asked, referring to the redhead.

"Claudia Church," Harris replied.

Riley hadn't heard the name before. So she had worked for Jack and was now running her own team. Equally irritating and interesting.

"From the limited information about Archers, they employ nearly forty operatives – techs, lab rats, medics, ex-soldiers..." Harris offered.

"Anyone we know?" Riley asked.

"A few of them came from Cactus. But no ringing bells."

Jack let her leave *and* take people with her? That certainly didn't sound like the Jack who Riley knew. *Do I really know him?* He supposed not.

"Also," Harris added tentatively, "Jack is a major shareholder of Archers."

Riley closed his eyes briefly. *He bankrolls them too? Whatever next?*

Harris handed Riley a tablet and retreated to a safe distance. Riley sat down heavily in the nearest chair and read through the report. It was the redhead's military record. He wanted to throw something and break things, but the control room was no place for a rampage. Instead, he ground his teeth, the muscles in his jaw twitching as he read the report thoroughly.

"H!" Riley roared some minutes later.

"Still right here," Harris said calmly from his station behind Riley.

Seeing Red

"Do you think they know we know who they are now?" Riley asked.

"It's possible, they are smart."

"Can we start being smarter?"

"Sure."

"How into you was the Amazonian?"

"Kat," Harris corrected. "Somewhat, I think."

"Now, see this is what happens when you think with your..."

"Understood," Harris said, cutting him off.

"Call her, act dumb. Find out what you can."

"The redhead is the ringleader, she's the one in charge."

"Leave Red to me," Riley growled, striding out of the control room.

Information Gathering

Riley

The next night, while Harris was entertaining his new Amazonian flavour of the week, Riley parked his black Ranger truck in a layby a mile away from Archers. Jonny sat beside him, face streaked with dark greasepaint, checking his gear. He had loaded the drone, night vision goggles, scope, rope, grappling hooks and other tactical equipment into a large backpack. Riley, preferring minimal kit, took only his sniper rifle. With a fist bump, the two ex-soldiers got out of the truck and headed in opposite directions.

Under cover of darkness, dressed in black combat gear, Riley sprinted across the fields until he could see Archers' perimeter wall. He slowed and silently circled the grounds, avoiding the intermittent security cameras.

He picked a suitable tree, an ancient oak, its leaves starting to turn yellow and began to climb. He pulled himself up with ease and wedged into a crook in the highest branches. Turning his baseball cap around, he trained the scope of the rifle slowly over the grounds. He saw meadows dotted with similar oaks, a large lake and finally the main house. It was a three-storey, red-brick manor house with tall white windows. Only one light was on. He zoomed in and saw Red sitting at a desk in what he assumed was her office.

Someone's working late, he thought and turned on his comms.

"Control, this is One," Riley said quietly.

"Welcome back, One," Ellis replied. "Five checked in about twenty minutes ago."

"Good for Five," Riley growled.

"See anything useful?" Ellis asked.

"CCTV covers the entire perimeter."

"ICU 4000, deterrent enough. Normal, night and thermal imaging. How far are you from it?"

"About thirty metres," Riley confirmed.

"That should be enough. Don't get any closer."

"Any joy getting into their system?" Riley asked.

"Nope," Ellis said. "Tighter than a proverbial duck's nether regions."

"Anyone home?" Tom asked, joining the conversation from the control room.

"Only one light on at the back," Riley said.

"Need a drone?" Tom asked. "Five, can you manage that?"

"Fuck you, Three," Jonny replied.

"Hold that," Riley said. "What are the chances they've considered that, judging by the overkill with the CCTV?"

"Good point," Ellis said. "Checking the purchase history from the security company now."

Riley watched Red. She had not moved from her desk. She was studying something, pure concentration on her face. *Was she doing her homework too?* He quickly scanned the rest of the buildings. No signs of movement.

"Yeah, don't bother with the drone," Ellis said. "They've got a proximity sensor that domes over the place."

"Parachuting in is off the cards, then," Tom said with a chuckle. "Pity. I miss dropping in unannounced."

"Five, anything?" Riley asked.

"Much the same," Jonny replied quietly. "Perimeter locked up tight. A few lights on in the building to the north. Medical centre, is my guess from the equipment I can see."

"Movement?" Riley asked.

"None," Jonny confirmed.

"Do we have schematics yet?" Riley asked.

"Just got them now," Ellis said. "In the main house there's a large reception area, commercial kitchen, dining room and a few meeting rooms. First-floor offices, bedrooms in the attic and two apartments. The basement has a conference room. In the middle building, a gym and pool. More bedrooms on the first floor. Converted stable block, control centre and an empty space below. The northern building is a medical centre with underground parking."

"Hmm," Riley growled thoughtfully.

"What next?" Jonny asked. "We can't get in and the USB could be anywhere."

Riley didn't answer. He turned off his comms, descended the tree and headed back to the layby. At the truck, he shrugged out of his combat vest and changed his boots. No need to give Red any clues about his covert surveillance. He considered putting on his fleece jacket but decided against it.

Seeing Red

He sat in the driver's seat and ran a hand through his hair, removing any trace of his baseball cap. He started the truck and drove towards the main gate.

A few minutes later, he pulled up to the intercom, reached out of the window and pressed the call button. He held his finger on it a bit longer than necessary.

"Can I help you?" a female voice said through the speaker.

Riley wondered if he had met this person. "Yes, I very much hope you can," he said politely. "I'm here to see Claudia Church." He smiled up at the camera pointing in his direction from the stone gatepost. He noted the brass nameplate.

"Do you have an appointment?" the voice asked. "There's nothing in her diary and we normally don't have visitors at this time of night."

"No appointment, no. But I am sure she's expecting me. Would you mind calling her?"

"May I ask who you are and the purpose of your visit?"

"Justin Riley, Team Echo and Club Enigma. I'm sure Miss Church knows exactly why I'm here."

That should get her attention.

Riley waited patiently for Archers to scramble. Plenty of time for her to assemble her team before he could get into the building. He relaxed his hands on the steering wheel and nonchalantly leant his elbow out of the window.

"Please follow the drive up to the main house," the voice eventually said.

There was a quiet buzzing sound and the gates swung slowly inwards.

Riley closed the window and reactivated his comms. "Control, I'm going in and going dark," he announced.

"In?" Ellis asked. "How?"

"Through the main gate, they just buzzed me in," Riley replied.

"Bold," Tom chuckled. "I like it. Just don't forget to smile."

"Fuck you, Three," Riley growled. "Five, I'll pick you up on my way out."

Riley switched off his comms, pulled out his earpiece, dumped it on the passenger seat and roared the truck up the drive.

Church

Working late, Church was sitting at her enormous black desk. It was set diagonally in one corner of the vast room, making the most of the views out of the large west-facing bay window. The thick carpet was cream, as were the walls, accented with luxurious black curtains. A huge painting of a moody Highland landscape hung over the large black marble fireplace. Two cream sofas with black velvet cushions were positioned either side of a black and glass coffee table. A matching dining table was positioned in front of the window.

Church's desk phone beeped with an incoming call from Ops.

"Justin Riley is at the gate wanting to see you," Kez said in one breath.

"Shit!" Church exclaimed.

"Yeah," Kez agreed.

Church's brain went into overdrive. This unscheduled meeting could go a number of ways. She needed to be prepared for all eventualities.

"Okay," she said confidently. "Let him in."

"You sure?" Kez asked uncertainly.

"Yes."

Church stood up and eyed her top drawer, where she kept her handgun locked away. With a shake of her head, she strode out of her office. She returned a moment later and retrieved her Bowie knife from the underside of her desk. She untucked the back of her shirt and secured the blade in its leather sheath, pointing upwards, over her bra strap. She raced down the wide staircase, the luxurious carpet softening her descent.

Standing behind the vast reception desk, Church watched the monitor. The black Ranger truck with blacked-out windows drove towards the house. It pulled up and came to a crunching stop on the gravelled area in front of the stone steps. She held her breath, waiting for her unannounced visitor to get out. He appeared to be in no rush.

Finally, the truck door opened and Justin Riley slid out gracefully. She let her breath out in a rush at the sight of him.

Get a grip! Battle stations!

Church felt under the reception desk and pulled out a handgun. She quickly checked it, loaded the magazine and tucked the gun into the waistband of her jeans, the grip less than an inch from the pommel of her knife. She relaxed as the cold metal touched her skin. She was ready.

The chief meathead took in his surroundings then athletically leapt up the stone steps. Church released the lock just before he reached the door. He walked straight in, scanned the room and then his eyes found hers.

They stared at each other for a long moment.

"Welcome to Archers, Mr Riley. We don't normally see people without an appointment," Church said.

"Claudia Church, I presume," he said. His voice was deep and gravelly. "Call me Riley."

So, he's done his homework!

The front door clicked as it closed behind him. He strode with purpose towards her. After a moment's hesitation, he offered her his hand. She shook it and ignored the spark she felt at his touch. Their hands parted and his face broke into a smile.

"How's your friend? Quick and full recovery, I hope," he said.

Church raised an eyebrow. "She's fine. Thank you for your concern. You couldn't ask that over the phone?"

"I like the personal touch," he replied, a flash of mischief in his eyes. "Good. I'm glad she's okay. We dealt with the kids, they won't be dealing or hurting anyone else."

What had he done to them? No police reports had been flagged. Church made a mental note to follow up on the two eager and very last-minute participants in Archers' impromptu charade. They had certainly been well compensated for their involvement. Had he killed them and disposed of their bodies?

Riley smiled again. "We taught them a valuable life lesson. We don't tolerate that kind of behaviour. Don't worry, they walked away afterwards."

Did he torture them? Did they give Archers up?

"I hope you and your four friends come back to the club, on the house, as an apology," he said.

An apology? Wait! Four friends? When did he spot Jen?

In the car, stupid!

The chief meathead was toying with her. She checked the monitor briefly. Was he creating his own diversion as payback? Were his team lurking outside the perimeter? They had no chance of getting in without being seen.

"That's very kind of you, thank you. So, if that was all . . ." She moved around the desk and gestured towards the door.

Riley stood his ground. "Nice place you have here," he said. He turned his back on her and wandered around the room. He studied the artwork on the walls, totally relaxed, hands in his pockets.

Church eyed him suspiciously. Fitted, tight black T-shirt, black combats, the pockets on his thighs appeared to be empty. His boots were clean and shone, even in the soft lighting. He wasn't carrying any sizeable weapon. She could take him down before he tried anything.

Careful! Look at the size of him!

Church snorted to herself. *When did a man's size ever stop me?* And she *was* looking at him. He looked like he had been carved out of marble, a Greek god, casually standing in her domain.

Oh, for the love of God! Jump him or get rid of him or… perhaps do both!

"Thank you," Church said, following him and watching his every move. She was ready for any sign of attack.

"So, what is it that you do here?" he asked conversationally.

When she didn't respond, he turned around to look at her.

He stared down the barrel of a Walther PPK.

Riley

No one points a gun at me and gets away with it!

It was aimed directly at his heart. Red's hand was rock steady. Why had she not fired? They stared at each other while he considered his options.

What happened to the creature from the club? he thought. *Admit it, she's just improved from a perfect ten to something else entirely!*

Seeing Red

Red looked like she meant business. Such fire in her eyes, daring him to make a move.

"Let's cut the crap," Red said firmly.

"Gladly," he replied.

Their eyes locked.

Riley lunged forward, clamping a hand around her right wrist, pushing her aim away from his chest. He expected the gun to fire, but it didn't. His right hand grabbed her neck. He forced her to step back until he had her pressed against the panelled wall.

Red didn't react. She didn't feel tense in his hands. He could barely feel her chest move as she breathed. She just looked up at him with those green eyes of hers. The gun dropped from her hand and landed on the thick carpet with a thud.

She tilted her head to the side, quizzically. "Why are you here?" she asked quietly.

Red smelt different today. Still good enough to eat, but something citrusy, laced with a different spice. Riley liked the feel of her this close. He loosened his grip on her but didn't let go.

"Sussing out the competition," he growled.

"How far did you think you would get?"

The corner of his mouth twitched. *How far do you wanna take this?*

He let his hands fall away from her and took a step back.

"Honestly? Not thought that far ahead."

Riley ran his fingers through his hair, brushing the curls away from his eyes and stepped back again.

Without warning, Red pushed herself away from the wall. She ran straight at him, wrapped her arm around his neck and swung herself around him. With a knee in his back and one foot planted on the floor, she flung him backwards. He landed heavily on his back and before he could blink, Red sat squarely on his chest, knees on his arms, her hand on his throat.

Riley stared up at her. *God, she's beautiful!*

He swiftly lifted his hip and shoulder together, flinging Red sideways. She was on her feet in an instant and spun out of his reach. Before he could straighten up, she leapt at him, wrapped her leg around his neck and spun him around with her momentum. He rolled twice and fluidly got to his feet.

She crouched, waiting.

"You wanna play?" he growled.

"Bring it on," she replied with a grin.

Archers

Jen, Miz and Kez stood fully armed, just outside the reception door, listening to the fight. They huddled together, watching the silent security footage on Kez's tablet.

"She's got this," Jen whispered confidently. "I'll deal with his buddy." She slipped down the corridor, tucking her blonde hair into a black woollen hat.

"Keep your comms open," Miz whispered after her.

"She's enjoying this!" Kez said, still glued to the screen.

"More so than at the club," Miz agreed.

"Should we break them up?" Kez asked.

"Nah, when was the last time you saw her smile like that?"

Clearing the Air

Church and Riley circled each other defensively. Poised, ready for anything. Their movements were graceful and deliberate. Riley lunged and ended up flat on his back in the middle of the reception floor, breathing heavily.

Church straddled him, breathing just as hard, one hand planted firmly on his chest. Her right fist was clenched. He was still smirking. She wanted nothing more than to wipe that smirk off his face.

"You come here, thinking you're so very clever!" Church hissed. "Let's dupe the silly little girl, play dumb, act all innocent, just checking up on your friend! You don't fool me, meathead!"

Kiss him!

Riley grabbed both her wrists, sat up and tried to reverse their positions. Church writhed out of his grip and kicked him in the head. He stumbled and reached for something from his boot. A glint of metal flashed in the soft lighting.

Church smiled wickedly, goading him to try it. He strode towards her, but stopped, feeling the cold, sharp steel of her blade pressed to the skin at his throat. Her Bowie knife was twice the size of his. The black handle was intricately carved and beautiful. The blade was about eight inches long. She pressed it a little harder.

"We saw what you did to that poor girl!" she hissed. "You can't force your way in here and expect the same result! You have no idea who you're dealing with!"

Kiss her!

"I see that," he said, grinning. He eyed her knife and let his drop to the floor. A frown then darkened his face. "Wait! What girl?" His arms relaxed.

Church stepped into him, leg between his, grabbed his arm, twisted and flipped him onto his back again.

"Collette. The girl who gave you the USB. You drugged her, ransacked her place. I get it. You like intimidating women!" She tightened her hold on his arm and gave it a twist. "You like exerting your dominance over them!"

"Hmm."

Riley twisted back, freeing his arm. He pulled her down on top of him as she gripped his T-shirt.

"I like you on top," he growled.

Church rolled her eyes and released him with a rough shove. She gracefully dismounted and stood. Riley got to his feet and made a show of brushing himself down.

"Cavendish's bit on the side?" he asked seriously. "We didn't lay a finger on her."

"You expect me to believe that?" Church sneered.

Perhaps Collette was telling the truth?

"Check the CCTV more closely," he said.

"We saw your two heavies enter the building, leaving one in the van."

"True, but they weren't the only ones to pay her a visit."

Church rolled her eyes again.

"Look for a stocky fucker… he was the one doing the attacking. My guys slipped out the back. Then your blonde turned up."

"Jen," Church corrected.

"Yes, her. My guys left."

"And took the USB with them."

"Collette willingly handed it over to Harris," Riley said.

Church looked at him critically. "Why were you there?" she asked.

"To obtain her security pass. We needed access to Cavendish's laptop," he replied.

"And I'm sure you were prepared to intimidate her or worse, to get it."

"You're insinuating you wouldn't have done exactly the same thing. Come on! We were hired to retrieve the files and we did."

"But you don't have them anymore," she said flatly.

"Well played on that one, by the way. We didn't see you coming," he said. "If I hadn't seen the blonde… Jen, driving your getaway car, I wouldn't have put two and two together."

Church snorted. She didn't believe him. She let out a breath and sheathed her knife. Riley picked his up from the floor and tucked it back into his boot.

They stared at each other for a long moment.

"Drink?" she asked suddenly and swept past him towards one of the inner doors.

Miz and Kez quickly ducked out of sight. Riley watched Red in disbelief for a moment. With a shrug of his shoulders, he followed her.

Barchers

Riley followed Red through the main house to the side door and out towards the old stable block. She opened one of the stable doors and disappeared inside. The lights flickered on revealing a small but well-stocked bar. The name *Barchers* was lit in blue neon behind the bar. The walls were bare brick and the place had an American saloon feel.

Red hopped onto the wooden bar, swung her legs over and landed gracefully on the other side.

"Bourbon?" she asked, already holding a bottle of Jack Daniels.

"Please," he replied, taking a seat on one of the wooden bar stools. He looked around the space. So Archers liked to drink. He wondered what else they got up to and why her team hadn't joined in the fun. Where was everybody? He couldn't hear any movement from outside.

Seeing Red

Riley watched her as she poured herself a healthy measure of Captain's Reserve rum. He held up his glass to her. "¡Salud!" he toasted.

"*Slàinte Mhath*," she replied and they drained their glasses.

"I owe you an apology," Church said.

"Hmm."

"Back at Enigma, I didn't..." Words failed her. She topped up their glasses. "I didn't know who you were. I wasn't trying to be the honey trap."

"Not trying, but you certainly succeeded. Spectacularly," he said, raising his glass again. "When did you realise who I was?"

Church looked him straight in the eye. "Jen filled me in when I got into the car. Moments before you came out of the side door with Kez."

"Hmm."

"I really had a good time..." she said.

"Me too."

"I'm sorry."

"Don't be."

"What did you do to the kids?"

"Why do you care?" he asked.

"I'm not completely heartless. Did you kill them?"

Riley laughed, his shoulders shaking.

"No. Like I said, they walked away following a little lesson in good manners and more gentlemanly behaviour." His eyes sparkled. "And no, before you ask, we didn't torture them and no, they didn't give you up. By that point, we had all the information we needed."

Church raised a questioning eyebrow.

"We ran your plates," he said in response.

"So, what now?" she asked.

"Well, that all depends on you," he replied thoughtfully. "Are you going to give the USB back?"

Church laughed.

"My client is a bit upset at the delay," Riley added.

"I'm sure he is. But that's not my problem."

"She," he corrected. "No, I guess not. But you can't blame a guy for trying."

"You thought asking would work?" Church asked in disbelief.

"I can ask nicer." Riley flashed a grin and slowly leant over the bar.

They were inches apart again. He liked the smell of rum on her, it complemented her fragrance perfectly. Her lips were slightly parted, her green eyes searched his. There were many questions in those eyes. If she would only ask them, he would tell her anything.

Church stepped away, breaking the spell. She frowned and shook her head. "We already returned the USB to its owner," she said.

"You sure about that?" he asked, the corner of his mouth twitching.

"Yes."

"You didn't consider that it didn't belong to Cavendish in the first place?" He watched her face, her eyes widened slightly. She hadn't considered that.

"And why should I believe you?" she asked, tilting her head to one side.

"I've no reason to lie to you. I need the files back."

"I can't help you."

"Can't or won't?" he asked.

Church didn't respond. They continued to look at each other, both wondering what the other was thinking.

"Do you have proof?" she eventually asked.

He smiled. "Yes."

"Show me."

"If I show you, will you give the USB back?"

"I said we returned it."

"I remember, but were you telling the truth?"

"Are you?" she countered.

"I find that with you, the truth is all I'm capable of."

Seriously? she thought. He looked sincere, though his eyes were still filled with mischief and something else that looked a lot like desire. She had to admit, he was captivating. *Don't be fooled by the face! He could be stringing you lie after lie! Find out the truth!*

"Fine," she said decisively. "I'll text you with a place to meet."

He grinned triumphantly. "If you wanted my number, you only had to ask!" He slipped a shiny midnight blue business card onto the bar.

"Get out," she said, laced with malice.

"Yes, ma'am." Riley finished his drink, lifted his empty glass in appreciation and left through the stable door.

Church followed and watched him stride back to his truck across the grass.

What the actual fuck just happened here?

The truck roared down the drive and Jen, Miz and Kez appeared out of the shadows to join her.

"Talk about fireworks," Kez said.

"Do you believe him?" Miz asked.

"I don't know what to believe," Church replied. She turned to them with concern on her face. "Have any of you heard from Kat?"

The girls shook their heads. Church patted her back pocket only to find it empty. Where was her phone? She snapped her head towards the drive, the chief meathead would have reached the gate by now. Had he taken her phone with him?

"Here," Miz said, holding Church's phone out.

"Oh, thank you," Church said, relieved.

"Found it in reception. You must have dropped it while you were dropping him."

"Have fun?" Jen asked.

"A little," Church admitted. "He was holding back though."

"So were you," Kez observed.

Church dialled Kat's number and put it on speaker. There was no answer, so she left a voicemail. "Two, Suspect Five paid us a little visit," she said.

"He wasn't alone," Jen added over Church's shoulder. "Suspect Four was lurking outside the perimeter."

Church looked at Jen with concern. Jen just shrugged her shoulders. "I sent him packing, left him by the gates. Shouldn't take the chief meathead long to find him," she said, grinning.

"Watch your back with Suspect Three," Church warned, continuing her voicemail message to Kat. "Check in when you can. If we don't hear from you in the next hour, the whole site is coming to get you." Church ended the call and sent a follow-up text message.

"Kat's fine," Kez said, checking her tablet. "She's at Charlie's apartment."

"So, what next?" Jen asked.

"I'm going to bed," Church said firmly. "I need time to think about everything, but I don't think I have any choice but to meet him and find out what I can. Let's look at this proof he claims to have."

The girls nodded, hugged and headed to their rooms.

C E Allardyce

Meeting at the Café

Church

Church chose the rendezvous point and barely gave Riley (or herself) time to get there. No time for him to plan anything. She had sent him a simple text with the name of the café, the town and the time. He had responded immediately.

Chief Meathead (Justin Riley):
It's a date! Looking forward to seeing you again ☺

Café Pour L'âme, *Coffee for the Soul*, was in the centre of a quiet market town, half an hour's drive from Archers. It was a Tudor, oak-framed, whitewashed building on the market square. A few brave patrons sat huddled under the awning outside, wrapped up against the chill of the autumn air.

Church picked a table for two inside the café by the floor-to-ceiling window. She sipped her third latte of the day, watching the people milling about the market square, one eye on the small parking area at the eastern end of the square. A steady stream of customers entered the café, most opting to take their coffees to go.

She knew the place well, it served the best coffee in the area. They supplied Archers with the coffee beans she bought by the sack. Church ground her own beans with her secret blend of three flavours.

Over the clinking of mugs and plates from the kitchen, the rumble of a large, powerful motorbike reverberated between the buildings on the narrow street that led to the square. A black Kawasaki Ninja swung into view. The rider could only be Riley, broad shoulders, narrow waist, clad in tight black leathers and a black carbon-fibre crash helmet with a tinted visor...

A fleeting feeling of déjà vu rippled through Church. She had heard that engine before. She had seen the bike and the rider, complete with the expensive crash helmet. She glanced at the time on her phone, it was two minutes before the rendezvous time she she'd given.

The bike idled for a moment, then powered onto the pavement outside the café, rattling the windows. The stand was kicked out and the handlebars turned. The rider dismounted, swinging his leg over the back of the bike.

Nice! she thought, admiring his leather-clad backside, completely forgetting their previous encounter. *I'd like to sink my teeth into his bare flesh, right there!*

Claudia Jean! her mother's scalding tone rang in her mind.

Oh, Mum! she sighed, mentally rolling her eyes. *Just lookin'!*

Riley pulled off his helmet and ran a gloved hand through his hair. His eyes found Church's and the corner of his mouth twitched. With purpose, he strode through the door, making the bell jingle. His leathers creaked as he shrugged off his backpack and jacket. He sat down opposite Church.

"Take a seat, why don't you," she said sarcastically.

"Thank you," he said, taking the printed menu from the small wooden holder on the table. He studied it carefully.

"Coffee?" she asked.

"Black. As large as they can make it."

Church stood and approached the oak counter. She returned a few moments later and set the coffee in front of him, then slid back into her chair.

"Thank you," he said.

"You're welcome."

See! I can be all sweetness and politeness too. Just don't push me!

The corner of his mouth twitched again as he stared at her. He looked relaxed, at ease. The twinkle in his eyes captivated her, pleasantly mingling with the smell of leather and that irresistible aftershave he was wearing.

Riley

Red looked radiant, even in the weak sunlight that shone through the large window beside her. The light caught the lighter strands of her hair. Riley marvelled at the colour, dark rusty tones, burnished copper with a hint of soft gold. Her hair was loose, the waves cascading over her shoulders.

She wore a white shirt with black jeans that hugged her curves and black flat-heeled suede boots that reached her knees.

Should've brought a spare helmet, he thought.

Riley glanced at the soft leather jacket draped over the back of her chair. That wouldn't do, she'd freeze.

The whirring and whining from the milk steamer echoed around them.

"So, do you have it?" Red asked, once the noise had settled.

"I do," he replied, taking a tablet out of his backpack. He turned it on, entered a passcode and handed it to her.

Red took it and scanned the document. Riley watched her read it thoroughly a second time, her eyes absorbing the irrefutable evidence.

When she had finished, she looked up. "May I have a copy?" she asked.

"Sure," he said, holding out his hand. She returned the tablet. He tapped the screen a couple of times, then offered it back to her. She shook her head, so he returned it to his pack.

Red looked at him expectantly. Riley simply grinned and waited for the notification to come through.

Her phone dinged and his mouth twitched. "Got it?" he asked, unnecessarily.

Red picked up her phone from the table and checked the screen.

"Yes," she replied. She placed the phone back on the table, screen-side down. "Why are you being so accommodating?"

"Well, Red, you have something I need."

Her eyes visibly twitched, though she tried hard to conceal it. "Why should I help you?" she asked.

"Because it's the right thing to do."

"And you're the king of doing the right thing?" she scoffed.

"On this occasion, yes, I am."

Church

Church studied Riley, trying to make sense of him. Stripping away the undeniable physical attraction, his behaviour still didn't add up. He was like her, same background, same training, same objectives. But how had he found her *personal* email? Hardly anyone knew it.

He had skills, ones she didn't like to admit he had.

And then there was the USB. Why hadn't he tried to take it by force? During their play-fighting at Archers, she'd felt him holding back. But why? Why back off? It made no sense.

"I won't break my contract," Church said.

"Hmm. I thought as much," Riley growled.

"Did you now?" Her voice dripping with sarcasm.

"I did." He flashed a grin.

"You seem to have all the answers."

"As a matter of fact, I do." His eyes twinkled with mischief.

She raised an eyebrow and waited.

"Return a dummy USB to Torenta, get paid." He shrugged. "Then give me the real one."

"Just like that?" she asked, sceptical.

"Just like that." He was still grinning. "Nice and simple. I'm sure your techs can dress up the files, make them look legit while corrupting the juicy bits."

"Of course they could. But that would be..." Church frowned slightly. "I can't accept payment from Torenta," she said firmly, looking out the window.

"Hmm," he growled in amusement.

"You *assume* a lot," she said, frowning at him.

"It's my job to *know* things… and to solve problems. You and your gang of kick-ass girls are my current problem."

"And what did you decide to do about us?"

She was poised to strike, coiled like a spring. Coffee in his face would be a good opener, mug and all. A knee to the balls was tempting, though less effective with those damn leathers. She held his gaze.

"My client agreed to pay you for your time and effort," Riley said.

That caught her off guard. That was certainly unexpected.

"And why would your client do that?"

"She wants her company's property back."

Church hated being on the wrong side of things. So much for a staying in the light. Mr Cavendish had lied to her and she'd fallen for it. Sloppy. Unforgivable. Rookie mistake.

"I need to corroborate the document," she said. Buy herself time. Cavendish owed her an explanation.

"Naturally," Riley said.

"And I want some answers."

"From me?" He raised an innocent brow, leaning back. "Fire away."

Church switched off her phone and tucked her hair behind her ears, revealing she wasn't wearing an earpiece. Riley didn't move.

"Your team listening?"

"Nope. Just us," he said, grinning as he waved to the server. "Another?" he asked, nodding to her mug.

"Not for me, thanks," Church replied.

The server brought Riley a fresh coffee, cleared the table and disappeared.

Church leaned in a little closer. "Have you thought about why this information has been stolen twice in a week?"

"Three times," he corrected.

She waved the jibe away and waited.

"Not really my concern. We were hired to do a job and we did it."

"Why offer to pay us?"

"She wants her stuff back," he repeated, like it was obvious.

"How much?"

"Forty K."

Church wouldn't accept a penny, even if the USB did truly belong to EMP, as the document suggested. "And if I don't accept?"

The muscles in Riley's jaw clenched. "Then we keep it, along with our fee and retrieve the information ourselves."

"By any means?" she asked.

He nodded.

"Good luck with that," she said, coolly.

Riley

Was that a challenge?

Oh, bring it on, Red!

She sat across from him, cool as a cucumber, her team was back at Archers. And yet, here she was. Alone.

God, she's mesmerising!

"I've got options," Riley said, eyes flashing. "I've considered them carefully."

"You and your bearded friend didn't get far in your little expedition around Archers walls," Red said.

Touché. Jonny had been knocked out cold. Riley found him slumped at the gates and had to haul him into the truck. Jonny came to on the drive back but "couldn't remember" what happened. Maybe he really didn't.

"And getting in wasn't all that successful either," Red added.

I was quite pleased with that, Riley thought. "Like I said, we were just sussing out the competition."

"And what did you conclude?"

"No conclusions. Yet."

Red nodded once. "I'll be in touch," she said, standing.

Conversation over.

She reached for her jacket. Riley stood, took it from her and shook it out, holding it open.

A small crease formed between her eyebrows, but she turned, slipped in her arms and let him ease it over her shoulders.

"Do you have a deadline?" she asked, facing him again.

"Not exactly. But sooner rather than later."

"Give me twenty-four hours."

Riley dipped his head in agreement and watched her leave. She walked up the street, disappearing around the corner.

He sat back down and finished his coffee.

Revelations

Archers

Church walked to her car, mind racing. Could she trust Riley? The evidence seemed solid. Her team would tear it apart. Should she take his client's offer? Forty grand was tempting for a few hours' work. But no. That wasn't the point anymore.

She drove past the café. In the rearview mirror, Riley was still sitting at the window. Damn, he was handsome. Too handsome. A distraction she didn't need.

Keep it professional, she warned herself.

But what if I don't wanna?

She scrunched that thought and mentally tossed it out the window, turning her irritation back to Edward Cavendish. The bastard had lied and he'd answer for it. In her old life, she'd have made him pay dearly and painfully. The thought soothed her as she drove.

Thirty minutes later, she pulled into the underground parking. Kat was waiting by the ramp.

"So?" Kat asked before Church had the chance to slide out of the driver's seat. "Which 'F' did you choose?"

Church gave her a look.

"Fighting or fucking?" Kat clarified, eyes twinkling.

An image of the latter flickered through Church's mind, which sent a not-so-unpleasant shiver down her spine.

"Neither," she said flatly. "I've now got more questions than answers."

Kat pouted in disappointment for her friend. "We'll figure it out. We always do." She linked arms with Church and they headed to the conference room, where the team were waiting.

Church summarised her meeting with Riley and forwarded his email to them. "We're on the wrong side of this," she said. "I'll update the op report. But first, problem one: we didn't verify that our objective was stolen property. That's on me. I should've dug deeper before accepting the op."

"Not the end of the world," Kat said. "We had to move quickly."

"It won't happen again," Church said firmly. "Now, problem two: do we report the theft?"

She wasn't sure that was the right move. The girls didn't have an answer either. The fuss around this information was setting off her alarm bells. Should she just return the USB to Riley and walk away?

"I'm going to talk to Mr Cavendish," she said decisively. "He signed our contract and broke it." She stood, grabbed a marker and started scribbling questions and thoughts on the whiteboard.

"I'll check on Collette," Kat offered. "She should be feeling better."

"Great," Church muttered, chewing the end of the pen as her eyes scanned the board.

"Before we move on," Kez said "I talked to Eve about the USB data. I know I shouldn't have, but we needed answers."

Everyone turned as she pulled up her summary on the main screen. Church returned to her seat.

"EMP have developed several major therapies," Kez explained. "Some were acquired from smaller companies. But the real money-makers? Those were Cavendish's, back when he was a scientist for EMP. He made them millions. Won awards. They took nearly all his projects to market."

She paused, then continued. "The USB holds one of his files. Project Warrior IV. EMP are crippled without it. They were conducting human trials, unsanctioned and illegal. The results are… horrific."

"Horrific how?" Kat asked.

"Severe side effects. Some of the test subjects had heart failure, respiratory collapse, psychological breakdowns. Some died."

"What were they testing?" Church asked.

"A human enhancement serum," Kez said. "Designed to increase stamina, strength, resilience. Recent trials show some promise, but the success rate is still low."

"Why cut corners? EMP aren't short on cash," Miz said.

"Greed," Kez replied. "They planned to sell it to governments, contractors, private defence firms. Global rollout. Not just domestic."

Church and Kat exchanged a look. In unison, they said, "Super soldiers."

"Any chatter about this?" Church asked.

"Nothing," Kez confirmed.

"But too many people already know," Church said, glancing at the whiteboard. "EMP, Torenta, whoever Collette is working for... Echo... and now us."

"Won't stay quiet for long," Kat added.

Church knew Archers were in danger. Possessing this information made them a target. Maybe the safest option was to get rid of it, fast.

"We need more," Church said. "Kez, see if you can get into EMP's systems."

Kez grimaced. "Already tried. Their new protections are tight since the breach. I threw everything I had at it, no luck." She sighed. "We'll need access to one of their buildings."

That was a dangerous step, especially if Church wanted Archers to stay in the light. But then a thought struck her. Riley had access to EMP and something to prove to Miss Romano. It was a risky idea. Riley wouldn't go for it easily. Still, it was worth mulling over.

"Thanks, Kez. I'll deal with Cavendish. Kat, check in with Collette. Everyone else, focus on EMP." She gestured toward the screen.

"What about Echo?" Kat asked.

"They can wait," Church said. "I have until tomorrow to give Riley our decision. I'd like some answers first."

Torenta Meeting

Armed with more information than she wanted, Church drove to meet Torenta's deceitful CEO. Kat had called minutes after visiting Collette at the safe house. Her summary was short and to the point.

The day after Edward took the USB, someone left explicit photos of Collette and Cavendish on her doorstep. Then came the stocky man – blackmail or else. If she didn't cooperate, Mrs Cavendish would find out. Divorce. Scandal. Job gone. Home lost. The man offered Collette twenty grand for her trouble, enough for a fresh start.

Cavendish had mentioned valuable information from an old colleague. Collette knew where he hid things, including videos from their hotel stays. She stole his access card, grabbed the USB and handed it to a tall, blond stranger who showed up the next day. Minutes later, the stocky man returned, furious to learn she'd already passed it on.

Whoever orchestrated this had moved fast. They must have shadowed Geoff Abraham and anyone he'd contacted. Church silently applauded the precision as she continued toward Torenta.

The more she'd dug into Cavendish, the more she disliked him. His scandalous departure from EMP was just the beginning.

By the time she reached the shabby business park, Church had formed a plan or two. She parked two hundred yards away, disconnected her phone from the car's console and scrolled to Cavendish's number. She jabbed at his name in quiet fury with her thumb.

He answered after a few rings. "Miss Church…"

"I have the USB," she said, cutting him off. "Are you free? I'm nearby."

In her rearview mirror, she caught movement from his office window. The grubby vertical blinds were quivering as he peeked through them.

"That's excellent news," he stuttered. "Yes, of course. How far away are you?"

"Not far. We'll wrap this up soon."

"Come straight up, you remember the way?"

"I do."

"Perfect. See you soon."

Church ended the call. Something was off. His tone was all wrong. He was obviously nervous. Jumpy. His cheeriness didn't match the fear she'd seen. She was prepared to show him something to really fear, when she got her hands on him.

She tapped her comms. "I'm outside Torenta," she said quietly, phone still at her ear. "Going in."

"Good luck," Kez said. "Wish you'd let us come."

"I'll be fine. If I'm not in touch in an hour, then send backup."

"They're two minutes away."

"Kerys!" Church scolded half-heartedly.

"Scorpio were nearby," Kez said. "'Use the resources we have.' Isn't that what you always say? 'Have a backup plan or three up your sleeve'. Isn't that another one? Or 'Plan for all possible and implausible eventualities'…"

"Okay, point taken," Church sighed. "Right, I'm going dark."

She ended the call and rolled her shoulders. The shift of the leather holster against her back, calmed her. With a steadying breath, she slid out of the car.

The Torenta office was eerily quiet again. Did anyone *work* here? Or was this just a shell company? Had Cavendish not noticed Collette's absence? She'd been the only employee Church had seen here. Maybe he didn't care.

Church climbed the stairs and knocked on his door.

"Come in," Cavendish called.

He looked relieved when she entered, offered a clammy handshake and gestured toward the chair across from his desk. "So, you have the USB?" he asked, sweating profusely.

Church resisted the urge to wipe her palm clean. "I have questions first," she said, sitting on the offered faded seat.

Cavendish blinked, caught off guard. "Can I offer you a cup of tea?"

"No. Thank you. I'll get straight to it. The property you hired us to retrieve, it doesn't belong to you. And it certainly doesn't belong to Torenta Pharmaceuticals."

He swallowed hard, eyes flicking to the phone on his desk, then to the door, then the window.

Church continued coolly. "May I remind you of clause twelve of our contract?"

Why was he so nervous? Church usually had to bare her dark side before provoking this level of fear.

"I... I can explain!" he stuttered.

I'm all ears, Church thought.

"I... this is... we..." Mr Cavendish finally managed, "We're experiencing a slight dip in our profits."

As if that's an explanation! Church said nothing, pressing him to fill the silence.

"I heard a rumour," he muttered. "I had to act quickly. Every man for himself! You don't understand. It's kill or be killed in pharma. I used to be a leader in research until that... that Italian whore ruined everything!"

Church arched an eyebrow, unimpressed by the insult. *So unimaginative!* she thought angrily. Yes, Romano was a ruthless businesswoman and probably ate men like Cavendish for breakfast. Was he just nursing his bruised ego at being outplayed by her?

"She screwed me over!" he snapped, his face flushing.

Church kept her voice calm, despite his whining grating on her nerves. "Miss Romano didn't force you to break the law, or your contract of employment. From what I've gathered, you heard EMP planned to use one of your ideas so you decided to steal it before they could."

"You can't steal something you developed!" he cried. "Years of research! Blood, sweat and tears. It nearly cost me my marriage!"

"I've read your termination letter from EMP. The information belongs to them. Intellectual property remains the company's, no matter who developed it. Then there's the matter of your dismissal for gross misconduct."

"That was a complete fabrication!" Mr Cavendish insisted. "Romano couldn't wait for me to retire."

"The evidence says otherwise. It would hold up in court... if the employee ever pressed charges."

His eyes widened.

"Yes, I've done my homework," Church said. "Speaking of which, where is she now? Shouldn't take long to find her. Much like your current relationship with Miss Millford... history seems to be repeating itself."

His mouth dropped open.

"Forgotten her already?" Church asked. "She's fine, by the way."

"I... we..."

"She stole the USB from the server room. But you knew that. Why else delete the security footage? And you kept the explicit content for insurance. In case things went cold between the two of you. Am I wrong?"

Cavendish squirmed.

"Did you ransack her place?" he asked quietly.

"No," Church replied evenly. "She was bribed to get the USB. She handed it to a third party. The briber trashed her place looking for it. We found her shortly after. Gave her medical attention and tracked down the USB."

"You have it?" he asked.

"I'm not giving it to you."

"We had an agreement!"

"And you broke it. You lied. Repeatedly."

"I had no choice!"

"There's always a choice, Mr Cavendish. For instance, not sexually harassing colleagues. Or not stealing information that doesn't belong to you."

"It was for the business... my wife expected a return on her investment… her expectations…!"

"Neither concern me."

"May said you came highly recommended! That you could get the job done!"

"I did. In less than twelve hours. But you won't profit from it."

"And you're letting *Romano* profit from it?" he hissed.

"I didn't say that."

He was unravelling fast. His forehead shone with sweat, his cheeks blotched red, hands trembling into fists against the desk.

"You won't get away with this!"

Church suppressed a laugh. *What exactly could this man do?*

"She won't stop!" he blurted. Then froze.

She? Church tilted her head. Had Romano found out he was behind the theft? Or was this something else? His eyes darted around the room, frantic. Still being watched? Bugged?

Church reached into her pocket and pulled out a small device. She activated it, then held up her phone screen. "No signal," she said. "You can speak freely. Tell me everything, or I walk and leave you to whatever mess you've got yourself into."

Cavendish hesitated, swallowing hard. He pulled his mobile from the inside pocket of his 'off the peg' jacket. Church doubted his wife's wealth extended to his wardrobe.

"Has someone else contacted you about the USB?" she asked.

"Where is it?"

"Safe. Give me a name."

He opened his mouth, then shut it again.

"Mr Cavendish," she said gently. "I can't help you if you don't talk."

"They'll kill me," he whispered. "I thought they'd killed Collette. Are you sure she's safe?"

"She is," Church assured him.

"My wife is next. Can you protect her too?"

"Of course." *Though I suspect you're more worried about her money than her wellbeing.* "But I need a name."

He slumped in his threadbare chair, defeated. "I don't know her name," he murmured.

"When did she contact you? How? What exactly did she say?"

"I can't."

Church softened her tone. "I can have a team at your house in minutes. Is your wife home? We can trace her phone."

"You can do that?" he asked, hesitant.

"That and more."

"They know you're here!"

"Let me worry about that. Talk. Fast."

He swallowed. "The day Collette stopped answering my calls, right after our meeting, I found these." He pulled out a thick envelope from his drawer. "They were just there, on my desk." He jabbed at the surface in front of his keyboard. "Then she called. A woman. The second I opened the envelope. She said copies of every photo would be delivered to May."

"I see," Church said coolly.

"I know they're listening. A man's been following me everywhere."

Church took an educated guess. "Short, stocky, always in a hood?"

He nodded.

"Leave him to me. Did you know EMP already started trials on the formula?"

"What? No. It's not ready! Kenny was still working on it, "

"Kenny Mackay? Deputy Research Scientist?"

He nodded again.

"He helped you steal the project file from EMP and scrub the evidence."

"Yes," he confirmed sheepishly.

"Who tipped you off to EMP's plans? Was it your poker buddy, Mr Abraham?"

Mr Cavendish gave a shaky nod.

"Tell me everything you know about this woman."

He sat trembling, eyes darting to the device on his desk. Confirming it was still active, he leaned forward. "The stocky man, he works for her," he whispered. "He called her *The Doctor*. She knows things, things no one should know. My wife…"

Progress. Not a name, but a title. It would have to do for now.

"Okay, here's what's going to happen." Church leaned in slightly. "I'm turning off this device. From that point on, we go back to how things were before I switched it on. Got it? Once I leave, lock yourself in and stay here. Do not move. I'll send someone to you. Don't open that door for anyone else until he identifies himself."

"Please don't leave," Mr Cavendish wailed. "Take me with you."

"A member of my team will be here in minutes, I promise."

"How will I know he's one of yours?"

"You'll know. Trust me."

He hesitated. "Do you trust him?"

"With my life," she said simply. "He wouldn't be on my team otherwise." She gave him a warm, fleeting smile. "Ready?"

Cavendish's eyes widened. He nodded.

Church switched off the jammer and rose from her chair.

"And why would I do that?" she asked, turning to face him once more.

Cavendish hesitated, then summoned what little confidence he had. "The contract, we can extend it."

"No." Her tone cut like glass. "You broke the contract. Our dealings ended the moment you lied to me. If you'd been honest from the start, I would've advised you differently. But now? I won't take a penny from you. And I'm certainly not helping you again."

"But… "

"You're on your own, Mr Cavendish. Good luck with that."

She walked out the door and left it open behind her.

Riley

Riley's mind buzzed with his encounter with Red as he rolled his motorbike into the club's garage. He draped the stretchy black dust cover over it, tightened the toggles and skipped the usual wipe-down – it would have to wait until tomorrow. He pulled down the up-and-over door, locked it and made his way to the side entrance.

The door didn't open immediately. Riley frowned up at the security camera. Where the hell was Ellis?

Seeing Red

With a growl he fished his keys from his inner pocket. Three locks and a security code later, he stepped inside.

The door clicked shut behind him, locking with finality.

The club was silent.

Only Ellis was supposed to be here. Riley had given the rest of the team time off until he figured out how to get the USB back. Red wasn't handing it over willingly and forcing it from her... well, that would more than likely result in failure.

He moved down the corridor toward his office, opened the door and froze.

A familiar scent wrapped around him like a noose – Marlboro smoke, laced with Black Opium perfume.

He flicked on the light.

And there she was.

Black, patent leather boots rested on his desk, ankles crossed, six-inch chrome heels catching the sterile overhead light. He remembered what those heels could do. What they *had* done.

His skin prickled.

The woman in his chair wore a long black skirt with a provocative slit revealing slender stockinged legs, a black silk blouse and long trench coat. Her long, manicured fingers tapped out a patient rhythm over her stomach. Nails black as lacquer. Her smoky hazel eyes followed a lazy cloud of cigarette smoke drifting toward the ceiling.

Mahogany hair, streaked with silver, was pulled back into a severe bun.

She exhaled slowly.

Her face bore a few more lines, but Riley remembered the texture of that olive skin, how it looked flushed with exertion, how it felt under his lips when he'd been allowed to touch her.

Gloria Pérez.

His former commanding officer. His abuser. The woman who had owned every part of him for far too long.

She didn't even acknowledge him. Just waited for the response she *knew* was coming.

His jaw clenched tight, muscles twitching. He wouldn't give her the satisfaction. She was nothing to him now.

But eight years wasn't long enough to forget.

Her head turned slowly. "*Soldado,*" she purred in Spanish.

"Ma'am," he replied, too fast, too automatic.

She held his gaze like *he* was the one intruding.

Movement behind him made him turn. A man, short, stocky, dressed in black combats, swaggered down the corridor.

Riley recognised him. The thug who'd been skulking outside Torenta, EMP and Cavendish's girlfriend's place. Stocky had a shaved head, a red tattoo curling up one arm and was built like a pit bull. About Riley's age, maybe younger.

Not her usual type.

Jealous?

Of him? Seriously?

He snorted inwardly. Let someone else scratch that particular itch.

Better him than me.

The man ignored Riley and stood silently at the door, waiting.

"Done?" Pérez asked him in crisp English.

"Aye," the man replied.

She gave a dismissive nod. He left without a word, boots thudding down the corridor.

Riley waited until the sound faded.

"Where's my team?" he asked.

Pérez's gaze turned colder as she caught his attempt at deception.
"You mean the one man you had on duty?" She tutted, dripping with disapproval. "I'm sure the mestizo won't kill him... but I might."

Riley didn't take the bait. She called her lackey, the stocky fucker, the mongrel, not referring to his heritage but his place in her ranks. Not her top dog. Primero, her First Officer, had been Riley's title. A title that had nearly cost him his career and his life.

"Why are you here?" he growled.

Pérez smiled, a slow, knowing curl of her lips.

"You know why."

He didn't. But he guessed. The USB.

"I don't have it."

"You let a bunch of girls get the better of you," she sneered. "Let them steal from you. No. I know you don't have it. But you will."

Riley crossed his arms, rigid. She inhaled deeply, then blew the smoke straight at him.

His mind spun. Where was Ellis? What had her mongrel done to him? Had she infiltrated Echo's systems? Was he followed from EMP? How had he missed that? He was in trouble. This woman could destroy everything he'd built, the club, his team... him, again.

You can't submit to her.

I don't intend to. Never again.

He needed to say something. He wasn't going to roll over for this woman.

"You left," he growled in accusation.

Pérez raised an eyebrow, surprised. She held his gaze, reading him like an open book, something she'd always been terrifyingly good at. Could he hide anything from her? He hadn't been able to before.

"I wasn't given a choice," she said quietly, venom lacing her words.

That cut deeper than he expected. Who had the power to force her to leave?

"You didn't contact me. I thought you were dead."

"Did you mourn me?" Her voice was silky, eyes boring into his soul.

Riley clenched his jaw, refusing to answer.

"You've bulked up," she said, admiring him slowly. "I like it."

She uncrossed her ankles, lifted her heels off his desk, then lowered her feet and stood with a predator's grace. Circling the desk, she settled on the edge, facing him. She drew from her cigarette, held it, then exhaled deliberately at the smoke detector. Riley's eyes flicked to it, no light.

Burn the place down! he thought wildly. Stocky was gone. Just knock her out, lock the door and let it burn with her inside. Then find Stocky. Get answers.

But could he really do it? Could he let her burn?

Pérez laughed, low and dangerous. "I'm not here to start a fire. Want to watch me burn, Justin?"

How does she do that?

"I'm just proving how useful the mestizo can be... when he puts his mind to it."

"Who is he?" Riley growled.

"James? He's a former friend of a foe," she said, vague and slippery. "He's nothing like you, don't worry. You're not that easily replaced. But he has certain... skills." Her eyes flashed wickedly.

She pushed off the desk and stepped close, her perfume intoxicating him.

"You're quite taken with the redhead, I see."

"You're misinformed."

"It'll take a lot to melt her ice... but we'll get to that later." She stepped closer, pressing herself against him.

"Did you miss me?" she whispered.

Journey Home

Church

Church surveyed the area discreetly as she returned to her car. There was no sign of anyone watching her. She called Kez and made her way back to Archers.

"Can you locate Mrs Cavendish and send Scorpio to her? I also need one of them to go to Torenta and collect Mr Cavendish."

"On it," Kez confirmed.

"Track down Kenny MacKay from EMP. He's the one who helped Mr Cavendish. Any more news from Kat?"

"Will do. She gave you pretty much everything," Kez said. "We found the photos in Collette's car."

"Mr Cavendish received the same, left on his desk in his office. Did Collette mention a woman?" Church asked.

"No. Why?"

"A woman threatened Mr Cavendish. Maybe that's who Stocky is working for."

"I widened the search for the stocky guy," Kez said. "And I've just got a hit."

"Where?" Church asked, intrigued.

"Outside Enigma," Kez said gravely.

Church took that in for a moment. What could that mean? Another incoming call beeped on the console.

"Shit! It's Riley calling. I'll play dumb. Can you summarise everything for me? Won't be long."

"Sure thing. Drive safe," Kez said and hung up.

Church accepted Riley's call using the button on the steering wheel.

"I thought I said that I would be in touch," she answered frostily, hearing little more than howling wind and the roar of a motorbike. From the sound of the engine, he was pushing it hard.

"You're driving," he growled over the noise.

"And you're riding."

"Where are you?" he asked.

By the desperation in his tone, he really needed to know.

"Why?" she asked suspiciously.

"Pull over."

"I'm on hands-free, if that's what you're worried about."

"It's not. Pull over."

Church passed a parking sign on the motorway – it was half a mile away. She shook her head in disbelief and berated herself for even considering listening to this meathead.

"What's up?" she asked, pressing down the accelerator a little harder.

Riley didn't reply. Was he waiting for her to comply?

Screw him! she thought.

Seeing Red

Leaving little time to stop the car elegantly, Church braked hard and swerved into the parking area. She put in her earbuds and transferred the call to them.

"I've pulled over and switched off the engine. Happy now?" she said sarcastically.

"Get out," he growled over the roar of his engine.

"Seriously?"

"Claudia! Get out of the fucking car – now!" he bellowed.

Before she could think, she launched herself out of the door and scrambled up the grassy bank. Breathing heavily, she turned to look at her car.

"Ha ha! Very fun..."

Church's car exploded in a ball of flames and thick smoke.

Riley

Riley heard the explosion through his headphones, then saw a flash of light against the dark sky. He dropped a gear and sped up the motorway.

"Can you hear me?" he shouted.

He pushed the bike faster still. Dread filled him and a shiver ran down his spine. He was too late.

Moments later, he could see the glow from a fire, flames reaching high into the sky and noxious black smoke blowing across the road.

Riley screeched to a halt behind the burning car and saw Red standing on the grass slope a few metres away. He huffed out a breath in relief. He swerved the bike around the fire and lifted his visor.

"Get on!" he shouted.

Red didn't move. She was staring at the car.

"Claudia! Get on!"

Perhaps she couldn't hear him – the blast could have temporarily deafened her. Riley kicked out the bike stand and dismounted. Just as he reached her, her knees gave way and she started to crumple. He grabbed her by the elbows and helped her down to the ground.

"Are you okay? Are you hurt?" he asked.

Riley patted her arms and legs, checking for obvious injuries. He placed a gloved finger under her chin and encouraged her to look at him. Her eyes were glazed and her pupils dilated. Eventually, she blinked and pushed his hands away.

"Let me get you out of here. It's not safe." Riley nodded towards the car.

Red shook her head. "I don't have a helmet," she croaked.

"That's the least of your worries," he said, grabbing her hands. He pulled her to her feet. "Come."

Red resisted for a moment, then allowed him to escort her to his bike. He got on and kicked back the stand. Red clambered on behind him and wrapped her arms around his waist.

"Hold on tight," he growled, speeding off.

Seeing Red

Red was a good passenger. She had ridden before, moving fluidly with the bike, her thighs gripping his. He patted her hand reassuringly. His comms crackled into life.

"Ri, what's going on?" Harris asked.

"Man, where to start?" Riley sighed.

"Where are you?"

"M11, northbound. Is Ellis okay?"

"He's fine. Bit sheepish. He's being babysat by Muscles and Tom."

"She's back, H."

"Who?"

"Gloria fucking Pérez."

"No way! When?"

"This afternoon. Brought the stocky fucker with her. Broke into the club. Disabled everything. I need everything scrubbed clean – check all systems, every corner."

Red's arms loosened around his waist. He patted her hand again and felt her thighs starting to relax against his.

"Claudia!" he shouted over his shoulder. "Stay with me!"

Red's hands nearly dropped away. Riley pressed her barely-laced fingers to his stomach with his arm and gripped her wrist, trying to stop her slipping off the bike. Her hold on him returned, but he wasn't going to risk it longer than he had to.

He approached the exit towards the city. At the last moment, he released her and smoothly roared up the slip road.

"Ri?" Harris called.

"I need to use your fuck pad. Can you let Wes know to expect me?"

"Sure, but why?"

"I'll tell you later."

The comms went quiet.

Archers

After Kez hung up from speaking to Church, she rallied the troops. Orders were sent to Scorpio One – Sebastian – who led the all-male backup team and Kez tasked the techs on duty to find Kenny MacKay. An alert sounded on her laptop. She frowned at the notification and clicked on the pop-up.

"Holy fuckin' hell!" she shouted at the empty surveillance room and immediately sent an emergency text message to the rest of Team Archers. She furiously clicked her mouse while staring at the screen. By the time the team appeared, breathless at the door, she had the answers she needed. She let out a breath in relief.

"What's going on?" Kat demanded.

"I just lost Church's car," Kez explained.

"Glitch?" Jen asked, looking at the screen. The map was empty – no flashing, solid red triangle showing the car's location.

"Nope. Look at this." Kez brought up CCTV footage of a fire on the motorway. "Last known location."

"Oh my God!" Kat cried.

"I've still got Church," Kez said quickly. "But she's nowhere near the car."

"Where is she?" Kat asked desperately.

"In town, by the river. Looks like Charlie's apartment on the river." Kez moved the map on the screen. It showed a solid red diamond – Church's tracker implant.

Kat frowned and dialled Harris's mobile. It went straight to voicemail.

"Hey babe, call me," she said and ended the call.

Riley

Riley sped through the town until he reached the private car park of the complex on the river where Harris's apartment was. He slid off the bike and held out his hand. Red lazily pushed it away. Leaning on the seat for support, she swung her leg over the back of the bike.

Her balance faltered. Riley was beside her in an instant. All the tension left her body. Before she slumped to the ground, Riley scooped her up in his arms and carried her towards the building. Her head slumped against his shoulder.

In the glass-fronted foyer, the night manager, Wes, remotely unlocked the door and it swung slowly inwards. Riley manoeuvred through the door, careful not to catch Red's feet.

"Evening, Wes," Riley said.

"Mr Riley," Wes said formally, standing up. He skirted the reception desk and slipped a keycard into Riley's hand. He didn't seem at all shocked at the semi-conscious woman in his arms. "You need anything, you know where I am."

"Thanks," Riley said as he entered the lift

Wes returned to his desk, his attention back on the security footage of the complex.

Inside the luxurious apartment, Riley gently laid Red on the white leather sofa. He adjusted a plush velvet cushion behind her head and covered her gently with a soft silver throw.

Riley knelt in front of her, hung his head to his chest and ran a gloved hand through his hair. She was alive, but she really needed to be checked over.

He pulled his gloves off with his teeth and shrugged off his leather jacket. Red looked so fragile lying there. He had nearly lost her. All because of that woman. Damn her! How did she know what Red meant to him? He barely knew himself – until her life was threatened. That had changed everything.

Red's eyelids fluttered open and she tried to sit up. Riley placed a hand on her shoulder and urged her back down.

"Easy now. You're okay." He removed his hand and sat on the coffee table.

Red looked around the apartment quickly – looking for weapons and exits, no doubt. She looked less than pleased, ready to plunge that knife of hers into his chest. He had felt it through her jacket when he carried her into the building. Riley sat back and raised his palms as Red sat up slowly

"Can I get you some water?"

Seeing Red

Red shook her head, immediately screwing her eyes shut and holding her head in her hands.

What could he do? He wasn't being particularly helpful.

"Did you have second thoughts?" she asked hoarsely, still looking at the floor. She raised her head slowly.

"No. It wasn't me." *She won't believe you.* Riley ran a hand through his hair.

"Your client ran out of patience?"

"It wasn't her either."

Red tilted her head. "The woman the stocky guy works for?"

Bingo.

How could Riley explain it to her? He knew he couldn't. He had taken a risk and there would be consequences for his actions. He didn't care what happened to him – as long as Red was safe. But it was more than unlikely that she would walk away from this. Not now.

"Claudia…" he said eventually.

Red pulled a face. "Call me Church."

The corner of Riley's mouth twitched. "I prefer Red, I'm afraid it's kinda stuck."

"That's worse! You want me to kill you right here, right now and mess up this amazing apartment, *handsome*?" she hissed.

Riley's heart practically sang at the return of her fiery, sassy side.

"Why did you bring me here?" she asked. "Is this your place?"

Riley smiled. "No, this is Harris's apartment. It was closer…"

Red was still looking at him warily.

"You're free to leave," Riley said. "You're not a prisoner."

She raised an eyebrow. "You're not going to ask for the USB?"

"Would you give it to me, if I did?"

"No," Red said firmly.

The sound of screeching tyres could be heard from their elevated position above the river. Riley stood and went to the glass wall, tugged the sliding door open and leaned over the balcony. "Your team's here," he growled. "Fully armed, by the looks of it."

He turned to see Red had already left the apartment.

A few moments later, Riley saw Team Archers surround Red and bundle her into the waiting car. It screeched its tyres again and sped away, out of sight.

Church

Church reported to medical, as instructed by the team. She just didn't have the energy to argue. She was fine. Her head was pounding like a kick drum, but it was nothing. She'd had worse. She just needed a shower and some sleep. The fuss was not necessary.

Eve, the Chief Medic, didn't agree. She diligently checked Church's vitals and took some blood samples – all with a disapproving look on her face.

"I'll run these now," Eve said, scribbling on one of the small tubes. "I'll send you the results in the morning, once you've had at least seven hours' sleep."

Church snorted. She barely had enough energy left to stand.

Eve looked over her glasses at Church. "The team said your car was blown up. Deliberately. That's a considerable concern."

"Professional hazard," Church said petulantly.

"I thought you were trying to get away from all that?"

"Seems like I've stumbled quite easily into something very similar to 'all that'."

Church stood in the shower, hands pressed against the tiles, knees locked in an attempt not to collapse. Her muscles shook with the effort. The powerful jet of water blasted between her shoulder blades, the scalding water filling the bathroom with steam.

The situation she found herself in was unpleasantly familiar. Her dark side was screaming to be let loose. The fury inside her was growing – building up to erupt spectacularly. She forced the feelings back down.

Not yet. The right time will present itself.

What felt like hours later, wrapped in a bathrobe, her hair in a towel, Church climbed into bed. A new phone and a welcome mug of hot chocolate were waiting for her on the bedside table. The drink had a smiley face drawn in the whipped cream on top.

Kat was mothering her and Church appreciated the gesture. Kat always knew how to bring Church back to herself, regardless of the situation.

Church grabbed the phone and logged into her iCloud account. While the apps loaded, she thought about what her next steps should be.

Was Riley involved – more so than he was letting on? Why did he stop it? Why save her? What was his connection to all this?

Church intended to find out. The urge to get out of bed and do her homework tugged at her. She needed answers, but she was exhausted. Sleep would settle her mind, reset her thoughts, ready for the morning and the next chapter. Slowly, her eyelids drooped and she fell asleep.

Church dreamt of old battered cars, lurking outside the gates. A man dressed in black scaling an old oak tree behind the main house. A net was closing in around her – something tightened around her neck and squeezed. The pressure built until she couldn't breathe.

Church woke up gasping, fingers clawing at her neck to loosen the restraint. Though nothing was choking her, she was in her room. She took a few deep breaths and let her heartbeat return to normal.

This wasn't going to stop her. If anything, it was spurring her on.

I will not let this get to me! They wanna kill me? Then they better try a lot harder than that!

Seeing Red

Church clambered out of bed, ignoring her pounding head. She dressed in her running gear and headed for the fire escape. After her second lap of the perimeter, she had a plan.

C E Allardyce

A New Threat

Archers

Team Archers gathered in the conference room, two hours later than usual. The table was filled with breakfast items ranging from pastries to bacon and sausage sandwiches. Tea and coffee pots were handed around and mugs were filled. A separate jug, filled with frothy, steamed milk, was placed in front of Church, in the centre of the table.

"We probably need to notch up our security rating," Church said, once everyone had settled.

"Defcon One?" Kat suggested.

"Not quite yet," Church said. "Kez, what news from Scorpio?"

"To hell with all that!" Kat cried. "Someone tried to kill you!"

"I'm aware, yet here I sit, in one piece. I'll come to that later," Church said firmly. "First things first. Collette corroborated Riley's story about handing the USB over to Harris and Jonny. *And* the fact that it wasn't them who attacked her."

"Stocky guy," Kez said. "Last seen outside Enigma yesterday afternoon."

"I've reviewed the feeds," Church said. "That's last on the agenda." She looked at Kez. "Scorpio?"

"Mr and Mrs Cavendish are tucked away in a safe house. Scorpio are rotating their shifts so at least two of them are on-site. Mrs Cavendish is not at all happy with the situation," Kez said.

Church nodded, unsurprised. "We need eyes on EMP too. That's the next priority. I want to know everything they do. Jen, can you follow up with Mr Abraham? See what he's willing to share. If he's uncooperative, bring him back here."

"Sure," Jen replied.

"I'll come with," Kat said. "I don't think anyone should work solo from now on."

Church ignored Kat's pointed look.

"As far as we can tell, Kenny MacKay is on holiday in Spain," Kez said. "The techs are checking that he's where he's supposed to be. And we got the wreckage of your car back to the garage. After consulting with the police – thank your brother for me, Kat – forensics are still working on it. The device was placed in the front nearside wheel arch. The techs are checking the CCTV outside the Torenta offices for any signs of tampering. It had to have happened there."

"Have you checked the feeds in the parking area here?" Church asked.

"Of course, nothing unusual," Kez said.

"Who went near it?" Church asked.

"It couldn't have been anyone here," Kez said.

"Check anyway. I want a list."

"Sure."

"The dealership is preparing a replacement car for you. That spec is pretty rare, so it may take a while," Jen said.

"Thanks, Jen," Church said. "Hope you don't mind me borrowing your car when needed?"

Jen shook her head.

"Did you get officially discharged by Eve?" Kat asked.

"The results showed no lasting effects," Church said. "Just some incapacitating agent." She waved it off. "Now the battered old Vauxhall out on the lane…"

"Huh?" Kez exclaimed in surprise.

"There's a faded yellow Astra outside the gates," Church explained. "It's been there since yesterday. It's still there now."

"I didn't see it," Kez said, frowning at her screen.

"It's just outside the zone, which I am sure is not a coincidence," Church said.

"Well, I'll go over there and tell them to go do one!" Kat cried.

"Leave them be, for now. They might be useful. I'll test them later."

"What do you have in mind?" Kat asked with a wicked grin.

"We'll see what happens," Church said casually. "I've adjusted the cameras so we're now watching them, watching us. In other news, the feed from Enigma from yesterday…"

All eyes focused on Church.

"Stocky lurker has a name and if I assume correctly, so does the mysterious doctor. James Doyle and Gloria Pérez."

"Our James Doyle?" Miz asked.

"None other," Church confirmed.

"Working for Bravo Control?" Jen asked. "Against us?"

"She's not Bravo Control anymore," Church said. "Not since after the Yankee op."

Yankee op – the op that nearly killed Church, leaving her in a critical condition, unable to walk – was her last op for Cactus.

"JD left Cactus?" Kat asked in disbelief.

Church shook her head. "He's been AWOL for six months."

"Shit," Kat said. "And how does Jack feel about that?"

Church shrugged her shoulders. "I need to know more before speaking with Jack. And he's the last person I want to know about all this."

"Probably a good idea," Kat muttered. "So, what does Pérez want with Warrior IV?"

"To sell it to the highest bidder, no doubt," Church replied, standing up. "Or build her own army of super soldiers … I'm going to talk to Riley. He has some explaining to do."

"You're not driving," Kat said firmly.

"Wasn't planning to," Church said, waving her phone.

Church

Church left the conference room and trudged up the stairs to her office. She hit the phone icon and selected Riley's name from her recent call list.

He answered immediately. "Hey. How are you? Everything okay?" he asked without preamble.

"Fine, thank you," she replied. "And it's nothing I can't handle."

"Have you reconsidered?" he asked.

"If you mean, am I going to give the USB back, then the answer is no."

"Claudia... Church," he corrected. "Please." The desperate tone had returned to his voice. "Romano's offer is fair. More than fair. The alternative is…"

"Is the car outside the gates to Archers anything to do with you?" she asked, cutting him off.

"What car? No, it's not."

"Never mind. Can you meet me? I'd much prefer to discuss this in person."

"Of course. Shall I come to Archers?" Riley asked.

"No, not here," she said, frowning at her laptop. The Astra was still there, but no sighting of its occupant – yet. He'd have to come out eventually.

"Where then?" Riley asked.

"I'll send you the co-ordinates."

She expected him to laugh.

"Fine."

Church hung up and re-watched the footage of the woman sitting behind Riley's desk. Gloria Pérez. Church hadn't seen her since just before she left Cactus – she was a hateful woman, Jack's second-in-command, Bravo Control.

Seeing Red

Pérez and her involvement with the Yankee op was the reason Church had left Cactus. The entire team were dead because of that woman – everyone except Church. Pérez should have finished the job to prevent Church from informing Jack who had sabotaged the op.

That had been her sole purpose in joining that team – find the person undermining Jack and take them out. Church hadn't had the opportunity to finish her mission – the only occasion where she hadn't been able to complete the job with pure efficiency.

Jack didn't react when Church told him the news. In the rescue helicopter, skimming the desert, barely able to see from the pain in her back, Hutchinson's hand firmly planted on her chest to prevent her from moving, Jack's lead operative had held the satellite phone to her ear as she croaked out the code that only she and Jack knew. She painstakingly spelled out the culprit – BRAVO CONTROL.

Jack was quiet for a few moments. "I'll deal with it," he eventually said. "Do not die! Do you hear me, Mana? That's an order!"

Church didn't respond. She finally succumbed to the pain and passed out.

So, Pérez was back. Vivid images of revenge crept into Church's mind. Old scores needed to be settled. Pérez had resurfaced after all this time – but now Church was less inclined to let anyone else deal with her on her behalf.

Using an app on her laptop, Church sent Riley an encrypted email from an untraceable account with the co-ordinates of a suitable meeting place and the time.

Another Meeting

Having avoided alerting her potential tail of her departure from Archers, Church waited for Riley at the co-ordinates. It was a spot between two country villages, a ten-minute walk from where she assumed Riley would park. It was a chilly late afternoon, her breath puffed out in front of her in little clouds. Winter was not far away.

As the sun dipped towards the horizon, Church had walked from her house, across the fields for nearly twenty minutes. From her position on the grassy footpath, she could see and hear anyone approaching. She didn't have to wait long before a large shape wandered towards her.

"Nice evening for a stroll," Riley said jovially. "How are you?" He stepped closer to her, his hands shoved deep into his leather jacket pockets.

"I'm fine," she replied.

"You said that earlier," he said. "But really?"

"It was nothing, just some incapacitating agent. No long-lasting effects, as you can see."

"Hmm," he growled. "So, why are we meeting here?"

"Convenience. Isolation. I had to be sure neither of us were followed. I've picked up a tail."

"But you shook it."

"I did."

"No one is following me," he said, glancing over his shoulder.

"No surprise there."

"Meaning?" he asked with a raised eyebrow.

Church studied him for a moment. "How do you know Gloria Pérez?" she asked bluntly.

The muscle in his jaw twitched, but his eyes never left hers. He didn't look surprised or shocked. He was trying to figure her out.

Good luck with that! she thought.

"I underestimated you," he said quietly. "For that, I apologise. So, you bugged the club too when you stole the USB."

"We did," Church admitted. "Video and audio. You're not the first to underestimate me… and I'm sure you won't be the last."

"Smart move."

"I thought so." Church shrugged unapologetically. "It paid off. Is Pérez the Doctor?"

Riley didn't answer. Church took out a small device from her pocket and activated it. A green light illuminated.

"You always come so prepared?" he asked.

"You never know," she replied.

Riley tugged his phone out of his back pocket and checked the screen. With the other hand, he pulled out a small black pouch from his jacket and placed his phone inside. He secured the Velcro fastening and stuffed it back into his pocket.

"No doubt you already know how I know her," he said.

"I know what's in your service history."

"As do I of yours. Why did you leave Cactus?"

"How come Jack never hired you?" she countered. "Give me something. You'll get the same in return."

"You're in a sharing mood?" he asked.

"I think we owe each other some honesty."

"Some?" Riley said with a raised eyebrow.

"I have questions," she said. "No doubt, you do too. Let's get it all out in the open."

"Why?" he asked.

"Because I have a favour to ask."

"You do?" he asked, surprised.

"Don't sound so surprised."

Riley laughed, making his shoulders shake. "Can we do this inside? It's cold and I need a drink."

"There's a pub in the village," Church said, pointing over her shoulder.

"They do food?"

"Yes."

"Any good?"

"Pretty good."

"May I buy you dinner?" he asked seriously.

Church shook her head. "No, you may not. My shout. My way of saying thank you."

"For what?"

"Getting me out of the car."

"Oh, that." Riley grinned and gestured for Church to lead the way. He walked beside her. "I honestly thought you weren't going to listen to me."

"I very nearly didn't. I don't take orders well. Never have."

"But you made an exception."

"God knows why."

Riley and Church sat at a quiet table in the corner of the gastropub in the heart of the small country village. The floor was covered in large dark slate tiles, the windows were draped with tiny white fairy lights. The open fire crackled delightfully, making the large space warm and inviting. A few other tables were occupied and the quiet chatter from the bar kept their conversation from being overheard.

"If I'd known, I would have made a little more effort," Riley said after the waiter took their order. He had ordered a rib-eye steak and Church had selected chicken tagliatelle.

"There's hardly a dress code here," Church said. "We look like walkers."

"Yeah, but this is our second date," he said, grinning. When he noticed the look on Church's face, he let it fade. He feigned concern. "Oh, this isn't a date?"

"This is not anything close to a date," she said firmly, not caring that the waiter had returned with their drinks.

"We'll make these bottomless," Riley said to the waiter, pointing to their glasses of bourbon. The waiter bowed his head and disappeared back to the bar.

"What would a date with you look like?" Riley asked.

"Stop deflecting. Charm me all you like, but can we get back to why I asked you to meet me?"

"You think I'm charming?" Riley grinned.

"You can turn it on like a tap."

"But you're immune?"

Church sat back in her chair. "Pérez," she pressed.

"You really want to know?"

"I want to know why she has a hold over you."

"You think she does?"

"I know she does," Church said. "She hasn't changed, from what I saw. Still the same manipulative, conniving..." Church struggled to find the right words. "Ball-breaker."

Spot on, he thought.

"She break yours?" Church asked.

"Once or twice." Riley swirled his glass and watched the dark liquor spiral. "I'm not working for her. God's honest truth." He looked across the table at Church. "I used to, but I've not seen her for years. Before yesterday. You saw and heard our conversation. It was pretty one-sided."

"She wants you to get the USB back. For her."

"She does. She's obviously aligned herself with Antonia Romano – temporarily, no doubt – just to get it." Riley sighed. "Just hand it over, please, with any copies you've made. I'll need all your findings on EMP too."

"No," Church said firmly. "So, which one of these women are you really working for?"

"My client is Romano. She's not a patient woman."

What woman is? he thought.

"She's not going to get the information back. You're not getting it. Neither is Pérez."

"You seem quite sure of that," he said. "Where is it?"

"You will never find it."

Riley ground his teeth.

"You think you could force me to tell you?" Church asked seriously.

"It would be fun finding out," he said with a glint in his eyes.

The waiter approached with their food. Church held Riley's gaze and waited for the waiter to retreat.

"Just try it, see how it pans out," Church warned.

"What are you going to do with it?" Riley asked.

"Do you know what all this is about? The information."

"Not interested," he said. "Best not to know. Just give it back and anything else you've found. I will ensure that'll be the end of it for you."

"That leads to yet another question," Church said. "Why the concern about my wellbeing and my involvement in all this?"

"You know why. You've been dragged into this. End it."

"No. I'll end this. My way."

Riley shook his head in disbelief. "There's no changing your mind, is there."

"I'm glad you realise that."

"What are you planning?" he asked.

"To take EMP down. They need to be stopped. They're killing people. Innocent people."

"And that bothers you?"

"Doesn't it bother you?" she asked.

"None of my business. Why waste your energy on EMP?"

"No energy required. That's the easy part. A little more evidence delivered to a friendly DCI and job done. With EMP out of the game, I can focus on Pérez."

"You trust me with that information?"

"Trust is earnt and proved," Church said. "What you do with the information is up to you. It's no secret. Pérez knows how I operate."

"You have history with her too?" Riley asked.

Church twisted her pasta around her fork. "She was Jack's right hand when I worked at Cactus... until she sabotaged my last op. She wiped out the entire team for her own gain. I hadn't known them long, but Yankee were still my teammates."

"What happened?" he asked.

Church shrugged. This was not a subject she wanted to talk about. She skirted the specifics. "I was battling to stay alive and learning how to walk again. Jack said he dealt with her, Pérez. I assumed he did. I never saw her again. I was kinda hoping she was dead."

"When was this?" he asked.

"Three years ago."

"I'm sorry about your team," he said quietly.

"Thanks."

"You hurt bad?"

"Worst injuries I've ever sustained. The rest of the team didn't fare so well... but I survived and proved the doctors wrong. Here I am." She waved her glass. "So, the car thing wasn't the first attempt she's made on my life and probably not the last. It's almost becoming a habit, but she needs to up her game..." Church frowned as her thoughts drifted from Pérez momentarily. "Why did you intervene?" she asked.

Riley chewed his food thoughtfully.

Eventually, he said, "I couldn't let her hurt you."

Church tilted her head as she looked at him, remembering when Pérez told him about Church's car. Nothing explicit, just a sinister insinuation. But it was enough for Riley to immediately walk away from Pérez and leave Enigma. How had he found her so quickly? Had he found a way to track her? She would have to look into that. But what if he hadn't called her?

You'd be dead.

"It makes no sense to off me," Church said. "Without me, the USB would be lost forever."

Riley took a sip of his drink. "It was more of a test for me. I showed my hand to her and by doing so, I've put you front and centre."

"Easy there, cowboy!" Church said. "I was already front and centre the moment we took the USB from the club. I stand by my choices."

"I do too. Saving you wasn't something I had to consider."

Church wasn't in the habit of needing to be saved. "Why?" she asked seriously.

Riley looked surprised. "You're really asking me that?"

"I am."

Riley sighed. "Because... I have feelings. For you."

Church laughed. "You don't know me."

"There's nothing I could find out about you that I don't already know, that could change my feelings," he said quietly.

Church raised both eyebrows and waited for him to continue.

"Claudia Jean Church," he said, with a hint of a smirk. "Youngest woman to receive her rank, selected over hundreds of applicants to complete several special ops programmes. Handpicked and singled out by Jack Williams at Cactus, becoming his padawan and flourishing as his prodigy girl. Your Cactus record is proving a little more difficult to obtain. But give me time." He winked. "You know, you intrigue me – not just a pretty face. A heavy drinker, you like to dance, you fight like a pro and you put me on my arse! What's not to like?" He continued. "Archers is more difficult to access, formed three years ago. CEO of your own business – and all this before your thirtieth birthday."

"There are no records from my time at Cactus," Church said. "Nothing on file, no trail. So don't waste your time."

"Black ops?" Riley asked.

"Something like that."

"Hmm."

"What does that mean exactly?" Church asked. "Your wolfish growl?"

"Depends on the situation. Right now, I still haven't heard anything I don't like the sound of. You're strong, stubborn – or should I say focused? You make your mind up and stick to it. You're fierce, in a gloriously sexy way. You're mysterious." He shrugged. "I just want to know everything. Even the bits you won't tell me."

Church rolled her eyes then closed them briefly, dismissing her scepticism. "Ask away."

"What's your relationship with Jack?" he asked.

Church laughed. Of all the questions to start with, he went straight there – to her sex life. Not – why did you leave the army to join the dark side when your career was blossoming? Or was it hard being female in a male-dominated environment for so long? But the insinuation that she screwed her way to where she was, didn't go unnoticed.

"You think we have a relationship? He's an investor and a friend. What were you expecting? That we were a thing?" She shook her head in disbelief. "You think that because he invested in Archers, I'm sleeping with him?"

Riley held his palms up. "No offence intended, but the Jack Williams I know doesn't offer his money to a potential rival set-up. Unless you're in his pocket and answer to him or..."

"Archers has no affiliation to Cactus. We are a separate entity," Church said. "He's a silent partner. It's purely a business thing. I'm the majority shareholder and I've worked very hard to get to this point."

That seemed to put Riley back in his place.

"So, what's your relationship with him?" Church countered.

"So, no boyfriend then?" Riley asked.

Church looked sceptical. "No. You?"

Riley nearly choked on his food.

Church couldn't resist. She kept her face neutral. "Charlie or Jonny, I wonder."

Riley recovered his composure and conceded. "No. Sorry to disappoint, but I'm hetero… Jack was my CO, before Pérez," he replied.

"I know that. Then what?"

"Then nothing. I haven't seen or heard from him since I was transferred from his unit."

Church believed him but knew there was more to it. "He never tried to recruit you to Cactus?" she asked. "You were a perfect candidate."

"On the face of it, I guess I would have been a good fit. But there were two major obstacles."

"Which were?"

"The main one was who trained me. I took a different path. One he didn't approve of."

Church frowned. Jack spent most of his adult life on the dark side – no holds barred. Why would Riley being trained by Pérez, then the commandos, put Jack off? "There's nothing in your service history that he wouldn't approve of," she said.

"You're not the only one with off-the-books activities," he said. "Did you learn anything interesting in your digging into my record?"

Church smiled in acknowledgement. "Mr Justin Riley, thirty-two, born in Barcelona to Maria Castillo, father unknown according to your birth certificate. Schooled in London after your mother married George Riley, British civil servant. You took his name shortly after. Good GCSE results and after obtaining three A-levels in History, English Literature and Computer Science, you joined the army. Trained at Sandhurst, achieved the rank of Lieutenant, served under Jack Williams for a time, then under Gloria Pérez and later transferred to commando training. All with a spotless record."

"Hmm, you have pretty extensive resources."

"You have no idea."

"Yet, you haven't heard the worst part."

"Care to share?" Church asked, casting a fleeting, longing glance at the few chunky chips remaining on his plate. Riley nudged his plate a little closer to her. She gratefully took a chip with her fingers and bit into it.

"Half the unit had no idea what was going on," Riley continued. "I don't think even Jack knew until it was too late. Blacker than black. The unit was given a nickname – the Perros."

"The dogs?" Church translated.

"Her dogs."

"Pérez's?"

Riley nodded. "I led them as her *Primero*. The Perros solved problems the regular guys couldn't. She has hundreds of them, in every unit, every force – maybe every outfit. An army of drones, prepared to do anything she commands."

Church knew Pérez had her own men under her command in Cactus. That was the only way she could have pulled off the hit on the Yankee op. Church mentally scrolled through the roster at Archers. Maybe an additional search for any connection to that woman was warranted.

"And she just left?" Church asked.

"Something happened. Something bad." Riley looked into his glass again. "The next day, she was gone."

Church didn't press for the details. She could investigate the circumstances later. "And she reappears a year or so later working for Jack at Cactus, after he retired from the service."

"Apparently so," Riley said. "I didn't hear from her after the incident. I guess she was done with me."

The waiter cleared their plates and offered them the dessert menu. Church chose a chocolate brownie and Riley an apple pie.

"I would have done anything she asked," Riley said solemnly. "I did do terrible things."

"We've both done bad things. Doesn't make us all bad. You were following orders."

"It was more than that."

"She hurt you?"

Riley sat back. "In every way imaginable – and then some."

"And you loved her," Church said, reading between the lines.

"I thought I did," he admitted. "There was no relationship. I see that now. I was her weapon. I was blind to it at the time. It wasn't until after she left that I realised it was toxic."

Church remained quiet. The waiter returned with their desserts.

"I don't feel the same anymore," Riley said. "I thought I had put it all behind me... until I saw her sitting in my office."

"You seemed to freeze," Church said quietly. "When she approached you in your office."

"Slipped straight back into the role of her sub."

Church didn't react. Riley had expected her to be shocked, or at least mildly surprised. He had never told anyone the true nature of his relationship with that woman. Harris had seen the result but never asked for details. Riley searched Church's face for a clue to what she was thinking. She appeared absorbed in her chocolate dessert.

"You're not surprised?" he asked eventually.

"Nothing about that woman would surprise me. Why does she call herself the Doctor?"

"Nickname from university. She did her PhD in psychology. Her initials are GP."

"How un-sinister," Church mused.

"You may think you know her. Walk away – that's my advice. She'll come after you and she'll go after everything you care about, Archers, your team..."

"I *am* going to stop her. She has a debt to pay."

"You think you can stop her?"

"I know I can, I…"

"What?" Riley asked when Church didn't finish her thought.

She shook her head. "I'm sorry," she said. "I was going to ask you something… it doesn't matter now."

"What? You can ask me anything. I'll tell you the honest answer, if I know it. You mentioned earlier that you wanted to ask me a favour. Ask – if it's in my power, it's yours."

"You've been very open with me," Church said.

"That's not a favour. But yes, I have."

"Are you playing me?"

"Don't you trust me?"

"I trust no one, least of all you."

Riley smiled his winning smile. "I'd expect nothing less."

"Are you?" Church pressed.

"No."

Seeing Red

"You know, I would – if I were in your position," Church said candidly. "To get the job done."

"Hmm."

"And just to clarify – the night at the club…"

Riley held up his hand to stop her. "No need to explain."

"I think I do," Church insisted. "It's not something I do often. We rarely go out, I let my guard down and you were so…"

Riley raised his eyebrows in anticipation.

"Well-behaved – in an extremely dangerous way," Church finished.

Riley laughed. "You have no idea. So, you like to fight?" he asked, thinking of their play-fighting back at Archers.

"More than anything," Church whispered.

The temperature between them rose a few degrees. Church shook her head, as if to clear her mind. More drinks arrived, dissolving the moment.

Church sipped her bourbon thoughtfully. "This wasn't the favour, but answer me this – how much is Romano paying you?"

"Not enough," Riley growled. "Though admittedly, I've done a poor job so far – and it looks like I'm still failing."

"Sorry about that. But seriously, how much?"

"Why?"

"Because I'll double it."

"For what?"

"To flip."

"What?" Riley cried, a little too loudly, causing some patrons to turn their heads towards them.

"You heard," Church hissed quietly. "Work for me."

"You're joking, right?"

"Deadly serious. EMP needs to be stopped. They're crippled right now. Help me bring them down."

"How?"

"Willingly hand over your little recordings of Romano's phone conversations. Break your contract with her – really piss her off."

"You already accessed my system. Why didn't you just take them?"

"That would be rude."

Riley laughed loudly.

"I need more," Church said. "You can get into EMP. I can't, not without force or a lot of background work. I'd like you to deposit something."

"I could do that," Riley said contemplatively.

"Will you?"

"Why not? I'm not going to be able to fulfil our contract, so might as well. You really don't need to double the fee."

"That wasn't everything," Church said.

"Okay. You going to ask?"

Church sat back and took a deep breath. "There's no better way to take down an organisation than from the inside." She watched Riley closely. "Pérez wants you to get close... to me and get the USB."

"But you won't hand it over."

"The USB is off the table. As far as you're concerned, it's gone. You'll never get it."

"So why team up?"

"Can you deceive her?" Church asked seriously.

"I've never been able to before. She's always at least two steps ahead. It's like she can read my every thought."

"Then don't try to deceive her. Agree to do whatever she asks of you. Without question – like before."

"What if she asks me to kill you?"

"She may well ask that. Then you do it – or at least try," Church said, with a wicked smile.

"You think I couldn't?" Riley asked. "Actually kill you – not just try."

"Could you?" she asked.

Riley ground his teeth, considering it. "No. I don't think I could," he admitted. "Not unless you really pissed me off."

Church took that as a challenge. "You wouldn't succeed."

"If I wanted you dead, you'd be dead," Riley said seriously. "I'm pretty handy with a sniper rifle. I've already had my sight trained on your pretty little forehead. One squeeze and poof."

"The oak tree on the other side of the lake?" Church asked, deadpan. "Just before you buzzed the gate?" She shook her head. "Bulletproof glass."

Riley dipped his head and raised his glass. "You're something else."

"Thanks," Church said.

"Seriously – if she asks and I fail... she doesn't take failure well. She'd have me killed."

"But you're special to her."

"Hardly. So special she's avoided me for the past eight years," Riley said sarcastically.

"Trust me – you are. She won't kill you. And certainly not if I have anything to do with it."

"You really think you can stop her?" he asked.

"I know I can – but I need your help to do it."

Red was asking for his help. She actually said it.

The Deception Begins

After several more drinks, Church was finally starting to relax. This was going pretty well, all things considered.

"So, the Stocky Fucker," Riley said. "What did you find out about him?"

"James Doyle," Church confirmed with disdain. "Is Ellis okay?"

"He's fine. He was doped with something."

"We can run some tests at Archers. It might be the same stuff that was in the car bomb."

"You'd do that?"

"Sure," Church said.

"So you know the stocky half-pint?"

"I do. He was my second-in-command at Cactus."

Riley raised his eyebrows. "But he wasn't part of your last op?"

"No – and I now know why," Church mused. "He must have already been working for Pérez at that point… I was seconded to Yankee for that one op. The rest of my team – Doyle, Kat, Jen and Kez – were doing something else."

"And you didn't bring him to Archers with the others?"

"Before I left, I set him up to lead. I guess he fucked that up too – or Pérez had other ideas about his future."

"Have you known him long?" Riley asked.

"Long enough. We trained together. I'm not surprised that he sought out someone like Pérez, but I *am* surprised he went AWOL from Cactus. Alpha Team are slipping if they haven't found him yet."

"You know Hutch?" Riley asked.

"Yeah. Really good guy. We were friendly rivals at Cactus." Church's attention briefly shifted over Riley's shoulder. "I think he was relieved when I left – I think he tired of the competition. I wasn't seeking it, but you know…"

"I can imagine," Riley muttered. "Threatened by your spectacular performance."

"Are you threatened?"

"Not in the slightest," Riley replied. "Turned on? Definitely."

"I think my tail has finally found me," Church said quietly. "Would you walk me home?"

"It would be my pleasure." Riley summoned the waiter with a quick glance and a wave of his hand.

"I said it was my treat," Church said.

"Do as you're told for once, woman," Riley growled. "Let me maintain at least *some* masculinity."

Church hid her smile and stood up. Riley paid the bill, helped Church with her jacket and escorted her out of the pub. He took her hand and tucked it into the crook of his elbow. "Which way?" he asked.

Church pointed in the direction of her house and they walked down the street together.

"Nice, quiet place," Riley observed.

"I hardly spend any time at home these days. I stay at Archers – it's just easier to fall out of bed, work out and get to work."

"You know something?"

"What?"

"I like you drunk – your walls are almost scalable."

Church laughed. "You think *this* is drunk? Try a bucket more alcohol, a few pills and some good tunes…"

"Then?"

Church didn't respond. The fresh air had hit her hard and her head swam. Riley noticed and tightened his hold on her. "Not so infallible, after all," he chuckled.

"I could still put you on your arse," she muttered.

"I don't doubt it."

They crossed the road and turned a corner.

"Is he following?" Church asked quietly, her hearing dulled by the ringing in her ears. Perhaps drinking so much bourbon hadn't been such a good idea.

"Hmm," Riley confirmed. "You wanna confront him?"

Church shook her head. "Let him follow. Is he one of hers?"

"I don't recognise him – but I'm out of the loop."

"I'll find out who he is," Church said confidently.

They turned down a road that wound out of the village.

"How far?" he asked.

"About five more minutes."

Church's house was a quaint cottage, complete with a white picket fence and roses climbing the wall around the front door. A few remaining delicate yellow petals clung to the stems despite the chill. Their boots crunched on the gravel driveway.

Church rummaged in her pockets for her keys. She got the door open and stepped inside. Riley made no move to follow her.

"Waiting for an invitation?" she asked.

"I should go."

"Have you come to a decision?"

Riley didn't answer.

Church lowered her voice. "Please come in."

Riley stepped over the threshold.

The man watching them from the shadows a few hundred yards away, made a call. "He's in," he whispered, his binoculars focused on the front of Church's house.

"Let me know when he leaves," Pérez said.

"Yes, ma'am."

Archers

Kat knocked firmly on Geoff Abraham's front door and stepped back. Jen was standing a few paces behind her. There was no answer. After a few moments, Kat rang the doorbell. With a quick nod from Kat, Jen headed around the house to check the back door.

Kat rang the bell once more for good measure. Geoff's car was parked on the drive and he hadn't been seen at the EMP office for a few days. Things weren't looking good for Mr Abraham.

Jen reappeared beside the garage. "Nobody's home," she said. "Doors and windows locked – we're not getting in easily."

Kat looked up at the house. It was a nice place, on a leafy avenue in Stanmore. A respectable neighbourhood for businesspeople and well-off families. According to his records, Geoff lived alone. His kids were grown up and had moved away. His wife had left him several years earlier.

Geoff's car was badly parked in front of the garage.

"Why would you park on the drive and not keep it in the garage?" Kat wondered aloud.

"Good point," Jen agreed. "These trees drip sap – it ruins the paintwork." She wiped a finger across the bonnet to make her point. She walked around the car and looked more closely inside. Nothing out of the ordinary. She looked questioningly at Kat, then towards the garage.

"Think it's locked?" Kat asked.

"One way to find out," Jen replied. She tried the handle. It twisted easily in her hand and she pulled it open.

The smell hit Jen first – she immediately clamped her palm across her nose and mouth. Kat took in a sharp breath. The smell was unmistakable. Breathing through her mouth, Kat pulled a torch from her jacket pocket and ducked under the door, followed closely by Jen. Kat flicked on the torch, pointing it at her feet. She raised the beam of light and instantly found a gruesome scene.

Geoff Abraham was hanging by his neck from one of the rafters. The red nylon cord dug into his purple flesh, now bloated and mottled. His eyes were open and bulging from their sockets. There was no life in them – they were opaque and bloodshot. His tongue was swollen and protruded between his dark blue lips.

"Control. Are you seeing this?" Kat asked over comms.

"May he rest in peace," Kez said quietly. "Jen, activate your scanner. I'll inform Church."

"We'll update her later – leave her to whatever she's getting up to with Riley," Kat said. She found the light switch and turned it on. The harsh fluorescent tube blinked into life.

"Scanning now," Jen said and started slowly walking around the garage, ensuring the device captured all angles of the space.

"This is just too..." Kat mumbled.

"Too what?" Kez asked over comms.

"Too neat. Everything is in its place."

"The house is immaculate," Jen reported after a sweep. "Laundry still in the machine, post opened and stacked on the desk ready for filing. Breakfast things washed up and on the draining board."

"So, this wasn't planned," Kat said.

"Staged?" Jen asked.

Miz entered the surveillance room and sat beside Kez. She activated her comms. "Sorry I'm late. Two, can you show me the body?"

Kat moved her bodycam to give Miz a clear view. "Looks like he used a ladder to tie the rope to the rafter, then replaced it on its hooks. He used the kitchen chair and stepped off it."

The chair was lying on its side a few feet away.

"His neck doesn't look broken," Miz said. "Judging by the angle of his head."

Seeing Red

"There are scratch marks on his skin – he struggled," Kat said.

"Death by strangulation?" Jen asked.

"Most likely," Miz said.

"EMP or the Doctor?" Kat asked. "My money's on the Doctor."

"Could Echo have done this?" Jen asked.

"It's possible," Kat said. "But staging suicides isn't exactly their style."

"What *is* their style?" Miz asked. "We don't know what they're capable of."

"They're professionals. It'd be much easier to make him disappear than go to all this effort," Kat said, a little defensively. Jen gave Kat a pointed look. "What? I'll call Charlie if you want and ask him."

Jen smiled and shook her head to herself. They left the scene as they'd found it. Kat called her older brother once they got back into the car.

"Jor!" she cried when he answered. She knew it sounded like 'whore' and that it would irritate him.

"Hey, Kitty Kat," Jorge replied, having the same idea. Kat hated his pet names for her. "What trouble have you got yourself into this time?"

"None!" she said petulantly. "Can you send two uniforms and the on-call coroner to the address I'm about to send you?"

"What have you done?" Jorge asked.

"Nothing! Have a little faith! We've just found a disturbing scene at a residential address, is all. I'm doing the right thing by calling it in."

"Another anonymous tip?"

"Whatever," Kat said disinterestedly. It wasn't her fault Jorge was bound by boring red tape.

"I'll see what I can do," Jorge sighed. "Anything I should know?"

"It's not a suicide. The rest you can work out for yourself."

"Jeez, thanks, Kitty!"

Kat opened her mouth to retaliate, then decided against it. No doubt Church would fill him in later. Jorge listened to Church – appreciated her input. Church had more patience than Kat did with the finer details of police work.

"You're welcome," she said sarcastically and hung up.

Riley Visits EMP

The next morning, just before midday, dressed in a navy three-piece suit – no tie, collar unbuttoned – Riley approached the reception desk at EMP with purpose.

"Mr Riley!" Jessica, the receptionist, gushed when she looked up. He looked slightly dishevelled this morning. Not as groomed as on his first visit, but it certainly didn't detract from his general air of grace and confidence. "Such a pleasure to see you again…" Her eyes flicked to her screen. "Oh – I don't see you in Miss Romano's calendar." A crease appeared between her neat eyebrows.

"That's intentional," Riley said. "I'd like to surprise her."

"I'm sorry, Mr Riley, I'm simply not authorised to allow anyone entry without a scheduled appointment."

Riley leaned over the desk. "Would you make an exception – just for me?" he asked conspiratorially, flashing her a grin.

"I…" Jessica stuttered, losing her train of thought. He smelt divine – good enough to eat. She wondered what he had been up to the night before and was insanely jealous of any company he might have had.

"Is she in her office?" he asked.

"She is. But she's not to be disturbed."

"She asked me to come as soon as I had news of our venture. I should have called. My phone died an hour ago. I was finalising the details all night. I haven't slept a wink..."

Jessica wasn't listening, despite watching his lips intently. Her mind was elsewhere.

"I'm sorry to have bothered you." Riley smiled apologetically and turned to leave. "I suppose I'll have to find a payphone – Miss Romano may erupt at the delay." He strode back to the glass front doors.

"Wait!" Jessica called. "I can check with her assistant."

"Would you? That would be great."

Jessica held up a manicured finger and dialled a number on her desk phone. "Is Miss Romano still in her meeting?" she asked. "I have an unannounced visitor down here." She lowered her tone.

Riley half-tuned out Jessica and waited. The smell of coffee from the café was enticing. He decided to grab a tall black on his way out – all being well. He certainly needed it.

"Mr Riley?" Jessica called. "You can go up. Lily will greet you – you may have a long wait though."

"Thank you. You've really saved my bacon." He winked and offered his hand to her. She took it and allowed him to kiss her knuckles. She watched him stride towards the lift.

A young woman, who Riley assumed was Lily, was waiting for him as the lift doors opened on the top floor. She looked like the librarian type – but with a mischievous glint in her eyes.

"This way, please," she said ushering him towards a seating area overlooking the river. "Miss Romano is in a teleconference. I shall announce your arrival as soon as she is free."

"Thank you," Riley said, unbuttoning his jacket. Lily's eyes followed his hands, then flicked back up to meet his gaze. He sank slowly into a comfortable armchair and sat back. He draped one arm casually over the back of the chair.

Lily drank him in – a well-dressed, handsome young man. Not enough of them around here for her liking. "Can I get you anything?" she asked. "Miss Romano will be a while, I'm afraid."

"Happy to wait," Riley said smoothly. "Though an iced hazelnut oat milk mocha would be lovely."

Lily looked towards the office door for a moment, considering her options. She would have to go downstairs to the café for an order like that. There was nobody else she could call to help, so she nodded and returned to her desk. A moment later, mobile in hand, she trotted towards the lifts.

Riley waited for the lift door to close, then silently slipped over to Lily's desk. Her screen hadn't been locked. He pulled a small device from his pocket and inserted it into a port on her computer.

Shouting erupted from inside Antonia's office. She was calling for Lily. Riley waited for the light on the device to turn green before pulling it free and quickly returning to the waiting area.

The office door flew open and Antonia's voice echoed out. "Lily! Didn't you hear me?" When she didn't get the response she was expecting, she emerged and immediately saw Riley sitting casually in the armchair by the window.

"How did you get in here?" she asked frostily. "Where's my assistant?"

"Catering for your visitor's dire need of caffeine," Riley replied, getting to his feet.

"I wasn't aware we had an appointment," Antonia said icily.

"We don't."

"You have the information?" she asked hopefully. "You got it back?"

"No, ma'am."

"Then why are you here?" she snapped.

"To advise you that Echo are unable to continue with this particular project."

Any warm feelings Antonia had for this handsome man evaporated without a trace. "I don't understand," she hissed. "We had an agreement."

Riley didn't respond.

"What do you want? More money?"

"No, ma'am. I'm just informing you that Echo are no longer working for you."

"You haven't fulfilled the agreement," she said firmly.

"No, ma'am."

"Are you going to?"

"No, ma'am. We shall return the deposit."

"For the love of God, stop calling me *ma'am*!" Antonia took a breath in an attempt to regain her composure.

Riley could see she was more than angry. He walked towards her and she instinctively took a step back.

"Do you know where my information is?" she asked.

"Not exactly."

"What's *that* supposed to mean?" Antonia arched an eyebrow at him and watched him suspiciously. "This other team – you weren't able to negotiate with them?"

"Negotiations were unfortunately unsuccessful." Riley took another step forward. She wasn't used to someone standing up to her like this – that much was clear.

Antonia stood her ground and raised her chin. "You couldn't steal it back?"

"No."

Seeing Red

"Why not?"

"An attempt to steal it would also be unsuccessful. We are outmanned and outgunned. We're a team of five up against a small army. It's just not worth the risk to my team."

"And more money isn't enough of an incentive for you?"

"Money doesn't change the odds."

Antonia glared at him. "You came highly recommended. I was assured you could get the job done!"

"I *did* finish the job, but you were too busy to collect the information," Riley growled.

"This is *not* my fault!" Antonia spat. "You failed to keep hold of my information. This is on you and you need to fix it."

"I don't. Take my advice – watch your back. There's likely to be a target on it."

"Is that a threat, Mr Riley?" Antonia asked, glancing sideways towards Lily's desk.

"From me? No. You won't see me again. The funds will be returned within the hour."

Antonia opened her mouth but was distracted by the ding of the lift doors opening. Lily emerged with Riley's coffee.

Antonia's eyes darted towards her assistant. "You let him in without an appointment?" she barked. "You left your desk, leaving him unattended? For coffee? Call security."

"No need. I'm leaving," Riley said and started heading towards the lift.

Lily stood looking uncertainly between her boss and Riley.

"Don't just stand there!" Antonia cried at her assistant. "I gave you an order!"

Lily looked at the coffee cup in her hand, unsure what to do with it. She offered it to Riley.

Antonia lashed out and knocked the coffee out of Lily's hand. Before it hit the floor, Riley slipped between the two women. He gently urged Lily out of the way and held up a palm in front of Antonia. The coffee splattered across the white tiles. He glared down at the tiny woman, daring her to try anything further.

Antonia glared back at him, fury evident on her face, her cheeks flushed. "You're fired!" she screamed, leaning around Riley. "Effective immediately. Clear your desk. I want you gone. Now!"

Lily's bottom lip trembled.

Riley turned to Lily, keeping one eye on Antonia. "I'm sorry to have caused all this," he said gently.

"Get out! Both of you!" Antonia screamed.

Riley took Lily gently by the arm and ushered her towards the lift. Antonia retrieved Lily's handbag from under her desk and launched it across the room. Riley deftly caught it before it hit Lily in the face. He handed it to her and pressed the call button on the control panel. He kept himself between the two women and held Antonia's furious gaze until the doors opened.

Riley guided the trembling Lily inside. "I'm sorry about this – I've just cost you your job," he said gently. "Is she always like that?"

"Yes... well, no. She's usually worse, but I've not known anyone to fluster her like that."

"Hmm."

The lift doors opened on the ground floor. Jessica, the receptionist, craned her neck from her seat to get a better look at them from her position behind the desk.

"You two friends?" Riley asked Lily, nodding towards Jessica.

Lily nodded. Riley gestured for her to step out. He took her arm again and led her to the reception desk. He flashed a smile at Jessica. "I may have caused some upset upstairs with Miss Romano. Would you look after Lily? She's just lost her job."

Jessica stared wide-eyed at him, then looked worriedly at her friend.

"I'll let her explain," Riley nodded to Lily. He pulled a card from his inside pocket and slid it towards Jessica. "I really must go before security arrive. I can't come back, but please do contact me on this number. I can arrange alternative positions for you both – in a much friendlier environment. And Jessica, if you wouldn't mind hanging on for a few weeks, I could really use someone with your talents."

Jessica took the card and flipped it over. It was blank on one side and the other only had a telephone number on it. "Where do you work?" she asked quietly.

"I can't say. Not here," he looked furtively around. "But I can say I'm investigating some very serious allegations... my direct involvement here has unfortunately come to an abrupt end. So, I could really do with your help," he added, looking beseechingly at both young women.

The women exchanged glances and nodded in unison.

Riley flashed his smile. "I think you've just saved my bacon again. That's twice now."

The reception phone rang, making Jessica and Lily both jump.

"It's her!" Jessica wailed.

Riley noticed two security guards approaching the reception desk. "Tell her I'm leaving. Lily, you'd better come with me," he said quickly, taking her arm again.

Jessica nodded and answered the phone calmly. "Miss Romano."

With a wink at Jessica, Riley led Lily towards the main entrance doors.

"Yes, he's leaving as we speak, Miss Romano," Jessica said. "Yes, Lily too. Yes, Miss Romano, I'll get on that straight away."

Riley escorted Lily to his car. "Can I give you a lift somewhere?" he asked.

Lily shook her head. "I take the train."

"Can I walk you to the station?"

Lily shook her head again. "I'll be fine, thank you."

"Okay. I'd better go. I really am sorry," he said.

"I think you did me a favour... did you mean it about the job?" she asked.

"Absolutely. Send me your details and you'll soon see what a proper working environment should be like."

"Thank you."

Riley slid into the driver's seat. Coffee would have to wait – he needed to head back to the club. From his inside pocket, his mobile phone buzzed. He pulled it out and looked at the screen – a withheld number. He pressed the answer button but didn't speak.

"Soldier," Pérez purred.

Riley didn't respond.

"You've upset my friend and disappointed me. What do you think you're playing at?"

Riley was in an impossible situation. Trying to please one woman was work enough – but three? The news of what had transpired in the penthouse office had certainly travelled fast. He wondered if Antonia had called Pérez, or if Pérez had been watching the whole scene from the comfort of her dungeon.

"How did your evening with the ice queen go?" Pérez asked.

"Productive," he growled.

"Really? Not traumatised too much by the car bomb, I hope."

"It's made her more determined."

"What is she planning? Wait! Don't tell me – she wants to stop EMP and then she's coming for me."

Riley remained quiet.

"Are you in? Does she trust you?"

Riley ground his teeth.

Pérez laughed. "Make her trust you. Do whatever it takes."

"Your men," Riley growled. "They need to be less visible."

"That girl sees exactly what I want her to see. Get inside Archers. Do you think you can manage that?"

"I have an open invitation."

"See? Look at what you can achieve when you have the right incentive! You'll be by my side again in no time. Don't disappoint me further."

The call ended abruptly.

Negotiations

Church watched Riley closely over her desk as he signed the contract. He was showing no signs of hesitation. His questions were minimal and on the mundane side of their agreement.

Her suspicions prickled at her mind. This was risky. Riley had been casing the place the minute he stepped back into the main house at Archers. His eyes went to every corner, every potential hiding place.

You won't find it, she thought.

Church was ready for anything. Any sign of deception, diversion, or any other tactic he could think of. But Riley showed none – which left Church feeling a little disappointed.

"Old habits die hard," Riley growled.

"Excuse me?" Church said.

"I'm just getting a feel for the place."

"Whatever."

Riley's eyes fell on the chess board on a small table at the back of the room beside the fireplace. All the pieces were carved from marble and none were missing.

"No second thoughts?" he asked, looking back at her.

Church scoffed. "Second, third, fourth..."

"You didn't ask me to sign an NDA."

"That would be pointless – you'd have to break it."

Riley dipped his head. "So this," he said, pointing to the agreement he'd just signed. "This changes things... between us."

"Not necessarily," she said.

Riley raised an eyebrow. "I thought you'd want to keep things purely professional."

"They will be," she said firmly. "Until after this op."

Riley took her implication, hiding his smirk. He was willing to wait.

"I expected more questions, if I'm honest," Church said.

Riley shrugged. "It's simple enough."

"You don't have an issue with taking orders again?"

"Are you likely to deal out many?" Riley asked.

"No," Church admitted. "We can discuss certain aspects of the op behind closed doors, if that makes you more comfortable."

"Makes no difference to me." Riley sat back in his seat. "So, you really don't want to know everything she asks of me?"

"Taking all the fun out of it?" Church shook her head. "No. You do as she asks. That's it."

"And what if this arrangement – between Echo and Archers – doesn't pan out... for whatever reason?"

"We walk away. Nothing is permanent."

"You're putting a lot of trust in Echo – not just me."

"Trust is earned. You all need to prove you can be trusted to do what's asked. I assume your guys will follow your orders?"

"To the letter."

"Good," Church said with finality. She stood up and offered her hand to him, reaching over her desk. "Welcome to the team."

Arrivals

Echo

Team Echo drove towards Archers in two vehicles. Riley and Harris rode in Riley's Ranger, followed closely by Tom, driving their gunmetal grey van. Ellis and Jonny sat on the benches in the back, making sure their kit survived the journey. The team's comms were open.

"You sure about this?" Harris asked Riley.

"Ever known me to turn down a well-paying job?" Riley growled.

"I get that part. What about the other problem?" Harris pressed.

"I'll deal with that when the need arises," Riley replied. "Right now, I'm appeasing two out of the three women currently trying to crush my balls."

"They do kinda seek you out, don't they," Harris said with a grin.

"Hmm."

"It's the face," Tom added with a chuckle.

"Fuck you, Three!" Riley growled.

"Back at ya," Tom replied.

"I see you're not complaining," Riley said, looking briefly at Harris. "Surely, Kat could be a problem?"

"Kat is... perfection," Harris said with a satisfied sigh.

"Wait until she finds out about all the other girls you've strung along," Ellis said.

"What others?" Harris cried. "I've dropped them all. No competition. Kat's something else."

"We need to watch our backs once we enter their lair," Jonny said, rubbing the back of his head where he still sported a large lump.

"We need to watch *their* backs," Riley growled and pulled up to the intercom at the gates to Archers. He opened the window and pressed the intercom button. The gates immediately clicked and slowly swung inwards.

"Best behaviour," Riley said and drove through the gates.

Archers

Kat waited on the steps of the main house as Echo pulled onto the gravel drive. The guys piled out. Kat skipped over to Harris and kissed him on the cheek.

"Welcome to Archers," she said. "We're in the conference room." She took Harris's hand and led the way.

The conference table was covered with pots of tea and coffee and jugs filled with orange and grapefruit juice. The girls handed around plates laden with doorstep breakfast sandwiches.

"Is this normal?" Harris asked with his mouth full.

"Coffee is the most important thing," Kat said. "None of us care to spend long in the kitchen, so we ordered the sandwiches in."

Riley noticed that Jonny's attention was instantly piqued by the mention of the kitchen. "Muscles here is our resident chef."

"You cook?" Kat asked excitedly, looking at Jonny.

"Cook, bake," Jonny said with a shrug. "Someone had to learn, else these guys would starve."

"We'll give you the grand tour later," Kat said. "The kitchen is all yours. You can give Ruben a list of anything you want on the shopping list."

Kez handed out security passes on long, dark green lanyards to the guys.

Church had been quietly observing the team settling in. She wrapped her hands around her oversized mug. "The passes will give you access to the main house, the bar, gym and pool." She looked at Ellis. "We've emptied one of the rooms upstairs for your equipment."

"I just need a station in your ops room," Ellis said, with the intention of being helpful. "I don't want to put you out at all."

Riley looked at Ellis and shook his head slightly. Ellis closed his mouth with an apologetic look.

"One step at a time," Church said. "The surveillance room is top clearance only." She looked at Riley.

"Agreed," he said. "We're going to earn your trust."

"So, what's the pecking order?" Harris asked.

Church and Riley exchanged a look.

"We'll operate with our existing designations to avoid any confusion. We'll team up on this op only if everyone is comfortable with that," Church said.

"But who's calling the shots?" Harris asked, looking at Riley.

"I am," Church said.

"Church is," Riley said at the same time. The corner of his mouth twitched. Church bowed her head slightly in acknowledgement.

"My word is final," Church said. "All field work will be planned, discussed and agreed in advance. This is not a dictatorship. All opinions will be considered. Riley will be second-in-command for this op only."

"You sure you're okay with that?" Riley asked, looking at Kat.

Kat waved it off. "Makes no difference to me. I will always have her back, regardless," she said firmly.

"We'll have to use our full designations," Jen said. "If we call 'One,' we could be referring to either Church or Justin."

"Riley, please," Riley said.

"Will you be using your own comms or ours?" Kez asked.

"Both," Riley confirmed.

Church hid a smile. She had the same idea and instructed Kez not to give Echo access to the Archers channel. A new Archers / Echo channel would be created.

Kez nodded. "I'll issue your kits as soon as we're done here."

"Shall we go through what we know so far?" Church asked. Everyone nodded.

Kat led the meeting. "Mr Geoff Abraham, the guy who attempted to steal the information and who we believe informed Pérez of its existence. We found him dead yesterday. Definitely a staged suicide. Doyle's signature is all over the place."

Kat continued. "He went AWOL from Cactus some months ago. Dropped off the grid. We can't find him. No one from his usual circle has heard from him."

"What is Stocky's signature?" Riley asked.

"He likes to toy with his prey, loves a little drama and then stages the scene to throw off whoever finds it," Church said. "The police will get an update from us shortly."

"You called this in?" Riley asked.

"We did," Church replied. "We have a relationship with a DCI in the Met, we share relevant information and he turns a blind eye to our involvement."

"He's an ally," Kat said defensively. "He's not a problem."

"I wasn't suggesting he was," Riley said calmly. "It's just unusual to involve the police when your entire operation is in a very grey area, where the law is concerned."

"Leave him to us," Kat said.

Church nudged Kat with her shoulder. Kat glared at Church but said nothing more.

"He's family. End of," Church said firmly. "Our techs are tracking Doyle, it's just a matter of time."

"How many people work here?" Ellis asked, eager to change the subject and avoid any further tension.

Church replied, "We have two shifts of techs, so that's twelve, the five of us, Ruben heads ops and looks after the site, four forensic scientists, five in the medical centre led by Dr Douglas, Scorpio team is five more. We also have five apprentices who rotate through all departments and then choose their speciality."

Harris whistled, clearly impressed.

"Don't forget Lorenzo is starting tomorrow," Kat said, looking at Church.

"Who's Lorenzo?" Harris asked.

"Church's new assistant," Kat said.

"*Our* new assistant," Church corrected. "We needed someone to manage the meetings, diaries, you know, admin stuff. In time, he'll take the running of the site from Ruben."

The guys exchanged a glance. This company was something else. Nothing like they were used to.

"We're no further forward in locating Kenny MacKay," Kez interjected. "We really need to get inside EMP."

"I can help with that," Riley said, making everyone turn to look at him. He pulled a device from his pocket and slid it down the table towards Kez. She caught it and plugged it into her laptop.

"You did it already?" Church asked in surprise.

"I don't hang around," he replied with a grin.

Lorenzo

The next morning, a little later than usual, Church wandered down the stairs to her office. Her hair was still wet from her post-workout shower. She scrolled through the op information on her tablet, wishing she hadn't drunk as much as she had the night before. The welcome party for Echo had been a success and nearly every drop of alcohol on the premises had been consumed.

Church stepped into her office and instantly stopped on the plush cream carpet. The hairs on the back of her neck prickled as she sensed a strange presence. Her eyes flicked towards her desk, where she kept her gun, as she instinctively reached behind her back. Her hand found nothing, her blade was safely in its holster in her bedroom upstairs.

A man, in his early twenties, dressed in a white collared shirt, black trousers and very shiny shoes, was leaning over the black coffee table. He was in the process of placing Church's oversized coffee mug on a coaster. He froze when he heard Church enter the room. He looked nervously at her and slowly straightened up.

"Morning!" Kat chirped from behind Church, making her flinch inwardly. Kat sailed around her and sat on one of the cream sofas with her own mug in hand. She grinned broadly at Church, then beamed at the young man.

Church's hungover brain slowly caught up with the scenario. Her inner battle stations were stood down and the klaxons in her head were muted. The young man was Lorenzo, the new assistant. He wasn't the type of person she had been expecting. He was young and athletic, with a tanned complexion. Mediterranean descent, Church surmised and with a name like Lorenzo, very likely Italian. She thought she had better say something before her silence put him off.

"Welcome to Archers," Church said, regaining her composure.

"Don't worry about this one," Kat said conspiratorially to Lorenzo. "She was probably taken off guard by your presence in her inner sanctum and was considering which of her many weapons she could use to dispatch you with."

Lorenzo laughed nervously but looked uncertainly at Church. Church didn't notice, she was glaring at Kat.

"Her gun is in the top drawer," Kat said, pointing to the desk. "It's always locked and by the looks of her, she's just finished her morning workout... you're late!" Kat looked at her watch. "So, her knife is still upstairs."

Kat studied Church and noticed the weeping cut on her lip. She raised a questioning eyebrow.

"Thank you, Katherine," Church hissed, shaking her head discreetly in response to Kat's eyebrow.

"Don't mention it," Kat said, waving it off. Church sat down and reached for her coffee mug. Kat continued, "May I present Miss Claudia Church. Please only call her *Church*, anything else will likely result in immediate dismissal, castration or death."

"Kat!" Church protested.

Kat ignored her, still smiling at Lorenzo. "She's a pussycat if you follow the rules. Just don't cross her or you'll regret it." She looked pointedly at Church's lip.

Seeing Red

"You're making me out to be some sort of tyrant!" Church said.

Kat shrugged. "Just setting the scene for the guy."

"It's a pleasure to finally meet you," Lorenzo said, with only a slight hint of his native accent. He extended his hand and Church shook it. He had a firm grip, showing more confidence than the rest of him did.

"Likewise," Church said with a smile.

"I'll do my very best for you, Miss Church."

Kat winced.

"Church. Sorry, it just sounds a little disrespectful."

"And *Miss Church* is far too formal," Church countered. "Just *Church* is fine."

"I'll leave you two to it then," Kat said, jumping up. "I'll catch up with you after the briefing. I've got some things to do first."

"I noticed that Echo didn't go home last night," Church said.

Kat grinned. "After all that alcohol? Nah, they stayed… do we have to dredge the lake for Riley's body?" She looked at Church's lip again.

"He was very much alive last time I saw him," Church said innocently.

Kat raised another eyebrow in surprise, swung her hair over her shoulder and left the room, closing the door behind her.

"Can I get a first aid kit?" Lorenzo offered.

"You hurt?" Church asked, surprised by the question.

"Not me. You."

Church touched her fingers to her lip and they came away bloody. "It's nothing," she said absentmindedly. She relived the moment she had sustained the minor injury with a mixture of pleasure and irritation.

Lorenzo handed her a tissue from the box on the coffee table. Church took it and held it to the cut.

"You should see the other guy," she muttered.

Lorenzo picked up a tablet from the coffee table. "I took the liberty of checking the diary. We pushed the morning briefing to eleven."

"We?" Church asked.

"Miss Jones…"

"Kat," Church corrected gently. "Enough said, it's fine. We had a late night, let the team sleep in."

"Sebastian has requested a meeting with you this afternoon. He has an update on Kenny MacKay."

"Okay, put him in after the briefing, we can eat lunch together."

Church waved at the sofa, encouraging Lorenzo to sit. He straightened his shoulders and hesitated. Eventually, he sat down opposite Church.

"You came in early today," Church observed.

"First impressions are important," Lorenzo replied.

"Indeed."

"Apologies if I startled you."

Church laughed. "Being startled isn't something I do often. I was miles away, distracted. I should have been better prepared for your arrival." She studied him for a moment, berating herself for not reading up more on Kat's appointment beforehand. Church had delegated for once – and it had left her out of the loop. "So, tell me about yourself."

"Erm, not much to say. My older brothers and father enlisted, my uncle works with DCI Jackson."

The penny dropped, Lorenzo was a recommendation through Kat's brother, Jorge.

"What do you know about Archers?" Church asked.

"Not much, to be honest. I couldn't find your website."

Church smiled. "Don't be too concerned by that. There's a reason we keep a low profile, our reputation spreads through verbal recommendations. A bit old-school, but it's effective and necessary."

The door rattled in the frame, making the wall shudder. Someone was trying to open it without using a security pass. Lorenzo leapt up and strode to the door. He opened it to face Riley's chest. Riley raised his eyebrows in mild surprise but decided to ignore him.

"Church?" he called over Lorenzo's shoulder.

"May I help you?" Lorenzo said confidently.

"I doubt it," Riley growled, trying to sidestep him.

Lorenzo stood his ground and didn't let him pass. He regarded Riley critically, his right eye was swollen and the start of an impressive black eye was forming.

"Do you have an appointment? I don't recall seeing one in the calendar."

"Hmm." Riley had had enough of people blocking his way. He considered which window to throw the kid out of.

"Lorenzo, it's okay," Church called from the sofa. "Let him in."

Lorenzo bowed his head, released the door handle and Riley strode into the office.

"This is Justin Riley, Echo One," Church said, not looking up from her tablet.

"You need me to stay?" Lorenzo asked.

Church glanced up from her tablet. Lorenzo was looking concerned at the brute now standing in the office. "No, it's fine," she assured him.

Lorenzo left the office and closed the door. Church's eyes turned to Riley. She took in his injury and couldn't help but smile wickedly.

"What can I do you for?" she asked.

"About last night…" Riley growled.

"You bruise easily," she observed, cutting him off.

"And you're made of stone?" he countered, with a twitch to the corner of his mouth.

"Some would say ice."

"Hmm, you should put some ice on that," he said, pointing to her lip.

"It's nothing," Church shrugged. "And if you came to apologise, don't. I give as good as I get, as you no doubt now realise. I wanted a straight fight and I got one. You didn't hold back... I should thank you, I'd forgotten how good sparring was. I've not slept that well in weeks."

"Hmm," he agreed. "Round two still on the table?"

"I thought you'd never ask," Church said. "1800 hours suit you? Gives us a bit more time. How are you with Hanbō?"

Riley grinned. "Let's find out."

Scorpio

Sebastian, Scorpio One, updated Church on the team's findings on Kenny MacKay. They were sitting in Church's office at the table in the huge bay window. Lunch for all employees had been prepared by Jonny, a welcome change from a dull sandwich. Church studied her plate – chicken bean gribiche with homemade falafel. Seb had a sticky beef noodle dish with a doorstep of fresh crusty bread.

"He's not on holiday in Spain," Seb explained. "None of his family boarded the flight. They didn't enter the airport either."

"What do you think about that?" Church asked.

"Suspicious."

Church agreed.

Seb took another mouthful and closed his eyes in gratitude.

"So, how's your new recruit shaping up?"

"Good. He's got real potential," Church replied.

"What discipline?"

"We haven't had that conversation yet, but whatever he takes a liking to," Church shrugged. "Give him time to choose, it's only his first day."

"And Echo?"

Church raised an eyebrow. "What about them?"

"They're your new backup team."

"In addition to Scorpio," Church clarified.

"Not just new muscle then."

"Feeling threatened by the pretty boys?" Church joked. "We need their intel, Riley has already given us access to EMP's systems."

"You didn't need to hire them to get their intel," Seb said.

"It's not so bad, is it? Look at the food, that's a bonus, right?"

Seb remained quiet.

"You worried about them?" Church asked.

"Aren't you?"

"Worried? No. A little wary, perhaps," she admitted.

"They're way too close."

"To what? They're exactly where I want them to be."

Seb raised his eyebrows. "Oh, so you can keep an eye on them," he said quietly.

"No need to whisper, we do regular sweeps of all op-critical rooms, you know that."

Seb relaxed slightly and returned to his lunch.

"If you're that worried, how would you feel about some covert surveillance?" Church asked.

"Who?"

"Echo One."

Seb's face split into a wide grin.

Church Goes Solo

Church

After the briefing the next morning, Church headed back to her office. She collected a few things, then ran upstairs to her room. She threw some gear into a backpack and pulled her phone from her pocket. She looked at it for a moment, then left it on the bedside table.

She took off her T-shirt and shrugged her knife holster over one shoulder. After fastening the buckle, she pulled her T-shirt back on and smoothed it over an irregular lump on her stomach covered with surgical tape.

Glancing around the room, she grabbed a fleece and a waterproof jacket, shrugged on the bag and made her way down to the basement garage.

Sitting in the driver's seat of one of the pool cars, Church leaned forward and pulled her knife from its holster. She flipped open the vanity mirror, her fingers probing the skin at the back of her neck. She closed her eyes and placed the tip of the blade between her fingers. With a deep breath, she increased the pressure on her skin.

The car door suddenly opened and Riley slid into the passenger seat, the car dipping with his weight.

"Need a hand?" Riley asked.

"What are you doing?" Church asked, eyeing him critically.

He shrugged, looking at the knife in her hand then to the first aid kit on the dashboard. He raised a questioning eyebrow. "It's none of my business but…"

"You're right, it's not," Church said coolly, cutting him off. "I was aiming for a little privacy."

"In the garage?" he asked with a chuckle. "Solo knife play?"

"I'm heading out. I won't be back for a while, so you and the rest of Echo can go do… whatever it is you do when you're off duty."

"An op, huh?"

"Something like that."

"Need some company?"

"I'll be fine," she said, her patience wearing a little thin.

"Whatever you're planning, you're gonna do some serious damage with that," he said, indicating her blade. He shoved a hand into his back pocket and pulled out his own knife, which was half the size of Church's. "Two eyes and two hands will make light work of whatever you're trying to do."

Church studied him for a moment, judging whether to tell him what she was doing or not. "Keep this to yourself," she said.

"My lips are sealed," he said solemnly.

"I just need a few hours of being undetectable… electronically."

"You're hot?"

"Why, thank you, Mr Riley, not so shabby yourself." Church rolled her eyes at him.

"You know what I mean," he said quietly, then grinned again. "But you *are* hot, in so many ways."

"All field operatives have trackers implanted under their skin, for security reasons. It won't take Archers long to realise I've gone AWOL. There'll be hell to pay when they find out."

"Need me to cover for you?"

It was Church's turn to raise an eyebrow.

Riley continued. "I can plant it somewhere, your room, perhaps. Tell them that you've gone for a lie-down with a headache or something. Would that work?"

"My room?" she said dubiously.

"Bedroom," he said with a glint in his eye. "Shame you won't be joining me there."

Church gave him a look that told him to pack it in. She huffed out a breath. "Fine," she said. "Take my keycard so your entry doesn't set anything off in the surveillance room."

Riley took the offered keycard. "Thanks," he said, still grinning. "I promise not to rummage through your stuff while I'm in there."

"Knock yourself out," Church said disinterestedly.

"So, you wanna do this here or somewhere with better light so I can actually see what I'm doing?"

Church reached over his knees and opened the glovebox. She grabbed a torch and handed it to him.

Riley

"You don't have to do this. Feels like we're crossing a line," Red said, looking uncertainly at his knife.

"A friend in need." He shrugged. "And as for crossing lines... haven't we crossed a few already?" He spun his knife in his fingers, demonstrating his dexterity. "Are you sure you wanna do this? This is gonna hurt."

"Just do it," she whispered.

Red took in a deep breath, let it out slowly and her shoulders relaxed. She turned her back to him and swept her hair away from her neck.

"You have a hair tie?" he asked.

Red pulled an elastic tie from around her wrist. Riley snatched it from her fingers and expertly gathered her hair in his hands. Before she could protest, he gently pulled and smoothed her hair into a high ponytail and used the tie. He kept the ends of her hair neatly captured so her neck was clear.

"I won't ask where you learned to do that," she muttered.

"I like the feel of a woman's hair, especially when it's like yours," he replied quietly. "It's like silk."

And smells like heaven, he thought.

Red tapped a spot on the back of her neck, to the left of her spine. Riley held his knife, poised over the spot, his fingertip replacing hers as he felt for the tracker. He could barely feel it, but it was there, just under the skin.

An alcohol wipe appeared in her hand. Riley took it and wiped her pale skin clean. He quickly made a small incision – Red not making a sound – and squeezed either side of the cut with his thumb and forefinger. He held the knife between his teeth, pinching the blue pellet with his fingertips. Blood trickled from the wound as he pulled it out.

Red held a gauze pad over her shoulder. Riley took it and pressed it firmly over the wound. She readied another pad, more alcohol wipes and an adhesive dressing. He took them in turn as she handed them to him.

"Thank you," Red said quietly when he was done. She turned to face him and held out her hand. Riley placed the bloody tracker into her waiting palm. She offered Riley the pack of wipes to clean his hands. She cleaned the tracker and gave it back to him.

"In front of my pillow would be best, I think."

"Okay," he said. "Should you really go it alone with someone out there trying to take you out?"

"I'll be fine. It's not like I haven't done this kinda thing before," she said firmly. "I'd better go."

Riley made no move to get out of the car. He shoved his hand into his pocket and pulled out his keys.

"The tail is only interested in you," he said. "Take my truck, give yourself a head start."

"I thought we agreed…"

Riley held up his hand to stop her. "Watch your back," he said, getting out of the car.

Seeing Red

Riley returned to Echo's room on the first floor of the main house, which had been set up with their equipment. The rest of the team were at their stations.

"Security seems pretty tight. No holes as far as I can see," Ellis reported once Riley sat down. "Though one of the cameras in the basement garage has moved."

"That was Church," Riley said.

"What? Why?" Ellis asked.

Riley gave Ellis a look that told him to stop asking questions. He lifted a finger, spun it in a circle and looked pointedly around the room. Ellis gave the all-clear signal.

Riley tugged his phone from his back pocket and made a call.

"I've a job for you," he growled. "My truck has just left Archers. Church is driving it. Follow her. Keep out of sight and watch for anyone else following." He hung up.

"The young ladies at EMP have been in contact," Ellis said. "Lily wants to meet you."

"Where?" Riley asked.

"She left you to decide."

"Find somewhere suitable close to a station. Text me the location," Riley said, turning to Tom. "I need to go back to the club. I need a lift."

Tom grabbed the keys to the van and followed Riley down to the garage.

In the surveillance room at Archers, Kez watched Echo's van leave the gates.

"You're on," she said over comms.

"Copy that," Seb replied.

Church

Church drove through the gates with one eye on the rear-view mirror. The blacked-out windows of Riley's truck shielded her from anyone who cared to look. The tail's Vauxhall was still in the layby as she roared past. It didn't pull out to follow her and she relaxed for a moment. The tail might be fooled for a short time, but she wasn't going to take any chances.

Church had the techs sweep both of Echo's vehicles twice daily, at random intervals. Each time they hadn't found any trackers or anything else of interest. Did Riley know she had their vehicles checked? Possibly. She shrugged to herself. It didn't matter if he did, she knew how to avoid being followed and if she spotted anyone attempting to, she knew how to shake them.

Her journey would take several hours, so she had plenty of time to think things through. She drove for an hour before reaching her first checkpoint. She parked the truck in the train station car park and left the keys in a magnetic secure box under the wheel arch. She pulled on her coat and her backpack and headed for the ticket office.

Behind her sunglasses, her eyes constantly scanned her surroundings as she waited patiently in the queue. She noted every person she saw, height, build, sex, clothing, gait, hair colour, skin tone, demeanour. She looked for anything out of the ordinary and more importantly, any nondescript, grey people who excelled at not being noticed.

She purchased a ticket with cash and boarded the next train heading south. She got off at the next station, bought a large latte from the café and another ticket at the manned booth. She crossed the bridge over the track and waited for the next northbound train. She leaned against the station wall, head lowered towards the book she held open in front of her. She didn't read a single word. No familiar passengers from the previous platform had joined her.

The train screeched into the station and Church waited. She watched her fellow passengers board. Once the platform was empty, she stepped away from the wall and moved towards the train. The doors beeped in warning and glided shut. The train departed without her.

Under the shelter of the waiting area, Church opened her backpack, shoved her well-read book into it and rummaged around for a few moments. She left the station and walked into town. She passed shops and businesses until she reached the market square. She made a slow circuit of the farmers' market, bought some lunch and walked back towards the station.

The northbound platform was deserted. Church visited the ladies' loos, changed her outerwear and pulled on a black woolly hat, tucking her hair under it. The announcement about the next approaching train echoed around the platform. She waited until the last moment to emerge from the toilets and leapt straight onto the train.

Church walked through each of the carriages and back again, eventually taking a seat in the first carriage, facing the rear of the train. She was confident that all the passengers were unfamiliar to her. She would not leave the train for a couple of hours, so she made herself comfortable. She watched the countryside fly past her window and ate her lunch, noting any movement in the reflection. At each station, she mentally ticked off passengers as they disembarked and added new ones to her mental list as they boarded.

At the last station, Church waited until the doors were about to close before she leapt up from her seat and slipped between them. She was the only passenger on the platform. She shrugged on her backpack and headed towards the bus stop.

Church took the number forty-four bus. The only other passenger was an elderly woman in a tweed jacket. The bus trundled out of the small town and into the countryside. Church disembarked twenty minutes later in a small village and headed out beyond it, following a well-trodden track into the hills.

After nearly an hour of trekking into the trees, Church finally reached her the last checkpoint. The bothy was nestled among a small cluster of trees. She went in and shrugged off her backpack. The room was clean yet sparse. The only furnishings were a small wooden table with two chairs, a basic and bare camp bed and a small wood-burning stove. She set a timer on her watch and settled herself on the camp bed. She would rest until after dark.

Under the cover of darkness, Church set out into the chilly night with the bothy's shovel wedged through the straps of

Seeing Red

her backpack. Thirty minutes of walking away from the track led her to a small clearing in the trees. She stopped, held her breath and listened. All she heard was the light breeze in the leaves and the occasional owl. She was truly alone. She turned north and walked for another ten minutes.

Vaulting over an ancient stone wall, Church made her way to the centre of the grassy field. She turned in a slow circle and surveyed her surroundings. No movement, no noise. She walked back to the wall and knelt down on the damp grass. Removing her backpack, she started to dig.

After a few minutes, Church reached the desired depth. She undid her coat and untucked the layers of her gear. Taped to her stomach was the chess piece-shaped USB stick. The queen, the most powerful piece.

Church ripped off the tape and held the queen in her hand for a moment. The blueprints for death and destruction. The cause of all this fuss.

Decisively, Church wrapped the USB in the tape and placed it into a small plastic box from her backpack. She dropped it into the hole and started to fill it in. She patted down the loose soil and covered the disturbed earth with stones and leaves.

Sitting back on her heels, Church looked at her watch and memorised the co-ordinates. She did up her coat and stood up. The skin on the back of her neck prickled. She was no longer alone. Someone was watching her.

Not bad, she thought to whoever was out there in the dark. *You nearly made a clean run of it.*

With a small smile to herself, Church returned to the bothy.

The silence around the bothy was reassuring. It was still unoccupied. She placed the shovel back in a wooden crate by the door. Removing all traces of her brief stay, Church left the bothy and descended into the trees. She took a direct route down the slope towards the nearest village.

When Church eventually got back onto the train, she pulled up her hood and let herself rest. She leaned her head against the window and closed her eyes.

Church woke with a start, her eyes flashing open, but she remained perfectly still. It took a few seconds for her to remember where she was. The train slowed as it approached a station – this was her stop. She gathered her things, got up and waited by the doors.

She retrieved the keys to Riley's truck and drove back to Archers.

Riley

In Echo's room at Archers, Riley growled in affirmation. He ended the call and returned his mobile to his back pocket. His truck was two minutes from the gates.

Letting his truck through, he made his way down to meet Red. She was getting out of the truck when he arrived.

"Welcome back," he growled from the shadows. "Want me to scrub the footage so you can get to your room unseen?"

"That won't be necessary," she replied. "Keeping tabs on me?"

"Just maintaining your cover. Took the night shift."

"Thanks for the loan," Church said, throwing his keys in his direction.

"Anytime," he said, catching them. "How did it go?"

"Uneventful," Red shrugged. "But successful. Anything to report here?"

"No, your tail hasn't moved from the layby."

Had his tail really managed to evade her? Riley couldn't be sure. Would she say anything? Unlikely.

"You been here the whole time?" she asked.

"I met with one of the girls from EMP," Riley replied. "But that can wait until the morning briefing."

Red nodded. She looked tired and a little pale.

"Can I make you something to eat?" he asked.

"I'll grab something from the kitchen on my way upstairs."

"Jonny left you something in the fridge. I'll heat it up for you."

"No need."

Red made to leave the garage. Riley reached out a hand to stop her.

"I told the girls you weren't feeling well, something you ate."

"Thanks."

"See you at the briefing," she said, leaving him to watch her walk away.

Irritation

Briefing

The team gathered in the conference room, though Church's seat was conspicuously empty.

"Boss still under the weather?" Riley asked Kat as he took his seat.

"She's on a call," Kat said evasively. "She asked me to lead this meeting in her absence." She addressed the team. "So, what news?"

"Access to EMP's systems failed," Kez said, avoiding looking at Riley. "Lily just didn't have the credentials. We needed senior managers or above. There's nothing of note in the files we could access from her computer."

Kat looked pointedly at Riley. He calmly held her gaze. Fortunately, he had a contingency in place.

"My assets in EMP have provided some interesting information," he said, gesturing to Ellis. "Not everything useful can be found on their servers," he added.

A bio on Leonard Adams appeared on the main screen. The team scanned the information about the small, mousy man. He was a legendary IT genius who had developed impenetrable computer systems. His catalogue was impressive.

Kat looked at Riley questioningly.

"This guy is the key," Riley continued. "Romano is hiring this lone IT wolf to scour their systems to find the leak and then he'll upgrade them. Once he applies the update, we'll be shut out for good, whether we have people on the inside or not. I suggest we make him give us all his findings first.

"Church wants to take EMP down, so the more information we have on them, the easier that'll be. I'm sure this project isn't the only time they've crossed the legal line. It won't be long before he finds the evidence you need."

Kat raised a sceptical eyebrow.

"First, we need to find him," Riley said. "Our attempts to follow the guy proved fruitless, he's as slippery as they come."

"You lost him?" Kat asked.

"We know where he'll be, in two weeks' time," Riley said. "The Gladstone Hotel. Black tie exclusive charity event. He wants to meet the special guest."

"Who's not been announced yet," Kez said, having just looked up the event online. "Tickets are all sold out too."

"Adams knows who the special guest is," Riley said. "And now, so do we. Maddy Lagos."

"Oh," Kat sat back in surprise.

"So, we get close to Adams and make him help us."

"Make him?" Kat asked. "How do you suggest we do that?"

"He has a daughter…"

The girls looked at Riley in shock, Kez sucked in a breath.

"Absolutely not!" Kat cried. "No way we're going to threaten a child."

"I wasn't suggesting we did," Riley growled. "*Romano* has threatened Adams's daughter, we need to ensure her protection."

"God help Romano, when Church finds out," Jen muttered.

Riley continued, "We get close to Adams, ask him for the evidence against EMP and make sure his daughter is safe as a sweetener."

"We can do better than that," Kat said. "Church can ask Maddy to assist, so she'll have to be front and centre on this one." Kat looked at Jen. "Call, Kris, get us two tickets." She turned to Lorenzo. "We'll have to keep Church out of this for the time being so please leave this out of the minutes."

Lorenzo looked up from his tablet in surprise.

"It's okay," Kat explained. "Leave Church to me. If she asks, tell her no lies, just don't mention the guest's name."

"Who's Kris?" Riley asked.

"Head of Maddy's Security Team," Kat replied. "We've worked with him before. He'll get us in."

"You think keeping Church in the dark is a good idea?" Riley asked.

"I know her better than anyone. Trust me. It'll be fine."

Church

Church sat in her office, scrolling through hours of CCTV footage. She was mapping her tail's movements since she had first spotted him, the day after her car was blown to smithereens.

Seeing Red

It was not the first time she had reviewed the footage. She liked to keep his movements fresh in her mind as she searched for more recent encounters. He was not particularly careful, sloppy, at times. Riley was right – he was only interested in her. He did not follow anyone else.

The tail did not appear at the station on her little solo expedition, but she reviewed her movements regardless, checking to see if anyone else had been watching her. A young man had been standing behind her in the queue at the ticket office. His face was obscured by a baseball cap. He had spent most of the time with his head lowered, looking at his phone. But his body language screamed at Church.

"Now who are you?" she asked the blurry image on her screen.

Church tried to get a different angle to get a better look at his face. He was several inches taller than her. If he stood up straight, he might just make six foot three. Fair complexion. No visual yet on his hair colour. Slim build.

She watched the young man with interest. He shuffled forward when Church approached the ticket booth and with a lightning-fast hand, he delved into his pocket and flicked something towards Church's backpack.

"You sneaky bastard!" she exclaimed.

Church had not been followed, she had been tagged before her journey even began. She had to be impressed. She followed the young man's movements. He did not buy a ticket when he reached the desk. He spoke briefly with the attendant, then left the station building.

Church switched to a different camera and found him in the station car park. He was standing next to a motorbike with a top box. He unlocked it and pulled out a backpack and a crash helmet.

Church ran his plates. Moments later, she had all the information she needed. She could not help but smile.

"Got ya!"

A knock on her door dulled her moment of jubilation.

Seb appeared in the doorway. "Thought you'd be in the briefing," he said.

"I'm delegating that," Church replied.

Seb raised his eyebrows and sank into the chair in front of Church's desk.

"Cat got the cream," he observed, noting her jubilant expression.

"A little spy, who just so happens to work at a familiar nightclub, tagged me on my expedition."

"Want me to bring him in?" Seb asked.

Church shook her head. "It was a goose chase, let them figure that out for themselves. So, what news?"

"Nothing untoward," Seb said, sounding more than a little disappointed. "Handsome left here with their medic. They went back to the club, he changed clothes and met with Lily, formerly of EMP. He came straight back here."

"Any calls?" Church asked.

"None outside the team and the club."

Church nodded.

Seeing Red

The next day, a notification appeared on Church's screen. She clicked on it and frowned. It was surveillance footage from a few days ago, with a message from Kez.

Kez:
Thought you should see this 😮

Church hit play. Lorenzo was walking towards the car park at Archers. The video was time-stamped, he was late leaving for the day. Riley was waiting by Lorenzo's VW Golf. They spoke briefly, then Lorenzo followed Riley to his truck and got in. The clip switched to another camera and showed Riley's truck speeding up the drive and out of the gates.

Church drummed her fingers on her desk as she considered how to approach this. Decision made, she called out through her open door.

"Lorenzo, do you have a minute?"

"Problem?" Lorenzo asked, poking his head round the door.

"No, not at all," Church said. "Come in."

She stood up and gestured towards the cream sofas. Lorenzo stepped in and sat down. Church closed the door.

"Everything okay? Any issues?" she asked.

"Issues?" Lorenzo repeated, looking confused.

Church sat opposite him. "You can talk to me, you know. If you have any questions or concerns."

"I know."

"We have to trust each other," Church said.

"Essential part of the job," Lorenzo recited.

"Exactly. So, if you ever need to say something, to get anything straight in your own mind, just ask, okay?"

"Will do."

Lorenzo did not appear concerned.

"Even if I'm busy or preoccupied," Church added. "Just speak up. I'll make time for you."

"I appreciate that."

Church studied him. "So, no one's been bothering you?" she asked.

"Not at all. Everyone's been great."

"Good," she said. "So, what do you get up to after hours?"

Lorenzo looked surprised by the question. "I train, mostly."

"You know you've got free rein here. If you want to train, you can use the gym any time, even after hours. It's fine."

"Thanks."

"You drink?"

"Not much. My brother's got a bit of a problem... put me off, I suppose."

Church nodded. She leaned back and relaxed her shoulders. "You hang out with Echo?" she asked.

"Yeah, they've been helping me."

"How so?"

"Training."

Church did not detect any untruths. "What sort of training?"

Lorenzo did not respond.

"I'm not interrogating you," Church said. "I'm just concerned that Echo may be leading you in a particular direction, away from your responsibilities here."

"Not at all!" Lorenzo said. "My duty is to you."

He looked sincere.

"Duty? To me, or to Archers?" she asked.

"You first. Then Archers," he said. "Echo are worried about you."

"Are they now?" Church said suspiciously. "And what else did they say?"

"Well..." Lorenzo sounded uncertain. "That I should learn..."

Church raised an eyebrow. What could Echo possibly teach Lorenzo that Archers could not, or were not already?

"Protection," he said finally.

Church could not hide her surprise. "Protection?" she repeated.

"Yes. That I should watch your back. Stop you from..."

Church held up her hand to stop him. "I don't need protection," she said firmly.

"They said you'd say that."

Riley

Early the next morning, Riley found Red in the gym. The light was dim in the huge space. He made sure the doors didn't bang shut behind him. He kept to the edge, in the shadows.

Red was attacking the punching bag with ferocity. She huffed out a breath with every strike, growing louder as her frustration built. She pivoted on one foot and kicked the bag with her shin. She danced around the bag, left, right, left, right, shin, shin. He enjoyed watching her. Her guttural cries were very erotic.

"FUCK!" she cried at the bag and unleashed everything she had.

Riley could not help but chuckle. Red heard him and spun to face him.

"Sorry, did I disturb you?" he said.

Red returned to her attack, her back to him. She was clearly pissed off about something and the bag was going to pay for it.

"What are you doing?" she asked breathlessly.

"Not much."

"Why are you watching me?"

"No reason."

Riley saw the muscles in her shoulders tense for a fraction of a second. Perhaps now was not the time to goad her further.

"Bit early for you," she said, dropping her arms. She turned to face him.

"I couldn't sleep, so I was going to train," Riley said.

"What's stopping you?"

Riley looked at her with a raised eyebrow, then pushed himself away from the wall.

"Couldn't sleep either?" he asked.

Red didn't reply.

"What made you scream out like that?"

In the dim light, he thought he saw a flush appear on her already rosy complexion. She turned abruptly, swiped up a towel from the gym floor and buried her face in it.

"Just stuff," she said through the towel.

"Anything I can help with?"

Red stopped rubbing and looked at him over the towel. "That's unlikely," she said.

"A problem shared and all that," he said, stepping closer to her.

"Who said it was a problem?" she snapped.

Riley chuckled again. "Definitely sounded like a problem to me... or one hell of an orgasm."

Red stared at him for a moment, then swept past and disappeared through the doors to the changing rooms without a word.

That was no fun. Red needed to stop running away from him. He followed her. She was sitting on a bench, head in hands, elbows on her knees.

"Get out," she said without looking at him.

"No," he said firmly, crossing his arms and leaning against the doorframe.

Red lifted her head and glared at him. "You want to know what my problem is?" she asked.

He gestured with his hand – *by all means*.

She narrowed her eyes. "You asked Lorenzo to *protect* me," she hissed.

The corner of his mouth twitched. So the pup had squealed. He wasn't surprised. "I did," he said.

"Why?"

"You need people to look out for you. If he's going to be your padawan, then he needs to start learning. And quickly."

"I don't need protection."

"I disagree."

"Padawan?" she said disbelievingly. "He's our assistant."

"So you chose a jacked kid for no reason?"

"Kat made the appointment," Red said defensively.

"Whoa! You delegated something?"

Red folded her arms.

"I offered our insight and experience to him, that's all," Riley said.

"What can *you* offer that we can't?" Red asked.

Riley raised an eyebrow. "I'll teach him all the stuff *you* won't," he said flatly.

"Such as?"

Riley didn't answer.

"Leave him alone," she said.

"I didn't force him," Riley said quietly. He took a breath. "You done here? I was going for a run."

Church

It was just starting to get light as Church and Riley jogged around the perimeter path. The only sound was that of their trainers on the worn track. She kept pace with Riley, his stride was considerably larger than hers, but he had started slow and steady.

"Why did you send Harris's nephew, Benjamin, to tag me?" Church asked suddenly.

"Why do you think?"

"To fuck with me," Church huffed. "He did a pretty good job. You trained him well."

"Thanks," Riley replied.

"Learn anything?" Church asked.

"That you're a nightmare to follow. So, when did you spot him?"

"I didn't. I had a feeling at my final destination, but nothing concrete. It wasn't until I checked the CCTV at the station that I saw him."

"Hmm," Riley growled.

They continued in silence for a while. Riley maintained his pace.

"No need to hold back on my account," she said.

"Wouldn't dream of it. I know how much that irks you," he replied.

"You like irking me though. You've made a sport out of it."

"Blood sport, more like," Riley muttered. "Though, I think you miss beating the crap out of me. Your frustration seems to be reaching a peak. There are other ways to let loose you know."

Church remained quiet for a while.

"Wanna race?" she asked.

Riley didn't respond. Church sped up and he matched her pace. On their third circuit, Riley slowed down and held up his hands in defeat.

"Enough," he gasped. Church turned her head and started to slow.

"You proved your point," he said, hands on knees. "You won. Again. I lost. You beat me fair and square. Again. You are the endurance queen."

"Fuck you," Church said breathlessly, walking back to him.

"Fuck you too. I'm done with all this."

"Spoilsport."

"And you make a sport out of beating me." Riley straightened up. "Losing is getting a bit tedious. Is there anything you're not great at?"

Church laughed. "Trusting people. Not being competitive. Relationships."

"Hmm."

"Truce?" she asked.

"Never."

Their breathing now under control, they walked back towards the house.

"Would you have stopped?" he asked.

"Hadn't considered it," she admitted.

"Didn't it hurt?"

"Oh, it hurt, but that's not the point."

"What was then?" he asked.

Church shrugged.

"You don't have to prove anything to me. I get it. You're strong, you're fast, all that. It's not a competition," he said.

Tension

Church and Riley remained in the conference room after the rest of the team had left. The tension between them had simmered throughout the entire meeting.

"What do you want from me?" Riley growled quietly.

"Honesty," Church replied.

"I haven't lied to you. We have an agreement and I'm following it."

"Are you?" Church accused. "You're keeping things to yourselves."

"I wasn't aware micromanagement was part of the agreement."

Kat and Harris lingered in the corridor outside and could hear the raised voices.

"What should we do?" Harris asked quietly.

"Leave it to me," Kat said. "We need a night out. She needs to let her hair down and expel all this frustration."

"Sounds like that involves bloodshed."

"It'll be fine," Kat assured him.

"You're not totally forthcoming either," Riley countered. "I understand why you're having us all followed, but really, there's no need. We're not the problem here."

Church and Riley were standing with the conference table between them, arms crossed defensively.

"I don't need to explain myself to you," Church said, her chin raised. "I'm protecting Archers. I thought you understood that."

"You don't need to protect yourselves against us," Riley said. "We're on your side."

Seeing Red

"But you're not, are you?" Church said, narrowing her eyes at him.

Riley ground his teeth.

"You have something to say, say it," Church hissed.

"Stop following us," Riley growled.

Church knew that her team following Echo wasn't what was really bothering him.

"No."

Riley ran a hand through his hair. "Shall we take this to the gym?" he asked. "You only seem to be satisfied when you've beaten the shit out of me."

"That won't help," Church said quietly.

Their fighting, while very stimulating, was not the kind of example she wanted to set for the teams. Kat was right, it was weird and it really didn't look good to the newer members.

"Bedroom?" Riley arched an eyebrow. He instantly regretted it. The second the word left his mouth, he wished he could take it back. Now was not the time for his suggestive innuendos.

Church looked like she was going to launch herself across the table at him. He half wished she would.

"Not happening," Church said, her tone plummeting.

Riley held up his hands apologetically. He had crossed a line. The op came first.

Church seemed to take his gesture like a slap. She was seething.

Riley dropped his arms to his sides in defeat. He wasn't getting anywhere.

"You're the boss," he said, leaving the room.

Church grabbed the nearest mug and hurled it at the closed door. It opened moments later and Kat poked her head inside. She looked quizzically at the pieces of ceramic on the polished wooden floorboards, then at Church.

"We're heading out in thirty minutes. Go get ready," she said.

"Where?" Church asked. She was still fuming and barely paying attention as she stared at the tablet in front of her.

"Enigma," Kat said flatly.

"No." Church shook her head. "You go. Have fun. I'm not in the mood."

"Get in the mood," Kat said, grabbing Church by the wrist and dragging her out of the room. "It's been a hell of a few weeks. You need to decompress. Let's get drunk and hit the dancefloor. It'll do you the world of good."

Night Out

Church held a bottle of beer in front of Riley's face as a peace offering. He frowned at it, so she pulled it away and offered a bottle of bourbon instead.

"I hope you paid for that," he growled.

"My credit card's behind the bar. Drinks are on me."

"You didn't need to do that."

Seeing Red

Church slid into the booth beside him. She raised her eyebrows in question as she poured. He didn't respond, so she kept pouring a more than generous measure into his crystal glass.

Church watched him drink heavily. "I'm sorry," she said. "I know I'm a total bitch."

"Hmm."

"I was being unreasonable."

"You want space. You can have it."

"I was expecting too much. This is more difficult than I thought. The waiting…"

"The op or us?"

The million dollar question. What was eating Church? She couldn't tell which was the issue.

Church looked at Riley, but he was staring into his glass. She slid out of the booth without answering, leaving both bottles on the table.

Riley watched her sidle onto the dancefloor to join the girls.

"Trouble in paradise?" Harris asked with a smirk, hands flat on the table in front of Riley.

"Fuck off," Riley growled.

"You know what you need?"

"I'm sure you're going to tell me."

"I am. Glad you appreciate that," Harris grinned. "Get on those decks and do your thing. It's been ages. Show her what you've got. She's no DJ, but she does love to dance."

Riley looked blankly at Harris.

Harris read his thoughts. "You'll find the vibe soon enough. Get those girls grooving. I challenge you."

Riley grabbed the bottle of bourbon and left the booth.

Riley had a better view of the dancefloor from his position on the stage. It was a busy night and the floor was filled with hot bodies. He caught glimpses of Red, she seemed totally absorbed in the music. But he also saw sadness in her eyes. A loneliness, until one of the girls spoke to her, then she would smile and seem happy. He wondered what she was hiding from her friends. Was she more concerned about the op than she let on?

The barman, Matt, hopped up onto the stage. Riley pulled one of his headphones from his ear to listen. There was a call for him on the club's landline. Riley frowned and looked at his watch. Who would be calling the club at this time of night?

Matt shrugged apologetically. It was urgent, whoever it was. Riley replaced his headphones and started to mix the current track with a prerecorded section so he could leave the decks and take the call. It was a smooth and seamless transition. He jumped down and headed to his office.

Riley was gone for only a matter of minutes, taking a booking for a stag night in six months' time. The music was still pumping, the dancefloor still packed, but the atmosphere had changed.

Matt appeared at Riley's side. "Trouble," he shouted in Riley's ear, nodding towards the dancefloor near the booths.

Seeing Red

People were pushing and shoving. Riley could hear aggressive, raised voices over the music. It looked like a fight was about to break out. He put his thumb and forefinger into his mouth and whistled, nearly blowing Matt's eardrums.

Riley strode through the crowd, pushing people aside to find the eye of the storm. A clearing had formed on the dancefloor. A young man was face-down on the floor with Kat kneeling on his back, bending one of his arms behind him. He was wheezing and struggling to breathe. Harris was holding back the guy's friend, who was trying to get at Kat.

Riley placed a hand on Kat's shoulder. She spun her head towards him, her eyes filled with rage.

"Care to explain?" he growled, scanning the scene in front of him. Then he saw Red, being shielded by Jen, Kez, and Miz. She was hurt.

Jonny and Ellis appeared at Riley's shoulder. He pointed to the guy on the floor and indicated with his thumb for the guys to remove him.

Riley strode over to Red. "Are you okay? What happened?" he asked.

She rolled her eyes at him. Her cheek was red and starting to swell. "I'm fine," she said.

"You hurt?"

"Hardly! I think I hurt him more." Red glanced in the direction of the guys dragging the man away. "It's dealt with. Done. No need for you to intervene."

"C'mon," Miz urged, pulling Red towards the bar. The girls followed. Riley grabbed Kat by the wrist to stop her following them. She glared at his hand in disgust. He released her and raised a questioning eyebrow.

"The guy on the floor tried it on, that's all," Kat sighed. Riley's other eyebrow shot up. "Fine," she conceded with another sigh. "He grabbed her from behind and was getting very handsy. Church obviously dealt with him herself, but his buddy tried to get involved. The floor guy started swinging at his friend and Church got in between them to split them up." Kat shrugged, the rest was obvious. She turned and headed for the bar, leaving Riley on the dancefloor.

A little later, Riley found Red in the booth. The rest of the girls had returned to the dancefloor, the scuffle clearly forgotten. Riley slid a large crystal glass across the table towards her and sat beside her.

"Thanks," she said. She gave it a quick sniff, then downed the entire contents.

"You always go for the throat?" he asked.

Red shrugged. "I didn't have my knife."

"You usually go dancing armed?"

"Maybe I should consider it."

"I'd rather you didn't," he said.

Red's mouth twitched and she eyed Riley. "What did you do with the body?" she asked.

"Hmm," he growled with amusement. "No body. He's still breathing."

Seeing Red

"And his friend?"

"Same."

"Hmm," Red mused, not entirely convinced. She looked pointedly at Riley's red knuckles. "*We* had dealt with it," she said.

"This is my place. We don't tolerate shit like that."

"What shit?" Red asked. "Fighting? Check the footage, I struck first."

Riley looked at her. "He didn't take no for an answer, did he?"

"I gave him ample warning."

"As did I," he said.

They were quiet for a while.

"I'm sorry," Red said suddenly.

"What for?"

"Everything. Snapping at you, being so competitive with you. You know." She shrugged. "This was supposed to be fun."

"You didn't have fun? Before the guy, I mean," Riley said.

"Oh, before? I was getting there. A gallon more rum would have done the trick or..."

"Or?"

"A locked room, my blade and that guy. I'd like to teach him a thing or two."

Riley smiled knowingly.

"What did you do to them?" she asked.

"Not much," he said, flexing his fingers.

"You could've extended an invite to *that* party," she said.

Riley's eyebrow shot up in surprise, making Red laugh.

"Didn't consider it, did you? No, you just jumped straight in, defending my honour. Well, I don't need your protection. I thought I made that clear. Next time... let's hope this doesn't happen again. Oh, you know what I mean! Don't keep all the fun to yourself. Okay?"

"Noted."

They were silent again for a while. It was getting quieter in the club. People were leaving in small groups.

"So, you like hands-on, close contact stuff?" Riley asked.

Church shook her head. "You know I do. But I shouldn't go there."

"Why not?"

She sighed. "Responsibilities, setting a good example. I'm meant to be staying in the light, remember."

"Fuck the light," he growled. "It's fine for a time, but doesn't it get a little… you know… boring?"

Red leaned back in the seat and sighed again. "You've no idea."

"So, sparring with me wasn't enough to quell this thirst of yours?" Riley asked, grinning.

Red rolled her eyes.

"Leave it with me," he said.

"There's no need. Honestly."

"What harm would a few days do?" he asked. "Truly? Even you, the mighty machine, need to take a break. And if getting dirty and bloody is how you unwind..."

Red looked at him but didn't respond.

"I can take it. To a point. But it's affecting the rest of the team," he said.

That got her attention. "Take what?" she asked defensively.

"Your temper."

"I apologised for that."

"You did. Don't worry about it. I can handle it."

"But I did hurt your feelings," she said.

"Takes more than a few sharp words to hurt me, Red."

She sucked in a breath. "You don't understand, *Handsome*, how much I so wanna break you when you call me that."

"You haven't come close yet."

"We'll see about that."

"I look forward to it," he replied with a smirk.

C E Allardyce

Charity Fundraiser

Glamour

A week later, Church swept into the crowded ballroom in the luxurious Gladstone Hotel, looking like a movie star. She was dressed in a full-length, sleeveless black velvet dress that hugged her figure, the sweetheart neckline accentuating her curves. The diamond-encrusted choker at her throat twinkled in the lights, matching the bracelet on her wrist and the dangling earrings that brushed her bare shoulders. She wore black high heels and her hair was piled in ringlets on top of her head.

"You look amazing," Kez whispered in Church's ear over comms. The team had set up their surveillance kit in a hotel room across the street.

"Ridiculous, more like," Church replied quietly.

This was about as far away from her romp with Riley and a bunch of psycho ex-marines in the Lake District as you could get. Attending the Annual Warrior Competition was his idea of a team building exercise. Beating – and mostly bludgeoning – the opposition had resulted in the fearsome duo walking away victorious. The rest of the competitors hadn't been so lucky.

The air had been cleared and trust had been earnt – they were in this together… for the time being.

Kat had diligently covered Church's minor cuts and fading bruises with make-up. Even her latest injury, just below her shoulder at the top of her biceps, where the new tracker had been fitted, was almost invisible.

Church opened her clutch bag and frowned. "What's this?" she asked quietly.

"What?" Kez replied nonchalantly.

"A taser, a burner phone, a cloning device and what looks like a backup earpiece," Church muttered. "Where's the tracker?"

"Erm..." Kez said uncertainly. "Where's the tracker?" she asked, looking at Riley. He was sitting beside her, scouring the security footage of the ballroom on the screen in front of him. He had been in charge of Church's kit.

"This'll be a whole lot easier if you switch back to the inclusive channel," Riley growled. "She's wearing it." He watched Church on the screen, looking at herself in confusion. "The brooch, it's clipped to the back of it."

Kez relayed the information. Church was surrounded by people, all waiting to get to the bar. She looked down and adjusted the brooch in acknowledgement. It matched her jewellery perfectly, glittering with diamonds. She couldn't tell if it was a cheap knock-off or not.

"Possible target is ten feet behind her at her eight o'clock," Riley said.

Kez zoomed in to confirm.

"One, the target is behind you. Brown suit, mousy curly hair, about five-five, looks uncomfortable and very nervous."

Church scanned the crowd casually as she waited in line. She spotted her target by the fountain.

"Popstar, incoming," Riley said, watching another screen showing a side room.

"Potential asset inbound," Kez said quietly.

Asset? Church thought. *What asset?* Did she hear Riley say *popstar*?

The master of ceremonies appeared on the stage, beaming at the gathered crowd. "Ladies and gentlemen!" he cried over the chatter. He waited for the room to quieten down. "Our very special guest for tonight, the international sensation, every woman's fantasy, the one and only... Mr Maddy Lagos!"

The double doors beside the bar opened. The crowd turned towards them and erupted into cheers and applause. Maddy Lagos, the famous American singer, songwriter and actor, slid into the room. He gracefully glided to a stop, spun around and bowed deeply to the adoring crowd.

Church sucked in a breath and nearly lost her cool in that moment. She turned away and squeezed her way through the well-dressed bodies in the opposite direction, heading for the toilets. Her dress was too tight. She couldn't breathe.

"Three, explain!" she hissed as soon as she was out of earshot from the other guests.

"Erm, yeah, sorry," Kez said apologetically. "Maddy is the special guest."

"You've got to be kidding me!" Church muttered under her breath.

"The target is desperate to meet him. We thought you could ask Maddy for a favour. He could be useful, you know, as an asset," Kez explained.

Riley

Riley got up from his seat and walked into the other room, closing the door firmly behind him.

"Control, what's Red saying?" he demanded over comms, on the 'Echo only' channel. Two could play that game.

"You honestly don't want to know," Ellis replied from his location in the van parked in the loading bay of the hotel.

"Hmm."

Ellis cringed at the tone of Riley's growl. "Fine, fine," he conceded. "She's going to skin Kat and Kez in their sleep and feed it to them for breakfast. Then she's going to remove Kat's eyes and shove them up her skinny arse," Ellis chuckled. "Jen and Miz are getting off lightly."

"Patch it through," Riley growled.

"What?"

"You heard."

There was a series of clicks and Riley heard the girls' conversation.

"*Hi, Maddy, it's been a while!*" Church cried quietly in parody of her potential conversation with Maddy. "*So sorry things ended so abruptly. Hope I didn't break your heart too much, you know how things are, right? Anyhoo, you know that part of me you despised, my work? Well, I'm on a job right now and I need you to do your thing while I nobble this poor guy here!*" Church was seething.

"I don't see what the problem is," Kat insisted calmly.

Riley absorbed the information. So Red and the popstar had history? That was interesting. He wouldn't have pegged her for the groupie type. Sure, the guy was good-looking, loaded and successful. But a popstar? All that attention!

And more importantly, did she make a habit of breaking guys' hearts?

"He'll do anything for you, you know that," Kat pleaded.

"How can I ask him? Now, after all this time. We've not spoken since..." Church's words trailed away.

"He still cares. You know he does," Kat said firmly. "Just ask, no harm done."

"No harm!"

"Oh, for fuck's sake!" Kat cried. "Take one for the team! Not exactly a hardship, is it? I mean, look at him. All gift-wrapped and... "

"Kat!" Church warned.

"You don't have to sleep with him! It's not as if we're pimping you out!" Kat protested. "Unless you're preoccupied by a certain brooding Alpha male, a little closer to home."

Riley's phone vibrated against his chest. He pulled it out of his inside pocket and glared at the screen. An unknown number was calling.

Why now?

He turned off his comms.

"Riley," he growled.

"Soldier," Pérez purred.

Seeing Red

Riley screwed his eyes shut for a moment. "Ma'am."

"Having fun, are we?"

"Not exactly," he replied quietly.

"I'm not seeing any results. I thought you would have provided me with an update by now. What's taking so long?"

"We're about to obtain the target's home address."

Pérez sucked her teeth, making a soft hissing sound. Riley knew that the USB and the project files were far more important to her than some insignificant IT geek.

"Soon, ma'am," he said. "There's no sign of the USB and it wasn't downloaded onto the servers. It's not been seen since they took possession of it."

"And her little jaunt away from Archers?"

"A diversion. I'm sure of it, ma'am."

"Doyle doesn't believe it was a diversion. Give him the co-ordinates of her little expedition and let him follow up. So, she's not disclosed anything? No pillow talk?" she asked. "You have succeeded in that, I trust?"

"Yes, ma'am. But no mention of the USB nor the files."

Pérez hissed again in dissatisfaction. "Try harder! Do what you have to do. You must find a way."

"Yes, ma'am."

The thought of *her* Justin with Church made Pérez feel sick. She wondered when Church had finally given in. Was it after their cosy dinner date in the pub in Church's village, when she had invited him into her house? Or after their playfighting at Archers? Or perhaps they'd roughed it while sharing a tent at the AWC...

"What was it like?" Pérez asked.

"Ma'am?" Riley said, not understanding her.

"Don't be coy. What was *she* like?"

Riley didn't respond.

"Vanilla, I'm sure," Pérez said with disdain.

Riley mentally scoffed at the thought, then checked himself. Pérez was more than adept at knowing when she was being lied to.

"Surprisingly not, ma'am."

Pérez made an approving sound in the back of her throat. "You enjoyed it?"

A loaded question.

"Not the worst time I've had, ma'am," Riley replied.

Pérez sighed. "It pleases me that it wasn't too much of a chore for you. But you deserve so much more than *her*."

"I will earn the right, ma'am, to please you again. I just need a little more time."

"You have four days. If you still find nothing, then we clean house and move forward regardless. Understood?"

"Yes, ma'am."

"Is your team read in?"

"No, ma'am."

"Good. Keep it that way."

Four days! That was not enough time. He hadn't even got halfway through his search of the premises at Archers. Without his team assisting, it would take weeks. He'd have to up his game.

"Ma'am?" Riley said.

"Yes?"

"I look forward to presenting you with the files."

"If you do that, you can have anything you desire," she said silkily. "Anything," she repeated for emphasis and hung up.

Riley took a deep breath, rolled his shoulders and returned to his station.

Church

"The target is now alone. He's not moved from the fountain," Riley growled next to Kez.

Kez fumbled with the controls. "Archer One, good time to intercept the target, while everyone else is swamping Maddy."

Church, having calmed a little, took a deep breath, smoothed down her dress and headed back towards the bar. She wondered how much of her heated discussion with the team Riley had overheard. How much did he know already? She threw the distracting thoughts away and waited in line.

A few minutes later, Church had a tall Cuba Libre in her hand and her clutch bag tucked under her arm. She retreated to the calm of the marble fountain. Her target, Mr Adams, was only a few feet away, intently watching the commotion around Maddy Lagos, international sensation, singer, songwriter, actor... and her former lover.

Maddy hadn't managed to get more than a few feet into the room. He was surrounded by people taking selfies and putting their arms around him. Church shuddered inwardly. She would never get used to the attention Maddy attracted, or how overly familiar strangers were around him.

She had to admit that he looked good. Really good, as he always did. Immaculate black fitted suit, no tie, white shirt collar undone and he was wearing his red Nike trainers.

It had been nearly two years since Church had last seen him. She had ended their whirlwind romance, which had quickly turned into something far more serious. Maddy hated her job, hated the thought of her getting hurt, of her putting herself in harm's way. If it wasn't for that, he could easily have been the *one*.

"Is that really him?" an unfamiliar male voice said, breaking her reverie. Church found that her target had moved closer and was now standing right beside her.

"Yes, that's really him," Church sighed.

"He's even better looking in person, if that's even possible."

Church smiled in agreement, sipping her drink to keep her face from betraying her true feelings.

"My name is Lenny, by the way," Mr Adams said, holding out his hand.

Church shook the offered hand delicately. "Claudia."

"Pleasure to meet you," he said politely.

Seeing Red

A loud American drawl called out over the excited chatter of the crowd in front of them.

"Claudia! Is that you?"

Church cringed inwardly as all heads within earshot of Maddy turned, eager to see who had attracted his attention. The urge to run in the opposite direction took some combatting.

The crowd parted and Maddy swept determinedly towards her, a huge grin on his face. Church gave Lenny an apologetic look and braced herself.

Maddy greeted her with open arms, eyes surveying her from head to toe. Spotting the drink in her hand, he quickly took it from her and handed it to a stunned Lenny. Maddy stretched out his arms again and waited for Church to step into them. When she did, he clamped his arms around her and lifted her up.

"It's been too long!" he cried, spinning her around.

"I'm working," Church whispered in his ear, her hands on his shoulders. "I'm sorry. Act normal. It's fine that you know me."

His grip immediately relaxed and he stopped spinning. It felt like the entire room was watching them as she slowly slid down him until her heels touched the floor.

Maddy stepped back and took her in again, critically judging every inch of her.

"You look stunning," he said finally, taking one of her hands. A cheeky grin appeared on his face. "Then again, you always do! How are you?"

He kissed her hand, his thumb brushing over her knuckles and rubbing her ring finger in slow circles. Was he pleased to find no ring there?

"I'm good, thank you," Church said, a little flushed.

"Staying in town?" he asked, the question laced with promise.

"I am."

Maddy's grin broadened. "Dinner later, then? After all this?"

"I'd love to..."

"Great!"

"But unfortunately, I can't."

Maddy still had hold of her left hand and he smiled wickedly, his eyes sparkling with mischief. Lenny cleared his throat quietly.

"Who's your friend?" Maddy asked, tearing his eyes away from Church.

"We've only just met," Church said, retrieving her hand from Maddy's loosened hold. "This is Larry."

"Lenny," Lenny corrected, holding out his hand.

Church looked down, an embarrassed giggle escaping her lips. The sound made Maddy glance at her in surprise for a moment as he shook the offered hand.

"Hey, nice to meet you," he said jovially.

"My daughter's a huge fan," Lenny gushed.

"She is?" Maddy asked with genuine surprise. "What's her name?"

"Amelia," Lenny replied.

"Be sure to say hi from me, won't you."

"I will, I will. Do you mind if we have a picture or two together? My daughter won't believe me otherwise."

"Sure," Maddy said with a smile.

"I'll take it," Church offered.

Lenny awkwardly held the two drinks in his hands. He looked around, then placed the glasses on the edge of the fountain, rummaged in his pocket and eagerly gave Church his phone.

"You'll need ninety seconds at least," Kez whispered over comms.

Maddy draped his arm around Lenny's shoulders and Church held up the phone, fumbling with the screen for a moment.

Maddy rolled his eyes. "Need a hand, sugar?" he drawled.

"I think I've got it," Church replied. "Scooch in."

She took several photos in quick succession. Maddy with his boyish grin, Lenny with both thumbs up, leaning into Maddy.

Maddy turned to Lenny and shook his hand again. "Real nice to meet you," he said, pulling his own phone from his inside pocket. "Would you do the same for me and my dearest friend here?" he asked, eyes roving over Church again.

"Of course," Lenny replied, taking Maddy's phone with shaking hands.

Maddy grabbed hold of Church and dipped her low, his eyes never leaving hers. She was all laughter and smiles, her eyes sparkling.

"Talk about hot!" Kat said, fanning her face with her hand while watching the footage from the ballroom on a tablet. "The entire female contingent will be jealous as hell. Just look at the two of them!"

Harris leant across the seat beside her. This wasn't good. Riley wouldn't take the competition well. The popstar would likely disappear without a trace...

"They make such a beautiful couple," Kez whispered from the hotel room. "Shame he hates her job."

Riley growled something incomprehensible and got up from his station and left the room.

Kez watched the bedroom door close behind him. "Charlie Mike has just walked out again."

"Well Chief Meathead needs to seriously up his game if he wants to compete with Maddylicious," Kat muttered.

Startled, Harris looked at Kat. "You're still calling us meatheads?" he asked.

Kat shrugged. "Not to your faces."

Seeing Red

"The pleasure was all mine!" Lenny assured Maddy, gripping his hand in both of his. "Thank you, I know you must hear this all the time."

"We've got it," Kez announced quietly over comms. "Tracking his movements now."

Lenny was explaining to Maddy about his daughter, that she was in hospital and receiving chemotherapy. Maddy listened intently.

Church admired Maddy, taking everything in his stride, taking time to listen to the babbling Mr Adams. His interest was genuine. Fame, fortune and the constant attention didn't faze him in the slightest.

Church noticed two very anxious-looking hotel employees practically hopping on the spot behind Lenny, trying desperately to catch Maddy's attention. She laid a hand on Maddy's forearm.

"I think you're needed," she said quietly, indicating the two employees.

"Man, so sorry to cut this short," Maddy said to Lenny. "I have to present some award, then perform."

"Oh, don't let me keep you!" Lenny insisted.

"Tell Claudia where your daughter is, I'll pay her a visit tomorrow. If that's okay with you, of course."

"Amelia will be thrilled!" Lenny cried. "But you don't have to do that. No, it's too much. Just to know that you wished her well and that you were so concerned about her, it'll make her year."

"I would be honoured. Sorry, I've gotta go."

Maddy looked longingly at Church. He took her hand again and gave it a squeeze.

"Don't go far," he said. He leant in and kissed her cheek tenderly before he was practically dragged away by the two hotel employees.

"Do you think he means it or was he just being polite?" Lenny asked Church.

"Oh, he means it," Church replied.

"We're working back through his movements," Kez whispered. "We've pinpointed his house, Jen is heading there now."

Church touched her necklace in acknowledgement.

"Amelia's in Great Ormond Street Hospital," Lenny explained.

Church nodded. "Maddy's team will make the arrangements."

"Team?"

"His security."

Lenny looked impressed. "So, you two are...?"

"We're just friends," Church said, cutting him off.

Lenny nodded but didn't look convinced.

"So, what do you do?" he asked. "Socialite? Model? Actress?"

Church laughed. "Never judge a book by its cover," she said.

"I've offended you," Lenny said. "Apologies, but you're too attractive for something mundane."

"Mundane is underrated. What about you?"

"IT. Not as boring as people make out."

"I'm sure," Church agreed. "Access all areas, a field where no one can have any secrets."

Lenny laughed. "You have no idea!" He leaned in closer to Church. "Maddy is still looking at you, like you're the only person in the room."

"He's making sure I don't run away," Church said.

"Do you run away a lot?" Lenny asked.

Church shook her head. "Quite the opposite, despite the overwhelming feeling, sometimes, that I'd be much better off if I did."

The award ceremony passed without incident. The meaningless and ridiculous awards were presented to the highest donors and sponsors of the event. Maddy had offered to double all donations to the chosen charities, to a raucous round of applause.

Church made her excuses to Lenny and left him standing at the fountain. He smiled but didn't look away from his phone.

"He's texting his daughter," Kez explained. "She can't believe he's spoken to Maddy. She's over the moon. He hasn't mentioned the visit, he wants to surprise her. So sweet!"

Church made her way through the crowd to the bar. The lights in the ballroom dimmed and the stage was illuminated in a soft blue hue. A spotlight focused on the rich velvet curtains. They swept open and the band was revealed. They started to play and Maddy appeared, the spotlight following him as he sauntered onto the stage. He perched on a stool and began to sing. The crowd were instantly captivated.

A familiar sensation prickled at the back of Church's neck as a presence materialised behind her with an unmistakable male scent. Church kept her eyes on the stage, deciding to ignore the tingling she felt.

"May I have this dance?" Riley growled quietly in Church's ear.

"You shouldn't be here," she whispered. "You could be seen."

"I doubt anyone has night vision trained on the crowd."

Church couldn't help a twitch of her lips in amusement. "We do."

"Hmm, then the team can all look away for the next five minutes."

Church felt the vibration in his chest as he spoke.

"Can't it wait?"

"No."

Riley took her hand firmly and led her to a space on the dancefloor.

Turning to face Riley for the first time, Church was surprised by his appearance. Full tux, clean-shaven, product in his hair and that aftershave! He looked and smelt good enough to eat.

Riley wrapped his arm around her and pulled her close. Church didn't resist. He rested his cheek against her head and they swayed to the crooning Maddy.

Church turned off her comms as Riley lowered his lips to her ear.

"I've been contacted," he whispered.

Church didn't react but held him a little tighter.

"The timeline has moved up."

"How long do we have?" she asked quietly.

Riley didn't respond.

"Not long, then."

Riley spun Church in a pirouette and pulled her back to him.

"Was it serious?" he asked.

Church leant back, looking at Riley questioningly.

"You and the popstar?" he clarified.

"Jealous?"

"Hmm," he growled.

It sounded like an agreement to Church.

"So, you came in here to stake your claim?"

"You are nobody's property."

Church raised an eyebrow. Did he mean that?

"How much did you hear?" she asked.

"Enough."

"We're friends, I'm not going to apologise for having a history with someone."

"No apologies necessary."

"I declined his invitation to dinner, didn't you hear that part?"

"Hmm." Riley sounded pleased about that.

"He knows my work comes first," Church said.

As before, time slipped away from them. Church's mind half on the man in her arms, the other half realigning her strategy for the shortened timeline. They hadn't noticed that Maddy had finished singing until he approached them through the crowd. Riley spotted him first.

"Incoming," he growled in Church's ear and released her. "I'll leave you two to…"

Church took Riley's hand to stop him from leaving.

"There you are!" Maddy drawled. He smiled warmly as Church turned to face him. It faded a fraction when he looked up at Riley. "Another friend?"

"Yes, this is Justin," she said, still holding Riley's hand. She glanced at Riley. His face showed no sign of what he was thinking.

"Pleasure," Maddy said, holding out his hand. Surprisingly, Riley shook it amiably and without crushing it.

"Great set," Riley said.

"Gee, thanks!"

Seeing Red

"Erm, guys?" Kez whispered over comms. "Sorry to interrupt. But Lenny is leaving!"

Riley glanced at Church, the corner of his mouth twitching. He inclined his head slightly, suggesting that Church turn her comms back on.

"I'll see you later," he said to her with a wink and left.

Maddy watched him stride away. "Wow!"

Church nudged Maddy with her elbow. "What?"

Maddy shook his head. "Wow," he repeated. "Now I understand why you refused to come to dinner."

"Madera," Church said seriously, using his full name.

Maddy looked at her, startled. "Shit, I'm in trouble! What'd I do now?"

"Nothing. I'd love to catch up and I can see you're bursting with questions. I also need to explain what's going on here."

"Then come to dinner," Maddy insisted. "Surely that beast of a man wouldn't mind, or would he? Is he like you? Will he kill me, my body never to be found?"

"Maddy," Church pleaded. "I can't do this now. Not tonight and not for a while. If I get this job done, then we can do dinner."

"*If?*" Maddy cried quietly, instantly serious. "Since when do you ever have doubts about your work?"

"This is an utter shitstorm, it will be messy."

"Claudia!" He took her hand gently, nothing but concern on his face. "Anything I can do to help? You know I will."

"Thanks for the offer. One of these days I will take you up on it. But I really have to go, the team..."

"I understand," he said, kissing her knuckles.

Church kissed his cheek, surprising him.

"Why do I feel like that's a goodbye?" he asked quietly.

Church smiled without answering and left him on the dancefloor.

Leonard Adams

Much later than intended, Lenny returned home and approached his back door. Scanning his thumb print and using three separate keys he opened the door. He flicked on the kitchen light and nearly leapt out of his skin. He stumbled back in shock, staring at a muscular man with huge shoulders, sitting at the kitchen table, drinking a cup of coffee. The man was wearing a tuxedo with the bow tie loose around his neck, the shirt collar unbuttoned.

"Good evening, Mr Adams," the handsome man said.

"Who are you? What do you want? How did you get in here?" Lenny cried, looking around the kitchen nervously.

"I'm not here to hurt you, Mr Adams. I need a favour, that's all."

The man stood up slowly, pulled out a chair and gestured for Lenny to sit.

Lenny took another step backwards and collided with the back door.

"Answer my questions," Lenny said breathlessly.

Seeing Red

He was going to die, he could feel it. His instincts told him to defend himself. He scanned the kitchen for a weapon, despite knowing it would be useless against this monster of a man.

"My name is Justin," Riley said, sitting back down. "I need a favour from you and I walked in through your front door."

"But it was locked!"

"It was," Riley admitted. "My colleague opened it for me."

Lenny looked around, expecting another hitman to leap out at him at any moment. He considered running out of the back door when a blonde woman appeared silently in the doorway to the hall. She was dressed like the man from the old Milk Tray ads, all in black with what looked like a utility belt strung around her hips. Catwoman? Batgirl?

"Mr Adams," she said, just as politely as the big man had.

"How did you find me?" Lenny stuttered. "Have you been following me? Did Romano send you? I gave her my answer already! I wouldn't risk..."

"Please, sit." Riley waved his hand at the chair.

"Can I make you a cup of tea, Mr Adams? Earl Grey, right?" the woman asked.

"How do you know what tea I drink?"

"We know a lot of things, Mr Adams. Please don't be alarmed. You're not who we want, but we do need your help," she said.

A frown appeared between Lenny's eyes. He looked between the two strangers and back again.

"What do you want?" he asked, tentatively perching on the edge of the wooden chair.

Jen smiled, then reached over to switch the kettle on and took his mug from the drainer next to the sink. Wide-eyed, Lenny watched her.

"Mr Adams," Riley said gently. "We need all the information you find for Miss Romano. Before you give it to her, we'd like you to provide it to us first."

"What?"

"Miss Romano, the head of EMP, has asked you to upgrade her systems, correct? To find a leak in her organisation and monitor all communications in and out of the company," Riley clarified.

"How do you know that?" Lenny asked. "Did she send you?"

Riley shook his head. "We've been monitoring Miss Romano for a while now. She's involved in something... bad. We're trying to stop her and would appreciate your help. She has no idea we are here."

"You're trying to stop her?" Lenny wasn't convinced.

"Yes, we are," Riley said.

"You're with the police?" Lenny asked, with a quizzical look at Riley's appearance. "MI5?"

Riley remained silent and Lenny nodded, he accepted that this man couldn't tell him and it was probably safer for him not to know.

"She's..." Lenny struggled to find the words. In the end, he just shrugged.

"We know," Riley said.

Lenny's eyes flicked between the strangers as he thought about what he was being asked to do. Jen placed his mug on the table in front of him.

"Who are you working for?" he asked.

"We report to Claudia, you met her at the ball," Riley said.

"The pretty redhead? She's your boss?" Lenny asked incredulously.

"Looks can be deceiving, Mr Adams," Riley said.

Lenny looked astonished and let out a long breath. The redhead was also an agent? Were these people really working for her? He considered his options. Claudia had been kind, friendly even. But was it all a lie? He thought about what she had said. She avoided mentioning what she did for a living. Of course she scoffed at the mention of mundane, she was a spy! And she had introduced him to Maddy, there was no doubt that he knew her, he called her Claudia. Or was he in on it too?

He had been set up! But these people couldn't have followed him, they were already inside his house, and his security system wasn't exactly easy to disable. What was going on here?

"Can I speak to her?" Lenny asked suddenly. "Your boss. Claudia, if that's her real name."

"Of course," Riley said.

He moved to pull his phone from the inside pocket of his jacket, causing Lenny to visibly flinch. Riley raised his hands gently.

"Just reaching for my phone."

Lenny nodded and watched as Riley sent a text message.

A few moments later, the redhead walked through the back door. She was now dressed similarly to the blonde woman – all in black, but with no utility belt. A redheaded, shorter version of Lara Croft.

"Is your name really Claudia?" Lenny asked her.

"Yes, Mr Adams. My name is Claudia Church," Church replied. "May I sit down?"

Lenny nodded. Who knew hit people could be so polite?

"Are you okay?" Church asked.

"A little concerned. I come home to find two strangers in my kitchen, my security system has been disabled with no notification... you're all being very polite, but I get the feeling that if I don't do as you say, I'll end up in the river."

Church smiled but shook her head.

"Not quite our style, Mr Adams." She watched Lenny closely, he was looking like he was about to throw up. "I understand this is unnerving, but we really do need your help. We're not going to force you."

"That stunt with Maddy Lagos..."

"No stunt, Mr Adams. Maddy really is a friend of mine. I've already spoken with his team. He'll visit your daughter tomorrow at the hospital, the arrangements have been made. We just need your okay."

"I really should be there," Lenny said.

"Of course you should, that's not a problem."

"So, what do you want me to do?"

"We need your help, nothing more. A copy of anything you find on the missing project files. That's it."

Lenny looked at the attractive, sinister people in front of him. Surely he was dreaming this!

"If I do this... can you assure my safety?" he asked.

"Absolutely," Church replied.

"And my daughter? Miss Romano has already threatened her. If I don't do as she says..."

"Your daughter is safe. Two of my team are already there."

Lenny's heart stopped and felt like it turned to stone.

"How do I know you won't hurt her?"

"You have my word, Mr Adams. I know this is a lot to take in. We are not in the business of threatening or using children. We're asking for your help, that's all."

"You're the good guys?" Lenny asked.

"We try to be," Church replied. "What did Miss Romano threaten to do?"

Lenny swallowed. "She said she'd poison Amelia's medication. Something deadly and untraceable!"

"And you agreed to work with Miss Romano?" Church asked gently.

"Of course I did! What father would refuse? Amelia's all I've got."

"We'll check her meds. Trust me, no harm will come to your daughter," Church said firmly.

Lenny looked at them as he considered his options. He didn't have many.

"Okay," he said eventually. "I'll help. Now what happens?"

"Get some rest," Church said. "Jen will stay with you, if you're okay with that. She'll prep you for your start at EMP on Monday."

"You'll stop Romano?" Lenny asked.

"Yes," Church replied. "We will."

Jen

On Monday morning, dressed in a conservative navy-blue skirt and white blouse, Jen drove Lenny to EMP. He was sweating in the passenger seat and dabbed at his forehead with a handkerchief. Jen had spent the weekend coaching him and talking him through the plan.

"You have nothing to worry about," Jen assured him as she parked the car.

"They'll know!" Lenny whispered.

"They don't know anything. We've been listening to all of Antonia's calls. She's hired you to do a job and she expects you to do it."

"You make it sound easy."

"Because it *is* easy. You know what you're doing. Find the leak and report your findings to her."

"How do I explain you?"

Seeing Red

"We've been through this," Jen said patiently. "I'm your personal assistant. Where you go, I go. I'll be with you every step of the way. They won't question it."

"What if they do?"

"I'll explain. You can let me do the talking if you prefer." Jen smiled warmly at him. Lenny nodded but shrank back into the seat.

"Come on. Game on." She got out of the car and opened the door for him.

Some hours later, Jen passed Lenny another cup of Earl Grey tea across the table where he had set up his station.

"Kenny MacKay," Lenny said, not looking up from his screen.

"One of the research scientists," Jen said. "We suspect he was the one who stole the information for Edward Cavendish."

"It was definitely him. He tried to cover his tracks, but it was him."

"Any idea where he is now?" Jen asked. "We've been looking for him."

"His calendar says he's on holiday in Spain."

"He didn't go. We already checked the passenger list for the flight he booked."

"How do you know that?" Lenny asked.

Jen winked at him but didn't reply.

"Can I ask you a question?" Lenny asked quietly.

"Of course. I may not be able to answer you, though."

"Why me? You don't need me. You're perfectly capable of getting this information yourselves."

"Lenny, you are vital to this. We couldn't do this without you. You were invited here. It would take us weeks to prepare a suitable background. We needed to move quickly. You understand that, right?"

Lenny nodded.

"And we really appreciate your help," Jen continued.

"What if they find out?" he whispered.

"They won't."

"But they could..."

"We have contingencies in place. If they suspected anything, you wouldn't have free rein in their systems. We've got this."

Lenny swallowed.

"Now let's focus on this warehouse in Norfolk," she suggested.

Joint Op

Briefing

Later that morning, the team gathered in the conference room for the briefing. Jen called in from Lenny's laptop from the offices at EMP.

"Lenny has ensured this line is secure. He's set up a bubble around the office we're in. We can't be overheard and there's no one else on this floor at the moment," she explained.

"The techs are trawling through the data you've already sent us," Kez said. "Our own attempts at infiltrating the system at EMP were less than successful."

"EMP were spooked," Jen explained. "They stopped communicating using their usual channels and anything new about Warrior IV has been moved to a new system. But you should have access to everything now."

"Thanks," Kez said. "We've also managed to procure the police and coroner's reports from the last six months, from all the bodies found along the Thames. Nothing really stood out, but this appeared on half a dozen of them."

Kez brought up a photo showing one of the unidentified dead bodies. The deceased man had been pulled from the river outside the city. He was in his mid-thirties and well built. His face was so badly beaten that facial recognition was useless. Kez clicked her mouse and a close-up appeared on the screen of a faded brown henna tattoo on the inside of his wrist.

"Similar tattoos have been found on four more bodies. But as they're inked with henna, they do eventually fade away," Kez said. "So, there could be more."

"What is that design?" Kat asked. "It seems familiar."

"It's the Dara Celtic Knot," Kez explained.

The team exchanged blank looks.

"It represents the oak tree, which symbolises strength, longevity, endurance and power," Church said, making everyone look at her.

"So, a warrior symbol," Kat said.

"Exactly," Church said.

"I've seen that symbol," Jen said from the screen.

"Yes, that's it!" she exclaimed. "Some invoices and emails mention Dara, but we found no corresponding project name, just that same symbol."

"Warrior IV," Kat said jubilantly.

"Wait, there's more," Jen said. "Some emails mention a satellite office. A lab, by the looks of it. Something about stability tests."

"Where?" Church asked.

"It's remote, outside a small town in Oxfordshire," Jen confirmed. "I don't think Romano knows anything about it."

"Can you be sure?" Church asked.

Jen's head momentarily disappeared from view. The team could hear Lenny talking in the background but couldn't make out what he was saying.

"It's part of the development process," Jen said. "It's a standard requirement. MacKay arranged the testing, no authorisation required from senior management."

"So, this lab will have samples of the formula?" Church asked.

"Yes," Jen confirmed.

Church looked at Kez, who nodded and was already tapping away on her laptop, Ellis mirroring her actions on his.

"Minimal security. One guard on shift overnight," Kez said, reading her screen. "We could knock out the power. Might set off alarms. If it is a lab, they'll need backup power for the fridges. System's pretty basic."

"What are you thinking?" Riley asked, who had been quietly observing the team's progress.

"We need to know what's there," Church said.

"Smash and grab?" Riley asked incredulously. "That's your plan?"

"I can get you in," Lenny said, still out of view of the camera. He leaned over Jen's shoulder. "No smashing required."

"Thank you, Lenny," Church said.

"I can create you a pass, access all areas and bury the trail in their system. Essentially untraceable... unless you're me." Lenny grinned. He was warming up to this spy malarkey.

Church looked at Riley. This was it, the moment of truth. If she got her hands on the only remaining prototype of this cursed formula, what would Riley do? Would he take it from her? Whose orders would he follow? For Church to take down EMP and stop Gloria Pérez, she needed every last scrap of information about the formula.

"Echo One and I will go," Church said firmly.

Riley dipped his head in agreement. Harris passed him a tablet that had originated further down the table from Ellis.

"There's a spot two clicks from the lab," Ellis explained. "Perfect place to leave the truck."

Ellis gestured to the main screen and Kez gave him control. A map of the area appeared and plans were made.

Prep

Later, Church and Riley met in the garage, dressed for the night op. Kat and Harris joined them. Kat handed Church a backpack. Church looked at it with a frown.

"I packed it myself," Kat said. "It's all there. You can check it on the way."

"Thanks," Church said. She liked the process of packing her kit herself.

Harris and Riley were talking contingencies, leaning against the bonnet of the truck.

"Ellis is control for this one. Curvy is his backup," Harris said quietly.

"Chat lines?" Riley asked in a low voice, while the girls were loading the kit into the truck.

"Not with Curvy breathing down his neck," Harris replied. "Would feel a lot happier if we went with you."

"This isn't anything I can't handle," Riley responded.

"I know, but..."

"Keys?" Church called, interrupting them.

Riley tossed his keys over. Church caught them and jumped into the driver's seat.

"Good luck, mate," Harris said, clapping Riley on the shoulder.

"Hmm," Riley growled, climbing into the truck. He barely had time to settle before Church roared out of the garage.

Teamwork

Church and Riley were standing with their backs to the lab wall, the fire escape door between them. Riley glanced at Church and placed his hand on the handle. With a nod from him, Church swiped the security pass through the reader and Riley opened the door for her. She slipped through, with Riley directly behind. Once the door was closed, they crept down the corridor in darkness.

At the end of the corridor, Church peered through the small window in the door. All was dark. She could only see the green glow of the emergency light above the door on the other side of the room. Riley checked the stairwell to their right and patted Church on the shoulder. She turned and he followed her up the stairs.

"First floor, west side," Ellis said quietly over comms. "The guard is in his room, hasn't moved for a while. Sounds like he's watching a soap."

Church reached the top of the stairs.

"Corridor is clear. No movement," Ellis said.

Church swiped the pass and Riley pulled the door open. They entered the lab. Church turned right to the fridges and Riley approached a cluster of desks to the left. He inserted a USB device into one of the computer ports and waited for the green light.

Church opened the first fridge. It was filled with racks of vials. She ran a gloved finger over the rows, scanning the labels until she reached the bottom shelf. She closed the door and repeated the process with the next fridge. Halfway down, she paused and glanced over her shoulder towards Riley.

Riley removed the USB, pocketed it and joined in the search. He started with the fridge furthest from Church. After some agonising minutes, they met in the middle of the row. It wasn't there.

Church scanned the lab for any other fridges. Riley paced the rows of counters, checking under each one. He shook his head with a frown. Then their eyes simultaneously rested on a door leading to an office off the lab. They approached and looked inside. Church went in first and scanned the room.

A quiet hum caught her attention. She approached the cupboard and ran her hand over the door. It was warm to the touch. An integral fridge. She opened the cupboard door to find the fridge was padlocked with a heavy-duty, five-digit combination lock.

"Guys, the guard is on the move," Ellis warned.

"Hmm," Riley growled quietly to confirm he'd received the message.

Church raised an eyebrow at him. He pulled out a set of bolt cutters from his backpack, positioned them on the shank and started to apply force. The tendons in his arm quivered with the force he exerted. Church held her breath until the lock finally gave way. She opened the fridge to find a single rack of vials filled with blue liquid. The vials had no labels, but each lid bore a stamped Dara Celtic knot.

"The guard is heading up the stairs. Time to move," Ellis said.

Church and Riley exchanged a glance. Church motioned for Riley to head out. He turned on his heel and silently crept back into the lab. Church grabbed the rack and was about to shove the vials into her backpack when she hesitated.

Then the alarm sounded, reverberating against the walls.

Church joined Riley at the lab doors. He pulled open the door, she slipped past him and flew down the stairs, Riley right behind her.

Church reached the bottom, grabbed the rail, swung around the corner and sprinted down the corridor. The alarm was deafening. She swiped the pass against the reader but the light stayed red. She swiped again, a fraction slower. Riley stood directly behind her, his back to hers, eyes on the corridor behind them.

"Shit," Church whispered. Resisting the urge to shout, she gasped, "Guys, we need a hand here." She waited for a response. Nothing. "Control?" She looked at Riley, who frowning at her over his shoulder.

With a nod, they swapped places, pirouetting on the spot. Church covered their six. Riley urged her back a few steps, then launched his foot at the door near the handle. He kicked it again. It started to give. Church appeared on his right and, with a nod, they both braced and hurled themselves, shoulders first, into the door. It burst open and they fell out together. They rolled into the fall and were back on their feet, sprinting for the fence moments later.

Riley skidded to a stop at the wire fence, leant under the gap in the chain and braced his legs, allowing Church to slide through, feet first. He ducked under the wire and followed her into the trees.

Archers

"What the fuck is going on?" Kat cried to the crowded surveillance room.

Everyone was working hard to regain contact with their teammates. Ellis was clicking furiously on his laptop, Kez beside him, eyes scrutinising their screens.

"Archer One. Come in!" Kat switched channels. "Archer One!" She looked at Harris.

"Echo One. Do you read?" Harris said more calmly after switching to the Echo-only channel.

Nothing. No crackle. No interference. Nothing.

"It's like the plug's been pulled," Kez muttered.

"We need eyes on them!" Kat said.

Seeing Red

"I've lost contact with the drone too," Kez called. "Roobs, can you send a backup?"

"Already on its way," Ruben, Head of Operations, said quietly.

"It'll take too long!" Kat complained. "Shit. Shit. Shit!"

"If it's any consolation, Lenny is covering their tracks," Jen said from one of the monitors. She'd dialled in from their office at EMP.

"What the hell is happening?" Kat asked.

"No idea. Lenny's baffled," Jen replied. Lenny muttered something beside her. "He says it must be your end. Let him take a look."

Kat shook her head. Now wasn't the time to let someone else into their systems. Church would have a fit.

"It's probably fine," Harris said.

Kat spun towards him.

Harris shrugged. "Don't think the worst," he said. "They're pretty capable people, right?"

Kat didn't respond.

"Should me and Tom take the bikes?" Jonny asked.

Kat shook her head again. Jonny looked at Harris, who confirmed her answer with a shake of his head.

"Okay, this is what we'll do..." Kat said decisively, smoothing her hair away from her face. "Let's focus on our systems, find out what the actual fuck is going on. Archer One is a big girl. Harris is right. They both can look after themselves for a bit."

"Lenny can help," Jen said again from the screen.

"Kez?" Kat asked.

Kez looked up at Kat with a worried expression. "It's not protocol," she said. "But we could use all the help we can get right now. We're chasing our tails here."

"Okay. Kez, give Lenny the access he needs. Work with him," Kat turned to Harris. "Secure the premises. No one in or out. Full lockdown. Full sweep. Find out who did this. It can only have been done from the inside, they must still be here."

"Yes, ma'am," Harris replied, leaving the room, closely followed by Jonny and Tom.

Moments later, Kez slammed her palms onto the desk, hard enough to make it rattle. Ellis looked at her in disbelief, his fingers hovering over his keyboard.

"What now?" Kat asked.

"I'm locked out," Kez said.

"Me too," Ellis added.

"Me three," Ruben called from his station.

Then the power failed, plunging the surveillance room into an eerie green gloom from the emergency lighting than ran on batteries.

"What the fuck!" Kat cried.

"We've lost power," Kez said in the darkness. "Backup should kick in any min..."

The lights flickered on, but the screens remained black.

"We'll have to restart. Might take a while," Kez said, nodding to Ruben, who started the sequence.

"This is no fucking coincidence!" Kat said. Using her mobile, she dialled Jen's number, but the call failed. She looked at her phone screen. No signal. "Kez, is the jammer active?"

"Nothing's online right now," Kez replied.

"Shit," Kat muttered.

"What can I do?" Miz asked.

"Go to the armoury. We're under attack," Kat said.

Ellis looked up from his station with concern. Miz flew out of the door. Kat picked up a desk phone and dialled Jen's number.

"We're compromised..." was all she managed before the room descended into darkness again.

"The genny must've failed," Ellis said from the shadows. "I'll grab a can of fuel from the garage and get it back up and running."

"Thanks," Kat said, hearing him leave the room. "We're flying blind here, people."

The room fell silent for a while.

"Thing is," Kez said quietly. "The genny is checked every morning. It was full of fuel or I'd have been notified."

"Shit," Kat said again.

Miz returned, laden with kit. The girls each took a gun and donned their vests. Ruben took only a vest and returned to his station.

"I pulled out the old radios. Of course, Church kept them," Miz said.

"Thanks. Good job she did," Kat said, clipping the radio to the strap of her vest.

"Did you pass Ellis on your way back?" Kez asked Miz.

"No. Why? Where's he off to?"

"To check the genny... oh, fuck my life!" Kat said and flew out of the door.

Sabotage

Kat stalked around the small wooden compound in full stealth mode. The genny inside the fenced area was silent, but the problem was obvious. The smell of fuel hung thick in the air. It was wet underfoot. She reached the gate. The padlock had been cleanly cut and the gate hung limply open. Kat slipped inside. There was a gaping hole in the bottom edge of the tank and petrol was still dripping out.

Kat retreated into the shadows and made a quick circuit of the medical building. At the top of the fire escape, she had a good view of the main house and part of the rear gardens. All was in darkness. All was quiet. She used the butt of her torch and banged a code in Morse on the door. Dot, dash. Kat took a breath. Dot, dot, dash, dash, dash.

The door opened, revealing Dr Eve Douglas aiming a rifle at Kat's chest.

"Stand down. It's only me," Kat said gently.

Eve lowered the gun. "What's going on?" she asked.

"Full FUBAR."

"Thought as much."

"Any problems here?"

Eve shook her head. "No patients. Just me and one other medic on duty tonight."

"Does Church know about that?" Kat asked, nodding at the rifle.

"Yes. She provided me with the locker herself."

"Of course she did," Kat mused. She raised her radio. "Control, this is Two."

"Reading you, Two," Ruben replied formally.

"Six," Kat said, surprised Ruben had stepped in. "Is Three okay?"

"All good. She's currently under her desk, head in the connections."

"Copy that," Kat said, relieved. "Medical is secure. Two in situ, well protected. Genny is out of action long-term. Definite sabotage."

"Copy that."

"Any joy your end?"

"That's a negative."

"Shit," Kat muttered to herself.

Kat and Miz met outside the surveillance room by the steps.

"Echo's gone. Most of their stuff along with them," Miz said breathlessly.

"Fuckers!" Kat whispered.

"Should we go after Church?" Miz asked.

"We've no idea where she is. If she got out of the lab okay, she wouldn't have hung around."

"But she's with Riley. Alone."

"Have faith. She's put him on his arse a few times already. She can do it again," Kat said confidently.

"What do you think is going on?" Miz asked.

"We'll find out, preferably before Church gets here."

Church

Church and Riley crouched side by side in the darkness, looking towards the truck. Two of the tyres had been punctured and the windscreen had been smashed.

My fucking phone was in there! Church thought angrily. It was totally useless to any thief but she needed to make contact with Archers. Quickly.

Once they were sure the area was clear, they slowly approached the truck. Riley checked every inch of the outside, including the chassis.

"Clean," he muttered.

Church jumped up onto the bonnet and clambered through the broken windscreen to retrieve their kit. Their bags were gone. She checked the centre console. It was empty, just as she had expected. She climbed out and Riley held out his hand. She took it without complaint and he helped her back to the ground.

With a glance at each other, they retreated further into the trees and began their long jog towards the nearest civilisation.

Comms had been silent since the alarm sounded in the lab. Church wondered how it had been triggered and if it was somehow connected to their loss of communication with Archers. She firmly did not believe in coincidences. This was not random.

They jogged in silence, Church leading the way. After several miles, they approached a small cluster of farm buildings. Church disappeared into one of the sheds. Moments later, she reappeared and pushed the huge double doors open wide. She ducked back inside and emerged driving an ancient Land Rover. She idled long enough for Riley to hop in, then powered down the muddy track.

"I didn't think carjacking was your thing," Riley said, bracing himself against the dashboard with both gloved hands.

"Needs must," Church replied.

"Hmm."

"I'll return it with suitable compensation, if that's what you're worried about."

"Who's worried?" Riley replied. "You hotwired it?"

"Didn't need to. Keys were in the ignition."

"Hmm."

The gates at Archers were in complete darkness when they arrived. Church slowed down fractionally, then continued driving.

"Enigma?" Riley suggested, looking back at the gates.

"I can drop you off there," Church said and sped up.

A crease formed between her eyebrows. What else was there to say? This was it. Time to step things up a gear or two.

Archers had been compromised. Something Church wouldn't have believed possible, but had planned for, just in case. She had allowed it to be compromised. Unforgivable.

Church pulled into the car park at Enigma and left the engine idling. Riley unbuckled his seat belt and leant over, cupped her face and stared into her eyes. He then pulled her closer and kissed her deeply.

Church was stunned for a moment, but then soon melted into him. Just a moment. No more, or she risked having second thoughts. A seed of doubt threatened to embed itself in her mind. Was he still playing her? Could she count on him?

Riley pulled away. "Good luck," he whispered against her lips.

They rested their foreheads together, eyes closed, for a moment.

"I meant what I said," Church said quietly. "You follow her orders, whatever they are. Promise me."

"I'll do what needs to be done."

Seeing Red

Church briefly kissed him again. Was this a final goodbye? If only the circumstances were different.

Riley glanced at her pack on the back seat.

"I should probably take those," he said.

Church shook her head. "I wouldn't bother. Trust me on that."

Site B

Church

Church drove the Land Rover towards her house. She brushed her fingers lightly over her lips as she considered her next steps.

When she pulled up in front of her garage, she left the engine running. She got out and slipped around the house to the small blue garden shed. Inside, she retrieved an old biscuit tin, rusted with age. Inside was a lockbox that only her fingerprint would open. Inside that was a spare set of house keys. She returned to the front of the house, unlocked the garage door and parked the Landy inside.

"Welcome home," she muttered to herself as she unlocked the internal garage door and stepped into her kitchen.

It had been months since Church had last spent any decent amount of time here, not including the night Riley had stayed. They had spent the whole night talking, plotting and scheming. The alcohol slowly faded as it was replaced by several cups of coffee.

The temptation to take things further had been ever present. He looked good enough to eat, sitting on the rug in front of the fire he had lit…She pushed thoughts of that time out of her mind. Now was not the time to dwell on it.

Church's house was beautiful, secluded and quiet but she much preferred to stay in her attic rooms at Archers. The original plan had been to have somewhere separate to get away from it all. But she didn't want to get away from it. Archers was everything to her.

Seeing Red

Church filled the reservoir on the coffee machine with water. There was no milk in the fridge, so she would have to settle for a healthy dose of Coffee Mate and a few sugars. She headed upstairs to her bedroom, shed her clothes and had a quick shower. She dressed in clean combat gear, tied her wet hair into a ponytail and went back downstairs.

Church rummaged through one of the kitchen drawers while she drank her coffee. She found an old burner phone, inserted a new SIM and switched it on. Then dialled a number and wedged the phone between her ear and shoulder.

The line just rang out. Even if the desk at Archers wasn't manned, it should divert to one of the company mobiles and answered by whoever was on call. But it didn't. Church frowned at the phone and dialled Kez's emergency number. The same thing happened. Absolutely nothing. She tried Kat's mobile next. It went straight to voicemail. The fine hair on the back of her neck prickled.

Don't panic. Not yet.

She dialled Jen's number, who should still be with Lenny and nowhere near Archers.

"Hello?" Jen answered tentatively.

"Four, One. Sit rep."

Jen let out a long breath of relief. "Thank God you're okay! Where are you?"

Church remained silent. Emergency protocols were needed here and Jen should remember that.

"Church?" Jen asked.

"Control is not responding. Can't get through to Two, Three, or Five. Base is in darkness."

"We lost contact too," Jen said. "Lenny offered to help, but they must have lost power. Is Echo One with you?"

"He's at their base."

"And you're okay?" Jen asked.

"I'm fine."

"Okay," Jen said, unconvinced. "So, Lenny thinks sabotage if the whole system is down."

"The mobile signal must've been jammed too," Church said.

"Who?"

Church didn't want to answer that.

"Stay with Lenny, get somewhere safe. Get yourself a burner. Text me the number. I'll ditch this number later."

"Copy that," Jen said.

"I'm going to set up Site B."

"Okay."

Church ended the call and immediately made another.

"Hello?" a sleepy Lorenzo answered.

"Did I wake you?" she asked quietly.

"What time is it?" Lorenzo asked.

Church looked at her watch. "Just after five. I need you to come in. Archers is compromised, so we're setting up at our Site B."

"Site B?"

Seeing Red

"I'll text you the address. Only, you can't drive here. I'll send you two locations, one where you can park your car, then a second location. You'll have to run the rest of the way. Got it?"

"Yeah, gimme two minutes and I'll be on the move."

"Thanks," Church said gratefully.

"What's going on?" Lorenzo asked.

Church could hear him rustling about as he got ready.

"It's all kicking off. And soon it'll be showtime."

Church started to make her second coffee and found a sliced loaf of brown bread in the freezer. She put four slices into the toaster. She made another call, this time to Scorpio One.

"Yes," Sebastian barked in answer.

"Scorpio One," Church said quietly.

"Archer One. Apologies. What's with the number change?"

"No time to explain. Base is compromised. I need you guys to secure it, then strip it clean."

Sebastian listened but didn't react.

"Charlie Juliet Charlie, order station protocol, Foxtrot Uniform Bravo Alpha Romeo, zero four six one nine," Church said, confirming the code.

"Understood," Seb said.

"Watch your backs."

"Copy that. You too."

Church ended the call, buttered the toast and filled a travel mug with coffee. She approached the French doors and switched on the outside light, illuminating the back garden. A path led over the grass to a large summer house, surrounded by a decked veranda. The red and white checked curtains were drawn over the large windows.

Turning off the garden light, Church followed the path, unlocked the reinforced double doors and switched on the lights. Inside were two white-painted wrought iron garden chairs either side of a Mediterranean-tile-topped table. She dragged the furniture from the centre of the room, set her breakfast on the table and rolled back the rug revealing a trapdoor. On the back wall, she removed a wooden photo frame showing a pile of Scottish stones. Behind it was a scanner. She pressed her palm to it. The trapdoor unlocked with a soft clink.

Church pulled the trapdoor open, grabbed her breakfast, and descended the smooth concrete steps. The air was stale until the HVAC system could be fired up.

At the bottom of the steps, Church pressed a switch and the trapdoor closed silently above her. In the darkness in front of her was a short corridor with a steel door at the end. She felt along the wall, pressed her thumb on a small pad and entered a twelve-digit code on the dimly backlit keypad. The door sucked open and swung inwards, revealing a replica of the surveillance room at Archers.

Church ate her toast as she started to switch on the equipment. She settled herself at the helm and got to work.

Recall

Lorenzo arrived first. Church watched his approach on her hidden surveillance cameras. She met him in front of the closed doors to the summer house.

"Nice place," Lorenzo said, looking at her with more than concern.

"Thanks. Do come in." She gestured for him to pass her. She closed the doors behind them and opened the trapdoor.

Once inside the underground bunker, Church gave him a quick tour.

"Kitchen, bathroom and bunks are through there," she said, pointing to another door at the back of the room.

"This is just like Archers," he observed.

"With one major difference," Church said. "I can access the systems from here, but we don't know the extent of the problem, so we'll have to wait. In the meantime, we can access a backup from..." She looked at her watch. "About fourteen hours ago."

"Okay," Lorenzo said.

"You don't look surprised," Church said.

"I suppose I expect the unexpected. This is just normal. For you."

"I hoped we'd never need this."

"What's going on?" he asked.

"We're going to find out."

Church wheeled out a chair at a station beside hers and Lorenzo sat down.

"There are a few cameras at Archers that aren't connected to the system there."

She clicked on an icon on the laptop. An image of the reception area at Archers appeared on the screen in front of them.

"Scroll back and look for anything unusual. Note all comings and goings for each camera."

"Got it," Lorenzo said, taking control of the footage.

Church received a text message from Jen with her new burner number. She scribbled it down on a Post-it note and stuck it to the desk between her and Lorenzo.

A notification beeped on her laptop. One of the cameras had picked up movement just beyond her garden wall.

"Back in a sec," Church said.

Church followed the same process as when Lorenzo arrived. She waited just outside the summer house doors, having locked Lorenzo inside the bunker. This time, she was armed. She whistled a short pip and it was returned with a similar call, signalling all was good.

Kat appeared a moment later, jumping over the wall. Kez and Miz walked more leisurely through the garden gate. The four of them embraced.

"Thank God you're okay," Kat whispered.

Seeing Red

With everyone sitting at their stations, the team updated Church.

"Both shifts of techs are on standby," Kez said. "They're all working remotely once we get the system online."

"Temporary medical has been set up in the back of the vets," Miz confirmed.

"I'll ensure everyone checks in and is accounted for," Kat said.

"Jen's making her way to a safe location with Lenny," Church added. "Her number's here." She pointed to the Post-it note. "I've initiated the clean-up with Scorpio."

"We swept the place," Miz said.

"They do a full clean," Church said solemnly. "So, what happened to Echo?"

"Last we saw of them was just after we lost comms," Kat said. "I sent Harris, Tom and Jonny to secure and sweep. Never saw them again. Then the backup power failed. Ellis offered to check the genny, then – poof!"

"What happened to Riley?" Kez asked.

"Nothing," Church said. "After we saw the gates were in darkness, I kept driving. I dropped him off at the club and came back here."

"So, he doesn't know where Site B is?" Kat asked.

"I doubt he even knows we have a Site B," Church replied.

"We thought the worst, you know, when Echo disappeared..." Kat said. "You were alone with Riley."

"Forget about them for now," Church said. "This wasn't Echo. Focus on getting our systems functional and finding out what exactly is going on."

Moles

"Only one person unaccounted for, not including Echo," Kat said.

"Who?" Church asked.

"Dante."

"One of the apprentices?" Kez asked, disbelievingly.

"Okay, let's find him," Church said. "We know he's not at Archers."

"Last location of his phone was at his house. No signal now. Must be switched off," Lorenzo said.

"That's a good place to start," Church said, standing up.

"Shall we come with you?" Miz asked.

Church shook her head.

"Lorenzo, with me, please. I have a job for you."

Lorenzo followed Church out of the bunker, into the kitchen and then into the garage.

"I need you to drive this back to its owner."

She handed Lorenzo a fat envelope and the keys to the borrowed Land Rover.

"Fill it full of diesel." She tapped him a quick message with the location. "Just leave it anywhere on the premises where you won't be seen. Leave the envelope in the glove box. You can drop me off at Dante's house on the way."

Lorenzo took the keys and got into the driver's seat. The garage doors opened and he backed out. Church jumped in and he drove towards Dante's house.

The street was quiet. Lorenzo pulled up to the kerb and Church got out.

"Shall I hang around for a bit?" he asked.

"I'll be fine. Call Scorp One to send someone to follow you and pick you up. Don't be seen."

"Got it."

He hesitated again.

"Go," she said.

With a nod, he drove away and Church started walking towards Dante's house. She made a mental note of the parked cars on both sides of the narrow street. Her usual tail's car was nowhere to be seen. There was no foot traffic – it was still early. Church pushed open the gate and stepped up to the front door. She was about to knock when she stopped – the door was slightly ajar. A familiar shiver ran up her spine.

"Dante?" she called, slowly pushing the door open with her gloved hand. The house was gloomy and silent. All the curtains were still drawn. She stepped over the threshold.

"Dante?" she called again. "It's Claudia."

Church peered into the small front room. With one glance she could tell it was empty. The narrow staircase was in front of her, the kitchen down the hall. The door was closed. She approached it silently and pushed it open.

Dante was dead, slumped over the kitchen table, head to one side, cold sightless eyes staring at his hand – which was pinned to the table with a kitchen knife. His left arm was secured behind his back, tied to the chair by a leather belt. From the amount of dry blood on the table and the floor below, his throat must also have been cut.

A noise sounded behind Church in the hallway, making her spin around and draw her gun. She immediately straightened, took a silent breath and holstered her weapon. She strode through the door and closed it behind her.

A little girl of about seven or eight was standing by the front door.

"Is it safe to come out now?" the little girl asked, hiding most of her face behind her teddy bear.

"Hello, you must be Dante's little sister. Sophie, right?" Church said gently, kneeling in front of her. The girl nodded. "I'm Claudia, it's nice to meet you."

"Dante told me to wait for you," she said. "Are you the police?"

"No sweetie, I'm not. But you are safe with me."

The little girl threw her arms around Church's neck suddenly, taking her by surprise. She clung on with such force. Church slowly wrapped her arms around the small body and closed her eyes. This little girl had just lost her entire world. What would become of her? The barriers around Church's heart threatened to crumble and a tear formed in the corner of her eye.

"Dante told me to hide," Sophie said, pulling away.

"You hid really well," Church said with a smile, quickly wiping away the tear. "Come with me."

The little girl nodded but then dashed up the stairs. She returned a moment later with a small backpack. She reached for her coat and Church helped her put it on and pulled the straps of the bag over her little shoulders. They walked down the street hand in hand.

They walked further into town and went into Café Pour L'âme, where Church had previously met with Riley. Church sat Sophie at the table in the window and ordered her a hot chocolate and fully loaded pancakes. She stepped outside and made a call to Kez.

"Dante's dead. He's in his kitchen. I found his little sister, Sophie. She's okay, she was hiding. Call it in. We're in the café in town."

"On it. I'm sending Kat to your position," Kez replied.

"No need. You guys stay where you are. I've got something to follow up on, once the police collect Sophie."

"If you're sure," Kez said uncertainly.

Church ended the call and watched the little girl through the window. She looked happy with her pancakes, swimming in chocolate sauce and ice cream. Sophie smiled at Church, her mouth covered in chocolate. Church went back in and sat down.

"Pancakes good?" she asked.

"Yes," Sophie replied, still smiling. "I never get pudding for breakfast! Dante said you would come."

"He did?"

"He said trouble was coming. Told me to hide. I'm good at hiding. We play hide and seek all the time. He told me to wait until you came."

Church nodded and kept an eye on the street outside. One of the cars that had been parked near Dante's house was now parked on the opposite side of the road, facing towards the car park.

"Were you hiding long?" Church asked.

Sophie shrugged. "I was in my jammies. Dante told me to get dressed but it was dark. Past my bedtime. Then the bad man came. We heard him come in the back way. I hid."

"That must have been really scary."

Sophie didn't answer. She pulled her teddy bear from the seat beside her and thrust her hand into its dungaree pocket. She pulled out a small sheet of paper folded into four and handed it to Church.

"Dante told me to give you this."

Church opened it. It was a name, telephone number and address.

"You call my auntie?" Sophie asked. "Dante said I'm going to live with her now."

"Of course," Church said. She felt relieved. Dante had trusted her to make sure Sophie was cared for, despite everything.

"He said to tell you that he's sorry. He didn't mean to... betray you. He said he had no choice. What does betray mean?"

"Erm... it means to give information or do something that might hurt someone else. It's okay, though. I understand what he meant. He's not in any trouble with me." Church patted her little hand. "I'm sorry."

"Dante said he might not be able to come with me. Did the bad man hurt him?"

"Yes, he did."

"Dante's not coming back, is he?"

"No, sweetie. He's not."

"He said you would find the bad man."

"I will. I promise."

Sophie nodded in complete faith.

DCI Jorge Jackson entered the café looking stressed. Church smiled at Sophie and slid away from the table. She beckoned Jorge towards the counter so Sophie couldn't hear them speak.

"Thanks for coming," Church said quietly.

"I was in the area. I told the local station this is part of an open investigation. Uniform are at the address now. Pretty gruesome, by all accounts," he said. "Any ideas who did this?"

"I have my suspicions, but no evidence. You won't find any either."

Jorge frowned. "And what am I supposed to do with the case?"

"I'll get you evidence or a confession, but it may take me a while."

"Give me a name at least. Something to follow up on."

"A name won't help you. We've been trying to locate him for weeks." She held out the piece of paper. "These are the contact details for Sophie's next of kin. Her and Dante's aunt. I can get my team to check her out."

"I'm sure we can manage that." He tucked the paper into his inside pocket. "So, is it the same guy who killed the EMP finance guy?"

"More than likely."

"And that's all you're going to give me?"

"For now, yes. When I have proof, you'll be the first to know."

"Fine."

Church returned to Sophie.

"Sophie, this is my friend Jorge. He's with the police."

Sophie looked up at Jorge and studied his brown suit. Church guessed what she was thinking.

"He's a detective, so he doesn't wear a uniform."

Seeing Red

Sophie nodded at Church. "Shall I go with him now?"

"Yes, sweetie. I've got work to do."

"Get the bad man?"

"Yes."

"Okay." Sophie gathered her things and looked expectantly at Jorge.

"So, you'll keep in contact?" Jorge asked Church.

"The team will," Church said. "Kat will be your contact."

"Not you?"

Church shook her head. She looked down at Sophie and kissed the top of her head.

"Are you okay?" Jorge asked gently.

"My defences are a little battered, is all. You'll be surprised to know that children are my Kryptonite."

"What's Kryptonite?" Sophie asked, looking up at them both.

"Something that weakens a person's powers," Church replied.

"You have superpowers?" Sophie asked in amazement.

"She sure does," Jorge said.

Church watched from the café door as Jorge put Sophie into the back of his car. Sophie was complaining that he didn't have a booster seat for her. It made Church smile. What a strong, brave little girl. They both waved at her as Jorge pulled away.

Church took a deep breath and studied the car she had seen earlier outside Dante's house. It was still parked across the street and it was still bothering her.

It was a good place to start.

She focused her attention further down the street and strode to the other side of the road. From the corner of her eye, she saw the driver duck a little lower behind a newspaper. That was confirmation enough. Once she was out of his line of sight, she quickly doubled back and slid over the bonnet. She wrenched the car door open, grabbed the man's collar and dragged him out. She disabled him with a jab to the throat and he dropped to the tarmac. She pinned his head to the ground with her boot and frisked him for his phone. He was limp and gasping for breath.

She straightened up, ignoring a few passers-by who hesitated at the spectacle, then trotted nervously away. She scrolled through the phone. No saved contacts and only one number was in the recent call list. She hit the redial button and held the phone to her ear.

"Well?" a familiar voice with a Geordie accent answered.

"James fucking Doyle!" she hissed. "Long time no speak, you son of a bitch!" She heard a rustling, probably him signalling to whoever was with him to pay attention. He didn't respond.

"You killed one of my employees... you killed Geoff Abraham. Why are you fucking with me without actually facing me? Fucking coward!"

"You know why," Doyle growled back.

"You want this shit?" Church asked. "Then come get it."

Seeing Red

"Now, now, pet, that's not how this works! You're not calling the shots here..."

"Neither are you," Church interrupted.

"We'll be in contact. We'll name the time and place. You bring the files and the prototype and we'll go from there."

"Is the Doctor there with you?" she asked.

"Who would that be?" Doyle said nonchalantly.

"You know who! Your new boss," Church smiled a wicked smile. "Ballsy, going AWOL from Cactus. I didn't think you had it in you."

"Fuck you!"

"Fuck you right back!"

Doyle hung up and the guy under Church's boot started to squirm. She released his head and squatted in front of his face.

"Let's have a little chat," she said, tilting her head at him.

Team Scorpio arrived in their van. Scorp Two and Three got out and bundled the man into the back. Church got into the driver's seat of the tail's car and Scorpio One got in beside her. She pulled away and the van followed.

She drove to a safe house. Two and Three supported the man between them and took him inside. Church and Scorpio One stayed in the car.

"We'll get him to talk," Seb said confidently. "What are you going to do?"

"End this. One way or another," she said firmly.

"Want us to pay the Echo meatheads a little visit?"

"Leave them."

"They deserve a little payback, don't you think? Especially Mr Frowny."

Church shook her head. "They played their part but let's not waste our time."

"He played you!" Seb persisted.

Church looked at him. Seb widened his eyes in realisation.

"Oh, you knew," he said, shaking his head in disbelief.

"I knew things would escalate soon enough. Riley failed in finding the USB so the Doctor stepped things up."

The tail's phone beeped with a text message. Church looked at the screen, just a time and a set of co-ordinates.

"Showtime," she said.

"Good luck," Seb said as he got out of the car. He tapped the roof three times and Church pulled out of the drive.

Showtime

Sacrifice

The journey to the location Doyle had sent her would take at least an hour. An hour to prepare. Was there another way? Had she missed anything? Would she have done anything differently?

Her reverie was broken by the tail's phone vibrating angrily on the seat beside her. With nothing to lose, she picked up the phone and pressed the green answer button.

"Hey," Riley growled.

"Hey," Church replied, mildly surprised.

"Now don't go postal!"

"I can't promise that. What have you done?"

"Nothing yet, I just wanted to check that you were okay."

"It's only been a few hours, I'm fine. Can't say the same for Dante though."

"Dante?"

"He was one of my apprentices. Doyle got to him, threatened his sister, no doubt. I found Dante dead on his kitchen table. His little sister was hiding upstairs."

"I'm sorry," Riley said quietly.

"I don't need your apologies. Did you know?"

"No," he sighed.

"So, *she* has her contingencies too. Did she not trust you to get the job done?"

"I couldn't find the USB, nor the files."

"Where did you look?"

"Not in the right places, obviously."

"Are your team in on this?"

"No... they know I'm back with *her*, but they're following my orders."

"Which are?"

"To look out for you and the rest of the team."

Church rolled her eyes.

"Now don't go rolling your eyes!" he growled. "The rendezvous, it's a trap."

"No shit," Church said quietly, making a turn off the A-road.

"You can't fight your way out of this one, trust me."

"I'm not intending to," Church replied.

"Don't do this," he pleaded.

"Do what?" she sighed. "Save lives, save my team, stop this shit from starting a war?"

"You're sacrificing yourself."

"Do what you've got to do, right?"

"They've got MacKay. Had him for weeks. They're continuing the tests. He's close to figuring it all out."

Church's shoulders sagged a little. Withholding the project files and the prototype had just made them more determined to cut corners. She wondered how close MacKay was to succeeding.

Seeing Red

"There's a derelict warehouse, out in the country. That's where they've been holding and using their guinea pigs," Riley continued.

"Norfolk?"

"Yes. How did you know that?"

"I pay attention."

Riley shouldn't have been surprised.

"The place is surrounded," he said. "But it's not where she is. I don't know where yet."

"I wouldn't expect anything less. How many guinea pigs?"

"Twenty or so. Can't be sure exactly."

"And you're risking your life to tell me this, why?"

"My soul is already damned, so my life is irrelevant. If this goes the way I think it will, we'll both be dead before too long."

"Not if I have anything to do with it!" Church said firmly. "Continue as we agreed. Forget about playing the hero. I make my own choices. Whatever happens, take her out, whatever the cost."

Riley sighed. "One successful subject, that's all she needs. She's already set the auction, invites have gone out to all the major players."

So far the testing been unsuccessful. That was both good and bad. How many more people were going to die because of this?

"Do you know how much is she expecting?" Church asked.

"I don't know, tens of millions, who knows."

"That narrows it down," Church mused to herself. "When?"

"Next week," Riley confirmed.

"Shit!"

"Indeed."

Plans swirled around in her head. Let the auction take place. Get the players in the room or at least connected remotely. They would need to simultaneously trace all the participants, a team in place for each player, wherever they were. She needed an army, more resources. International teams. Who could she trust with this?

"Justin?"

"I'm here," he breathed. "What do you need?"

"You're going to hate this."

"I'm not liking it much so far," he growled. "Just hit me with it."

Church left the car on the side of the road with the keys in the ignition and walked into the woods. She reached the co-ordinates with a few minutes to spare. The spot seemed deserted. She circled the clearing a few times, no sign of any movement. She knew it was a trap, but she wasn't about to make this easy for them. She climbed up into one of the trees on the edge of the clearing and waited, hidden amongst the evergreen branches.

The specified time came and went. Church focused on her breathing, she needed a level head. Her heart pounded in her chest and ears.

Seeing Red

Some minutes later Doyle sauntered into the centre of the clearing.

"I know you're here!" he called.

Church remained quiet and watched him. He turned slowly in a circle, surveying his surroundings.

"The files, CJ. Hand them over with the prototype and we can talk."

Church leapt down from the tree while he had his back turned. He spun to face her.

"JD," she said, her tone laced with hatred.

They glared at each other, twenty feet of patchy grass and rocky earth separated them.

"I didn't think you would come, pet."

"Yet here I stand."

Doyle smirked at her. "This is the end of the road, CJ. You've been fooled, pet. Hook, line and sinker."

"Have I?"

"Yeah. You have. From the moment you walked into the offices at Torenta."

"Enlighten me," she said, tilting her head.

Doyle stuck his thumb and forefinger in his mouth and whistled. Five men dressed in black emerged from the shadows under the trees and stepped into the clearing. Riley was among them. He strode over to stand beside Doyle and the four others approached Church. Her eyes flicked between the men but rested on Riley. Riley's mouth twitched into a cocky grin.

Doyle chuckled. "Like I said, hook, line and sinker."

Church remained silent.

"Come on now, nothing to say to him? That's not like you, pet."

Church tore her eyes away from Riley and glared at Doyle.

"No?" Doyle shrugged. He turned to Riley. "What was she like in the sack?"

Riley winked at Church. She glared back at him.

Doyle was still looking smug. "Well, let's clear a few things up while we can."

"Such as?" Church spat.

"Your little trip to Yorkshire..."

"What about it?"

"Thought you outwitted us there, didn't you?"

Church said nothing. Doyle was fond of the sound of his own voice, so she let him yabber on.

"Your beau here took the reins on keeping tabs on you." He tipped his head towards Riley but kept his eyes on her. He was waiting for her reaction. She gave none.

"We're retrieving the package you buried as we speak... Riley kindly gave us its location."

Church looked back to Riley in accusation. He calmly returned her gaze. He had held on to that information for as long as he could. He gave her time. She should be thankful.

"If looks could kill, mate, you'd be in serious trouble," Doyle said, nudging Riley with his elbow. He raised his voice and addressed Church again. "Any moment now, we'll have the prototype."

The corner of Church's mouth twitched.

"She knew," Riley growled.

Doyle looked at Riley, then back at Church, then pulled his phone out of his pocket, dialled a number and held it to his ear. When the call was answered, he stepped away towards the line of trees. Church kept her eyes on the men in front of her, judging their ability, speed and weight. They were giving her plenty of time to plan her attack.

"You're fucking kidding me!" Doyle yelled down the phone. He strode back towards Church, face reddened and lips pursed.

"Where is it?" he spat.

"Where's what?" Church asked, as if she had no idea what he was talking about.

"Don't fuck with me, CJ! You know what! The files. The USB you buried up there is empty. Where are the files? Where's the prototype?"

Church shrugged.

"Do you have it?" Doyle asked.

Church raised her hands, palms up, suggesting he come and search her.

Doyle glared at her. "We're not fooling around, you know. We're not going to kill you yet, but we will hurt you."

"Come and try," Church said.

"The prototype," Doyle said impatiently. "Where is it? We know you have it. You took it from the lab. Riley made sure you got out with it."

Church looked at Riley, then back to Doyle. She lowered her arms.

"I don't know," she said with a shrug.

Doyle spun towards Riley.

"You saw her take it!"

"We found the vials. I cleared our exit," Riley said calmly.

"Where are they?" Doyle bellowed at her.

"Not a clue," she said.

"And the files?" he asked.

Church shrugged.

"You haven't found them, have you? All that time wasted infiltrating our systems... they were never there!"

"Fuck!" Doyle cried and ran a hand over his shaved head. "Search her!" he barked at the four men.

Church relaxed her knees into a slight crouch and prepared to fight.

She fought the men with ferocity despite being outnumbered and outweighed. She caught the younger man with an elbow to his nose. He fell to the ground clutching his face, blood seeping through his gloved fingers. Two more approached from either side. Church swung a fist in one direction and pivoted on one foot, kicking out with the other, both blows connecting with her opponents. The last man aimed a boot at her stomach.

The blow caused her to double over. Two of the men grabbed her arms. She twisted and writhed to break free from their grip. The man who'd kicked her was standing behind her and she caught his chin with the full force of her head as she threw it backwards. She nearly managed to pull the two men over.

"Enough of this shit!" Doyle bellowed and strode towards the fighting. "Hold her still!" he ordered.

The men tightened their grip. Church's eyes found Doyle's and she bared her teeth in a silent snarl. He didn't hesitate and shot her in the thigh with a dart gun.

"Coward!" she screamed at him, still wrestling with her captors. "Fight me like a man!"

A haze descended over Church's vision and she visibly relaxed. The two men loosened their grip prematurely and instantly regretted it. She pulled her right arm free and thrust her fist into the nearest throat. She pivoted, bent low and kicked the other man in the chest. Her head swam and nausea threatened to overwhelm her. Doyle fired another shot into her leg.

Before Church could strike again, her arms and shoulders were grabbed and she was forced down to her knees. Her arms were pinned painfully behind her back, her hair gripped, pulling her head back while another man cautiously patted her down. He retrieved her phone, gun and knife, but shook his head at Doyle. No USB. No prototype.

"It's time!" Riley bellowed across the clearing, moments later, they all heard the sound of an approaching vehicle. The engine roared in protest.

Doyle swapped the tranquilliser gun to his left hand and pulled his Desert Eagle from its holster with his right. Team Archers burst into the clearing, their guns aimed at the men. Doyle calmly held the barrel of his oversized pistol to Church's temple.

"One step further, ladies and we'll all see what she's really made of," Doyle snarled.

The girls froze but kept their respective targets in their sights. Kat's eyes scanned the scene and then stopped when she saw Riley. He held her gaze. A slight frown appeared between her eyebrows, but her look soon turned to one of disgust. She dragged her eyes away from him and focused on Doyle.

Doyle had a smug look of victory on his face. His hand was steady as he pressed the barrel into Church's head, making her stretch her neck further to one side. Her eyes rolled drunkenly towards Kat.

"Stand down," Church slurred.

Kat's grip tightened on her rifle and she steadied her stance. She was less than two metres away from Doyle, her finger on the trigger.

"That's an order!" Church said, struggling to sound coherent.

Kat looked between Church and Doyle. "What have you done to her?" she hissed at Doyle.

"Insurance," he said, waving the tranquilliser gun loosely in his left hand. "Wanna dose?" He jerked his head towards Church. "She's had two already. Your choice, you can watch us leave, or she gets one of these." He waved the Desert Eagle. "Or another of these." He wiggled the tranq gun again.

The girls looked at Kat for updated orders with fleeting glances. Kat kept her eyes on Doyle but moved her finger away from the trigger.

"Good choice," Doyle said with a smirk. "Time to go."

Church was dragged to her feet and the men retreated into the trees.

Kat

Kat watched as her best friend was dragged from the clearing. Doyle was the first to disappear, but his aim never left Church's head, which was rolling limply on her shoulders. The men melted away and Kat spun around, but Riley had gone. Team Archers closed in behind her.

Something shiny and metallic skittered across the ground at their feet. The grenade went off with a deafening boom. The girls barely had time to throw themselves to the ground and cover their heads with their arms as soil and stones rained down on them. Noxious smoke filled the clearing.

Church

Through the fuzziness in her head, Church heard the explosion and felt it through the ground.

The team! Oh my God, the team!

Church was powerless. She was being manhandled across the uneven ground. It passed beneath her, her feet dragging over dry grass and rocks.

The group stopped, but her world kept spinning. Everything was blurred. She was bundled into the back of an ATV and they roared along a bumpy track. A black sack was thrown over her head. She had lost the feeling in her hands. Her muscles had no strength left. She was limp and helpless, a knee painfully pressing between her shoulder blades.

After some time, Church couldn't tell how long, the vehicle slowed to a stop and she was dragged out. She tried to make sense of the sounds she heard. The wind in the trees sounded like whispers. A chanting.

You're done for, this is the end.

She could hear another noise, a repetitive whomping sound, she could feel it in her chest.

Another hand grabbed her upper arm roughly.

"Let's go, pet."

Church lifted her head slowly. She could just about make out a blurry face inches from hers. She recognised the voice and the smell of cheap aftershave.

As the hood was ripped off, Church bit the inside of her cheek hard, drawing blood. She threw back her head and spat in Doyle's face.

"Argh!" Doyle cried in disgust. "Bitch!"

Doyle tightened his grip on his gun and slammed his fist into her face.

Sierra Building

Bad Guys

The helicopter landed on the painted letter H on the roof of a building in a small, deserted industrial area on the outskirts of London. The doors slid open and Doyle jumped down. Church's limp body was hauled over the shoulder of one of the Perros.

Riley disembarked last. He watched as the helo took off and disappeared over the cityscape. He followed the group to the stairway. The sound of their boots echoed off the concrete walls. They descended a flight of stairs and the group split. The man carrying Church turned right, followed by the other Perros. Doyle continued down another flight, with Riley behind him.

Doyle swaggered ahead of him, grating Riley's already tense nerves. He didn't know this guy well, but what he did know irritated him to his core. Doyle thought he was in charge, thought he was important here. He obviously didn't realise that he was just another expendable soldier, just like all the other Perros in the Doctor's circle.

Doyle knocked on a door and waited obediently for the occupant to respond. Riley heard the scrape of a chair – then silence. Doyle tapped his foot impatiently and lifted his hand to knock again. He hesitated, then lowered his arm. Riley knew knocking a second time would mean instant punishment. Severe and brutal punishment. Everything had to be on her timing. No one else's.

"¡Venir!" *Come!* A stern, feminine voice barked from inside the room, speaking in her native Spanish.

Doyle looked blankly at Riley. Riley just shook his head in disbelief, opened the door and sarcastically waved Doyle inside.

Gloria Pérez was sitting behind the desk, dressed in smart black trousers and a black buttoned shirt. Her brunette hair was scraped back into a neat bun at the nape of her neck. Her fingernails and lips were both dark, almost black.

Before Echo, Riley had been her number one operative. Her Primero. Back then, he would have done anything she commanded. He had killed for this woman and would likely have to kill again. She gazed with contempt at Doyle for a moment, then her eyes rested on Riley and her features immediately softened.

She purred in Spanish, "Welcome home, soldier."

"Señora," Riley replied formally.

"It's done?" she asked.

"Partly," Riley said. "She's here, but no files and no prototype."

She flashed a glare at Doyle. He had failed. Her orders had been clear. Doyle's smug grin slowly dropped when he realised she was not pleased.

"Tell him to leave us," she said sharply.

Riley looked at Doyle and nodded towards the door. Doyle didn't move.

"You can go now," Riley growled in English.

"What?" Doyle blurted, then immediately closed his mouth. He dipped his head sheepishly towards Pérez and ducked out the door.

Pérez remained seated and gazed at Riley. He was standing straight-backed, arms by his side, chin up. She relaxed in her chair.

"What happened?" she asked.

"I failed." There was no point in making excuses.

She closed her eyes briefly in disappointment. "I should have guessed *she'd* fuck everything up!" she hissed.

"But you have her."

"I do." She sounded pleased about that. "What does her team know?" she asked.

"Next to nothing. She kept almost everything from them," Riley replied.

"And you, it seems."

"Some things, yes," he admitted.

"Where are they now?"

"I don't know, but I will find out, ma'am."

"Make sure you do."

Riley dipped his head obediently.

"The house rules," Pérez said, standing up and smoothing her hands over her immaculate clothes.

"Stay away from Church. Leave her to me. You're confined to this floor only. You're not free to leave without my express permission. We'll get you set up with the appropriate access. Your every move will be monitored. Is that clear?"

"Yes, ma'am."

She stepped up in front of him, her eyes fixed on his.

"You understand why we used one of her young employees?"

"Yes, ma'am."

"As you spectacularly failed in your task, I ordered Doyle to implement a little backup plan. If your team got caught up in it…" She waved it off as irrelevant. "Prove to me you can continue to follow my orders... just like you used to."

"Yes, ma'am. I will."

Her perfume wafted over him. The smell transported him back years. His body remembered the pain. He forced himself not to react, but all he wanted to do was grit his teeth and clench his fists. He studied a spot on the wall behind her.

Sometimes the pain she inflicted ended in pure ecstatic pleasure – if he managed to please her. But she was extremely difficult to please. Her expectations were high. He wondered how Doyle had managed under her command. The man was a walking disaster.

"You need to earn your title back," she said.

"Yes, ma'am."

"You know how this works."

"I do."

"You answer to me, just like the rest of the Perros. Clear?"

"Yes, ma'am."

"You look tired. At the end of the hall, you'll find your room. Rest up now. I'll send for you."

"Ma'am."

Dismissed, he turned on his heel and left the room.

The Doctor

"Doyle!" Pérez called from outside his door. She heard him scramble to his feet and come running to the door.

"Yes, ma'am, I'm here," he said breathlessly.

"With me!" she barked.

"What about him?" Doyle asked, gesturing to Riley's room.

Pérez arched an eyebrow briefly and ignored his question. She strode to the stairs and waited for him to open the door for her. He was so undisciplined, so uncouth. He made her skin crawl. Not her usual choice, but his previous position at Cactus had its advantages. But she still wondered how long his usefulness would last.

At the next door, Pérez didn't have to wait for Doyle to open it. He reached it first but nearly knocked into her in his eagerness. She refrained from visibly cringing. She needed him on side, for the time being.

Pérez entered the room and found Church unconscious. She was bloody and tethered to the hospital bed, her wrists and ankles in thick leather cuffs. Her face was a mess. Dried blood covered her nose and mouth.

"What is this?" she hissed at Doyle.

"She resisted."

"Was I unclear?" Pérez asked.

"No... ma'am." He added the formality as an afterthought.

"Then explain to me why she looks like that. You were given enough darts to make this quick and easy. Seems to me you wanted a little fun of your own. Payback, maybe?"

"No!" Doyle cried. "It wasn't like that!"

"Enough!" Pérez seethed quietly. "Leave. Now."

Doyle left the room. Pérez approached the bed and motioned for the medic to update her.

"We found the tracker, it was in her upper arm. The incision was fresh. Riley blocked the signal with a Faraday patch. We removed the tracker. It's still active and currently with one of the soldiers."

"Perros," Pérez corrected.

The medic dipped his head in acknowledgement.

"Her wounds are superficial, medically speaking. Nothing broken. Her vitals are normal."

"How many darts did she take?"

"I found two puncture marks in her thigh."

Two? she thought. One was enough to floor a man the size of Riley.

"Bring her round," she demanded.

"I would advise against that."

"If I wanted your advice, I would ask for it!" Pérez hissed. "Bring her round."

The medic nodded curtly, then prepared a needle and syringe. He injected the substance into a vein and stepped away.

"Leave us," Pérez ordered, moving to the end of the bed. She would wait.

Pérez studied the monitor and eventually Church's heartrate changed slightly. Slowly, she opened her eyes but didn't move.

"Good morning, Claudia," Pérez said brightly. "Welcome back to Sierra."

Church frowned.

"Yes, we're hiding in plain sight. Right under the Almighty's nose. Yet he doesn't have a clue."

Church turned her head on the pillow and stared at the woman in front of her.

"Gloria," she croaked.

"It's been a while," Pérez said conversationally. "Last time I saw you, you'd just been blown up by two attack helos."

"At your command."

"An insignificant detail," Pérez said. "Yet here we are again." She smiled down at Church.

"What do you want?" Church hissed.

"To cause you much pain. Emotionally as well as physically."

"Go right ahead," Church said.

"There's plenty of time... we have all the time in the world."

"Is that so?"

Pérez smiled knowingly and left the room.

Church

Once the door closed, a sense of panic washed over Church.

My team! What had happened to my team?

She remembered hearing the explosion as she was dragged away from the clearing. The team should have been heading to the warehouse in Norfolk and not following her. She regretted having a new tracker fitted. She should have gone dark, like before.

Had the team followed any of her instructions? Were the preparations being made? She had no idea.

She was on her own.

Church tugged frantically at her restraints. The leather cuffs on her wrists and ankles were unbreakable and unpadded. If she struggled, they would start to rub and bite into her skin. There was nothing she could do.

She took a deep, calming breath and gave herself a stern talking to.

Breathe. Keep calm. You're stuck here for now. Rest. Bide your time. If an opportunity arises, take it.

Seeing Red

But my team! They killed my fucking team!

What can you do? Exactly nothing! Listen to me!

Church listened. She let her detached inner self take control and she relaxed her tense muscles. Struggling against her restraints would get her nowhere.

She surveyed her own injuries. Her face was numb and on fire at the same time. She couldn't breathe through her nose, but it didn't feel broken when she rubbed it against the pillow, just swollen and very sore. Nothing else was broken. Several bruises. A few cuts. Her head pounded from the tranquilliser and whatever else they'd injected her with. She had got off lightly, all things considered. She had certainly expected worse. It was likely that worse was yet to come.

Church considered what Pérez had said. *The Doctor*, she scoffed. *Ridiculous*. Pérez had said *Welcome to Sierra*. Sierra was a codename for one of Jack's buildings. Owned by Cactus and used by operatives for various reasons. Church had used it as a base for many of her solo ops. Somewhere to crash, store equipment, clean up and plan, a basic operative's hotel without any staff.

Is Jack in on this? she thought wildly. That wasn't beyond the realms of possibility, but she doubted it. Pérez had spectacularly burnt that bridge after Church found out she was working against Jack right under his nose.

She considered why Pérez had told her all this. Was it a show of strength? A demonstration of the reach of her conniving fuckery? Jack would take real pleasure in gutting Pérez, once he got his hands on her. And here she was, in one of his buildings. How come Jack didn't know? Or did he know and was letting Pérez get away with it?

How had she survived crossing him on the Yankee op?

And then there was Riley. Whose side was he really on? She couldn't be sure.

The door to her room opened and the medic returned. He didn't look at Church directly. He prepared another needle and syringe and jabbed it in her arm. He didn't look particularly happy about it. He had a tense and stern expression on his face. All business. Just following orders.

The medic turned his back to her and scribbled notes on a clipboard.

So, he had proper training and was keeping medical records. But what was the point?

Church thought no more as she faded back into oblivion.

Doyle

Several hours later, Doyle was leaning casually against a small table against the back wall of a windowless room, Church's Bowie knife in his hand. He admired the ripple in the metal of the blade. It was a deadly weapon and slightly ridiculous. Forged Japanese steel! Who did she think she was?

Two Perros burst through the door dragging Church between them. They shoved her on to the floor and stepped away. On all fours, she coughed and gagged, looking like she was going to throw up. She was weak and vulnerable. Not like the Church he knew.

Seeing Red

Doyle holstered the blade, placed it on the table and gestured with his thumb for the Perros to leave. He waited until they shut the door behind them.

"Wakey, wakey," he crooned, pushing himself away from the table.

Church slowly got to her feet. He could see the effort it took her to stand up straight.

"James," Church said with disdain.

"We need to have a little chat."

"Do we?" Church said sarcastically.

"We do. The vials, CJ, where are they?"

"Don't call me that!" she hissed.

Doyle chuckled. This was going to be fun.

"You *will* tell me. You know how this goes."

Church raised her chin defiantly. "Do your worst."

Doyle's phone beeped twice. He pulled it from his pocket and looked at the screen. Without reacting, he turned it off and placed it beside Church's knife. He caught her glancing between the table and the door, judging the distance.

"You'll never make it," he sneered, rolling his neck until it cracked.

Without another thought, he launched himself towards her.

Church tried to spin away but wasn't fast enough. Doyle ploughed into her, his thick arm wrapped around her neck. He took a handful of her hair in his fist, pulling her head back.

"Not so high and mighty now, are we?" he snarled in her ear. "You think you're so clever, burying the empty USB. You had us there for a moment. Where's the information? It's only a matter of time before we find it."

Church didn't respond.

"No matter how deep you put it in your system, we'll find it. Your newbie was very helpful with that."

"Did you enjoy killing an innocent kid?" Church wheezed.

Doyle snorted. If only she knew what was coming. "It had to be done, you know that."

"I'm not going to fight you," Church gasped, limp in his vice-like grip.

"No? We'll see about that."

Doyle smiled wickedly and brushed his nose down her neck, smelling her skin. He felt her immediately tense in his arms.

"Fight me," he whispered. "I know it really gets you going." He flicked out his tongue and slowly licked her, closing his eyes in brief ecstasy.

Church's reaction was immediate. She bucked and twisted, trying to unbalance him. She whipped her head away, leaving clumps of her hair in his fist.

Doyle held on, reasserting his dominance and cut off her airway with his biceps. With a fast jab to her kidney, he forced her down to her knees, his other arm pressed against the back of her neck.

"Fight me," he repeated.

"Ke."

Seeing Red

It was the only sound she could make. She was choking, unable to speak, unable to breathe. He had her and she was powerless to stop him.

From the corner of his eye, he could see her face was turning purple, eyes bulging, teeth gritted. She gripped his arm at her throat, her nails broken and ragged.

He expected a little more from her. She never went down without a fight. He'd seen her beat men twice her size. Doyle wasn't much taller than her but he did outweigh her.

Disappointed, he released her with a shove and rocked back on his heels. Church slumped to the floor gasping. He waited two breaths, dragged her onto her back and straddled her chest, knees pinning her arms to her sides. He clamped a large hand over her windpipe and started to squeeze.

"The prototype," he demanded.

Tears spilled from her red, sore eyes. They trailed down and disappeared into her hair. Doyle had never seen her cry before. He didn't think she was capable, having a heart of stone.

She was refusing to look at him. He leant down, increasing the pressure further.

"Look at me!" he roared.

Church screwed her eyes shut.

"Look at me and tell me where the fuck those vials are!"

She opened her mouth but no sound came out. Doyle released the pressure by the smallest of fractions and allowed her one desperate mouthful of air.

"Where?" he demanded.

Church shook her head, making him slap her across the cheek. The sound echoed around the sparse room.

He tightened his grip again until he felt things crack and pop beneath his fingers. He leant his full weight onto her chest.

"Tell me, pet," he whispered into her ear. "I won't think any less of you."

He could smell the fear on her. Another first. She was shaking like a leaf beneath him. It was intoxicating. A power he never had with her before. He breathed it in, savouring the feeling.

"Tell me," he urged.

Her body relaxed as her consciousness slipped away. He licked her neck again and her head turned towards him. Was she finally giving in?

She wasn't.

Church clamped her teeth into his neck and bit down hard.

Doyle roared in pain and tried to pull away. She sank her teeth in further, tasting the metallic blood filling her mouth. The pressure on her neck increased then suddenly disappeared. With a gasp, Church let go and tried to shove Doyle off her.

With another roar, he swung his fist into her face and Church's world went black.

Tormented Dreams

Church was dreaming. A luxury, considering her current situation. They had been depriving her of sleep since she had been brought to this place. She was lucky to get more than a few minutes at a time.

Church dreamt she was back in her office. The team were standing around her desk, the air gapped laptop open in front of her, the queen shaped USB stick plugged into the only port. One click of the mouse and all the information they had about Warrior IV would be deleted. Gone. For good.

Kat smiled with encouragement. This was the right thing to do.

Church clicked on the delete button.

Without warning the scene in her mind changed, she was dreaming about the lab in Oxfordshire, with Riley. The rack of vials were right there, on the shelf in the fridge, a Dara Celtic knot stamped on each of the lids.

The only remaining prototype of Warrior IV. There only by chance because one research scientist felt compelled to follow normal protocols and send the sample for testing.

It was now or never. She had to do something. But how would Riley react? Would he stop her?

Their comms crackled and Ellis advised that the guard was on the move, heading to their floor. She motioned for Riley to head out.

The second he was out of sight, Church unscrewed the lids and poured the blue liquid down the sink.

As she watched it swirl down the drain, the alarm went off, filling the room with a deafening siren. Unperturbed, Church refilled the vials with a mix of water and blue handwash. Shoving the rack into her pack she followed Riley out of the lab.

She had done it. The formula and any evidence that it existed was gone. All that remained were the people who knew about it. Was their knowledge a problem? She planned to find out.

After finding Archers in darkness and dropping Riley off at Enigma. Church took a detour and dumped the useless vials. She didn't even get out of the Land Rover. She just slowed down, hurled the pack out of the window towards a group of industrial skips and drove home.

Kenny MacKay

Kenny MacKay, formerly Deputy Research Scientist at EMP, worked day and night in the makeshift lab. He slept on a camp bed in the corner. He was only allowed out of the lab every other day for a short, escorted walk to the nearest shower room. His ankles were shackled in chains, which clinked and clunked as he shuffled around the lab. The metal had already rubbed the skin on his ankles raw.

He had been locked in the lab for weeks and had quickly lost track of the days. He saw no daylight. They had taken his watch and there wasn't a clock in the lab. His paper notes were spread everywhere, on every surface. He wasn't allowed to use a computer.

He was guarded twenty-four-seven. Two men, dressed in camouflage combats, kept sentry outside the locked door. They didn't speak to him and they certainly didn't answer his questions. They would just dump his food tray on the desk without a word. They didn't even speak to each other.

Seeing Red

Occasionally, a short, stocky man visited him. He also wore combats. He seemed to be in charge and was constantly checking on Kenny's progress. Kenny explained the intricacies of the work, but he knew the man didn't understand.

Kenny had worked tirelessly since they abducted him. They said they had his family – if his wife and their two daughters were still alive. He had no idea what these people were capable of.

He looked down the lens of the ancient microscope and scribbled more notes without looking at what he was writing. He was close. He could feel it. He hoped he was close. For his family's sake.

He had to perfect the formula. He had been forced by these people to start from scratch, to try to remember every detail, every step, with nothing to work from. He had to recall the variations, the previous errors. He meticulously made notes as he worked. He kept his notebook beside him and jotted down any ideas or questions as and when they came to him.

Hearing the door being unlocked, he struggled to his feet. Was it mealtime already? He shuffled backwards and watched as a hospital bed, with a person-shaped form on top, was wheeled into the lab.

The guards said nothing and left the room, but the door remained open. Kenny looked uncertainly from the bed to the door. What was going on?

The stocky man strode into the lab. "We've brought you a new test subject," he said proudly, waving his thick hand at the bed.

"I don't test on humans!" Kenny protested. "It's nowhere near ready for human testing!"

The man snorted. "We've been testing for weeks now, man. One more subject won't hurt. She's heavily sedated, so you can do anything you like to her but..." He waggled a finger at him. "Don't go killing her, okay?"

Kenny looked at the bed again. Before he could respond, the man was striding back out.

"Wait!" Kenny called after him. "I can't! It's not right!"

"You can and you will, if you ever want to see that pretty family of yours again," the man sneered. "Just bang on the door if she shows signs of waking up. She's pretty feisty." He pointed to a blood-soaked dressing taped to his neck.

He left, leaving Kenny staring at the battered young woman on the bed.

Archers, Scorpio and Echo

Kat

The grenade blast obliterated the centre of the clearing. Kat had thrown herself to the ground, hands over her head. Moments later she forced herself to move. Struggling to her hands and knees, her ears ringing, she tried to shake away the fogginess, blinking profusely. She soon realised that her vision was obscured by actual fog. It hung thick in the air, close to the ground and was choking her. She staggered to her feet.

"Jen!" she croaked. "Kez! Miz!"

She felt the ground shudder and instantly took a defensive position. Kneeling on one knee, she swung her rifle towards the sound. She couldn't see a damn thing.

"Fuck!"

She heard the familiar voice over the ringing in her ears – it came from behind her. She spun towards it, breathing hard and prepared to fire. Then the strength left her body and she slumped to the ground.

Echo

Harris sprinted through the smoke into the clearing, searching for the girls. He scanned the ground around him, praying the girls were okay, unhurt, in one piece at least. The rest of the team were with him, each of them searching their designated zone.

If only they had got here sooner. Echo had heard the blast when they were only a few hundred yards from the clearing. Riley had warned them that contingencies might be deployed. Suspect the worst, he had said.

Harris was facing the possibility of finding the girls broken and bloody. They were too late. Not fast enough, despite Jonny almost breaking the sound barrier getting the team there after Riley's call. What if the girls were hurt, or worse?

The thought of losing Kat made him suck in a choking lungful of rancid gas through his gritted teeth. She was the one for him. He knew it. Someone he didn't have to hide his true self from.

Was that the attraction in these fearless, feisty vixens? Archers knew what Echo did after dark and didn't care. They had likely done worse. Church certainly had. A buddy of his still worked at Cactus and the stories he told were like modern legends, Church in Africa, almost single-handedly saving a royal family from execution. Church in Russia, taking out a warlord... the list was seemingly endless.

Did Kat know Church's history? They were pretty close, so he assumed she did. And now Church had just upped and handed herself over to the bad guys. Harris shook his head in disbelief and wonder. God, she's got some balls. No wonder Riley got it so bad... but to stand there and watch while the bad guys took her...

Through the smoke, he heard a croaking voice and breathed a sigh of relief. It was Kat, calling for the girls. He followed the sound.

"Fuck!" he cried at the sight of her covered in blood.

Kat spun to face him, aiming straight at him. Her aim faltered and she slumped to the ground.

Harris dropped to his knees, swinging his rifle behind his back.

"Babe, get up!"

Kat was alive, in one piece, just about. She still had her limbs. Harris thanked God for that. Everything else could wait. He grabbed her by the vest straps and hauled her to her feet. Shoving his shoulder under her arm, he urged her forward. Over comms, the guys confirmed that they'd found the other girls.

Kat was coming round and he could feel her tense up.

"Get your filthy hands off me!" she screamed.

"I would, if you could move faster. We need to get outta here!" he gasped.

"You fuckers!"

"Can you wait until we're clear? Then you can shout all you like. We were attempting to be stealthy."

"Fuck you!"

"Any time, babe. Just not right now, okay?"

Kat wrestled free and spun to face him. "How could you?" she screamed in his face.

"I haven't done anything," Harris said firmly. He resumed helping her along with an arm around her waist.

"He just stood there and watched!" she cried. "How could he? I thought... he cared... Bastard!"

"Let's not judge his parentage right now, babe. Now get in." Harris held the van door open for her.

"I'm not going anywhere with you!"

"The girls will need to see that you're okay and I'm not about to leave you here on your own. You need medical attention."

"Screw that!" Kat spun away from him and bolted back towards the clearing.

Harris sprinted after her and tackled her to a stop. Wrapping his arms around her, pinning her arms to her chest, he held her tightly against his chest.

"Let's go. It's not safe. Who knows what other tricks they've left," he whispered in her ear.

She suddenly collapsed in his arms, tears streaming down her cheeks. He squeezed her a little tighter. Lifting her into his arms, he made his way back to the truck. She finally gave in and rested her head on his shoulder.

Tom jumped out of the van when Harris approached.

"One broken ankle, several abrasions, some partial hearing loss," he reported.

Harris clambered in, with Tom behind him. Tom slid the side door closed and Jonny sped the van away. Tom turned his attention to Kat and started a quick examination.

Kat sat up on the bench and batted his hand away. "Touch me again and you will regret it!" she hissed.

Tom backed off, palms raised. Kat glanced at the rest of Archers. Miz looked pointedly at Kez's ankle with concern.

Kat nodded in acknowledgement. She could see it was broken from the angle of her boot.

"Take us to Orwell Vets," she demanded, looking at Jonny. "Know where that is?" she asked.

"Sure," Jonny replied. "Two?" he asked Harris for confirmation.

"Whatever the lady commands," Harris said.

The van finally made it to a tarmacked road and Jonny put his foot down.

Temporary Medical

Echo piled out of the van and helped the girls to the back doors of the veterinary surgery. Eve was waiting for them. She held the door open, allowing Tom through as he carried Kez. Eve directed him towards the consultation room and the rest of the team to the waiting room. Two medics started cleaning and dressing the minor wounds on the girls.

Kat sat down heavily in one of the plastic chairs.

"Is the bubble active?" she asked no one in particular as one of the medics dabbed at the wound on her forehead.

"Confirmed," Lorenzo said, his voice coming from a laptop on the small table in the corner of the room. Leaflets about pet insurance and doggy daycare services had been hastily swept aside.

"Is Lenny online?" Kat asked.

"Lenny here, all present and correct." Lenny's face appeared on the split screen, next to Lorenzo's.

"Scorpio One," Seb confirmed from the third box on the screen.

"Archer Six reporting." Ruben appeared next.

Echo waited patiently for their orders, but Kat ignored them. They exchanged glances between them, Harris giving a look – *let's wait and see*.

"Great," Kat said. "Seven, where are we with tracking Church?"

"I lost her signal about thirty minutes ago, just four clicks from the clearing," Lorenzo replied.

"Was the signal interrupted or is it offline?" Kat asked.

"Interrupted."

"Send me the location. I'll find her," Seb said.

"Don't bother," Kat said. "Riley knows she has a tracker, so if the signal returns we should assume it's to send us on a wild goose chase. Seven, keep your eye on it and let Scorp One know if anything significant happens."

"Copy that," Lorenzo said.

"We're working on locating Mrs MacKay and her daughters," Seb said. "It's just a matter of time now."

"Keep me updated," Kat said. "Lenny, how did you get on with Archers systems?"

"Everything is shut down. I'm scrubbing the system and rebuilding it. The site is completely clear of personnel," Lenny said. "And the evidence against EMP is complete."

"Thanks, Lenny. Send it to DCI Jackson," Kat said. "Six, instruct all available personnel to scour every CCTV angle for either Church, Riley, Doyle or anyone else of interest."

"Already on it," Ruben confirmed.

Kat nodded with satisfaction. Harris cleared his throat, making Kat look at him.

"Yes?" she asked.

"Instructions for Echo?" Harris asked.

Kat snorted. She had a few suggestions but decided to keep them to herself for the time being.

"Do you know where Riley is?" she asked instead.

"He went dark," Harris said.

"Can you contact him?" Kat pressed.

"He went dark."

"I heard you," Kat snapped. "But can you contact him, or will he check in with you?"

Harris ground his teeth, debating what to tell her. Help the girls, protect the girls. Those were his orders.

"If he can, he'll check in," Harris replied.

"Let me know when he does, we may need to co-ordinate." Kat stood up. "Right, people, let's get to it."

DCI Jackson

DCI Jorge Jackson read the evidence thoroughly, several times. It had arrived in his inbox from an unknown sender.

Pinching the bridge of his nose, trying to abate one hell of a headache, he called his younger sister.

"Kitty Kat," he said. "Did you send me an early birthday present?"

"I don't know what you're talking about... but if I did, it's never too early to tell you how much I care," Kat said sarcastically. "Can you use it?"

"Of course I can use it. It's very thorough and very... concerning."

Kat snorted in agreement. "You're welcome," she said. "When can you take them down?"

"Patience, Kit Kat. Legal cogs turn slowly."

"You've seen what they've been doing, right? Why the delay?"

Jorge sighed. "I'll assemble a team. Apologies if you think we're slow, but we need to get this right."

"You need to hit the head office and the warehouse at the same time, before they can do anything once they know you're on to them."

"Yes, dear," Jorge said in exasperation. "This is not my first rodeo... Tell me something. Why am I not talking to Claudia? Why did she tell me to contact you?"

"She delegated to me," Kat replied.

"Right," Jorge said, not convinced that was the whole story. When Kat didn't respond, his concern about Church notched up a level. "Katherine?" he pressed.

Seeing Red

Kat huffed out a breath. "How was she, the last time you saw her?"

"You know, preoccupied. More concerned than I've ever seen her before. The little girl... she really affected her."

"How is Sophie?" Kat asked.

"Safe with her aunt and on their way back to the Wirral."

"Good," Kat said quietly.

"Now, back to Claudia. What's happened?"

Kat hesitated. This was Archers business and a total shitstorm. She decided she could trust her own brother. Church trusted him and that meant more than a lot.

"A few hours after you met her, she willingly walked into a trap, just handed herself over... I tried to stop her. As soon as I figured out what she was doing... we arrived two minutes too late. I tried. I really tried."

Jorge heard the heartbreak in Kat's voice but didn't understand why she wasn't doing anything more. More super commando, special ops stuff.

"Can't you track her?" he asked.

"The bad guys know about her tracker. No doubt they've removed it. It's currently on the M25, on its twentieth circuit."

"I'll put the word out. She has friends here and in the security services... we'll do what we can, you know we will. Give me some names, at least. Something to enable us to help you."

"They're bad people, Jorge. They'll kill any uniforms they see."

"So we go in plain clothes. Names, Kit Kat."

"We've been trying to locate them for weeks... what do you think you can do that we can't do better and faster?"

"Let us help."

"Take down EMP. That's what you can do."

Takedown

Scorpio

Team Scorpio followed up on a lead on Kenny MacKay's wife and daughters. The family were last seen by their neighbours. It looked as though they were heading away for their holidays, suitcases packed, summer clothes worn. But none of them had boarded the flight to Madrid.

With Lenny's help, they discovered the youngest daughter suffered from a rare disorder that needed specialised medication. It didn't take long, trawling through all the pharmacy prescription records, to narrow down the search. As soon as the medication request was processed, a notification was sent to Site B.

Seb and Oliver staked out the chemist in a nondescript old vehicle and waited for the prescription to be collected. There was no CCTV in the small town, so a drone hovered silently above the streets and Lorenzo ran facial recognition from the safety of Site B.

"Nothing to report," Lorenzo said over comms. "Nothing more than a few driving offences."

"It's a sleepy town. Low crime rate," Seb muttered.

"What are we looking for?" Lorenzo asked.

"We'll know it when we see it," Seb said.

"Well, that narrows it down," Lorenzo said sarcastically.

"Patience. Just keep your eye on the pharmacy logs. As soon as the prescription is collected, we're in business."

A steady stream of people entered the chemist and came out a few minutes later. Seb and Oliver assessed each one. None of them looked out of place.

"They're really slow at updating their records," Lorenzo grumbled.

"What's the rush?" Oliver asked. "If they're getting the kid the medication, then they're looking after them."

"Bad guys with a conscience?" Lorenzo said incredulously.

"Dead hostages don't make good hostages," Oliver muttered.

A woman trotted along the path towards the chemist. She kept looking behind her. Both Seb and Oliver watched her, their attention instantly piqued.

"We're in business," Seb said quietly.

"She's not in the system," Lorenzo said.

"That's Mrs MacKay."

"Wrong hair colour."

"Heard of wigs, probie?" Oliver snorted. "Her demeanour is screaming out."

"Maybe she's late for something?"

"Maybe she's nervous as hell because her captors are holding her and her daughters."

The woman came out of the chemist a short while later and fumbled with a white paper bag. Seb got out of the car and walked towards her.

"What are you doing?" Lorenzo asked. "She's likely being watched."

Seeing Red

"Just watch and learn," Oliver said patiently.

Seb bumped into her, making her drop the paper bag.

"My apologies!" Seb said, bending down to pick up the bag. He handed it back to her with a smile. "Sorry, I was miles away."

"No harm done," she said.

"Are you okay?" he asked. She was a nervous wreck, her hands shaking and her lip trembling.

"Fine. Fine," she insisted. "Thank you." She gestured to the bag, turned away and trotted back the way she came.

Seb entered the chemist, bought two granola bars and returned to the car.

"Definitely her," Seb said, sliding back into the driver's seat.

"Drone's following," Oliver said, looking at his tablet screen. "She's just got into an old Ford."

Seb and Oliver followed the Ford Fiesta into the countryside outside the town. From the drone surveillance, they watched a man drag Mrs MacKay from the car and roughly escort her to the isolated cottage. Another man waited at the front door, smoking a cigarette. All three disappeared inside. The unfinished cigarette was flicked towards the road.

After dark, all members of Team Scorpio surrounded the cottage. From the heat signatures, they confirmed MacKay and her daughters being kept in the attic room. Two other bodies were in the kitchen.

"Three, it's all yours," Seb said quietly.

"Copy that, One."

Scorpio Three turned on the tap on the canister he held in his gloved hands. The narrow hose led from the nozzle to a small hole in the window frame. He looked at his watch and waited. Scorpio Two watched the screen of his tablet and waited for the shapes in the kitchen to stop moving. After a few moments, they both slumped over the table.

On Seb's command, the team simultaneously entered the cottage from the front and back. Scorpio Three, Four and Five secured the men in the kitchen and dragged them out to the waiting van while Seb and Scorpio Two went upstairs. They broke the padlock on the attic door and found Mrs MacKay and her daughters huddled together on a threadbare mattress.

Seb held out his hand. "Mrs MacKay, my name is Sebastian. You're safe now, come with us."

Her wide eyes widened further in fright. She clung to her daughters.

"We've secured the men downstairs," he assured her.

She took his hand and hoisted the youngest girl onto her hip. Oliver picked up the older daughter and they ushered them out of the house.

Edward Cavendish

"May, darling..." Edward said.

"Don't you dare *darling* me!" May snapped. "Who is she this time? Not your PA, I made sure of that." May waved the explicit photograph in his face.

Seeing Red

Edward swallowed hard. How had she got the photo of him and Collette? Who had given it to her? They were meant to be safe and secluded in this safe house, dingy as it was. Not to their taste at all.

"I can explain..." he stuttered.

"Explain what? You're screwing around with another employee! What is there to explain?"

"May, I love *you*!" Edward pleaded.

"Ha!" May scoffed. "You love the money, that's all. What did you promise this one? Money? Promotion?... *Babies*?"

"It wasn't like that!" Edward cried.

May stood up. "I'm going to the clubhouse. I've had enough of this flea pit."

"May, please!" Edward reached out a hand towards her. "It's still not safe..."

May pulled her arm out of his reach. "Don't touch me! If I see you again, I'll take Jack up on his offer."

"Jack? Jack who?" Edward asked, confused.

"Doesn't matter. Just know that I do know people, people who are more than capable of making people like you disappear. He's offered more than once... free of charge, too!"

"You wouldn't!"

"Try me!" May hissed. "Your bank accounts have been frozen and you will be hearing from my solicitor shortly. I assume you'll move in with your sister... if she'll have you."

"May!"

May stormed towards the front door. The operative guarding them was holding it open for her.

"You're finished, Edward. I'm selling Torenta, stripping the assets, whatever is left of them. You'll never work in Pharma again."

Edward glanced between the operative and his irate wife. Why wasn't he trying to stop her from leaving? The man had a glint in his eye as if he was enjoying this.

"Please," he begged.

May left the small house and disappeared into the darkness.

EMP

Antonia Romano was on a conference call in the boardroom, surrounded by her directors. This crisis was going from bad to worse. She had been well and truly screwed over. She had decided very early on that if she was going down, she wouldn't be doing it alone.

"I need you to clear up this mess," she hissed at the screen.

"Miss Romano, it isn't that straightforward," a man said. "Geoff must have emptied the company accounts…"

"I don't care. Get it done!" She glared at the screen.

"Can't your new IT specialist help sort this out?" Andrew Eakins, the Operations Director, asked calmly.

Antonia pressed her lips together. Where was that weasel of a man? Had he been compromised? Was he in on this too? He hadn't been seen at the office today.

Seeing Red

There was a knock on the door and all eyes turned towards the sound. Who dared to interrupt?

A head tentatively appeared around the door. "Apologies," Jessica, the receptionist, said breathlessly. "Miss Romano, you're needed downstairs."

"Whatever it is, it can wait!" Antonia snapped.

"Erm, it's a little... delicate."

"Does it look like I care?" Antonia seethed.

"It's the police. They have a warrant for your arrest," Jessica blurted out quickly.

"Don't be ridiculous!" Antonia said, standing up. Could she make a run for it? Certainly not in these heels. She smoothed down her suit. "Gentlemen, one moment. I will sort this out and be back with you shortly."

She strode out of the room and headed for her office. Jessica had to trot to keep up. Antonia grabbed her mobile from her desk and spun to face Jessica. "Stall them!" she snapped, waving Jessica away. Once the door was closed, Antonia made a call. "The police are here!" she barked into the phone.

"Congratulations," Pérez sneered.

"What shall I do?"

"Why are you asking me?"

"You promised to help me."

The line went quiet.

"Get me out of this," Antonia pleaded.

"Reap what you sow. You let me down, Antonia."

"We're so close..."

"Not close enough. I don't need you or your failures anymore."

Pérez hung up.

Antonia's office door opened and a smartly dressed man with a ridiculous tie entered without preamble. The lights flickered and the computer screen on her desk turned black.

"Antonia Romano, you are under arrest," DCI Jorge Jackson said firmly. "We are seizing all your assets and you are to cease all operations immediately."

Antonia stepped back a few paces. The area outside her office was filled with police officers and her Directors. Andrew Eakins had a disdainful look on his face. He was talking animatedly to one of the officers.

"We had no idea!" he said. "Deaths? That's unimaginable! No, we had no idea!"

DCI Jorge Jackson approached Antonia with a set of handcuffs.

"Please," she said. "There's no need for those. What are the charges?"

Jorge didn't reply and took her arm firmly, just above the elbow. As she was escorted out of her office, she desperately searched the growing crowd for allies. She spotted Jessica filming the entire scene with her mobile.

"Jessica!" she called. "Call legal."

Andrew stepped into their path. "Our legal team can't help you. You are relieved of your position here. I have full agreement of the board." He turned to the DCI. "You have our full co-operation. Anything you need."

"Thank you, Mr...?" Jorge said.

"Andrew Eakins, interim CEO," Andrew said proudly.

"One of the officers will need to speak to you. Please shut down all activities. And no further calls to anyone. Wait for the officer in the boardroom."

"Certainly," Andrew said and stepped away.

Jorge escorted Antonia into the lift.

The Warehouse

The warehouse, in a deserted and derelict part of Norfolk, was surrounded by armed police officers. On receiving the command, they entered the building using bolt cutters and handheld battering rams. Officers streamed in and searched the building from top to bottom. Every room, every inch.

"Sir," the officer gasped into his radio. "There's nothing here. Nothing."

Jorge closed his eyes and took a deep breath. Of course it wouldn't be that easy. What the hell was going on here?

"Sir?" the officer pressed.

"Ma'am?" A Perro lieutenant approached Pérez. She dragged her eyes away from her screen.

"The warehouse has been hit by armed police," he reported.

A knowing smile tugged at the corner of her lips. "And we're secure?" she asked.

"Yes, ma'am. No movement, ma'am."

Sibling Rivalry

"Did you know?" Jorge asked patiently into his mobile phone. He paced the pavement outside EMP offices having received an update from the team who were at the warehouse. He wondered if this had been just a hoax. Heads would roll after this shitshow – mostly likely his.

Kat felt like she was being told off, Jorge's tone sounded like he was talking to a petulant child. She tried her best not to get riled.

"Of course not," she replied.

"You're not there."

"Just because your team can't see us, doesn't mean we're not here," she said. "We have eyes everywhere… What did I tell you about that bloody tie?"

Jorge looked down and straightened his favourite tie. What was wrong with it? Navy blue with dinosaurs, a birthday present from his kids. Nothing wrong with a little humour, particularly in his line of work. Was Kat just guessing that he was wearing it? He casually surveyed the area. Okay, she was good at her job. He had no idea where she was. He looked up into the sky, expecting to see a drone hovering above him.

"We've been sent on a wild goose chase, that's all," Kat said.

Seeing Red

"This could cost me my job, Kitty."

"Look, just give us two minutes."

"It's too late! Do you have any idea how much an operation like this costs?"

"Actually, I do... I'm sorry you're drowning in boring red tape." Kat stopped herself from preaching to him about his life choices. "Look, you got EMP. That's a big win for you, surely. Even without the evidence of their testing. The other stuff is more than enough."

"But this..."

"This? This is a whole other level, Jorge. It's gonna be messy, best you stay out of it until we're done. Okay?"

Jorge could hear movement down the phone line.

"You're leaving?" he asked, incredulously.

"No point hanging around," Kat replied. "We have another lead to tug on. I'll call if we need you and the boys in blue."

Kat didn't give him a chance to respond before she ended the call.

C E Allardyce

The Demonstration

Prisoner

Church tried her best not to throw up. Her stomach was empty. Bile rose up into her throat, stinging and burning. She resisted – she wouldn't give them the satisfaction. Instead, keeping her eyes lowered, she spat on the floor.

"So ladylike," Doyle sneered.

Fuck you, she thought. It was better for her to think rather than articulating her feelings.

How long had she been here? She had lost count of the days. Or was it weeks? She hadn't seen daylight since before she arrived here, wherever here was. She could be anywhere.

Her new tracker was gone, surgically sliced out of her and expertly stitched back up again. A clue to suggest they weren't prepared to kill her. Yet.

Not that they hadn't tried. First Doyle beat her into oblivion, she retaliated by taking a chunk out of his neck. He didn't appreciate that much. Church had woken up hours later with her mouth filled with his blood and shackled by her ankles to the ceiling.

She didn't have the energy to try and free herself. So she just hung there, biding her time, conserving what little reserves she had left. They let her down eventually, after hosing her down with ice cold water. She was returned to her six by six cell and left to freeze.

Then she was taken to the scientist, Kenny MacKay. He had injected her with more drugs. The pale blue liquid burned cold as it entered her vein. What if she couldn't fight it? Would it kill her like all the other test subjects? She supposed she would find out.

Doyle barked inane orders at her, over and over. Do this, do that. He enjoyed every moment of it. Church played along until she couldn't stand. She crumpled to the floor with exhaustion.

Doyle tutted and she was knocked out again. When she woke, she felt a new pain in the base of her spine. Her fingers tentatively explored the stitches. She felt something rectangular, just under the skin. What the hell was it?

The implanted device was tested a few hours later. She was dragged into Doyle's playroom for another round of humiliation. Just as Church's legs gave out, Doyle whipped out a small black box from his pocket and made a show of pressing the button on it.

His grin split his face as Church writhed on the floor in agony. Just a quick sharp shock was all it needed.

"Hesitate again, CJ and you'll get zapped. Get it?"

Church got it. Now, here she was, with Doyle again. His new play thing. Enjoying her compliance and subservience. Whatever they had drugged her with kept her just about conscious but everything was distorted – her vision, her perception of time, her pain. Whatever it was, it helped her push all feelings deep down inside her.

She wouldn't give in. No matter how much her inner self begged.

"Best behaviour now, pet," Doyle muttered, dragging Church to her feet. "We've a little demonstration for the punters."

The cell door opened and two Perros appeared.

Was this it? Was it time for a performance of a lifetime?

Warrior

Church's semi-conscious body was dragged across the dark concrete floor, supported between two Perros. They dumped her in the centre of the huge space, under a wide circle of harsh white light.

Her shoulders were hunched, her chin on her chest. One of the Perros roughly injected something into her arm and both retreated into the shadows.

Via video link, distorted and unrecognisable faces inched closer to their screens. The bidders were hundreds or even thousands of miles away. Everyone Pérez wanted to attend was there, including several she hadn't expected to be interested or willing to risk delving into the underworld. The bidding would get very interesting with the level of players present.

She turned on her camera, the software similarly distorting her face and disguising her voice.

"Gentlemen, ladies," she said. "This is our most successful participant in this trial. She is military-trained, at the height of her fitness."

"But... a woman," one of the faces said with disdain.

Pérez continued, ignoring the interruption.

"A solid, disciplined background appears to have its benefits."

"She's barely conscious," another face observed.

"For good reason," Pérez said. "The formula is designed to inhibit the subject, remove those irritating human emotions and focus their attention. She will follow my orders. Without question."

"A human drone," a face said.

"Indeed," Pérez confirmed.

"How would you transfer her to another commander?" another face asked.

"By simply instructing her to follow their orders."

"You expect us to believe that this young woman is a killing machine?"

"She was already a killing machine. Don't let her gender, size or build fool you. I could give you a list of her accomplishments, but I'd rather demonstrate what she is capable of."

Two more Perros, younger than the others, entered the pool of light and faced Church, standing on either side of her.

"Is she armed?" a face asked.

"She doesn't need to be," Pérez said.

"Are the soldiers armed?" another asked.

"No weapons for this demonstration. That will come later."

Church struggled to her hands and knees. The Perros stood their ground, feet wide, poised and ready to fight.

"Are your men well-trained?" another face asked.

"They have to be, to work for me. These two Perros are young, eager and strong."

And expendable, she thought.

Pérez leaned towards the intercom on her desk and held down the button. "Perra!" she commanded. "Incapacitate them, but don't kill them."

Church got to her feet and an uncertain look passed between the two Perros. She straightened her spine and rolled back her shoulders. Then she ran straight at the Perro on her left and tackled him. He held her at arm's length by the shoulders as she forced him backwards, out of the pool of light.

Moments later, more lights were switched on, revealing Church standing over the Perro. He was on the floor, dragging himself away from her. His left foot drooped at a sickening angle.

Church turned her back to him and launched herself at the remaining Perro. He took a swing at her, his fist connecting with her cheek. She fell to the floor but immediately leapt to her feet. With a lightning-fast uppercut, she stunned the Perro long enough to get him into a chokehold. Increasing the pressure on his throat, she forced him lower to the floor. He clawed at her arm, trying to twist himself out of her grasp.

Church held on, his face turning purple, his gasps becoming more ragged and desperate. She tightened her arm, forcing his head sideways. Bones in his neck cracked under the pressure. Suddenly, she released him, stomping her boot on his ankle.

Church straightened up, bowed her head and knelt on the floor beside his body, palms flat on top of her thighs.

Eventually, one of the bidders broke the silence of the call. "I would need to see more compelling evidence before investing."

"I didn't invite you to *invest*," Pérez sneered. "This is an auction, not a pitch." She scanned the faces on her screen. "Are there any questions?"

"Does she disobey?" a face asked.

"Never," Pérez said. "If she did, she would suffer the consequences."

"What consequences?" another face asked.

Pérez smiled and held up a small black box. "Insurance against the subject's non-compliance. It doesn't take many doses for the subject to get the idea. It's very effective, just like training canines."

Pérez pressed a button on the device and Church's screams echoed through the warehouse.

Church arched her back and fell sideways, her muscles quivering as the electricity pulsed through her system from the device implanted at the base of her spine. Her fists clenched and unclenched reflexively, her teeth gritted in pain.

The pulses subsided and Pérez pressed the button again for good measure. The results were the same. After a few moments, Church's body slumped to the floor. Gasping and drenched in sweat, she sat up and returned to a kneeling position.

"Your bids shall remain anonymous," Pérez said. "There is enough formula for thirty subjects. Within two weeks there will be enough for a regiment."

The participants remained silent.

Pérez was unfazed. "Perhaps another demonstration?"

A small figure staggered into the circle of light. It was a boy, no more than eight years old. He looked around him with wide, glassy eyes. Church's head remained bowed in submission.

"Perra! Slaughter the child," Pérez ordered.

A knife clattered across the smooth concrete floor and came to a stop in front of Church's knees. She picked up the knife and stood.

Church strode towards the child, spun him around and clamped him to her with her arm across his chest. Her hand quickly drew across his throat. She turned towards the camera revealing blood flowing over her arm and down his chest. The boy collapsed and Church sank to one knee as she held him until his small body went limp.

Church released the child and stood up. The bloody knife clattered to the floor.

"Your bids can now be submitted. You have one hour," Pérez said and left the conference call.

Doyle

The harsh spotlights were switched off and an eerie quiet descended over the loading bay floor. Numerous blood splatters and one pool of drying blood remained, the only evidence of the events that had occurred there.

The two sacrificial Perros were taken down to the east side of the basement where Doyle was waiting for them. Their cries of agony wouldn't be heard on this side of the building, far from the Doctor and even further from Church's cell.

Golden boy Riley had been ordered to dispose of the kid's body.

That will teach him! Doyle thought.

It was about time he got his hands dirty. Doyle smirked to himself. Riley would not see Church in the same light now. Not after she had done something so unforgivable. She would never forgive herself... if she ever found her conscience again. Doyle supposed that mindless drones had no need for that kind of thing. He shrugged the thought off. None of it mattered now.

Doyle entered the dark cell. "Medic's on his way," he said cheerfully to the two Perros. "Lots of lovely opiates for you. Now stop your snivelling and squealing. The Doctor is pleased with your performance. The rewards will be extensive, she told me so herself."

The young men calmed a little. One Perro wiped away a tear from his blood-streaked face, the other was slipping out of consciousness. Doyle grinned and pulled the Desert Eagle from his waistband and shot them both in the head, dead centre between the eyes. He turned on his heel and closed the door behind him.

Riley

Riley carried the small, limp body of the child, wrapped in a sheet, over his shoulder. He laid the body in the back of the van beside the two young Perros with holes in their heads. He jumped in and slid the door closed behind him. He tugged the sheet away from the kid's face. In the dim light of the underground parking area, Riley could see that the boy was covered in blood, darkened to almost black, from his chin down to his narrow waist. He muttered a silent prayer to himself. How could he have let this go so far? *A kid! A fucking kid!*

Riley took the child's dirty hand with the intention of laying it across his narrow chest. He was surprised to find his skin was still warm. A hell of a lot warmer than it should have been. Riley leant down and felt a faint whisper of breath against his cheek. How was this kid still breathing?

Riley clambered into the driver's seat, fired up the engine and roared up the ramp. He sped the van out of the loading bay.

A few miles outside the city, he pulled into an isolated lay-by on a quiet stretch of road and returned to the back of the van. He checked the kid over. He was still unconscious, pulse faint but breathing. No injuries other than a few bruises. No cuts. The skin on his neck was intact.

Reaching under the bench seat, Riley pulled out the first aid box and grabbed a bundle of oily rags from underneath it.

Seeing Red

Wrapped in a slightly cleaner cloth was a small burner phone. Riley turned it on, dialled a number and prayed someone would answer.

Operation Cerberus

A Call for Help

Before Church handed herself over to Doyle, she lingered on the phone with Riley.

"You're going to hate this," she said quietly.

"I'm not liking it much so far," he growled. "Just hit me with it."

"I'm going to call Jack."

She expected some fallout from Riley but all she heard was silence. She waited for him to process it.

"He'll want this shit for himself," Riley eventually growled. "He's probably already signed up for the auction. He wouldn't pass on an opportunity like this."

"More than likely," Church agreed. "But it's a risk we'll have to take. Leave that to me."

She said *we*. Riley was momentarily stunned. Did she mean them? Him and her – a team.

"Claudia…" he sighed.

"I know you can't stand him. You have history. I get it."

"You can't trust that man!"

"I know," she said firmly. "But he owes me… and more importantly he has serious beef with Pérez. And Doyle for going AWOL. All those things are in our favour."

Our. She said it again.

"No better time than now to call that favour in," she added.

Seeing Red

"You want my approval?" Riley asked.

"No," Church said. "But thought you should know."

Riley didn't answer.

"See you on the other side," she said.

"You can count on it."

Church hung up and dialled Jack's number. It rang for several moments before he answered.

"Williams," he said angrily.

"Hunter, it's Mana," Church said, using their Cactus call signs. It should be enough to express the seriousness of her call.

"Mana," Jack said without surprise.

"That favour you owe me…"

"What do you need?"

"Everything you've got."

"When and where?"

"Right now. Where, no idea. We need a wide net."

"Who's co-ordinating?"

"Davies."

"Patch her through," Jack said.

Church could hear a door closing in the background.

"I've severed contact with the team. You'll have to call her at Archers."

"Going rogue?" Jack asked with amusement.

"Something like that. I won't beat around the bush… Pérez is back. Doyle's also working for her… I don't suppose you've received an invitation to an auction recently?"

"An auction? No."

"Check, it's real…"

"Leave it with me," Jack said firmly.

Church couldn't be sure if she had said enough or too much. Was he going to help?

"Be safe," he said quietly.

Was Jack being sentimental? Not his usual style.

Church laughed without any humour. "You know I don't make promises I can't keep."

"Try!"

Jack hung up. The three beeps in Church's ear seemed spectacularly final.

Archers and Echo

The team sped away from the Norfolk warehouse in two vehicles and Kat reactivated her comms.

"Where?" she demanded.

"Head towards London. Lenny's closing in," Kez confirmed.

"That narrows it down," Kat hissed.

"He's only just got the invite to the auction, give him a break," Kez said, trying to placate Kat.

"Church's life depends on this!" Kat snapped.

"Wait a sec..." Kez's voice faded from comms.

Kez took the phone that Lorenzo was thrusting at her.

"Archer Three," she said into it when Lorenzo just shrugged in response to her questioning eyebrow.

"Kerys," Jack said politely.

"Mr Williams," Kez said in surprise. "Erm, is everything okay?"

"Not exactly," Jack replied. "Time is of the essence. My best teams are otherwise engaged, so I need *your* best team."

"Erm, they're currently in the field, sir."

"I understand that," Jack said patiently. "We're working the same op, are we not?"

"Yes, sir. The warehouse in Norfolk was a dead end, Archers and Echo have just left..."

"Send them to Sierra. Jones should know where it is."

"Sierra?" Kez asked.

"Yes. That woman is using one of my buildings..." Jack's tone rippled with something that terrified Kez.

"On it, sir."

Jack hung up.

Kez took a calming breath. No time to question his motives. She spoke into her comms.

"Archer Two, don't know how much of that you heard… does the name Sierra mean anything to you?"

"Sierra?" Kat said incredulously.

"Yes. That was Jack on the phone and asked if you could go there. Now."

Kat looked at her watch. "Why?" she asked.

"That's where Pérez is."

"Copy that."

Kat gestured for Harris to speed up and pointed towards the next exit on the A11.

Command

Kez fidgeted in her seat. She was unable to pace the floor due to her ankle being in a cast, resting on a small stool under the desk. A bottle of painkillers sat beside her left hand. Her eyes systematically flicked between each screen in front of her, fingers impatiently drumming on the desk. It wasn't enough to dispel her anxiety.

Lorenzo and Lenny were sitting either side of her in the control room of Site B, each screen showing multiple feeds.

Operation Cerberus, named after the three-headed dog from Greek mythology that guarded the entrance to Hades, involved multiple teams and organisations. Co-ordination was vital. Kez had not led such a vast op before. She needed to time everything perfectly.

Louie, Jack Williams's right-hand woman, call sign Bravo Control, was first to report in over comms.

"Cactus teams are now in position." Nearly all available teams in Cactus had been dispatched on Jack's orders.

Mallorie Amell led an all-female outfit, long-time rival of Cactus. She had eight teams in eight countries waiting on standby.

"Mercury teams are set, ready for the green light," she drawled.

"Scorpio, ready," Seb confirmed.

"Stand by," Kez said, looking at Lenny. His eyes were fixed on the screen of his laptop.

"Two minutes," he whispered.

"Two mikes," Kez said repeated for the team over comms.

Archers and Echo were lagging behind schedule. Harris was driving the van, Jonny the truck, both speeding towards Sierra. The building had once been Cactus's most depraved team's base of operations.

Team Sierra had a reputation for being the wild boys, the only ones mad enough to deploy into no-win situations. Their successes were many, but eventually the team was disbanded due to too many deaths and injuries. Without a resident team, the building had been repurposed as a safe haven for any Cactus operative to store equipment, crash, train and prepare for ops.

It was Church's base when she was working on her super dark, black ops for Jack. Kat had delivered a few care packages to her there. It was a bleak place, more like a prison than a suitable base for one of Jack's star operatives.

Kez switched the comms to the Archers-only channel. "Archer Two, you have time," she said reassuringly.

"We're going to miss the start!" Kat snapped.

"We have to let it play out," Kez said. "You can't go in there guns blazing. We'll patch you through to the call as soon as we're in."

"Jen's got the tablet," Kat said, looking at Jen over her shoulder. Jen nodded with the tablet in her hands.

Lenny – Archer Eight

Lenny took a deep breath and dialled into the conference call. He joined the auction, masquerading as a representative from Mercury Corps, with access to the company's funds and a buffer account belonging to Cactus. The software he had created started to trace all the participants, accurately revealing their exact locations.

The likely participants of the auction had been suggested by scary American lady, Mallorie and the even scarier Jack who had both reluctantly agreed to work together to help Church with her mission. Lenny wondered what on earth Church had done to earn such respect and gratitude from these people.

Lenny was moments away from his goal. His hands shook. The adrenaline coursing through his veins was alien to him. It was intoxicating. He had never experienced anything like it. He gulped from his glass of water and dabbed his handkerchief over his sweating forehead.

Seeing Red

Lenny drowned out the background noise and the multiple images on the screens in front of him. He retreated into his own personal space – it was him and his laptop. Just how he liked it.

Lenny tried his best to ignore the images on the screen showing the live feed from the auction's demonstration. He had just witnessed Church killing a child. He hadn't seen a person die before, let alone be executed. An innocent, defenceless child! He swallowed hard, trying his best not to throw up. He entered the first bid.

Lenny's fingers hovered over the numbers on his keyboard. Sway the auction – that was all he needed to do. Keep bidding, keep raising the offer. Sweat trickled down his face, despite the cool air of the creepy underground bunker. He glanced at Kez. She gave him an encouraging yet pitiful smile and waved her fingers in an upward movement for him to keep going. Her face was pale. Even she was affected by what she had seen her friend do.

He felt all eyes were on him. He had promised the owners of the significant amount of money that he could retrieve every penny before the transaction was finalised.

"You don't have to trust me," he had said. "The results will speak for themselves."

It was done. Lenny's last bid had been accepted.

"Congratulations!" the evil voice said.

Lenny didn't hear anything more. He let out a breath with as much control as he could muster. The ringing in his ears drowned out the voice. He opened his mouth to speak, hoping sound would emerge.

"I expect delivery within two hours," he managed to say. The software would mask the fear and exhaustion in his voice.

The evil voice said something else, then abruptly exited the call. With shaking hands, he muted all the participants and seamlessly looped the video feeds.

"Go," he said quietly, looking at Kez.

"That's a go!" Kez repeated over comms. "Go. Go. Go."

In ten different countries, thirteen elite teams burst through doors. Flashbangs were thrown, shots were fired. Lenny covered his ears and rested his forehead on the desk in front of him.

Archers and Echo

Outside Sierra, Archers and Echo lay in wait, armed and ready to move. The tension was building.

Kat heard a quiet buzz from behind her. Someone's phone was vibrating. She rolled her eyes. *Rookie move!* Whoever it belonged to, they didn't seem to be in any hurry to answer it or turn the damn thing off.

"For fuck's sake," she hissed quietly under her breath, turning her head towards the sound. "Turn it the fuck off!"

Seeing Red

"They'll leave a message," Harris whispered, his eyes not leaving his scope, which was trained on the doors to the building.

The vibrating stopped, then immediately started again. Harris sighed in resignation and pulled the phone from his pocket.

"What!?" he barked in a whisper.

"Where are you?" Riley said.

"Bro! Where are you?" Harris exclaimed quietly.

Riley relayed his exact location. "Get a medic here. Now!"

"You hurt?" Harris asked.

"Not me – the kid."

"The dead kid?" Harris asked.

"H, please! He's not dead, he needs a medic. You need to position yourself outside Sierra – it's one of Jack's buildings..."

"It's Echo One. The kid's not dead! He needs a medic." Harris cried and repeated Riley's location so Kez could hear over comms. "Bro, we're already outside Sierra."

"Archer Five, Echo Three!" Kez ordered over comms. "You're closest with surgical training. Ten mikes if you leave now."

"Curly and Tom will be with you in ten," Harris said, as Miz sprinted with Tom back to the truck.

"There's not a scratch on him, no injuries that I can see. He must be drugged."

"But we saw Church slit his throat," Harris insisted.

"The kid's covered in blood, but it's not his," Riley said.

"We're coming," Harris said. "How...?"

"Fuck knows."

"But the zapper thing," Harris said, mixed with awe and disbelief. "Jeez!"

"I gotta get back," Riley said. "Wait for my signal, then hit that building with everything you've got."

"Copy that," Harris said. "I assume we'll know it when we see it?"

Riley didn't respond. He had already hung up.

Riley

Riley counted the minutes before Echo's truck roared up the road towards him. Miz jumped out before Tom had fully stopped. Riley got out of the van and slid the side door open. He pulled the kid into his arms and handed him over to Miz.

"Come with us," Tom said, helping Miz get the kid into the truck.

Riley shook his head solemnly. "I need to dump these two and get back. I need to get Church out," he said, shoving the burner phone under the driver's seat. He knew it would be found – each vehicle was thoroughly searched every time they returned to their base. It was just a matter of time.

Without another look at his teammates, Riley got back into the van and sped away.

The End?

Riley

Thirty minutes later, having left the bodies of the two Perros where they would be found, Riley arrived back at Sierra and drove down the ramp. He pulled to a stop near the stairs. Getting out, he threw the keys at the Perro on guard and headed for his room.

Once clean and in fresh clothes, Riley went to report to Pérez. On his way down a dimly lit corridor, a sound behind him made him stop in his tracks.

"Tut, tut, tut!" Doyle said smugly from the shadows. Riley turned to face him. "Making illicit calls, are we, mate?" Doyle held the burner phone in his thick fingers and gave it a wiggle.

"Fuck you, Doyle," Riley growled, turning back towards the door at the end of the corridor.

"Nah, mate. You're the one who's fucked!" Doyle said, striding after him.

Riley rolled his shoulders and cracked a few vertebrae in his neck. This fight would be one to savour. Weeks of irritation, watching this slimeball beat on Church, humiliate her, spit on her.

He clenched his fists at his sides and waited for Doyle to come meet his punishment.

Riley felt a sharp sting on the back of his neck. He spun around to find a Perro standing behind him, holding a dart gun. Riley squared his shoulders, reaching for the man as he started to blur. He tried to lift his arm but it wouldn't respond. The man melted out of sight and Doyle's shadow loomed towards him.

Riley was unconscious before he hit the ground.

Doyle

Doyle smirked down at Riley's slumped body. He wasn't stupid enough to take on Riley in a straight fistfight. Nor could he outrun him, so he had stacked the odds in his favour and cheated.

The Perro had fired the dart, injecting a triple dose of tranquilliser just to be sure. Another Perro appeared and between them, they dragged Riley away. Doyle followed, smug with the knowledge that the Doctor would be pleased with him. He had caught her precious *Primero* red-handed, calling for help. Help from who? he wondered. But it didn't matter. It was too late.

Riley was taken to a cell in the basement. His wrists and ankles were cable-tied, his bandana was ripped from his back pocket and used as a gag. They dumped him onto the cold concrete floor.

Doyle bolted the door from the outside and took one last look at the big man from the safety of the corridor. *Not so intimidating now!* he thought.

Church

After the demonstration, Church was escorted back to her cell and roughly shoved inside. The door slammed shut and was locked. She staggered and collapsed onto the narrow camp bed, her back to the door.

For once, they had not given her a sedative resulting in her feeling everything she had just encountered. Her arm particularly throbbed with every heartbeat.

With difficulty, she shrugged off her combat jacket and inspected the wound. Ripping her pillow case, she wrapped her arm with strips of rough cotton.

It had been worth it. Slashing deep into her own flesh was the only way she could think of to save that poor boy. Thankfully, the sight of her blood had made him pass out. She had heard from a loose-lipped Perro that Riley was ordered to dispose of the boy's body. Would he check for signs of life? Where would he take him? Dump his body like all the others?

The constant deception of being a compliant drone was taking its toll on her. It was exhausting. She retreated deep into herself and took whatever they threw at her.

The device in her spine was something else. Her first dose had been a shock – quite literally. But not nearly as bad as she imagined. Pain is a such an individual thing and Church had suffered deeply since her spinal injury in Africa, three years ago. The fire in her nerves at first was excruciating but somehow, she had got used to it. The burning subsided, dissipating to a dull fizzing.

It didn't stop her Oscar-winning performances. She hoped it had been enough.

Surely she could sleep now. Just for a short while. Until they sold her to the highest bidder.

Doyle

Doyle swaggered over to Church's cell and opened the hatch in the door. "Your beau has been a very naughty boy," he sneered.

Church didn't react. Doyle didn't expect her to. She was broken, finally beaten into submission after weeks of torture and being tested on like a lab rat.

He decided he had just enough time for a little fun of his own. Something long overdue.

He dismissed the two Perros guarding Church. "I'll keep an eye on her for a bit. We've got some unfinished business to discuss. Primero boy's just been demoted, why don't you get some payback of your own?"

Doyle closed the door to Church's cell. It was cold inside, colder than the corridor. The only furniture in the room was a small camp bed in one corner, a plastic table and one chair. One bare bulb, caged behind steel, lit the room with harsh white light.

Doyle dragged the chair to the corner of the room, its legs scraping against the concrete floor. He hopped up onto it and peered into the camera lens. The red light reflected in his cold, dark eyes. He tilted his head, wiggled his fingers in farewell and ripped the cable out of the wall.

Doyle jumped down and looked at Church. She lay motionless on the camp bed, her back to him.

With a sick grin, Doyle started to unbuckle his belt.

The Doctor

Pérez's eyes were fixed on the numerous counteroffers. Two organisations were fighting it out, increasing their bids in five-hundred-thousand increments. The other outfits appeared to have folded but remained on the call. Finally, there was a pause and the numbers stopped scrolling. Was this it? Did she finally have it in her grasp?

Pérez leaned forward with interest. The final total was staggering. Enough to disappear and never be found. But before she could do that, she had one last thing to do. Before Church was handed over to the highest bidder, Pérez would give her one final order – kill Jack Williams. Church was the only person who could get close enough to do it without him suspecting a thing.

Justice at last. Justice for the years Pérez had wasted living in that man's shadow. Justice for the physical pain he had inflicted on her. Justice for him taking everything she cared about. Once Jack was dead, Pérez would take over Cactus and obliterate it, wipe it off the face of the Earth. Every base, in every country. Pérez's heart skipped a beat at the thought of destroying the man and his life's work.

She had already taken his prodigy girl, third time lucky. Though Pérez had to admit that the second attempt on Church's life hadn't really been serious. It was more of a test, to see how tainted Riley had become. Was he really happy wearing the white hero's hat? That still remained to be seen.

Justin Riley had once been hers – and hers alone. Together, they were a formidable team. Him, following her orders to the letter, whatever the mission. Until Jack found out. Jack had been less than impressed with Pérez disregarding his direct order – play with any member of the unit she fancied, but Justin was off limits. Non-negotiable.

By the time Pérez found out why Justin was off-limits, it was too late. He was magnificent – in every way. A willing subject, more than willing to submit to her particular tastes and he was unquestioningly devoted to her. She just couldn't give him up.

Jack's wrath had been brutal and bloody. It had taken Pérez years to recover and even longer to escape his grip. She would never rest until Jack was dead. He had to pay. Eye for an eye. With both Church and Jack out of the picture, Justin would be free. Free to be hers once again.

Pérez's attention returned to the bidding. There had been no further movement, the numbers hadn't increased. It was done. With a smile to herself, she accepted the final bid with a satisfying click of the mouse. She turned on the microphone to the conference call.

"Congratulations! Once the transfer is complete, arrangements will be put into motion. I have a plane on standby."

Mercury had succeeded. Of all the organisations on the call, this one surprised Pérez the most. Who knew little Mallorie Amell had the balls and a dark side such as this. Pérez wondered who Mallorie had delegated this task to.

"I expect delivery within two hours," the highest bidder said.

That was cutting it fine. Berlin was nearly a two-hour flight from the private airfield a few miles away.

"Of course," Pérez said. "Gentlemen, ladies, it has been a pleasure." She exited the call.

Pérez gave the order for all Perros to leave the building immediately and gathered a few items from her desk. From the locked drawer, she armed herself with her stiletto blade and a retractable baton, which she hid up her sleeve.

She scanned the security footage one last time. The feed from Church's cell was dark static. With a guttural growl, she snatched up the black device and left her office.

Pérez headed down the stairway to the basement with two Perros following closely behind her.

"Get Justin to the car."

"He's not in his room," one of the Perros reported.

"Then find him!" she snapped.

The corridor was quiet as Pérez entered through the double doors. Ignoring the uneasy sensation she felt, she approached the door to Church's cell. Where were the guards? Where was Riley? Where was Doyle?

A muffled masculine grunt came from inside the cell. Pérez unbolted the door and flung it open to find Doyle on the camp bed, on top of a dishevelled Church.

"Mestizo!" she barked. "Out!"

Pérez waited as Doyle slid off the bed and made himself presentable. He tucked his T-Shirt back into his combats and straightened the leather holster over his shoulder. He patted the carved handle of Church's knife and opened his mouth to speak.

"Save it!" Pérez snapped. "Playtime is over. You've taken what you wanted, now get her to the car."

"But I…"

Pérez glared at Doyle then narrowed her eyes at him. "Where's Primero?"

Doyle grinned with satisfaction. "He's in cell two, Ma'am. Caught him red-handed. He betrayed you."

Pérez strode over to the other cell and pushed the door open. Riley was inside. He was down, unconscious with his wrists cable-tied behind his back.

She turned back to Doyle in quiet fury. "Get him to the car. I'll deal with you later."

Pérez glared at Doyle and without further protest, he did as he was told and went inside.

Doyle

Doyle squatted beside Riley's bloodied body.

"Wakey, wakey, big boy," he sneered.

He got no response, so he jabbed a finger into Riley's back.

"Boss lady dragged me away from CJ... what's left of her. We were having a little fun, me and her. God, she's something. Isn't she?"

Doyle leaned back and peered into the corridor, checking that Pérez had left. He pulled Church's knife from the holster and considered where to puncture him first. Lung or kidney?

The two Perros had worked Riley over good and proper. The back of his T-shirt was shredded and glistened with blood.

"I suppose you know how good she is," Doyle muttered. "When did you get your first taste?"

Doyle grabbed Riley's shoulder and pulled him onto his back.

"Holy fuck!" he exclaimed.

Riley's face was a mess.

Doyle chuckled. "Only a mother could love that now!"

"Mestizo!" Pérez cried from the other end of the corridor in exasperation.

Doyle sighed, shoved his hands under Riley's arms.

The Doctor

Pérez entered Church's cell.

"You can thank me later," Pérez sneered.

The Perra was still alive and breathing, curled up on the narrow camp bed. Pérez could see her shoulders moving with each slow breath.

"Look at me!" she ordered, fingers twitching at the defiance. "On your feet."

Church remained still.

"Perra!"

Pérez took a step closer.

With a flash of red hair, Church leapt off the bed and barrelled Pérez until she hit the opposite wall.

Pérez wrestled with the wildling, her hand reaching for the small black device in her pocket. She managed to press the button.

Nothing happened.

Church got her hand around Pérez's neck and squeezed. Vertebrae cracked.

Struggling to keep Church from snapping her neck, Pérez glanced at the device. It was operational, the light was illuminated. She pressed the button again.

Church tilted her head as she watched Pérez slowly suffocating while the realisation sank in. The device was useless.

Pérez dropped it to the concrete.

Church's lips curled into a grim smile. She shook Pérez, increasing the pressure on her neck and shoved her roughly. The back of Pérez's head connected with the wall, crumbling concrete falling to the floor. Pérez screwed her eyes shut at the impact and shoved back at Church with all her strength.

Church staggered back a step but didn't let go. Pérez shook out her arm and the baton dropped into her hand. She swung it at Church's face.

Church ducked and lifted her left arm instinctively, taking the full force of the blow. Something cracked.

Church held onto Pérez's neck and kneed her in the stomach. Pérez crumpled.

Church threw Pérez to the ground and leapt on top of her. Both of Church's hands returned to Pérez's throat and squeezed, her broken, ragged nails digging into her skin.

Gasping for breath, Pérez slammed the heel of her hand against Church's weakened left arm, immediately loosening her grip. Pérez had the briefest of moments to notice the crudely bandaged wound on Church's arm. The dressing was soaked with blood.

Church thrust her forehead into Pérez's nose. Blood spurted over Church's face and began to pour from Pérez's flaring nostrils. Church tightened her grip further.

Riley

Riley was being dragged backwards as he came to, his boots scraping on the dusty floor. Whoever had hold of him was struggling, their breathing laboured, clammy hands losing their grip.

With a huff, the dragging stopped and Riley's upper body was released. He landed heavily on the floor. Riley gritted his teeth and absorbed the pain in his back.

He listened and waited. Through his blurred vision they were at the bottom of the concrete stairs. He couldn't hear any other sounds over the gasping of the man behind him.

Doyle.

He wasn't strong enough to haul Riley up the stairs alone. Riley bided his time.

The second the cable ties were cut, weeks of irritation and repulsion exploded into fury as Riley leapt to his feet, his fist bearing down on Doyle's head. He clamped his hand around the back of Doyle's neck and forced his face down to meet his knee. Doyle slumped to the floor.

Riley loomed over him, hands grasping Doyle's sweaty T-shirt. With a glint of metal, Doyle slashed wildly at Riley with Church's knife. Riley grabbed his wrist and twisted.

Doyle feebly struggled to keep control, his free hand planted against Riley's shoulder. Riley twisted harder, ignoring every screaming, burning muscle in his body. He repeatedly slammed Doyle's hand to the floor until he finally let go of the knife.

Riley slammed his fist into the side of Doyle's head and gripped his neck. He leant down and stared into the terrified man's eyes.

His death would be slow and painful. Riley was going to relish every single moment.

Just Us Girls

Pérez managed to shove Church away and haul herself backwards towards the back of the cell, gasping for air. Church staggered to her feet and limped out of the door. Was she running away?

Coward! Pérez thought. *Is that all you've got?*

Church only needed a moment. If she could just reach the panel at the end of the corridor – all this would be over in a matter of minutes. She fell to her knees and clawed at the corner of the metal panel on the wall– her fingers slipping, slick with blood.

Eventually, she pried the panel open revealing a keypad and palm scanner. Wiping her hand on her T-shirt, Church pressed her hand to the cold surface and entered a twelve-digit code. A code she had stashed away in her brain for nearly five years. Back from her time spent here as a Cactus operative. A failsafe. Insurance. If the building was compromised then blow it all to hell.

Now was such a time.

Pérez watched Church with mild bewilderment as she headed the wrong way down the corridor, towards a dead end. What was she doing? Calling for help? Pérez snorted to herself. Who would come to her rescue? The rest of Archers had failed in locating their commander. No doubt they were still circling the dummy base of operations in Norfolk. Jack? Unlikely. If he knew Pérez was here, he would have turned up weeks ago. But not a whisper from him.

A rippling haze silently billowed through the ventilation grating, clinging to the ceiling and like heavy fog, drifted down to the floor. It filled the corridor and rolled towards the doors.

Church slumped to all fours, head hanging – summoning all the energy she could muster – she was running way past empty. She had no idea if the failsafe had worked. No beep, no green light. Nothing.

If she couldn't be sure the building would be destroyed then she had to finish the job herself. Woman to woman. Just as she was about to get to her feet, a sound came from behind her.

Pérez leapt towards Church with a stiletto blade in her fist. She drove it into Church's side. They fell together. Pérez twisted and forced the knife deeper. Rolling away, she scrambled towards the door.

Church attempted to stem the bleeding, both hands clamped around the hilt of the blade sticking out of her side.

She wouldn't let herself be beaten like this.

Get up!

I can't. I'm done.

Get up! Now!

Turning her head slowly towards Pérez, her decision made, she wrapped her fingers around the handle. With a sharp intake of breath, she pulled the knife out and pressed her other hand over the wound. Blood oozed between her fingers.

Finishing Pérez was more important in this moment. She could die later, when the job was done.

Church's hand slipped from her stomach, leaving a smear of dark blood. She staggered to her feet, leant on the wall for support and started her approach.

The building shuddered. A moment later, the sound of explosions thundered above their heads. Pérez laughed as the shuddering multiplied. The ceiling started to crack, dust and concrete raining down on them.

Riley

Riley burst through the doors.

"Claudia!" he roared, barely audible over the groaning of the building.

Pérez's eyes darted towards the sound, her brows furrowed.

Riley quickly scanned the scene, seeing Pérez was down, badly beaten and Church was on her feet. Barely.

"Out," Church gasped, dragging herself forward.

"Primero!" Pérez cried and reached her hand for him.

"You need to go," Church wheezed. "Now."

Riley stepped around Pérez.

"Hmm," he growled, wrapping his arm around Church's waist.

"Listen to me, Primero!" Pérez snapped. "Get us out of here! That's an order!"

"Get yourself out," Church whispered to Riley. "Please." She writhed in his arm, trying to get away from him.

A roar thundered around them and the grating from the ventilation vent glowed red.

Without another thought, Riley dragged Church away and headed for the door.

"Leave me," Church begged.

Riley kicked the door open.

"Never again," he vowed through gritted teeth.

Seconds later the corridor was engulfed in flames.

Archers and Echo

A thunderous boom shook the building, reverberating through the surrounding ground. The team ducked a little lower into the grass.

"Is that a go?" Ellis asked quietly.

"One's not a fan of explosions," Harris muttered.

"Control?" Kat asked desperately over comms.

"Not us," Kez confirmed.

"Are you still in contact with Jack?" Kat spoke fast, trying her hardest not to panic.

"Not right now," Kez said. "Gimme a sec." She looked at Lorenzo, who nodded and got on the phone.

Kat waited for a response. Every fibre in her body was telling her now was the time to hit that building. Her friend was in there!

"Hold your position!" Kez ordered a moment later, with a surprising amount of authority. Kat relaxed a fraction. Harris was still beside her, poised for action. The twitching muscles in his jaw told Kat he was also impatient to get on with it.

A series of explosions shook the ground. The team flattened themselves to the ground and covered their heads with their arms. Glass and brick rained down as clouds of smoke billowed into the night sky. Flames quickly followed. The building groaned and started to collapse inwards.

Kat screamed into her comms, "What the actual...?"

Seeing Red

The building slowly crumbled into a pile of rubble and ash. People shouted over comms, their words frantic but not making any sense to her. Kat tried to stand but fell to her knees, tears streaming down her cheeks. Harris crouched behind her, immobilised by the sight of the wreckage.

Eventually, an eerie quiet descended over the area – ash fell like snow through the smoke.

Kat gasped back a sob. "No!" she cried hoarsely. Harris gently laid his hand on her shoulder.

"I couldn't stop it!" Lenny wailed over comms. "It wasn't part of the system, I couldn't access it... and even if I could, there was no time to disable it... I'm so sorry!"

The team stood up, shoulders sagging, weapons dropped. There was no escaping the wreckage – the building was just gone.

"Some fuckin' signal," Harris muttered. "What are we supposed to hit exactly?" He looked forlornly at Echo.

Echo's van screeched to a stop and Tom and Miz leapt out and watched in horror.

Jen pulled Miz in a hug as they stood beside Kat. Tom rested his hand on Harris's shoulder.

"Hope is not lost," Jack said calmly from behind the teams. They spun simultaneously to face him, rifles raised.

As the flames started to subside, inhibited by the collapsed building, four armoured Cactus jeeps screeched to a halt and men piled out. Equipment was unloaded and the men spread out over the rubble. They scanned with handheld devices while two drones buzzed overhead in a grid pattern.

Jack strode over to greet one of the men.

Archers and Echo just stood and watched.

"We can help!" Kat called over to Jack.

"Stay where you are, Jones!" he barked back and continued his conversation.

Some of the men began clearing the rubble. Orders were shouted. Minutes later, more equipment arrived. A small digger was unloaded from a lorry. Men pointed and the digger started removing larger pieces of concrete.

One of Jack's men shouted something, work stopped and Jack strode over in the direction indicated. He suddenly jumped down out of sight, closely followed by one of his men.

Minutes or hours later – Kat couldn't tell – Jack re-emerged from the debris, dusty and dirty but intact. Kat and the team watched in silence as two body bags were hauled out of the hole in the ground by Cactus men.

A New Hell

Riley

Riley struggled to open his eyes. They were stinging like a thousand hot needles were jabbing his eyeballs. It was dark or he was blind – he couldn't tell which. His face felt sore and tight. He could barely move his arms. Where was he?

He could hear a distant roar and it was hot. Was he finally in hell? He tried to move and instantly regretted it. Pain flashed through every muscle in his body. What happened?

He wasn't dead. Death wouldn't be so painful.

Something was pressing against his chest, the only part of him that didn't hurt like a bitch. He lifted his hand, his fingers found something soft.

The realisation hit him like a thunderbolt.

Red!

She was hurt, her head rested on his chest. He sat up and cradled her.

"Claudia?" he whispered.

She stirred. "Need… to… move."

"Where exactly? I can't see a damn thing."

She pushed herself away from him. Feebly tugging on his T-shirt, urging him to move, she started to crawl away. He blindly followed the sound.

Church stopped. Something clicked and a dim blue light appeared in the wall beside her – a keypad. She entered a long code. There was a hiss and cool air brushed their faces.

A concrete hole, barely three feet wide, bathed in dim green light lay before them. Church crawled in, Riley followed.

They crawled for what felt like hours. They couldn't stop, the heat from the flames was catching up to them. Church was slowing down, his face inches from her boots. This hole was likely to become their tomb.

Everything hurt, every drag of his arms caused more pain. He ploughed on, Church needed medical attention. Hell, so did he, but she needed it more.

"You need anything?" he growled, his throat sore from the smoke that was filling the tunnel.

"A holiday," Church breathed.

"Deal. Where?"

She faltered, then slumped over onto her back. Riley took the opportunity to catch his breath. She struggled to pull something from her filthy combats.

"The nearest hospital then you choose where."

"Hmm," he growled in agreement.

Church placed something in his hand – a mobile phone with a black shiny case. It was Pérez's phone. Had she lifted it while fighting her?

"You know the PIN?" she asked.

He did.

"I could kiss you right now," he said, unlocking the phone.

Church pointed behind her, further down the tunnel. "Shaft. Signal."

"On it."

Riley scrambled past Church. As his face levelled with hers, she laid a hand on his chest.

"Thanks."

Archers and Echo

Helplessly watching the clean-up, Harris's phone started ringing again. He stepped away from the distraught team and answered the call. It was from another unknown number. He would give whoever was calling a piece of his mind. He was busy. He had just watched his best friend die.

Riley was dead. Buried under God knows how many tonnes of shit, along with his girl's best friend.

"Speak fast," Harris barked.

"H, trace this call. Now. We need an exfil."

Harris took a moment to register what he was hearing.

It was Riley's voice, urgent and demanding. Just like him to be snippy when he needed something done quick. No – *Hello, mate! How's things?*

Was it a trick? Was he hallucinating?

Riley said *we. We need an exfil.*

We? Harris thought. Who did he have with him?

Who else, dumbass? He's only gone and fucking done it. He got Church out! But how?

Harris turned back towards the team and made eye contact with Kat. He jerked his head, indicating that she should join him. Without question, she stepped towards him, not a glimmer of her usual sass.

"We?" Harris asked incredulously, holding the phone away from his ear so Kat could hear.

"Keep it on the down-low. We need to stay dead. Send Miz and Tom again, Church is hurt bad."

Kat listened wide-eyed to Riley's voice. She switched her comms back on and spoke quickly and quietly.

"Seven, trace the call on Echo Two's mobile. Now."

"On it," Lorenzo confirmed over comms.

"Archer Five and Echo Three?" Kat cried urgently towards the rest of the team. "Get to the van. Now."

Miz and Tom exchanged a glance then sprinted to the van.

"Got it!" Lorenzo exclaimed moments later and relayed the co-ordinates. "Echo One needs ropes, he's twenty feet underground."

"What?" Tom cried.

"Echo One has Archer One," Lorenzo explained patiently. "Twenty feet down a hole. Archer One is hurt."

Riley

Riley called back down the tunnel.

"Contact made,"

Only his voice echoed into the darkness.

"Roja?"

Leaving the phone on a tiny ledge in the shaft he closed the distance as quickly as he could.

Church didn't move as he approached, his pain forgotten.

"Claudia!"

He slid beside her and cradled her in his arms. She was limp in his gentle grip. Her skin was cold to the touch.

No. No. No. No!

Riley felt along her jaw and pressed two fingers to her carotid artery. He felt a faint pulse. Supporting her head, he laid her flat and knelt beside her. There was no resistance in her body.

No, you don't! Not now, not here!

"Claudia!" He rubbed his knuckles on her breastbone. "Wake up!" He leant over her and placed his cheek close to her lips. She was barely breathing. "Talk to me, Claudia! Shout at me. Hit me… anything!"

Riley took her hand and gave it a squeeze. "Please," he begged. "I'll kiss you again."

He stopped feeling her breath on his cheek. His heart sank. He rested his forehead against hers and prayed.

No!

Summoning his resolve, he locked his fingers together, placed the heel of his hand at the base of her breastbone and started chest compressions.

"Hold on. You've got this far. Just. Hold. On."

He lifted her chin, pinched her nose and gave two breaths. He resumed the compressions.

"Claudia! Come on, now."

His heart clenched in his chest. A black hole loomed, threatening to consume him.

"This is not how this goes! This wasn't the plan!"

Riley coughed, shielding his mouth against his shoulder and gave two more breaths.

"The team. They're coming."

He shook his head as he pounded on her chest.

"Hold on. Damn you."

Archers and Echo

"We're five mikes out," Tom confirmed. He was sprinting into the forest with Miz right behind him. Both had lengths of rope wrapped across their chests.

Tom arrived at the co-ordinates first and skidded to a halt. The area was covered in thick brambles. Miz waded through them, ripping at them with her gloved hands. Thorns caught her sleeves and combats. Tom made a path through the undergrowth beside her, hacking at the stubborn stems with his knife as the thorns shredded through his gloves.

Miz reached the heavy, wrought-iron grate in the ground first. It covered the top of the shaft and was concreted into place. Tom jabbed his thumb at his pack and spun around. Miz yanked open the zip and pulled out a small metal bar. Tom took it and jammed it into the grate.

"One!" Miz called down the shaft.

There was no response.

Miz helped Tom, both pushing all their weight onto the bar in an attempt to lever the grate open.

"This isn't working!" Miz gasped, letting go. She pulled the coil of rope over her head, crouched down and shrugged her own backpack from her shoulders. She retrieved a small rectangular box and placed it on the edge of the grate.

"Fire in the hole!" she screamed down the shaft and dragged Tom back through the thorns.

Seconds later, the device exploded.

Before the dust and debris settled, Tom and Miz peered down the hole. A shape at the bottom of the shaft emerged into the light. Miz scrabbled to secure the ropes around the nearest tree and flung them down.

A sharp double tug on the rope signalled he was ready. With a glance at each other, Tom and Miz took the slack and hauled.

Tom glanced down the hole, Church was hanging limply, the ropes looped under her arms. Riley was shuffling up beneath her, his boots and hands pinned to opposite sides of the shaft.

"Wait for the rope!" Tom called down to him.

He didn't receive a response. Tom and Miz pulled with everything they had.

Eventually Church's head appeared. Tom took the strain, allowing Miz to reach for her friend. She stumbled as she dragged Church out, Tom caught them both before they fell into the thorns.

Between them, they gently laid Church down and got to work. Minutes later, Riley appeared, huffing with the effort of hauling his own weight up the shaft.

Tom hesitated briefly while treating Church, with a concerned look at Riley. He only received a growl in response.

"Keep her alive," Riley ordered. "I can wait."

Tall Pines

Riley

Riley staggered out of the van almost before it screeched to a stop outside the solid oak double doors. The stone building in the sleepy Kent countryside didn't look like a hospital but he trusted Miz. Another contingency of theirs. Apparently it was safe and secure.

A hospital bed surrounded by four medics was waiting just inside the doors and before Riley could get Church out of the van, they wheeled it over the dark tarmac to meet them.

Riley gently laid Church on the bed and she was whisked away. Miz was talking with a stern looking older woman in a lab coat as they followed the bed into the building.

Miz relayed the detailed assessment of Church's condition. Emotionless. Factual. Riley listened in silent horror.

Deep laceration to left arm, suspected fracture to left ulna. Puncture wound to right side of the abdomen. Possible fractured ribs. Significant blood loss. Possible internal bleeding. Suspicious implanted device in her spine. Many minor cuts and abrasions. Full toxicology recommended.

Church was wheeled through solid white doors and disappeared from view. Riley was about to follow but was stopped by both Tom and Miz.

"They'll take the greatest of care," Miz said gently.

"Let us patch you up," Tom urged, trying to herd Riley in the opposite direction.

Riley stood his ground. He had to wait for news on Church.

Tom found a stool for Riley to sit on and between him, Miz and two nurses, they treated his wounds in the corridor.

After what seemed like hours of being prodded and poked, Riley sat alone in the corridor guarding the theatre doors. Miz had left to check in with the team. He had no idea where Tom was, probably doing the same with Echo or on another patrol of the grounds.

The stern female doctor appeared in front of Riley. He had since learned her name was Eve and was Archer's chief medic.

"How is she?" Riley asked, standing up with effort. He noticed her scrubs were immaculate.

"Critical, but stable," Eve said.

"Meaning?" Riley growled.

"Time will tell."

Riley glared past Eve towards the theatre doors. To hell with sterility, he needed to see her.

"Get some rest," Eve insisted, not moving from his path. "There's a room next to Church's. You can sleep there."

Riley's jaw twitched.

"She'll be brought out soon. She'll be out for a while. She needs rest."

"I'm staying," he said.

As if on cue, the theatre doors opened and a bed was wheeled out by two nurses. Church looked small and fragile. And barely recognisable with a tube down her throat, wires disappearing under the hospital gown she now wore, a monitor clamped onto her finger, several lines infusing her with fluids and blood. Her left arm was in a blue cast. What little skin was showing was either deathly pale or covered in bruises and dressings. Riley stepped aside to let them pass, then followed them.

"You won't get much rest in here," Eve muttered, as she and a nurse connected the tubes and gadgets keeping Church alive to contraptions in the wall behind the bed.

Eventually the medics left the room. Riley sank into the chair beside the bed and gently took Church's right hand.

A Visit from Harris

Riley woke suddenly, the door to Church's room had opened. He lifted his head and was about to launch himself at the presence when the pain hit him like a sledgehammer. His vision swam.

"Easy, easy. Just me," Harris whispered from the doorway.

Riley's shoulders relaxed. Church was still there. Still alive. She was unconscious, the monitors beeping softly and reassuringly, the ventilator hissing and huffing. She was alive. Barely.

"Mate," Harris urged, jerking his head towards the corridor. Reluctantly, Riley followed, wincing from the pain of standing.

"You okay?" Harris asked once the door was closed.

"I'm fine."

"Yeah, looks like it," Harris said, eyeing Riley's swollen, battered face. "I brought you some stuff." He pointed to a large kit bag on the floor in the waiting area outside Church's room.

"Thanks," Riley said.

"And this." Harris held out a large paper cup.

Riley sighed and took the cup gratefully. Fresh, hot, black coffee. He didn't wait for it to cool before gulping a mouthful. The burn felt like pure fire down his throat. It tasted good. It felt good.

"Report," Riley growled.

Harris nodded and gestured towards the brown leather sofa. Riley struggled to lower himself down, his muscles still protesting. He deserved every twinge, every ache and every single jab of molten lead that he felt.

Harris perched on the low table in front of him and spoke quietly.

"This place is secure, need-to-know basis and all that. The guys are prowling the perimeter..." Harris anticipated Riley's next question. "Five took over from Three and is literally outside," he pointed in Jonny's general direction. "I'm here and Four is back at base keeping eyes on the prize, virtually."

"Hmm," Riley growled appreciatively.

"EMP have been disabled. Romano was arrested by Kat's big bro. Nice guy. The warehouse was clean, no sign of any other test subjects. Poof!

Seeing Red

"Sierra's a wreck. Nothing but rubble, metal and dust. The research scientist, MacKay, was last to be found, what was left of him. The lab? Nothing left of that at all. Fire obliterated everything on that floor. No formula, no notes. Nothing.

"Scorpio found Mrs MacKay and her two daughters. They're all home. The kid you pulled out of Sierra is also safe and back with his family. He'd been drugged up to the eyeballs and remembers nothing. Small mercies, eh? He just needed a McDonald's, a good sleep and he's now right as rain." Harris looked at Riley. "How the hell did she pull that off?"

Riley shrugged and with a wave of his hand, encouraged Harris to continue.

"Jack took two body bags from the rubble. We thought they contained you and Church, but then you called. We hung around for a bit until Jack dismissed us... I can only assume…"

"You know what assuming does," Riley said gravely. "Move on."

Harris obliged.

"The girls are okay. Kez broke her ankle back in the clearing, after you… you know… took Church..."

Harris cleared his throat.

"All participants in the auction have been shown the error of their ways. Lenny played a blinder! You should have seen him. If the girls don't hire him, I think we should. He's really something."

"I can't think about that now," Riley said quietly, not taking his eyes off the door to Church's room.

"We've all the time in the world. Kat's running Archers while Church recovers. Kat suggests we occupy ourselves while they secure Archers. They're still paying us, you know."

Riley looked at Harris.

"Just sayin'," Harris said. "Did you know the girls had a backup base? A bunch of sunken shipping containers in Church's back garden. They certainly kept that quiet."

"They're smart."

"I'd say," Harris agreed, glancing at door. "She's going to be okay, right?"

"Time will tell," Riley quoted, without much enthusiasm.

"Jeez," Harris huffed.

A nurse appeared in the corridor and went into Church's room.

Riley stood up. "Thanks, H."

Harris clapped Riley on the shoulder, making Riley growl in discomfort.

"Soz. Holler if you need anything."

Riley followed the nurse. "Any change?" he asked her.

"All stable," she replied. "No change." She smiled kindly and finished making notes on her tablet.

Riley returned to the chair beside the bed and waited.

A Visit from Kat

It was dark when Riley was awoken by the monitors frantically beeping and alarming. He pressed the call button on the wall behind the bed as two medics burst into the room. He stepped out of the way but refused to leave.

Church's eyes were open, her fingers clawing at the tube in her mouth. The medics held her down by the shoulders. Church struggled and feebly tried to fend them off. She was choking, her heart rate through the roof. Something was injected into the cannula in the back of her right hand and slowly she began to calm down.

A slender, warm hand slipped through Riley's arm and led him out of the room. It took him a few moments to realise the hand belonged to Kat.

"I'll go get Eve," Kat whispered and left him standing outside the room.

Riley sank onto the sofa and held his head in his hands. Had Church given up? Did she have any fight left in her? She hadn't stopped fighting for weeks. A true warrior. Was it all coming to an end now?

Eve strode down the corridor. Riley lifted his head at the sound of her approach, but she ignored him. She entered the room without giving him the opportunity to see or hear anything from inside and she closed the door behind her.

Kat reappeared holding a tray and placed it on the table in front of Riley.

"Eat," she said with authority. Riley was still looking at the door.

"You're no use to her like this," Kat said. "When she wakes up, she'll need you."

Riley finally looked at Kat, but she didn't give him the opportunity to speak.

"She'll need to finish what she started. You have to be there for her."

Kat sat beside him.

"Church won't take our word for it. Jack took two body bags from the building, doesn't mean both occupants were dead, does it? He's not one for showing his hand, sneaky fucker. Don't get me wrong, I'm grateful for his help and all but..."

"You don't trust his motives," Riley growled.

"Exactly! Jack never does anything out of the kindness of his heart. There has to be an angle. Why not parade their dead bodies for all to see? Show the world who's really in charge? Everyone knows – no bodies, no confirmation. So, you have to be there for her. You understand. Maybe the only person who does. You were there. I can't begin to understand what went on in that place..."

Riley blinked. He certainly knew. And it was killing him.

"So eat that and get some sleep. I'll stay here and I promise to wake you the second anything changes."

Riley glanced at the tray for the first time. A full English breakfast with a pot of coffee. He looked back towards the door. What were they doing in there?

"The second anything changes," she repeated.

"I'll wait for Eve to come out," Riley said, then gave in and started to devour the breakfast.

Seeing Red

Kat chatted while he ate.

"Archers is on the way to being fully functional again. Lenny's helped with the system and stuff. Performed some upgrades here and there.

"Did you know Tom and Kez were a thing? They certainly kept that quiet! They make a cute couple, don't you think?"

Riley didn't answer, knowing he wasn't supposed to. Kat was distracting him and right now, he didn't mind.

"Charlie asked me to marry him yesterday."

Riley nearly choked on his food. He drank some coffee to hide it.

"It was a total surprise. Very romantic, silly old fool. Got down on one knee in front of everyone!" Kat waved her left hand at Riley.

The ring was a huge diamond surrounded by dark sapphires. Harris wasn't usually one for big romantic gestures. Perhaps making a rash decision after a particularly long and harrowing op wasn't such a good idea. But ops like that certainly made you question life in general. Life is short and is for living. Riley could understand that. But why hadn't H mentioned it himself?

"I think that was the first time in a long while I was completely lost for words. I said yes, of course."

"Congratulations," Riley said.

"You'll be Charlie's best man and Church will obviously be my maid of honour. Yuck! I hate that term. Church is no maid! She'll be my best woman." Kat shook her head. "No, that won't do either. She's just my person.

"You know, it's tradition for the best man and the maid of honour to get it on, right?"

Riley rolled his eyes. Church could be dying in there. One step at a time. Thankfully, his plate was now empty. He had a reason to leave. He drained his cup and stood up.

"Thanks, Kat," he growled.

Eve opened the door and let the other medics out of the room. She closed the door and stood in front of it, blocking Riley's path again. Kat stood at his elbow.

"She's stable. We had to sedate her," Eve explained. "No more visitors. She needs to rest, as do both of you." She looked at them both disapprovingly.

Begrudgingly, Riley entered the room next door with a look at Kat.

"The second anything changes," Kat vowed.

He closed the door and collapsed on the bed, not bothering to remove his boots.

Awake

A heart-wrenching scream dragged Riley awake.

"Get away from me!"

Had he been dreaming? Before Riley's brain caught up, he was on the move, nearly ripping his door from its hinges. He skidded on the shiny floor and burst into Church's room.

Church was sitting bolt upright on the bed, wielding a pair of forceps as a weapon. Two medics had retreated to the walls, hands up in surrender. The first thing that occurred to

Riley was, why had no one told him the ventilator had been removed? That was a change. Something new. Something different.

Riley calmly approached the bed, making Church focus on him. She looked terrified, her eyes wide, flicking between him and the medics. He closed his hand over hers and gently removed the forceps. Her hand was shaking uncontrollably.

He held the forceps behind his back and one of the medics took them from him. He sat on the edge of the bed, blocking her view of the strangers.

"Roja," he said quietly. He took her hand and gave it a squeeze. Fear, confusion and disbelief filled her eyes. "Let the medics here help you."

"Who? Where?" Church rasped, looking at the medics suspiciously, then wildly around the room.

"A private hospital in Kent. Eve is here, Miz arranged it all."

"Tall Pines?"

"Yes, Roja. You're okay. You're safe."

Church looked at one of the medics. "Who do you work for?" she asked.

"Dr Douglas, ma'am."

Church relaxed slightly.

"Let them help you," Riley said.

Church leant back onto her pillows and closed her eyes tightly. Riley indicated with his head for the medics to proceed. They quickly replaced the bags of fluids and checked the monitors. Church squeezed his hand and he felt her fingers tighten further.

"You in pain, Roja?"

Church avoided answering. Riley took the infusion pump controller and placed it gently into Church's hand.

"Press this for pain meds."

Church held her thumb on the button as the medics quietly left the room.

Confessions

Church slowly drifted back to sleep still clutching Riley's hand as if her life depended on it. Her skin looked paper thin, almost transparent, he could see her veins through the cuts and bruises.

"I'm sorry," he said quietly. "I should be angry, but how could I be with you? A true warrior to the last. I know you wanted to go down in that building. To finish it yourself. But I couldn't let you die in there."

He hung his head over her hand.

"I should have stopped it. What they were doing to you… they made me watch. Every fight, every test. They were watching me, watching you. *She* enjoyed that, I'm sure."

The sun started to rise over the surrounding trees. Soon the room would be bathed in sunlight, there was not a cloud in the sky.

Riley was still amazed that they had got out of that building in one piece. Though the journey wasn't a pleasant experience and was a situation he wouldn't ever want to repeat. But the end result was what mattered. Roja was out, she was alive.

"Remind me not to listen to you again," he muttered. "I won't let you throw yourself to the wolves like that."

A frown appeared between Church's eyes. Was she dreaming or was she in pain? He couldn't tell.

He gently lifted her hand in his and pressed it to his cheek. He closed his eyes.

"This isn't over but I owe it to you to finish it. Whatever it takes."

"Together."

Riley looked at her in surprise. Church's eyes were open and she was looking right at him. He gave her hand a gentle squeeze in agreement.

Darkness Descending

Finally alone for the first time since escaping Sierra, Church laid in the bed and steadied her breathing. Riley had left the room momentarily, promising to return with a latte. With a deep breath she tugged at the sheet covering her lower body. Forcing her legs to move under utter protest, she slowly eased them off the edge of the bed.

With considerable effort she made a staggering lurch to the bathroom door. Once inside, she pushed the door closed and slumped exhausted against it. Her legs gave way and she slid to the floor, unable to stand any longer.

By the time her backside hit the cold tiles, she was sobbing. Uncontrollable tears flowed down her cheeks as she cried. She covered her face with her hands and let it all go.

A few minutes of self-pity was all she would allow herself. Everything hurt. Her eyelids – dry and sore – down to her battered, aching toes. She was a mess. Inside and out.

You made it out! the voice in her head cried in anger.

Yeah, I did. Whose idea was that? she sneered in reply.

She hadn't considered surviving. She was fully prepared to go down with Sierra building. She very nearly did.

But Riley had got her out. Even if it was against her wishes. She needed to see that woman dead. Justice for the Yankee Op, trying to kill her, twice! For hiring Doyle, for him killing Geoff Abraham and Dante. For all the test subjects that were now dead because of her evil plan to make money. And for whatever she had done to Riley when he was a young officer.

She deserved to die and now who knew where she was.

Jack knows.

That was no use to her. She needed to keep as far from Jack as she possibly could. She wasn't safe. Not from him, not from anyone else who knew about Warrior IV.

It was a myth. Pure and simple. But would that stop Jack from pursuing it? Unlikely.

Church stopped her snivelling and hauled herself over to the sink. Grabbing the sides of the basin, she dragged herself to her feet and took a long, hard look in the mirror.

She barely recognised herself. Tugging at the hospital gown, she flung it to the floor in disgust. Her bruised and beaten body now in full view. Taking her time, she prodded and probed with her fingertips, assessing each injury and vividly remembering how she got them.

Seeing Red

Darkness descended and engulfed her soul completely. A blood-red mist filled her vision. Pain. Suffering. Torment. Everything she had suffered she needed to deal back in spades. She needed to take back what was taken from her and to hell with the consequences.

The dark side was calling her. Her inner demon was screaming to be unleashed and Church didn't have the energy to contain her anymore.

A gentle knock on the outer door brought Church back to focus. The darkness faded and she pushed the feelings aside. For now.

She grabbed a clean T-Shirt from the shelf and tugged it over her head. Wiping away the tears and the rage with them, she opened the bathroom door and hobbled back to bed.

Jack

Two weeks after Church's arrival, Jack's convoy sped towards the entrance to the Tall Pines medical facility. Jack slid out gracefully of the black Rolls Royce Callinan and strode towards the entrance. Eve hurried to greet him.

"Dr Douglas," he said in greeting, striding into the building.

"I'm sorry, Mr Williams, you're too late," Eve said.

Jack stopped and glared down at her.

"Explain!" he barked, with something close to a feeling fluttering in his chest.

"She's gone…"

Church, his prodigy, was gone? Dead? The most valuable asset he had ever had the pleasure to nurture and train. Even more so now, considering her recent participation in the human trials. He needed more time to see what he could do with those results. Could he do that without her?

"I mean, she's not here," Eve corrected. "The staff went to do their usual checks. Her bed was empty. No sign of Echo. No Archers either."

Jack opened his mouth but Eve interrupted before he had chance to speak or bark another order.

"We checked the security footage. Expert job but the cameras were hacked. Sometime this morning. They can't have got far. We'll find them."

"You said she couldn't be moved," Jack growled.

"I said *shouldn't*," Eve clarified. "She needs to rest and heal. I was working on a regimen to combat the withdrawal symptoms…"

Jack stormed towards the ward, Eve followed. He saw for himself that Church's room was empty. Was she taken or helped to leave? He intended to find out.

"Was Justin here last night?" he asked.

"Hadn't left her side since they arrived."

Jack made a disapproving sound in his throat and pulled his phone from his pocket.

"Hutchinson. Initiate a manhunt. Locate any member of Archers or Echo. Now."

Jack hung up, not waiting for a response or acknowledgement.

"The test results," Eve said, making Jack look back at her. "I can't say for certain…"

Jack held up his hand to stop her.

"A week, Eve! It took you a whole week to make contact. You were meant to be keeping her here and getting rid of Archers and Echo."

Eve raised her chin. "Claudia's health came first."

Jack snorted. "Yet you still betrayed her trust."

Eve didn't respond. What could she say? He was right, she did betray Church.

"Was my incentive not enough?" Jack asked, looming over her.

Eve swallowed, her mouth suddenly dry.

"I'll get my people to deal with this. You, you're coming with me. I have a few more things I need you to do."

"I have to get back to Archers. I will be missed."

Jack stopped by the front door.

"That ship has sailed, don't you think," he said. "I need your expertise in patching up another survivor from that building. I need her alive. I'll worry about the security."

Eve looked at Jack in shock.

"I'll wait in the car," he said. "You have three minutes."

About the Author

C E Allardyce was born in North Hertfordshire in the United Kingdom of Great Britain, grew up and schooled in South Cambridgeshire and moved to Central Bedfordshire in the late nineties. She now lives in a small village near Bedford with her teenage son and neurotic large-breed dog.

www.ceallardyce.com

Printed in Dunstable, United Kingdom